IMAGINING OURSELVES

IMAGINING OURSELVES

Classics of Canadian Non-Fiction

Selected by
DANIEL FRANCIS

ARSENAL PULP PRESS
Vancouver

IMAGINING OURSELVES
Selections copyright © by the Authors
Introductions copyright © 1994 by Daniel Francis

ARSENAL PULP PRESS
100-1062 Homer Street
Vancouver, B.C.
Canada V6B 2W9

The publisher gratefully acknowledges the assistance of the Canada Council and the Cultural Services Branch, B.C. Minstry of Small Business,
Tourism and Culture.

Printed and bound in Canada by Kromar Printing

CANADIAN CATALOGUING IN PUBLICATION DATA:
Main entry under title:
Imagining ourselves
  Includes bibliographical references.
  ISBN 1-55152-000-1
  1. Canadian prose literature (English)★ I. Francis, Daniel.
PS8365.I42 1994   C818'.08   C94-910400-0
PR9197.25.I42 1994

CONTENTS

INTRODUCTION

For almost twenty years I have been a writer of books and articles about Canada. Most of what I have written I think of as history, or more specifically popular history, but certainly all of it can easily be labelled non-fiction—a category of writing that had never impressed itself on me as very meaningful. For most of my writing career I was never aware that I might be working in a tradition. Naturally I read a lot of non-fiction, but I read it for information, and not for any imaginative experience. In fact, non-fiction writing has for most of my writing career been perceived generally as "easier" than fiction writing, engaging the imagination on a somewhat lower level than the more "serious" work of novelists and short story writers. Outside of the worlds of journalism and the academy, almost no writers made a living at it. When the historian Donald Creighton published his biography of John A. Macdonald in the 1950s, it was considered remarkable and even a little outrageous for a writer of non-fiction to strive for literary effects, or to describe what he was doing in literary terms, both of which Creighton was at pains to do. Non-fiction was not supposed to have literary pretensions.

But in recent years non-fiction writing in Canada has been finding a place in the literary world, although it's a place that remains hard to define, and books of non-fiction by Heather Robertson, Myrna Kostash, David Macfarlane, Terry Glavin, Maggie Siggins, Mary Meigs, Michael Ondaatje, Ronald Wright, and others are now among the finest writing in Canada in any genre. It is the appearance of these books that set me to wondering whether in fact there might not be such a thing as a Canadian non-fiction tradition. In particular, I wanted to know where this so-called "new non-fiction" came from. Did it have any relationship to its pre-modernist forebears? In an attempt to answer these questions I decided to read, in some cases re-read, a broad range of Canadian non-fiction published since the first explorers began writing about the country. The result is *Imagining Ourselves*, a collection of extracts from some of the most popular and interesting non-fiction writing in Canada over the past three centuries. I have chosen only from published books, not from essays or journalism or other forms of non-fiction writing. And I have chosen only English selections; this is an anthology of original writing, not translation.

Imagining Ourselves is not an attempt to create a canon. The books represented here are not presented as necessarily the *best* of anything. Each of the selections in *Imagining Ourselves* represents an interesting moment in the development of Canadian non-fiction writing, either because of their subject matter or the narrative skills they employ. Another editor would choose a completely different set of titles, and they might be just as valid. What I am attempting to do is to describe with examples the evolution of non-fiction writing in English Canada in the hopes of proving something, to myself if to no one else: that this country has a long tradition of excellent writing—literary writing—in the non-fiction genre. *Imagining Ourselves* is merely an appetizer; it is hoped that readers will go on to indulge themselves in the full menu.

But what about that term, non-fiction? Increasingly, it is a red flag guaranteed to infuriate the people who write it. Non-fiction, because it is defined by what it is not, seems an inadequate, even condescending, label to describe what they do. In fact, the expression *non-fiction* entered the language only as recently as about 1907, according to the Random House dictionary, perhaps as a category of display that booksellers found handy in arranging their shelves. Certainly the writers of previous centuries included here would have had no idea of themselves as writers of a thing called non-fiction. But in this century the anomaly seems to have taken a firm hold. Biography, autobiography, essay, memoir, cookbook, textbook, technical manual, all are "not fiction." Recently on the non-fiction best-seller list, Leonard Cohen's latest collection of poetry was sandwiched between *The Hidden Life of Dogs* and the memoirs of the victim of an incurable disease. Also on the list were a plea for a "new" feminism, three memoirs by retired politicians, and a how-to book about staying young through natural medicine. Can a term which encompasses so many different types of writing have any meaning?

More importantly, the basic distinction between fiction and non-fiction has broken down. Not so long ago everyone seemed to agree that the purpose of non-fiction was to convey information. It was writing which was empirical, fact-based. Fiction, on the other hand, conveyed experience. It did not describe things that had actually happened. But this distinction has never really been valid. As the selections in *Imagining Ourselves* reveal, non-fiction writers have always leavened their facts with generous portions of dramatic licence. From the beginning, writers of non-fiction have been self-consciously literary. By that I mean that they have worked and reworked their material, sometimes employing the devices of fiction, in an attempt, not to convey information, but to share experience with their readers.

Early explorers often hired editors to transform their raw journals into appealing narratives for the general public. One of the most famous incidents in Canadian history, the murderous attack on the Inuit at Bloody Fall near the Arctic coast, became so because of Samuel Hearne's harrowing description of it in his book, *A Journey to the Northern Ocean*, published in 1795. But recently, academic sleuths have determined that Hearne, perhaps with the help of a ghostwriter, may have invented some of the more lurid details, including the presence of a young Inuit girl impaled on a spear, a detail which contributed so much to the notoriety of the affair at Bloody Fall.[1] Hearne was not the first writer, and he was certainly not the last, to break the empirical constraints of non-fiction. In his own day he was very much in the mode of the sensationalist travel writer who sought to sell books by spinning exotic tales filled with hyperbole and even downright lies. More modern examples include the novelist Frederick Philip Grove, whose autobiography *In Search of Myself* won a Governor-General's award for non-fiction in 1946, then turned out to be largely a fabrication, and Grey Owl, the Englishman who wrote as an Indian. Unlike Hearne, Grey Owl and Grove were using autobiography to invent new identities for themselves (although this may be seen too as a strategy for selling more books). But whatever the motive, the point is that most non-fiction is factually suspect. Only the most unwary readers believe everything they read.

If Samuel Hearne invented the story of the Inuit girl and the spear, you might say he was lying. But lying is a word which has little meaning in literature; so often *liar* is just another word for *writer*. Of course, when we use a cookbook we expect that by combining the ingredients for spaghetti sauce we will not end up with a cheese soufflé. But cookbooks and car manuals aside, most non-fiction is, to say the least, unstable. Trying to match it to the real world is like trying to nail the proverbial jelly to the wall. For writers of non-fiction, the facts are only part of the story;

their response to the facts, what they make of them, is the rest of the story, and is often more important. The American journalist Janet Malcolm makes this point about non-fiction. It is actually fiction that is dependable, she argues, in the sense that the events of a novel are "true" in the context of its own imaginative world. In the case of non-fiction, however, we almost never get the truth. Instead, we get a version of the truth. "Only in nonfiction," writes Malcolm, "does the question of what happened and how people thought and felt remain open."[2]

If the distinction between fiction and non-fiction is not always clear, neither is the distinction between literary (or creative) non-fiction and its more prosaic variants. The term creative non-fiction has come into widespread use in the past decade to describe forms of non-fiction which employ fictional elements or strategies. Clearly, there is a distinction to be made between writing which merely wants to impart information and writing that wants to draw the reader into a shared experience. Whether or not creativity is the distinguishing feature is not as clear. Most writers seem to agree that it is not. The search for a new label will doubtless continue, but if non-fiction itself no longer means what it used to, it seems pointless simply to pile up adjectives in front of it. I am inclined to agree with Andreas Schroeder who proposes that we "just get rid of generalized, umbrella-type labels like Fiction and Non-fiction alto-gether—they've become hopelessly imprecise anyway—and just stick with the specific ones, such as novel, memoir, essay, parable, biography, history, poem, documentary, commentary and so on."[3]

We only really need a new label if we are dealing with a new phenomenon. Is there anything new about the "new" non-fiction? The selections included in this volume demonstrate one thing at least: that from the earliest days non-fiction writers in Canada have been producing books which deserve to be called literary. In other words, they have been recording their experience in imaginative ways. I have mentioned the example of Samuel Hearne. Susanna Moodie likewise took a form familiar in her day, the emigrant's handbook, and embellished it into what in the twentieth century is often called a non-fiction novel. Ernest Thompson Seton used his observations of animals to virtually invent a new genre, the realistic animal story. Wallace Stegner combined short story and memoir to recreate his prairie childhood. It turns out that creative non-fiction, or whatever you want to call it, has been around since the earliest explorers put quill to paper. It is a mistake to read early Canadian writers as if they were not every bit as "literary" as more modern ones; in other words, to think that there is no tradition of Canadian literary non-fiction.

If a tradition exists, what are its defining characteristics? Canadian non-fiction is about any number of things, from shamanism to lesbianism to hockey. Its earliest form was the explorer's narrative, very much in the mode of the travel account which had been in vogue since the invention of the printing press. The journals of early adventurers, rewritten or edited and published as books, proved immensely popular with reading audiences fascinated with the exotic details of life in "uncivilized" places. In Canada, the appeal of explorers' accounts continued into the twentieth century with the books of Vilhjalmur Stefansson, and still finds echoes in the contemporary popularity of travel writing. A close ally of the explorer's narrative is the "Frozen North" memoir, the recollections of life "North of 60" by a retired fur trader, Mountie, or missionary. The "Frozen North" memoir usually has a title something like *Memoirs of an Arctic Arab,* or *Land of the Frozen Tide,* or *Policing the Top of the World* and is invariably described with adjectives such as informative and useful. As yet, none of these books has achieved literary distinction, but each addition to the genre serves to keep alive our belief that we are a distinctively Northern nation, which is to say that they contribute to our imagination of ourselves.

Once the colonization of Canada was well underway, the settlement process became the major concern of non-fiction writers for several generations. Beginning with Susanna Moodie and her sister Catharine Parr Traill and continuing down to the modern period with Wallace Stegner and James Minifie, the "sod-hut memoir" proliferated. At its worst, this form was tedious and predictable, bogged down in the details of pioneer life. At its best, it helped a pioneer society take imaginative possession of its own landscape and provided the country with a myth of struggle and progress to justify its existence.

Other Canadian non-fiction writers were especially attracted to the natural world. Ernest Thompson Seton wrote animal stories; Grey Owl wrote about wilderness preservation; Emily Carr wrote about the isolated native villages of the B.C. coast; Roderick Haig-Brown wrote about the joys of sport fishing. Nature writing was a popular sub-genre that sought meaning in the wilderness and solace in the company of wild things.

Most recently, since the 1960s, non-fiction has attracted writers from marginalized communities which had not been able to get their concerns into print previously. It used to be very rare, for example, to have Aboriginal Canadians writing books about their own experience. That was left to sympathetic Whites, or Imaginary Indians like Grey Owl. Then writers like Maria Campbell and Harold Cardinal broke the silence, discovering in memoir and personal history a way to articulate the history and grievances of their people. Immigrant communities have also found their voices (examples in this anthology are Myrna Kostash, Michael Ondaatje, and Eva Hoffman), along with gays and lesbians (see the selection from Mary Meigs's memoir, *Lily Briscoe*), the sexually abused, and the politically progressive. Apparently this is where literature from the margins begins, in personal testimony. In fact, the most obvious feature of Canadian non-fiction writing today is the great variety of writers who are employing it, often in quite innovative ways, to tell their stories.

As it has become more inclusive, non-fiction writing in English has also changed its tone. Mainstream Canadian non-fiction writers adopted the romantic mode. Their work is hopeful, heroic, celebratory. It describes the ultimate triumph of civilization over the forces of nature, and the successful emergence of a new nationality. So, for example, William Francis Butler (*The Great Lone Land*, 1872) discovered in the prairie west a vast hinterland available for the civilizing. Susanna Moodie (*Roughing It In The Bush*, 1852), for all her negativity, argued that wonderful opportunities existed on the colonial frontier. Richard Maurice Bucke (*Cosmic Consciousness*, 1901), the religious mystic from London, Ontario, believed that mankind as a whole was on the verge of a spiritual revolution. All of these writers, and most of their contemporaries, were essentially optimistic in outlook.

Romance continues to be a popular mode, as evidenced by the success of popular historical writers such as Pierre Berton and Peter C. Newman, both of whom write unashamedly patriotic stories full of swashbuckling heroes and dramatic events (or, in Newman's own words, "feisty characters and remarkable circumstances"). However, best-sellers aside, the mood of Canadian non-fiction has darkened considerably in the past couple of decades. One does not look to writers like David Macfarlane or Michael Ondaatje or Mary Meigs in search of patriotic celebration.

For some it is irrelevant, for others a cruel joke. Triumph has been replaced by irony; life seems generally more complicated. In books like *Maps and Dreams* or *Lost in Translation*, language and imagination are the subject, along with the difficulty of using them to communicate experience. Today we read writers like Berton and Mowat with a comforting (or, perhaps, discomforting) sense of nostalgia.

This is, of course, the modern attitude; and there is nothing uniquely Canadian about it. But the more sombre mood also reflects the emergence of other voices in our literature—feminist, aboriginal, ethnic—which do not share the self-confident optimism of the dominant culture. These voices are more interested in subverting the mainstream than in upholding it.

Thirty years ago Northrop Frye argued that Canadian literature is notoriously preoccupied with the question "Where is here?"[4] No matter what they sit down to write about, our writers invariably end up writing about the kind of place they think Canada is, was, or ought to be. And by describing it, they imagine it into being for the rest of us. Most of the images we have of Canada, after all, are provided by the writers represented in this anthology, along with all the others. We imagine back to the prairie west before the White Man came and we think of it still as the "Great Lone Land" that William Butler described. Our knowledge of the Ontario backwoods comes to us through the memoirs of the genteel pioneers who lived there. We retain an appreciation for the wilderness, and for the North, though few of us ever go there, because so many of our writers have told us that we should.

In other words, I have found the non-fiction tradition for which I was looking, in the sense that I now realize that I have learned from books how to be a Canadian. And so have you, whether you have read the books or not. The images produced by the literature eventually transcend the literature; they become embedded in our knowledge of ourselves. They become the adjectives we use to describe ourselves: peaceable, unassuming, tolerant. The books contain the stories that produce the images that constitute the identity. What I have tried to do in *Imagining Ourselves* is to show this process taking place in the pages of some of our best non-fiction writing.

Notes

1. I.S. MacLaren, "Samuel Hearne's Accounts of the Massacre at Bloody Fall, 17 July 1771," *Ariel*, 22:1 (January 1991): 25-51.
2. Janet Malcolm, "The Silent Woman," *The New Yorker* (August 23 and 30, 1993): 138.
3. Andreas Schroeder, "Creative Non-Fiction Contest #5," *Event*, 21: 3 (Fall, 1992): 8.
4. Northrop Frye, *The Bush Garden* (Toronto: House of Anansi, 1971): 220.

CAPTURED BY THE IROQUOIS

PIERRE–ESPRIT RADISSON

From *The Explorations* (1668)

Pierre Esprit Radisson occupies a special place in the Canadian imagination. The memoirs that he wrote about his expeditions into "Indian Country" have been used by successive generations of historians and popular writers and regurgitated in scores of books. The more lurid details of his adventures among the Iroquois have been staple items in Canadian school books for more than a century. There was even a popular television show based on his life. Few people have read Radisson's original work, but its influence has been pervasive. So much of what we think we know about early Canada and its Aboriginal inhabitants comes from The Explorations. *They illustrate that a book does not have to be read widely to be influential.*

*   The Explorations, or Voyages, have a complicated publishing history. There are six narratives in total, each describing different expeditions undertaken by Radisson, sometimes in the company of his brother-in-law, the Sieur des Groseilliers. Some of them were written in 1668-69 when Radisson, then aged thirty-two, was supposed to be on a trading expedition to Hudson Bay. Bad weather forced him to stay in England and he passed the winter recording some of his exploits in New France for the benefit of the English monarch, Charles II. Apparently the narratives were dictated in English, a language Radisson knew only crudely, and recorded by a scribe. They were written with the expectation of making some money and a reputation for Radisson; their content conforms well to the tradition of sensationalist travel writing about the New World. Radisson*

9

interrupted his literary labours to resume his career as a trader-adventurer in Canada. It was not until after his retirement from the Hudson's Bay Company twenty years later that he completed The Explorations. *The manuscript then languished unpublished, virtually unread, in a library in Oxford for almost 200 years until it appeared in a small edition of 250 copies in Boston in 1885. The following selection is from a 1961 edition of the original manuscript.*

Radisson came to New France as a youngster. He was only fifteen years old in 1652 when he was abducted by a party of Mohawk and adopted into a Mohawk family. Not long afterwards Radisson and another captive, an Algonquin man, tried to escape. The selection below describes this escape attempt and subsequent events. The gruesome details are the raw material out of which the image of the Iroquois as bloodthirsty savage was created so many years later. Radisson survived his captivity, played a central role in the creation of the Hudson's Bay Company and served the company for many years. He died in London in 1710.

While the meat was aboiling, that wildman spoke to me [in] the Algonquin language. I wondered to hear this stranger. He told me that he was taken two years ago. He asked me concerning Three Rivers and Quebec. [He] wished himself there, and I said the same, though I did not intend it. He asked me if I loved the French. I inquired him also if he loved the Algonquins. "Mary," quoth he, and [I said], "So do I my own nation." Then replied he, "Brother, cheer up. Let us escape. Three Rivers are not afar off." I told him my three comrades would not permit me and that they promised my mother to bring me back again. Then he inquired whether I would live like the Hurons who were in bondage or have my own liberty with the French, where there was good bread to be eaten. "Fear not," quoth he. "We shall kill them all three this night when they will be asleep, which will be an easy matter with their own hatchets." At last I consented, considering they were mortal enemies to my country, that [they] had cut the throats of so many of my relations, burned and murdered them, promising him to succor him in his design.

They, not understanding our language, asked the Algonquin what is that he said, but [he] told them some other story, nor [did] they suspected us in the least. Their belly full, their mind without care, wearied to the utmost of the foremost day's journey, [they] fell asleep securely, leaning their arms up and down without the least danger.

Then my wildman pushed me, thinking I was asleep. He rises and sits him down by the fire, beholding them one after another. Taking their arms aside and having the hatchets in their hand, [he] gives me one. To tell the truth, I was loathsome to do them mischief that never did me any. Yet, for the above said reasons, I took the hatchet and began the execution, which was soon done. My fellow comes to him that was nearest to the fire (I dare say he never saw the stroke) and I have done the like to another, but I, hitting him with the edge of the hatchet, could not disengage [it] presently, being so deep in his head. [He] rises upon his breast, but fell back suddenly, making a great noise which almost awaked the third, but my comrade gave him a deadly blow of a hatchet, and presently after I shot him dead. Then we prepared ourselves with all speed—throwing their dead corpses, after the wildman took off their heads, into the water.

We took three guns (leaving the fourth), their two swords, their hatchets, their powder and shot, and all their porcelain. We took also some meal and meat. I was sorry for to have been in such an encounter, but too late to repent. We took our journey that night alongst the river. The break of day we landed on the side of a rock which was smooth. We carried our boat and equipage into the wood about a hundred paces from the waterside, where we stayed most sadly all that day, tormented by the maringoines [mosquitoes]. We turned our boat upside down; we put us under it from the rain. The night coming, which was the fittest time to leave that place, we go without any noise for our safety. We travelled fourteen nights in that manner, in great fear, hearing boats passing by. When we have perceived any fire, [we] left off rowing and went by with as little noise as could possible. At last, with many turnings by land and by water, we came to the Lake of St. Peter's.

We landed about four of the clock, leaving our skiff in among rushes, far out of the way from those that passes that way and [might] do us injury. We retired into the wood, where we made a fire some two hundred paces from the river. There we roasted some meat and boiled meal. After, we rested ourselves awhile from the many labours of the former night.

So, having slept, my companion awakes first and stirs me, saying it was high time, that we might by day come to our dwelling, of which counsel I did not approve. [I] told him the enemies commonly were lurking about the riverside and we should do very well to stay in that place till sunset.

"Then," said he, "let us begone. We [are] passed all fear. Let us shake the yoke of a company of whelps that killed so many French and black coats and so many of my nation. Nay," saith he, "brother, if you come not, I will leave you and will go through the woods till I shall be over against the French quarters. There I will make a fire for a sign that they may fetch me. I will tell to the governor that you stayed behind. Take courage, man," says he. With this he took his piece and things.

At this, I considered how if [I] were taken at the door by mere rashness. Next, the impossibility I saw to go by myself if my comrade would leave me; perhaps the wind might rise, that I could [only] come to the end of my journey in a long time and that I should be accounted a coward for not daring to hazard myself with him that had so much ventured for me. I resolved to go along through the woods, but the little constance that is to be expected in wildmen made me fear he should [take] to his heels, which approved [to me] his unfortunate advice: he hath lost his life by it, and I in great danger have escaped by the help of the Almighty. I consent to go by water with him.

In a short time we came to the lake. The water very calm and clear, no likelihood of any storm. We hazarded to the other side of the lake, thinking for more security. After we passed the third part of the lake, I being the foremost, have perceived [something] as if it were a black shadow, which proved a real thing. He at this rises and tells me that it was a company of buzzards, a kind of geese in that country. We went on. We soon perceived our own fatal blindness, for they were enemies. We went back again towards the land, with all speed, to escape the evident danger, but it was too late. Before we could come to the rushes that were within half a league of the waterside, we were tired. Seeing them approaching nigher and nigher, we threw the three heads in the water. They meet with these heads, which makes them to row harder after us, thinking that we runned away from their country. We were so near the land that we saw the bottom of the water, but yet too deep to step in, when these cruel inhumans came within a musket shot of us. Fearing lest the booty should get away from them [they] shot several times at us and deadly wounded my comrade, [he] falling dead. I expected such another shot. The little skiff was [so] pierced in several places with their shooting that water running in apace. I defended myself with the two arms. At last they environed me with their boats, took me just as I was sinking. They held up the wildman and throwed him into one of their boats, and me they brought with all diligence to land. I thought to die without mercy.

They made a great fire and took my comrade's heart out and chopped off his head, which they put on an end of a stick, and carried it to one of their boats. They cut off some of the flesh of that miserable, broiled it, and ate it. If he had not been so desperately wounded, they had done their best to keep him alive to make him suffer the more by burning him with small fires; but being wounded in the chin, and [a] bullet gone through the throat, and another in the shoulder that broke his arms, [these] made him incurable. They burned some part of his body and the rest they left there. That was the miserable end of that wretch.

Let us come now to the beginning of my miseries and calamities that I was to undergo. Whilst they were busy about my companion's head, the others tied me safe and fast in a strange manner. Having stripped me naked, they tied me above the elbows behind my back, and then they put a collar about me, not of porcelain as before, but a rope wrought about my middle, [and] so brought me in that pickle to the boat. As I was embarked, they asked me several questions. [I] being not able to answer, [they] gave me great blows with their fists, then pulled out one of my nails, and partly untied me. What a displeasure had I, to have seen myself taken again, being almost come to my journey's end, that I must now go back again to suffer such torments. Death was to be expected. Having lost all hopes, I resolved altogether to die, being a folly to think otherwise.

I was not the [only] one in the claws of those wolves. Their company was composed of a hundred and fifty men, [plus prisoners] took about Quebec and other places: two French men, one French woman, seventeen Hurons, men as [well as] women. They had eleven heads which they said were of the Algonquins, and I was the thirtieth [and] three victim with those cruels. The wildmen that were prisoners sang their fatal song, which was a mournful song or noise. The twelve colours (which were heads) stood out for a show.

We prisoners were separated, one in one boat, one in another. As for me, I was put into a boat with a Huron whose fingers were cut and burned, and very [few] amongst them but had the mark of those inhuman devils. They did not permit me to tarry long with my fellow prisoner, lest I should tell them any news (as I imagine), but sent me to another boat, where I remained the rest of the voyage by water, which proved somewhat to my disadvantage.

In this boat there was an old man who, having examined me, I answered him as I could best: told him how I was adopted by such as one by name and [how] as I was ahunting with my companions that wildman that was killed came to us and, after he had eaten, went his way; [how] in the evening [he] came back again and found us all asleep, took a hatchet and killed my three companions, and awaked me and so embarked me and brought me to this place. That old man believed me in some measure, which I perceived in him by his kindess towards me, but he was not able to protect me from those that had a will to do me mischief. Many slandered me, but I took no notice.

Some four leagues thence, they erected cottages by a small river very difficult to get to, for there is little water on [a] great sand [bar] a league wide. To this very hour I took notice how they tied their captives, though at my own cost. They planted several posts of the bigness of an arm, then laid us of a length, tied us to the said posts, far asunder from one another. Then [they] tied our knees, [next] our wrists and elbows and our hairs directly upon the crown of our heads. Then [they] cut four bars of the bigness of a leg and used [them] thus: they took two for the neck, putting one of each side, tying the two ends together so that our heads were fast in a hole like a trap; likewise they did to our legs. What tormented us most was the maringoines and great flies being in abundance. [We] did all night but puff and blow that by that means we saved our faces from the sting of those ugly creatures; having no use of our hands, we are cruelly tormented.

Our voyage was laborious and most miserable, suffering every night like misery.

When we came near our dwellings, we met several gangs of men, to our great disadvantage, for we were forced to sing, and those that came to see us gave porcelain to those that did us injury. One cut off a finger. Another plucked out a nail and put the end of our fingers into their burning pipes, and burned several parts in our bodies. Some took our fingers, and of a stick made a thing like a fork with which [they] gave several blows on the back of the hands, which caused our hands to swell and became at last insensible, as [if] dead. Having suffered all these cruelties, which were nothing to that they make usually suffer their prisoners, we arrived at last to the place of execution, which is at the coming-in to their village, where not [long] before I escaped very near to be soundly beaten with staves and fists. Now I must think to be no less treated, by reason of the murder of the three men. But the fear of death takes away the fear of blows.

Nineteen of us prisoners were brought thither and two left behind with the heads. In this place we had eight colours. Who would not shake at the sight of so many men, women, and children armed with all sorts of instruments?—staves, hand irons, heelskins wherein they put half a score of bullets. Others had brands, rods of thorn, and all such like that the cruelties could invent to put their prisoners to greater torments. Here [was] no help, no remedy. We must pass this dangerous passage in our extremity without help. He that is the fearfulest or that is observed to stay the last gets nothing by it but more blows, and put him to more pain: the meanest sort of people commonly is more cruel to the fearfulest than to the others that they see fearful; [the latter] suffer cheerfully and with constancy.

They begun to cry to both sides, we marching one after another, environed with a number of people from all parts to be witness to that hideous sight which seriously may be called the image of hell in this world. The men sings their fatal song; the women makes horrible cries. The victors cries of joy, and their wives make acclamations for mirth. In a word, all prepares for the ruin of these poor victims who are so tied—having not saving only our legs free—[and who] advance by little and little, according [to] the will of him that leads us. As he held us by a long rope, he stayed us to his will and often makes us fall for to show the cruelty, abusing you so to give them pleasure and you more torment. As our band was great, there was a greater crew of people to see the prisoners. The report of my taking being now made, and of the death of the three men, which afflicted the most of that nation, [a] great many of [them] came through a design of revenge and to molest me more than any other.

But it was altogether otherwise, for among the tumult I perceived my father and mother, with their two daughters. The mother pushes in among the crew directly to me, and when she was near enough she catches hold of my hair as one desperate, calling me often by my name. Drawing me out of my rank, she puts me into the hands of her husband, who then bid me have courage, conducting me another way home to his cabin.

He made me sit down [and] said to me, "You senseless! Thou was my son, and thou rendered thyself enemy. Thou rendered thyself enemy! Thou lovest not thy mother nor thy father that gave thee thy life, and thou notwithstanding will kill me. Be merry; Conharrassan, give him to eat." (That was the name of one of the sisters.)

My heart shaked with trembling and fear, which took away my stomach. Nevertheless, [I] signify a bold countenance, knowing well that a bold generous mind is always accounted among all sort of nations, especially among warriors that is very presumptuous and haughty because of their magnanimity and victories, opposing themselves into all dangers and encounters whatever, running over the whole land, slaining and killing all they meet in exercising their cruelties, or else showing mercy to whom they please to give liberty. God gave me the grace to forget nothing of my duty. I told my father the success of my voyage in the best terms I could and how all things passed, mixturing a little of their language with that of the Hurons, which I learned more fluently than theirs, being longer and more frequently with the Hurons. Everyone attentively gave ear to me, hoping by this means to save my life.

Upon this, here comes a great number of armed men, [who] enters the cabin, where finding me yet tied with my cords, sitting by my parents, [they] made their addresses to my father and spake to him very loud. After a while my father make me rise and delivers me into their hands. My mother, seeing this, cries and laments with both my sisters. I, believing in a terrible motion, [thought] to go directly on to the place of execution. I must march; I must yield where force is predominant at the public place.

I was conducted [to] where I found a good company of those miserable wretches altogether, beaten with blows, covered with blood, and burned. One miserable Frenchman, yet breathing, having now been consumed with blows of sticks, passed so through the hands of this enraged crew, and seeing he could [endure] no more [they] cut off his head and throwed it into the fire. This was the end of this execrable woeful body of this miserable.

They made me go up the scaffold, where were five men, three women, and two children captives. I made the eleventh. There were several scaffolds nigh one another, where were these wretches, who with a doleful singings replenished the heavens with their cries. I can say that an hour [passed] before the weather approved very fair, and in an instant the weather changed and rained extremely. The most part retired to avoid this hail, and now we must expect the rigor of the weather by the retiration of those perfidious, except one band of hell who stayed about us for to learn the trade of barbary. Those little devils, seeing themselves all alone, contrived a thousand inventions of wickedness. This is nothing strange, seeing that they are brought up [thus] and suck the cruelty from their mothers' breast.

I prolong a little from my purpose of my adventure for to say the torments that I have seen suffered at Coutu, after they [the prisoners] have passed the sallett at their entering into the village and the encounters that they meet ordinarily in the way, as above said. They tie the prisoners to a post by their hands, their backs turned towards the hangman, who hath a burning fire of dry wood and rind of trees, which doth not quench easily. They put into this fire hatchets, swords, and such like instruments of iron. They take these and quench them on human flesh. They pluck out their nails for the most part in this sort: they put a red coal of fire upon it and, when it's swollen, bits it out with their teeth; after, they stop the blood with a brand, which by little and little draws the veins the one after the another from off the fingers, and when they draw all as much as they can they cut it with pieces of red hot iron; they squeeze the fingers between two stones and so draw the marrow out of the bones, and when the flesh is all taken away, they put it [the fingers] in a dish full of burning sand. After, they tie the wrist with a cord, putting two for this effect, one drawing him one way, another of another way. If the sinews be not cut with a stick, putting it through and taking it, they make them come as fast as they can and cut them in the same way as the others. Some others cuts pieces of flesh from all parts of the body and broil them, gets you to eat it, thrusting them into your mouth, putting into it a stick of fire. They break your teeth with a stone or clubs. [They] use the handle of a kettle, and upon this do hang five or six hatchets red hot, which they hang about their [victim's] neck. [They] roast your legs with brands of fire, and thrusting into it some sticks pointed, wherein they put a lead melted and gunpowder, and [they] then give it fire like unto artificial fire and make the patient gather it by the stumps of his remaining fingers. If he cannot sing they make him quackle like a hen. I saw two men tied to a rope, one at each end, and hang them so all night, throwing red coals at them or burning sand and in such like burn their feet, legs, thighs, and breech. The little ones do exercise themselves about such cruelties. They deck the bodies all over with hard straw, putting in the end of this stray thorns. [They] so leave them now, then give them a little rest, sometimes give them fresh water, and make them repose on fresh leaves. They also give them to eat of the best they have that they come to themselves again, [in order] to give them more torments. Then, when they see that the patient can no more take up his hair, they cover his head with a platter made of rind full of burning sand, and often sets the platter afire. In the next place, they clothe you with a suit made of rind of a tree, and this they make burn out on your body. They cut off your stones, and the women play with them as with balls. When they see the miserable die, they open him and pluck out his heart. They drink some of his blood and wash the children's heads with the rest to make them valiant. If you have endured all the above-said torments patiently and without moans, and have defied death in singing, then they thrust burning blades all along your bones and, so ending the tragedy, cut off the head and put it on the end of a stick and draw his body in quarters, which they haul about their village. Lastly, [they] throws him into the water or leave [him] in the fields to be eaten by the crows or dogs.

Now let me come to our miserable poor captives that stayed all along [through] the rain upon the scaffold, to the mercy of two or three hundred rogues that shot us with little arrows and drew out our beards and the hair from those that had any. The shower of rain being over, all came together again and, having kindled fires, begun to burn some of those poor wretches.

That day they plucked four nails out of my fingers and made me sing, though I had no mind at that time. I became speechless oftentimes; then they gave me water wherein they boiled a certain herb that the gunsmiths use to polish their arms. That liquor brought me to my speech again. The night being come, they made me come down all naked as I was and brought [me] to a strange cottage. (I wished heartily it had been that of my parents.) They tied me to a post, where I stayed a full hour without the least molestation. A woman came there with her boy, enticed him to cut off one of my fingers with a flint stone. The boy was not four years old. This [child] takes my finger and begins to work, but in vain because he had not the strength to break my fingers; so my poor finger escaped, having no other hurt done to it but the flesh cut round about it. His mother made him suck the very blood that runned from my finger. I had no other torment all that day. At night I could not sleep because of the great pain. I did eat a little and drunk much water by reason of a fever I caught by the cruel torments I suffered.

The next morning I was brought back again to the scaffold, where there were company enough. They made me sing anew, but my mother came there and made [me] hold my peace, bidding me be cheerful and that I should not die. She brought me some meat. Her coming comforted me much, but that did not last long, for here comes several old people, one of which, being on the scaffold, sat him down by me, holding in his mouth a pewter pipe burning. [He] took my thumb and put it on the burning tobacco, and so smoked three pipes one after another, which made my thumb swell and the nail and flesh become as coal. My mother was always by me to comfort me, but [I] said not what I thought. That man having finished his hard work—but I am sure I felt it harder to suffer it—he trembled, whether for fear or for so much action I cannot tell. My mother tied my fingers with cloth, and when he was gone she greased my hair and combed my hair with a wooden comb [that was] fitter to comb a horse's tail than anything else. She goes back again.

That day they ended many of those poor wretches, flinging some all alive into the middle of a great fire. They burned a French woman. They pulled out her breasts and took a child out of her belly, which they broiled, and made the mother eat of it; so in short [she] died.

I was not abused all that day till the night. They burned the soles of my feet and legs. A soldier running through my foot a sword red hot out of the fire and plucked several of my nails. I stayed in that manner all night. I neither wanted in the meanwhile meat nor drink. I was supplied by my mother and sisters. My father also came to see me and told me I should have courage. There came a little boy to gnaw with his teeth the end of my fingers. There appears a man to cut off my thumb; being about it, [he instead] leaves me instantly and did no harm, for which I was glad. I believe that my father dissuaded him from it. A while after my father was gone, three came to the scaffold who swore they would [do] me a mischief. [One] tied his legs to mine, called for a brand of fire, laid it between his legs and mine, and sings; but by good luck it was out on my side and did none other effect than burn my skin, but [it] burned him to some purpose. In this posture I was to follow him. Being not able to hold me, [he] draweth me down. One of the company cut the rope that held us with his knife and make me go up again [on] the scaffold, and then [they] went on their way. There I stayed till midday alone.

There comes a multitude of people, who makes me come down and laid me into a cottage where there were a number of [about] sixty old men smoking tobacco. Here they make me sit down among them, and [they] stayed about half an hour without that they asked who and why I was brought thither; nor did I much care for the great torments I suffered; I know not whether I was dead or alive. Albeit I was in a hot fever and great pains, I rejoiced at the sight of my brother, that I had not seen since my arrivement. He comes in very sumptuously covered with several necklaces of porcelain, and a hatchet in his hand. [He] sat down by the company and cast an eye on me now and then. Presently comes in my father with a new and long cover and a new porcelain about him, with a hatchet in his hands; [he] likewise sat down with the company. He had a calumet of red stone in his hands, a cake upon his shoulders that hanged down his back, and so had the rest of the old men.

In that same cake are enclosed all the things in the world, as they told me often, advertising me that I should [not] disoblige them in the least nor make them angry, by reason they had in their power the sun and moon and the heavens, and consequently all the earth. You must know in this cake there is nothing but tobacco, and roots to heal some wounds or sores. Some others keep in it the bones of their deceased friends. Most of them [keep] wolves' heads, squirrels' or any other beast's head. When they have any debatement among them, they sacrifice to this tobacco; that they throw into the fire, and make smoke of that they puff out of their pipes. Whether for peace or adversity, or prosperity or war, such ceremonies they make very often.

My father, taking his place, lights his pipe and smokes as the rest. They held great silence during this. They bring prisoners: to wit, seven women and two men, more [than] ten children from the age of three to twelve years. They placed them all by me, who as yet had my arms tied, the others all at liberty, being not tied, which put me into some despair lest I should pay for all. A while after, one of the company rises and makes a long speech, now showing the heavens with his hands, and then the earth and fire. This good man put himself into a sweat through the earnest discourse. Having finished his panegyric, another begins, and also many [more], one after another.

They gave then liberty to some, but killed two children with hatchets, and a woman of fifty years old, and threw the rest out of the cottage (saving only myself) at full liberty. I was left alone for a stake.

They contested together. [Upon] which my father rise and made a speech which lasted above an hour. Being naked, having nothing on but his drawers and the cover of his head, [he] put himself all in a heat; his eyes were hollow in his head; he appeared to me like mad, naming often the Algonquins, in their language Attiseruata, which made me believe he spoke in my behalf. In that very time [my mother] comes with two necklaces of porcelain, one in her arms and another about her like a belt. As soon as she came in she begun to sing and dance and fling off one of her necklaces in the middle of the place, having made many turns from one end to the other. She takes the other necklace and gives it [to] me, then goes her way. Then my brother rises and, holding his hatchet in his hand, sings a military song. Having finished, [he] departs. I feared much that he was first to knock me in the head, and happy are those that can escape so well rather than be burned. My father rises for a second time and sings. So done, [he] retired himself. I thought all their gifts, songs, and speeches should prevail nothing with me.

Those that stayed held a council and spoke one to another very low, throwing tobacco into the fire, making exclamations. Then the cottage was open[ed on] all sides by those that came to view. Some of the company retires, and place was made for them as if they were kings. Forty stays with me, and nigh two thousand about my cottage, of men, women, and children. Those that went their way returned presently. Being set down, [they] smoked again whilst my father, mother, brothers, and sisters were present. My father sings awhile [and] so done, makes a speech. Taking the porcelain necklace from off me, [he] throws [it] at the feet of an old man and cuts the cord that held me, then makes me rise. The joy that I received at that time was incomparable, for suddenly all my pains and griefs ceased, not feeling the least pain. He bids me be merry, makes me sing, to which I consented with all my heart. Whilst I did sing they whooped and hallooed on all sides. The old man bid me, "Ever be cheerful, my son." My mother, sisters, and the rest of their friends [sang] and danced.

Then my father takes me by the arm and leads me to his cabin. As we went along, nothing was heard but whooping and hallooing on all parts, bidding me to take great courage. My mother was not long after me, with the rest of her friends. Now I see myself free from death.

SWORD SWALLOWING
ON THE TUNDRA

SAMUEL HEARNE

From *A Journey to the Northern Ocean* (1795)

Even though they were written for a European audience, the narratives of fur traders and explorers are now recognized as the origins of a distinctive literature about Canada. The best of the genre take the daily experience of frontier travel and trade and transform it into narrative accounts which are the first attempts to describe the country. The three pillars of this genre, in English at least, are David Thompson's Narrative, 1784–1812, *Alexander Mackenzie's* Voyages from Montreal, *and Samuel Hearne's* A Journey from Prince of Wales's Fort in Hudson's Bay to the Northern Ocean, 1769–1772. *Mackenzie's book, written with the help of literary hack William Combe, won him a knighthood and was the only one to achieve success in its author's lifetime. Thompson and Hearne hoped to support themselves from the proceeds of their books, but both died before their books were published.*

Hearne's account describes a trek he made with a party of Chipewyan hunters across the Barren Lands of the Northwest Territories. It was published in London in 1795, three years after his death, and immediately established itself as the first popular book about the Canadian hinterland. German, French, and Dutch editions appeared almost immediately. There is some question as to the authorship of A Journey, *which is an embellishment of field notes Hearne kept during the expedition and, like Mackenzie, he may have had help preparing the published version.*

Samuel Hearne was born in London in 1745. He enlisted in the Royal Navy as a young boy, then joined the Hudson's Bay Company as a sailor. However, it was as a landsman that he made his mark with the company. In 1769 he led an expedition overland from the shores of Hudson Bay to search for copper at the mouth of the optimistically named Coppermine River and to make contact with native groups outside the HBC trading network. After two false starts, Hearne obtained the services of a Chipewyan guide named Matonabbee, and the success of the excursion was assured. The return trip took a year and a half and covered 5,600 kilometres, all on foot. Most of what Hearne saw had never been seen by any other White person.

That Hearne could not escape his own cultural biases the following extract makes clear. However, he was impressed by many aspects of Aboriginal culture, was not reluctant to say so, and was clear-eyed about some of the negative results of contact with White civilization. He offers us a fascinating portrait of a man struggling to come to terms with experiences completely outside his normal frame of reference. The following extract describes an example of Chipewyan conjuring.

When a friend for whom they have a particular regard is, as they suppose, dangerously ill, beside the above methods, they have recourse to another very extraordinary piece of superstition; which is no less than that of pretending to swallow hatchets, ice-chissels, broad bayonets, knives, and the like; out of a superstitious notion that undertaking such desperate feats will have some influence in appeasing death, and procure a respite for their patient.

On such extraordinary occasions a conjuring-house is erected, by driving the ends of four long small sticks, or poles, into the ground at right angles, so as to form a square of four, five, six, or seven feet, as may be required. The tops of the poles are tied together, and all is close covered with a tent-cloth or other skin, exactly in the shape of a small square tent, except that there is no vacancy left at the top to admit the light. In the middle of this house, or tent, the patient is laid, and is soon followed by the conjurer, or conjurers. Sometimes five or six of them give their joint-assistance; but before they enter, they strip themselves quite naked, and as soon as they get into the house, the door being well closed, they kneel round the sick person or persons, and begin to suck and blow at the parts affected, and then in a very short space of time sing and talk as if conversing with familiar spirits, which they say appear to them in the shape of different beasts and birds of prey. When they have had sufficient conference with those necessary agents, or shadows, as they term them, they ask for the hatchet, bayonet, or the like, which is always prepared by another person, with a long string fastened to it by the haft, for the convenience of hauling it up again after they have swallowed it; for they very wisely admit this to be a very necessary precaution, as hard and compact bodies, such as iron and steel, would be very difficult to digest, even by the men who are enabled to swallow them. Besides, as these tools are in themselves very useful, and not always to be procured, it would be very ungenerous in the conjurers to digest them, when it is known that barely swallowing them and hauling them up again is fully sufficient to answer every purpose that is expected from them.

At the time when the forty and odd tents of Indians joined us, one man was so dangerously ill, that it was thought necessary the conjurers should use some of those wonderful experiments for his recovery; one of them therefore immediately consented to swallow a broad bayonet. Accordingly, a conjuring-house was erected in the manner above described, into which the patient was conveyed, and he was soon followed by the conjurer, who, after a long preparatory discourse, and the necessary conference with his familiar spirits, or shadows, as they call them, advanced to the door and asked for the bayonet, which was then ready prepared, by having a string fastened to it, and a short piece of wood tied to the other end of the string, to prevent him from swallowing it. I could not help observing that the length of the bit of wood was not more than the breadth of the bayonet; however, as it answered the intended purpose, it did equally well as if it had been as long as a handspike.

Though I am not so credulous as to believe that the conjurer absolutely swallowed the bayonet, yet I must acknowledge that in the twinkling of an eye he conveyed it to—God knows where; and the small piece of wood, or one exactly like it, was confined close to his teeth. He then paraded backward and forward before the conjuring-house for a short time, when he feigned to be greatly disordered in his stomach and bowels; and, after making many wry faces, and groaning most hideously, he put his body into several distorted attitudes, very suitable to the occasion. He then returned to the door of the conjuring-house, and after making many strong efforts to vomit, by the help of the string he at length, and after tugging at it some time, produced the bayonet, which apparently he hauled out of his mouth, to the no small surprise of all present. He then looked round with an air of exultation, and strutted into the conjuring-house, where he renewed his incantations, and continued them without intermission twenty-four hours. Though I was not close to his elbow when he performed the above feat, yet I thought myself near enough (and I can assure my readers I was all attention) to have detected him. Indeed I must confess that it appeared to me to be a very nice piece of deception, especially as it was performed by a man quite naked.

Not long after this slight-of-hand work was over, some of the Indians asked me what I thought of it; to which I answered, that I was too far off to see it so plain as I could wish; which indeed was no more than the strictest truth, because I was not near enough to detect the deception. The sick man, however, soon recovered; and in a few days afterwards we left that place and proceeded to the South West.

As during our stay at Anaw'd Lake several of the Indians were sickly, the doctors undertook to administer relief; particularly to one man, who had been hauled on a sledge by his brother for two months. His disorder was the dead palsey, which affected one side, from the crown of his head to the sole of his foot. Besides this dreadful disorder, he had some inward complaints, with a total lack of appetite; so that he was reduced to a mere skeleton, and so weak as to be scarcely capable of speaking. In this deplorable condition, he was laid in the centre of a large conjuring-house, made much after the manner as that which has been already described. And that nothing might be wanting toward his recovery, the same man who deceived me in swallowing a bayonet in the Summer, now offered to swallow a large piece of board, about the size of a barrel-stave, in order to effect his recovery. The piece of board was prepared by another man, and painted according to the direction of the juggler, with a rude representation of some beast of prey on one side, and on the reverse was painted, according to their rude method, a resemblance of the sky.

Without entering into a long detail of the preparations for this feat, I shall at once proceed to observe, that after the conjurer had held the necessary conference with his invisible spirits, or shadows, he asked if I was present; for he had heard of my saying that I did not see him swallow the bayonet fair; and on being answered in the affirmative, he desired me to come nearer; on which the mob made a lane for me to pass, and I advanced close to him, and found him standing at the conjuring-house door as naked as he was born.

When the piece of board was delivered to him, he proposed at first only to shove one-third of it down his throat, and then walk round the company afterward to shove down another third; and so proceed till he had swallowed the whole, except a small piece of the end, which was left behind to haul it up again. When he put it to his mouth it apparently slipped down his throat like lightning, and only left about three inches sticking without his lips; after walking backwards and forwards three times, he hauled it up again, and ran into the conjuring-house with great precipitation. This he did to all appearance with great ease and composure; and notwithstanding I was all attention on the occasion, I could not detect the deceit; and as to the reality of its being a piece of wood that he pretended to swallow, there is not the least reason to doubt it, for I had it in my hand, both before and immediately after the ceremony.

To prevent a variety of opinions on this occasion, and to lessen the apparent magnitude of the miracle, as well as to give some colour to my scepticism, which might otherwise perhaps appear ridiculous, it is necessary to observe, that this feat was performed in a dark and excessively cold night; and although there was a large fire at some distance, which reflected a good light, yet there was great room for collusion: for though the conjurer himself was quite naked, there were several of his fraternity well-clothed, who attended him very close during the time of his attempting to swallow the board, as well as at the time of his hauling it up again.

For these reasons it is necessary also to observe, that on the day preceding the performance of this piece of deception, in one of my hunting excursions, I accidentally came across the conjurer as he was sitting under a bush, several miles from the tents, where he was busily employed shaping a piece of wood exactly like that part which stuck out of his mouth after he had pretended to swallow the remainder of the piece. The shape of the piece which I saw him making was this, ; which exactly resembled the forked end of the main piece, the shape of which was this, . So that when his attendants had concealed the main piece, it was easy for him to stick the small point into his mouth, as it was reduced at the small end to a proper size for the purpose.

Similar proofs may easily be urged against his swallowing the bayonet in the Summer, as no person less ignorant than themselves can possibly place any belief in the reality of those feats; yet on the whole, they must be allowed a considerable share of dexterity in the performance of those tricks, and a wonderful deal of perseverance in what they do for the relief of those whom they undertake to cure.

Not long after the above performance had taken place, some of the Indians began to ask me what I thought of it. As I could not have any plea for saying that I was far off, and at the time not caring to affront them by hinting my suspicions of deceit, I was some time at a loss for an answer: I urged, however, the impossibility of a man's swallowing a piece of wood, that was not only much longer than his whole back, but nearly twice as broad as he could extend his mouth. On which some of them laughed at my ignorance, as they were pleased to call it; and said, that the spirits in waiting swallowed, or otherwise concealed, the stick, and only left the forked end apparently sticking out of the conjurer's mouth. My guide, Matonabbee, with all his other good sense, was so bigotted to the reality of those performances, that he assured me in the strongest terms, he had seen a man, who was then in company, swallow a child's cradle, with as much ease as he could fold up a piece of paper, and put it into his mouth; and that when he hauled it up again, not the mark of a tooth, or of any violence, was to be discovered about it.

This story so far exceeded the feats which I had seen with the bayonet and board that, for the sake of keeping up the farce, I began to be very inquisitive about the spirits which appear to them on those occasions, and their form; when I was told that they appeared in various shapes, for almost every conjurer had his peculiar attendant; but that the spirit which attended the man who pretended to swallow the piece of wood, they said, generally appeared to him in the shape of a cloud. This I thought very a-propos to the present occasion; and I must confess that I never had so thick a cloud thrown before my eyes before or since; and had it not been by accident, that I saw him make a counterpart to the piece of wood said to be swallowed, I should have been still at a loss how to account for so extraordinary a piece of deception, performed by a man who was entirely naked.

As soon as our conjurer had executed the above feat, and entered the conjuring-house, as already mentioned, five other men and an old woman, all of whom were great professors of the art, stripped themselves quite naked and followed him, when they soon began to suck, blow, sing, and dance, round the poor paralytic; and continued so to do for three days and four nights, without taking the least rest or refreshment, not even so much as a drop of water. When these poor deluding and deluded people came out of the conjuring-house, their mouths were so parched with thirst as to be quite black, and their throats so sore, that they were scarcely able to articulate a single word, except those that stand for *yes* and *no* in their language.

After so long an abstinence they were careful not to eat or drink too much at one time, particularly for the first day; and indeed some of them, to appearance, were almost as bad as the poor man they had been endeavouring to relieve. But great part of this was feigned; for they lay on their backs with their eyes fixed, as if in the agonies of death, and were treated like young children; one person sat constantly by them, moistening their mouths with fat, and now and then giving them a drop of water. At other times a small bit of meat was put into their mouths, or a pipe held for them to smoke. This farce only lasted for the first day; after which they seemed to be perfectly well, except the hoarseness, which continued for a considerable time afterwards. And it is truly wonderful, though the strictest truth, that when the poor sick man was taken from the conjuring-house, he had not only recovered his appetite to an amazing degree, but was able to move all the fingers and toes of the side that had been so long dead. In three weeks he recovered so far as to be capable of walking, and at the end of six weeks went a hunting for his family. He was one of the persons particularly engaged to provide for me during my journey; and after his recovery from this dreadful disorder, accompanied me back to Prince of Wales's Fort in June one thousand seven hundred and seventy-two; and since that time he has frequently visited the Factory, though he never had a healthy look afterwards, and at times seemed troubled with a nervous complaint. It may be added, that he had been formerly of a remarkable lively disposition; but after his last illness he always appeared thoughtful, sometimes gloomy, and in fact, the disorder seemed to have changed his whole nature; for before that dreadful paralytic stroke, he was distinguished for his good-nature and benevolent disposition; was entirely free from every appearance of avarice; and the whole of his wishes seemed confined within the narrow limits of possessing as many goods as were absolutely necessary, with his own industry, to enable him to support his family from season to season; but after this event, he was the most fractious, quarrelsome, discontented, and covetous wretch alive.

Though the ordinary trick of these conjurers may be easily detected, and justly exploded, being no more than the tricks of common jugglers, yet the apparent good effect of their labours on the sick and diseased is not so easily accounted for. Perhaps the implicit confidence placed in them by the sick may, at times, leave the mind so perfectly at rest, as to cause the disorder to take a favourable turn; and a few successful cases are quite sufficient to establish the doctor's character and reputation: But how this consideration could operate in the case I have just mentioned I am at a loss to say; such, however, was the fact, and I leave it to be accounted for by others.

NOOTKA CUSTOMS

JOHN JEWITT

From *Narrative of the Adventures and Sufferings* (1815)

The captivity narrative has been a popular form of travel writing since the first Europeans arrived in North America. Aboriginal people often seized early traders or settlers and held them captive, sometimes adopting them into their tribes for periods of many years. Likewise, Europeans captured Aboriginals and took them home to display to a curious public. Aboriginal captives did not usually survive their sojourns among the Whites, and those who did did not write books about their experiences. White captives, on the other hand, often hurried into print with accounts of their treatment at the hands of the "savages." Pierre Radisson is one example. Another is John Jewitt's book about his twenty-seven months among the Nuu-chah-nulth (Nootka) people on Vancouver Island's west coast.

John Jewitt (1783-1821) was born in England where he trained as a blacksmith. At the age of nineteen, he sailed as an armourer aboard the vessel Boston *bound for the Pacific Northwest on a trading voyage. At this time coastal British Columbia was attracting dozens of trading ships to its shores annually to collect sea-otter pelts from the Native groups who were its sole inhabitants. In Nootka Sound on the west coast of Vancouver Island, a group of Nuu-chah-nulth people, led by their chief, Maquinna, attacked the* Boston, *probably in retaliation for insults they had suffered at the hands of other traders. They murdered every member of the crew except for Jewitt and the sailmaker, John Thompson. The two men lived among*

the Nuu-chah-nulth until 1805 when
they managed to convince Maquinna to
release them.

After his rescue John Jewitt returned
to New England where he immediately
published the journal he had been keep-
ing during his captivity. This volume
impressed the writer Richard Alsop who
collaborated with Jewitt on a longer
version of his story. Narrative of the
Adventures and Sufferings of John
R. Jewitt *appeared in 1815 and has*
been reprinted many times since then.
It is the only first-hand account of the
Nuu-chah-nulth by an outside observer
who lived on intimate terms with the
people for an extended period of time. With the appearance of the Narrative,
Jewitt became something of a celebrity in New England. He toured the countryside
selling his book at public lectures and even appeared as himself in a dramatization
of his experiences. He died in 1821.

Early on the morning of the 7th of January, Maquina took me with
him in his canoe on a visit to *Upquesta*, chief of the A-i-tiz-zarts,
who had invited him to attend an exhibition at his village, similar to the
one with which he had been entertained at Tashees. This place is between
twenty and thirty miles distant up the sound, and stands on the banks of
a small river about the size of that of Cooptee, just within its entrance,
in a valley of much greater extent than that of Tashees; it consists of
fourteen or fifteen houses, built and disposed in the manner of those at
Nootka. The tribe, which is considered as tributary to Maquina, amounts
to about three hundred warriors, and the inhabitants, both men and
women, are among the best looking of any people on the coast.

On our arrival we were received at the shore by the inhabitants, a few
of whom were armed with muskets, which they fired, with loud shouts
and exclamations of *Wocash, wocash.*

We were welcomed by the chief's messenger, or master of ceremonies,
dressed in his best garments, with his hair powdered with white down,

and holding in his hand the cheetoolth, the badge of his office. This man preceded us to the chief's house, where he introduced and pointed out to us our respective seats. On entering, the visitors took off their hats, which they always wear on similar occasions, and Maquina his outer robes, of which he has several on whenever he pays a visit, and seated himself near the chief. As I was dressed in European clothes I became quite an object of curiosity to these people, very few of whom had ever seen a white man. They crowded around me in numbers, taking hold of my clothes, examining my face, hands, and feet, and even opening my mouth to see if I had a tongue, for notwithstanding I had by this time become well acquainted with their language, I preserved the strictest silence, Maquina on our first landing having enjoined me not to speak, until he should direct. Having undergone this examination for some time, Maquina at length made a sign to me to speak to them. On hearing me address them in their own language, they were greatly astonished and delighted, and told Maquina that they now perceived that I was a man like themselves, except that I was white and looked like a seal, alluding to my blue jacket and trowsers, which they wanted to persuade me to take off, as they did not like their appearance. Maquina in the mean time gave an account to the chief, of the scheme he had formed for surprising our ship, and the manner in which he and his people had carried it into execution, with such particular and horrid details of that transaction as chilled the blood in my veins. Trays of boiled herring spawn and train oil were soon after brought in and placed before us, neither the chief or any of his people eating at the same time, it being contrary to the ideas of hospitality entertained by these nations, to eat any part of the food that is provided for strangers, always waiting until their visitors have finished, before they have their own brought in.

The following day closed their festival with an exhibition of a similar kind, to that which had been given at Tashees, but still more cruel, the different tribes appearing on these occasions to endeavour to surpass each other, in their proofs of fortitude and endurance of pain. In the morning twenty men entered the chief's house, with each an arrow run through the flesh of his sides, and either arm, with a cord fastened to the end, which as the performers advanced, singing and boasting, was forcibly drawn back by a person having hold of it. After this performance was closed we returned to Cooptee, which we reached at midnight, our men keeping time with their songs to the stroke of their paddles.

The natives now began to take herring and sprat in immense quantities, with some salmon, and there was nothing but feasting from morning till night. The following is the method they employ to take the herring. A stick of about seven feet long, two inches broad, and half an inch thick, is formed from some hard wood, one side of which is set with sharp teeth, made from whale bone, at about half an inch apart. Provided with this instrument, the fisherman seats himself in the prow of a canoe, which is paddled by another, and whenever he comes to a shoal of herring, which covers the water in great quantities, he strikes it with both hands upon them, and at the same moment turning it up, brings it over the side of the canoe, into which he lets those that are taken drop. It is astonishing to see how many are caught by those who are dexterous at this kind of fishing, as they seldom fail when the shoals are numerous, of taking as many as ten to twelve at a stroke, and in a very short time will fill a canoe with them. Sprats are likewise caught in a similar manner.

About the beginning of February, Maquina gave a great feast, at which were present not only all the inhabitants, but one hundred persons from A-i-tiz-zart, and a number from Wickinninish, who had been invited to attend it. It is customary with them to give an annual entertainment of this kind, and it is astonishing to see what a quantity of provision is expended, or rather wasted on such an occasion, when they always eat to the greatest excess. It was at this feast that I saw upwards of a hundred salmon cooked in one tub. The whole residence at Cooptee presents an almost uninterrupted succession of feasting and gormondizing, and it would seem as if the principal object of these people was to consume their whole stock of provision before leaving it, trusting entirely to their success in fishing and whaling, for a supply at Nootka.

On the 25th of February, we quitted Cooptee, and returned to Nootka. With much joy did Thompson and myself again find ourselves in a place, where notwithstanding the melancholy recollections which it excited, we hoped before long to see some vessel arrive to our relief; and for this we became the more solicitous, as of late we had become much more apprehensive of our safety in consequence of information brought Maquina a few days before we left Cooptee, by some of the Cayuquets, that there were twenty ships at the northward preparing to come against him, with an intention of destroying him and his whole tribe, for cutting off the *Boston*. This story which was wholly without foundation, and discovered afterwards to have been invented by these people, for the purpose of disquieting him, threw him into great alarm, and notwithstanding all I could say to convince him that it was an unfounded report, so great was his jealousy of us, especially after it had been confirmed to him by some others of the same nation, that he treated us with much harshness, and kept a very suspicious eye upon us. Nothing indeed could be more unpleasant than our present situation, when I reflected that our lives were altogether dependent on the will of a savage, on whose caprice and suspicions no rational calculation could be made.

Not long after our return, a son of Maquina's sister, a boy about eleven years old, who had been for some time declining, died. Immediately on his death, which was about midnight, all the men and women in the house set up loud cries and shrieks, which awakening Thompson and myself, so disturbed us that we left the house. This lamentation was kept up during the remainder of the night. In the morning, a great fire was kindled, in which Maquina burned in honour of the deceased, ten fathoms of cloth, and buried with him ten fathoms more, eight of I-whaw, four prime sea otter skins, and two small trunks, containing our unfortunate captain's clothes and watch. This boy was considered as a Tyee or chief, being the only son of Tootoosch, one of their principal chiefs, who had married Maquina's sister, whence arose this ceremony on his interment; it being an established custom with these people, that whenever a chief dies, his most valuable property is burned or buried with him; it is, however, wholly confined to the chiefs, and appears to be a mark of honour appropriate to them. In this instance Maquina furnished the articles, in order that his nephew might have the proper honours rendered him. Tootoosch his father was esteemed the first warrior of the tribe, and was one who had been particularly active in the destruction of our ship, having killed two of our poor comrades, who were ashore, whose names were Hall and Wood. About the time of our removal to Tashees, while in the enjoyment of the highest health, he was suddenly seized with a fit of delirium, in which he fancied that he saw the ghosts of those two men constantly standing by him, and threatening him, so that he would take no food, except what was forced into his mouth. A short time before this, he had lost a daughter of about fifteen years of age, which afflicted him greatly, and whether his insanity, a disorder very uncommon amongst these savages, no instance of the kind having occurred within the memory of the oldest man amongst them, proceeded from this cause, or that it was the special interposition of an all merciful God in our favour, who by this means thought proper to induce these barbarians still farther to respect our lives, or that for hidden purposes, the Supreme Disposer of events, sometimes permits the spirits of the dead to revisit the world, and haunt the murderer I know not, but his mind from this period until his death, which took place but a few weeks after that of his son was incessantly occupied with the images of the men whom he had killed. This circumstance made much impression upon the tribe, particularly the chiefs, whose uniform opposition to putting us to death, at the various councils that were held on our account, I could not but in part attribute to this cause, and Maquina used frequently in speaking of Tootoosch's sickness, to express much satisfaction that his hands had not been stained with the blood of any of our men. When Maquina was first informed by his sister, of the strange conduct of her husband, he immediately went to his house, taking us with him; suspecting that his disease had been caused by us, and that the ghosts of our countrymen had been called thither by us, to torment him. We found him raving about Hall and Wood, saying that they were *peshak*, that is bad. Maquina then placed some provision before him to see if he would eat. On perceiving it, he put forth his hand to take some, but instantly withdrew it with signs of horror, saying that Hall and Wood were there, and would not let him eat. Maquina then pointing to us, asked if it was not John and Thompson who troubled him. *Wik*, he replied, that is, no, *John klushish—Thompson klushish*—John and Thompson are both good; then turning to me, and patting me on the shoulder, he made signs to me to eat. I tried to persuade him that Hall and Wood were not there, and that none were near him but ourselves: he said, I know very well you do not see them, but I do. At first Maquina endeavoured to convince him that he saw nothing, and to laugh him out of his belief, but finding that all was to no purpose, he at length became serious, and asked me if I had ever seen any one affected in this manner, and what was the matter with him. I gave him to understand, pointing to his head, that his brain was injured, and that he did not see things as formerly. Being convinced by Tootoosch's conduct, that we had no agency in his indisposition, on our return home, Maquina asked me what was done in my country in similar cases. I told him that such persons were closely confined, and sometimes tied up and whipped, in order to make them better. After pondering for some time, he said that he should be glad to do any thing to relieve him, and that he should be whipped, and immediately gave orders to some of his men, to go to Tootoosch's house, bind him, and bring him to his, in order to undergo the operation. Thompson was the person selected to administer this remedy, which he undertook very readily, and for that purpose provided himself with a good number of spruce branches, with which he whipped him most severely, laying it on with the best will imaginable, while Tootoosch displayed the greatest rage, kicking, spitting, and attempting to bite all who came near him. This was too much for Maquina, who, at length, unable to endure it longer, ordered Thompson to desist, and Tootoosch to be carried back, saying that if there was no other way of curing him but by whipping, he must remain mad.

The application of the whip produced no beneficial effect on Tootoosch, for he afterwards became still more deranged; in his fits of fury sometimes seizing a club, and beating his slaves in a most dreadful manner, and striking and spitting at all who came near him, till at length his wife no longer daring to remain in the house with him, came with her son to Maquina's.

A BACKWOODS HOUSE-RAISING

CATHARINE PARR TRAILL

From *The Backwoods of Canada* (1836)

With Catharine Parr Traill we move from exploration, or travel, writing to settlement literature, a very different genre. Whereas explorers were interested in highlighting the exoticism of the Canadian frontier, settler writers wanted to convey the ordinary details of daily life. They usually wrote either to encourage or to discourage others like themselves who might be planning to seek a new life in Canada. The Backwoods of Canada, *for example, is basically a guidebook, written to forewarn British emigrants, especially female emigrants, that life in the colonies could be arduous and dispiriting. For members of the genteel middle class, unused to physical labour and spartan living, Mrs. Traill warned her readers, "Canada is the worst country in the world." Indeed, in its cautionary tone,* Backwoods *resembles that other classic of Ontario pioneer literature,* Roughing It in the Bush, *written by Mrs. Traill's sister, Susanna Moodie. But unlike Moodie, Traill herself was happy in her new home on the Otonabee River near Peterborough and her book, which is a collection of letters written to friends and relatives in England, strikes a much more positive note. For settlers willing to bend their backs to the labour, "Canada is the land of hope," she writes; "here everything is new; everything is going forward. . . . "*

When Catharine Parr Traill (1802-1899) arrived in Upper Canada from England with her husband, a retired soldier, in 1832, she was already a published author of childrens' books. Backwoods *was her first work of non-fiction; she went*

on to write other juvenile novels, three studies of Ontario flora, and a guide to pioneer housekeeping. Backwoods met with an appreciative audience when it appeared in London in 1836. British emigrants were flooding into the overseas colonies and eagerly sought information about conditions there. German and French translations soon followed.

But it is time that I should give you some account of our log-house, into which we moved a few days before Christmas. Many unlooked-for delays having hindered its completion before that time, I began to think it would never be habitable.

The first misfortune that happened was the loss of a fine yoke of oxen that were purchased to draw in the house-logs, that is, the logs for raising the walls of the house. Not regarding the bush as pleasant as their former master's cleared pastures, or perhaps foreseeing some hard work to come, early one morning they took into their heads to ford the lake at the head of the rapids, and march off, leaving no trace of their route excepting their footing at the water's edge. After many days spent in vain search for them, the work was at a stand, and for one month they were gone, and we began to give up all expectation of hearing any news of them. At last we learned they were some twenty miles off, in a distant township, having made their way through bush and swamp, creek and lake, back to their former owner, with an instinct that supplied to them the want of roads and compass.

Oxen have been known to traverse a tract of wild country to a distance of thirty or forty miles going in a direct line for their former haunts by unknown paths, where memory could not avail them. In the dog we consider it is a scent as well as memory that guides him to his far-off home; —but how is this conduct of the oxen to be accounted for? They returned home through the mazes of interminable forests, where man, with all his reason and knowledge, would have been bewildered and lost.

It was the latter end of October before even the walls of our house were up. To effect this we called "a bee." Sixteen of our neighbours cheerfully obeyed our summons; and though the day was far from favourable, so faithfully did our hive perform their tasks, that by night the outer walls were raised.

The work went merrily on with the help of plenty of Canadian nectar (whiskey), the honey that our *bees* are solaced with. Some huge joints of salt pork, a peck of potatoes, with a rice-pudding, and a loaf as big as an enormous Cheshire cheese, formed the feast that was to regale them during the raising. This was spread out in the shanty, in a *very rural style*. In short, we laughed, and called it a *pic-nic in the backwoods*; and rude as was the fare, I can assure you, great was the satisfaction expressed by all the guests of every degree, our "bee" being considered as very well conducted. In spite of the difference of rank among those that assisted at the bee, the greatest possible harmony prevailed, and the party separated well pleased with the day's work and entertainment.

The following day I went to survey the newly-raised edifice, but was sorely puzzled, as it presented very little appearance of a house. It was merely an oblong square of logs raised one above the other, with open spaces between every row of logs. The spaces for the doors and windows were not then chopped out, and the rafters were not up. In short, it looked a very queer sort of place, and I returned home a little disappointed, and wondered that my husband should be so well pleased with the progress that had been made. A day or two after this I again visited it. The *sleepers* were laid to support the floors, and the places for the doors and windows cut out of the solid timbers, so that it had not quite so much the look of a bird-cage as before.

After the roof was shingled, we were again at a stand, as no boards could be procured nearer than Peterborough, a long day's journey through horrible roads. At that time no saw-mill was in progress; now there is a fine one building within a little distance of us. Our flooring-boards were all to be sawn by hand, and it was some time before any one could be found to perform this necessary work, and that at high wages—six-and-sixpence per day. Well, the boards were at length down, but of course of unseasoned timber: this was unavoidable; so as they could not be planed we were obliged to put up with their rough unsightly appearance, for no better were to be had. I began to recall to mind the observation of the old gentleman with whom we travelled from Cobourg to Rice Lake. We console ourselves with the prospect that by next summer the boards will all be seasoned, and then the house is to be turned topsy-turvy, by having the floors all relaid, jointed, and smoothed.

The next misfortune that happened, was, that the mixture of clay and lime that was to plaster the inside and outside of the house between the chinks of the logs was one night frozen to stone. Just as the work was about half completed, the frost suddenly setting in, put a stop to our proceeding for some time, as the frozen plaster yielded neither to fire nor to hot water, the latter freezing before it had any effect on the mass, and rather making bad worse. Then the workman that was hewing the inside walls to make them smooth, wounded himself with the broad axe, and was unable to resume his work for some time.

I state these things merely to show the difficulties that attend us in the fulfilment of our plans, and this accounts in a great measure for the humble dwellings that settlers of the most respectable description are obliged to content themselves with at first coming to this country, —not, you may be assured, from inclination, but necessity: I could give you such narratives of this kind as would astonish you. After all, it serves to make us more satisfied than we should be on casting our eyes around to see few better off than we are, and many not half so comfortable, yet of equal, and, in some instances, superior pretensions as to station and fortune.

Every man in this country is his own glazier; this you will laugh at: but if he does not wish to see and feel the discomfort of broken panes, he must learn to put them in his windows with his own hands. Workmen are not easily to be had in the backwoods when you want them, and it would be preposterous to hire a man at high wages to make two days' journey to and from the nearest town to mend your windows. Boxes of glass of several different sizes are to be bought at a very cheap rate in the stores. My husband amused himself by glazing the windows of the house preparatory to their being fixed in.

To understand the use of carpenter's tools, I assure you, is no despicable or useless kind of knowledge here. I would strongly recommend all young men coming to Canada to acquire a little acquaintance with this valuable art, as they will often be put to great inconvenience for the want of it.

I was once much amused with hearing the remarks made by a very fine lady, the reluctant sharer of her husband's emigration, on seeing the son of a naval officer of some rank in the service busily employed in making an axe-handle out of a piece of rock-elm.

"I wonder that you allow George to degrade himself so," she said, addressing his father.

The captain looked up with surprise. "Degrade himself! In what manner, madam? My boy neither swears, drinks whiskey, steals, nor tells lies."

"But you allow him to perform tasks of the most menial kind. What is he now better than a hedge carpenter; and I suppose you allow him to chop, too?"

"Most assuredly I do. That pile of logs in the cart there was all cut by him after he had left study yesterday," was the reply.

"I would see my boys dead before they should use an axe like common labourers."

"Idleness is the root of all evil," said the captain. "How much worse might my son be employed if he were running wild about streets with bad companions."

"You will allow this is not a country for gentlemen and ladies to live in," said the lady.

"It is the country for gentlemen that will not work and cannot live without, to starve in," replied the captain bluntly; "and for that reason I make my boys early accustom themselves to be usefully and actively employed."

"My boys shall never work like common mechanics," said the lady, indignantly.

"Then, madam, they will be good for nothing as settlers; and it is a pity you dragged them across the Atlantic."

"We were forced to come. We could not live as we had been used to at home, or I never would have come to this horrid country."

"Having come hither you would be wise to conform to circumstances. Canada is not the place for idle folks to retrench a lost fortune in. In some parts of the country you will find most articles of provision as dear as in London, clothing much dearer, and not so good, and a bad market to choose in."

"I should like to know, then, who Canada is good for?" said she, angrily.

"It is a good country for the honest, industrious artisan. It is a fine country for the poor labourer, who, after a few years of hard toil, can sit down in his own log-house, and look abroad on his own land, and see his children well settled in life as independent freeholders. It is a grand country for the rich speculator, who can afford to lay out a large sum in purchasing land in eligible situations; for if he have any judgment, he will make a hundred per cent, as interest for his money after waiting a few years. But it is a hard country for the poor gentleman, whose habits have rendered him unfit for manual labour. He brings with him a mind unfitted to his situation; and even if necessity compels him to exertion, his labour is of little value. He has a hard struggle to live. The certain expenses of wages and living are great, and he is obliged to endure many privations if he would keep within compass, and be free of debt. If he have a large family, and brings them up wisely, so as to adapt themselves early to a settler's life, why he does well for them, and soon feels the benefit on his own land; but if he is idle himself, his wife extravagant and discontented, and the children taught to despise labour, why, madam, they will soon be brought down to ruin. In short, the country is a good country for those to whom it is adapted; but if people will not conform to the doctrine of necessity and expediency, they have no business in it. It is plain Canada is not adapted to every class of people."

"It was never adapted for me or my family," said the lady, disdainfully.

"Very true," was the laconic reply; and so ended the dialogue.

UNCLE JOE AND HIS FAMILY

SUSANNA MOODIE

From *Roughing It in the Bush* (1852)

In Roughing It in the Bush, *Susanna Moodie takes the emigrant's handbook and stands it on its head. The conventional handbook, as it was produced and distributed by various promoters of emigration, was a collection of often spurious information, glowingly presented to encourage the unwary settler to come to the Canadian colonies. Mrs. Moodie had quite the opposite intention. Her book was written as a warning against the rigors of pioneer life. However, the book is far from being a long complaint. As Margaret Atwood has pointed out,* Roughing It in the Bush *has all the elements of fiction: an exotic setting, witty dialogue, a structured plot and several wonderfully-realized characters. Indeed, it has sometimes been called a novel. Unlike her sister, Catharine Parr Traill, who often seems content to pass along useful information, Moodie is more successful at conveying the actual experience of life in the bush.*

*   Roughing It in the Bush* was published in two volumes in London in 1852 by Richard Bentley, a leading British publisher. It met with very favourable reviews in the British literary press and a second edition appeared within months, along with several pirated editions in the United States. In Canada the response was a little less enthusiastic, mainly because of the unkind things Moodie has to say about some of her fellow settlers. A Canadian edition of the book did not appear until 1872, but it has since become a Canadian classic. Moodie is one of the earliest writers of non-fiction to think at all in terms of a Canadian audience. Most of her*

predecessors had a foreign market in mind; Canada was the scene of their adventures but not the audience for their books.

Susanna Strickland was born in Suffolk, England in 1803. When she was fifteen years old her father lost his fortune and died and it was partly to make a living that Susanna and her four sisters all turned to writing. In 1831 she married a half-pay officer, John Dunbar Moodie, and the following year the couple joined the flood of British emigrants then inundating Canada. They adapted poorly to backwoods life, but managed to muddle through and Moodie was later able to write about their experiences with a great deal of humour and insight. In 1840 Moodie and her husband moved to Belleville where he was appointed sheriff. It was here that she wrote the sketches which became Roughing It, along with its sequel, Life in the Clearings (1853), and several novels. After the death of her husband she lived mainly in Toronto, where she died in 1885.

The following selection, from the original edition, describes a family of Americans who lived next door to the Moodies.

Uncle Joe! I see him now before me, with his jolly red face, twinkling black eyes, and rubicund nose. No thin, weasel-faced Yankee was he, looking as if he had lived upon 'cute ideas and speculations all his life; yet Yankee he was by birth, ay, and in mind, too; for a more knowing fellow at a bargain never crossed the lakes to abuse British institutions and locate himself comfortably among the despised Britishers. But, then, he had such a good-natured, fat face, such a mischievous, mirth-loving smile, and such a merry, roguish expression in those small, jet-black, glittering eyes, that you suffered yourself to be taken in by him, without offering the least resistance to his impositions.

Uncle Joe's father had been a New England loyalist, and his doubtful attachment to the British government had been repaid by a grant of land in the township of H_____. He was the first settler in that township, and chose his location in a remote spot, for the sake of a beautiful natural spring, which bubbled up in a small stone basin in the green bank at the back of the house.

"Father might have had the pick of the township," quoth Uncle Joe; "but the old coon preferred that sup of good water to the site of a town. Well, I guess it's seldom I trouble the spring; and whenever I step that way to water the horses, I think what a tarnation fool the old one was, to throw away such a chance of making his fortune, for such cold lap."

"Your father was a temperance man?"

"Temperance!—He had been fond enough of the whiskey bottle in his day. He drank up a good farm in the United States, and then he thought he could not do better than turn loyal, and get one here for nothing. He did not care a cent, not he, for the King of England. He thought himself as good, any how. But he found that he would have to work hard here to scratch along, and he was mightily plagued with the rheumatics, and some old woman told him that good spring water was the best cure for that; so he chose this poor, light, stony land on account of the spring, and took to hard work and drinking cold water in his old age."

"How did the change agree with him?"

"I guess better than could have been expected. He planted that fine orchard, and cleared his hundred acres, and we got along slick enough as long as the old fellow lived."

"And what happened after his death, that obliged you to part with your land?"

"Bad times—bad crops," said Uncle Joe, lifting his shoulders. "I had not my father's way of scraping money together. I made some deuced clever speculations, but they all failed. I married young, and got a large family; and the women critters ran up heavy bills at the stores, and the crops did not yield enough to pay them; and from bad we got to worse, and Mr. C_____ put in an execution, and seized upon the whole concern. He sold it to your man for double what it cost him; and you got all that my father toiled for during the last twenty years of his life for less than half the cash he laid out upon clearing it."

"And had the whiskey nothing to do with this change?" said I, looking him in the face suspiciously.

"Not a bit! When a man gets into difficulties, it is the only thing to keep him from sinking outright. When your husband has had as many troubles as I have had, he will know how to value the whiskey bottle."

This conversation was interrupted by a queer-looking urchin of five years old, dressed in a long-tailed coat and trousers, popping his black shock head in at the door, and calling out,

"Uncle Joe!—You're wanted to hum."

"Is that your nephew?"

"No! I guess 'tis my woman's eldest son," said Uncle Joe, rising, "but they call me Uncle Joe. 'Tis a spry chap that—as cunning as a fox. I tell you what it is—he will make a smart man. Go home, Ammon, and tell your ma that I am coming."

"I won't," said the boy; "you may go hum and tell her yourself. She has wanted wood cut this hour, and you'll catch it!"

Away ran the dutiful son, but not before he had supplied his forefinger significantly to the side of his nose, and, with a knowing wink, pointed in the direction of home.

Uncle Joe obeyed the signal, drily remarking that he could not leave the barn door without the old hen clucking him back.

At this period we were still living in Old Satan's log house, and anxiously looking out for the first snow to put us in possession of the good substantial log dwelling occupied by Uncle Joe and his family, which consisted of a brown brood of seven girls, and the highly-prized boy who rejoiced in the extraordinary name of Ammon.

Strange names are to be found in this free country. What think you, gentle reader, of *Solomon Sly, Reynard Fox,* and *Hiram Dolittle*; all veritable names, and belonging to substantial yeomen? After Ammon and Ichabod, I should not be at all surprised to meet with Judas Iscariot, Pilate, and Herod. And then the female appellations! But the subject is a delicate one, and I will forbear to touch upon it. I have enjoyed many a hearty laugh over the strange affectations which people designate here *very handsome names*. I prefer the homely Jewish names, such as that which it pleased my godfather and godmothers to bestow upon me, to one of those high-sounding christianities, the Minervas, Cinderellas, and Almerias of Canada. The love of singular names is here carried to a marvelous extent. It is only yesterday that, in passing through one busy village, I stopped in astonishment before a tombstone headed thus:— "Sacred to the memory of *Silence* Sharman, the beloved wife of Asa

Sharman." Was the woman deaf and dumb, or did her friends hope by bestowing upon her such an impossible name to still the voice of Nature, and check, by an admonitory appellative, the active spirit that lives in the tongue of woman? Truly, Asa Sharman, if thy wife was silent by name as well as nature, thou wert a fortunate man!

But to return to Uncle Joe. He made many fair promises of leaving the residence we had bought, the moment he had sold his crops and could remove his family. We could see no interest which could be served by his deceiving us, and therefore we believed him, striving to make ourselves as comfortable as we could in the meantime in our present wretched abode. But matters are never so bad but that they may be worse. One day when we were at dinner, a waggon drove up to the door, and Mr. _____ alighted, accompanied by a fine-looking, middle-aged man, who proved to be Captain S_____, who had just arrived from Demerara with his wife and family. Mr. _____, who had purchased the farm of old Satan, had brought Captain S_____ over to inspect the land, as he wished to buy a farm, and settle in that neighbourhood. With some difficulty I contrived to accommodate the visitors with seats, and provide them with a tolerable dinner. Fortunately, Moodie had brought in a brace of fine fat partridges that morning; these the servant transferred to a pot of boiling water, in which she immersed them for the space of a minute—a novel but very expeditious way of removing the feathers, which then come off at the least touch. In less than ten minutes they were stuffed, trussed, and in the bake-kettle; and before the gentlemen returned from walking over the farm, the dinner was on the table.

To our utter consternation, Captain S_____ agreed to purchase, and asked if we could give him possession in a week!

"Good heavens!" cried I, glancing reproachfully at Mr. _____, who was discussing his partridge with stoical indifference. "What will become of us? Where are we to go?"

"Oh, make yourself easy; I will force that old witch, Joe's mother, to clear out."

"But 'tis impossible to stow ourselves into that pig-sty."

"It will only be for a week or two, at farthest. This is October; Joe will be sure to be off by the first of sleighing."

"But if she refuses to give up the place?"

"Oh, leave her to me. I'll talk her over," said the knowing land speculator. "Let it come to the worst," he said, turning to my husband, "she will go out for the sake of a few dollars. By-the-by, she refused to bar the dower when I bought the place; we must cajole her out of that. It is a fine afternoon; suppose we walk over the hill, and try our luck with the old nigger?"

I felt so anxious about the result of the negotiation, that, throwing my cloak over my shoulders, and tying on my bonnet without the assistance of a glass, I took my husband's arm, and we walked forth.

It was a bright, clear afternoon, the first week in October, and the fading woods, not yet denuded of their gorgeous foliage, glowed in a mellow, golden light. A soft purple haze rested on the bold outline of the Haldemand hills, and in the rugged beauty of the wild landscape I soon forgot the purport of our visit to the old woman's log hut.

On reaching the ridge of the hill, the lovely valley in which our future home lay smiled peacefully upon us from amidst its fruitful orchards, still loaded with their rich, ripe fruit.

"What a pretty place it is!" thought I, for the first time feeling something like a local interest in the spot springing up in my heart. "How I wish those odious people would give us possession of the home which for some time has been our own!"

The log hut that we were approaching, and in which the old woman, H_____, resided by herself—having quarrelled years ago with her son's wife—was of the smallest dimensions, only containing one room, which served the old dame for kitchen, and bed-room, and all. The open door, and a few glazed panes, supplied it with light and air; while a huge hearth, on which crackled two enormous logs—which are technically termed a front and a back stick—took up nearly half the domicile; and the old woman's bed, which was covered with an unexceptionably clean patched quilt, nearly the other half, leaving just room for a small home-made deal table, of the rudest workmanship, two basswood-bottomed chairs, stained red, one of which was a rocking-chair, appropriated solely to the old woman's use, and a spinning-wheel. Amidst this muddle of things—for small as was the quantum of furniture, it was all crowded into such a tiny space that you had to squeeze your way through it in the best manner you could—we found the old woman, with a red cotton handkerchief tied over her grey locks, hood-fashion, shelling white bush-beans into a wooden bowl. Without rising from her seat, she pointed to the only remaining chair. "I guess, miss, you can sit there; and if the others can't stand, they can make a seat of my bed."

The gentlemen assured her that they were not tired, and could dispense with seats. Mr. _____ then went up to the old woman, and proffering his hand, asked after her health in his blandest manner.

"I'm none the better for seeing you, or the like of you," was the ungracious reply. "You have cheated my poor boy out of his good farm; and I hope it may prove a bad bargain to you and yours."

"Mrs. H_____," returned the land speculator, nothing ruffled by her unceremonious greeting, "I could not help your son giving way to drink, and getting into my debt. If people will be so imprudent, they cannot be so stupid as to imagine that others can suffer for their folly."

"*Suffer!*" repeated the old woman, flashing her small, keen black eyes upon him with a glance of withering scorn. "You suffer! I wonder what the widows and orphans you have cheated would say to that? My son was a poor, weak, silly fool, to be sucked in by the like of you. For a debt of eight hundred dollars—the goods never cost you four hundred—you take from us our good farm; and these, I s'pose," pointing to my husband and me, "are the folk you sold it to. Pray, miss," turning quickly to me, "what might your man give for the place?"

"Three hundred pounds in cash."

"Poor sufferer!" again sneered the hag. "Four hundred dollars is a very *small* profit in as many weeks. Well, I guess, you beat the Yankees hollow. And pray, what brought you here to-day, scenting about you like a carrion-crow? We have no more land for you to seize from us."

Moodie now stepped forward, and briefly explained our situation, offering the old woman anything in reason to give up the cottage and reside with her son until he removed from the premises; which, he added, must be in a very short time.

The old dame regarded him with a sarcastic smile. "I guess, Joe will take his own time. The house is not built which is to receive him; and he is not a man to turn his back upon a warm hearth to camp in the wilderness. You were *green* when you bought a farm of that man, without getting along with it the right of possession."

"But, Mrs. H_____, your son promised to go out the first of sleighing."

"Wheugh!" said the old woman. "Would you have a man give away his hat and leave his own head bare? It's neither the first snow nor the last frost that will turn Joe out of his comfortable home. I tell you all that he will stay here, if it is only to plague you."

Threats and remonstrances were alike useless, the old woman remained inexorable; and we were just turning to leave the house, when the cunning old fox exclaimed, "And now, what will you give me to leave my place?"

"Twelve dollars, if you give us possession next Monday," said my husband.

"Twelve dollars! I guess you won't get me out for that."

"The rent would not be worth more than a dollar a month," said Mr. _____, pointing with his cane to the dilapidated walls. "Mr. Moodie has offered you a year's rent for the place."

"It may not be worth a cent," returned the woman, "for it will give everybody the rheumatism that stays a week in it—but it is worth that to me, and more nor double that just now to him. But I will not be hard with him," continued she, rocking herself to and fro. "Say twenty dollars, and I will turn out on Monday."

"I dare say you will," said Mr. _____, "and who do you think would be fool enough to give you such an exorbitant sum for a ruined old shed like this?"

"Mind your own business, and make your own bargains," returned the old woman, tartly. "The devil himself could not deal with you, for I guess he would have the worst of it. What do you say, sir?" and she fixed her keen eyes upon my husband, as if she would read his thoughts. "Will you agree to my price?"

"It is a very high one, Mrs. H_____; but as I cannot help myself, and you take advantage of that, I suppose I must give it."

"'Tis a bargain," cried the old crone, holding out her hard, bony hand. "Come, cash down!"

"Not until you give me possession on Monday next; or you might serve me as your son has done."

"Ha!" said the old woman, laughing and rubbing her eyes together; "you will begin to see daylight, do you? In a few months, with the help of him," pointing to Mr. _____, "you will be able to go alone; but have a care of your teacher, for it's no good that you will learn from him. But will you *really* stand to your word, mister?" she added, in a coaxing tone, "if I go out on Monday?"

"To be sure, I will; I never break my word."

"Well, I guess you are not so clever as our people, for they only keep it as long as it suits them. You have an honest look; I will trust you; but I will not trust them," nodding to Mr. _____, "he can buy and sell his word as fast as a horse can trot. So on Monday I will turn out my traps. I have lived here six-and-thirty years; 'tis a pretty place, and it vexes me to leave it," continued the poor creature, as a touch of natural feeling softened and agitated her world-hardened heart. "There is not an acre in cultivation but I helped to clear it, nor a tree in yonder orchard but I held it while my poor man, who is dead and gone, planted it; and I have watched the trees bud from year to year, until their boughs overshadowed the hut, where all my children, but Joe, were born. Yes, I came here young, and in my prime; and I must leave it in age and poverty. My children and husband are dead, and their bones rest beneath the turf in the burying-ground on the side of the hill. Of all that once gathered about my knees, Joe and his very young ones alone remain. And it is hard, very hard, that I must leave their graves to be turned by the plough of a stranger."

I felt for the desolate old creature—the tears rushed to my eyes; but there was no moisture in hers. No rain from the heart could filter through that iron soil.

"Be assured, Mrs. H_____," said Moodie, "that the dead will be held sacred; the place will never be disturbed by me."

"Perhaps not; but it is not long that you remain here. I have seen a good deal in my time; but I never saw a gentleman from the old country make a good Canadian farmer. The work is rough and hard, and they get out of humour with it, and leave it to their hired helps, and then all goes wrong. They are cheated on all sides, and in despair take to the whiskey bottle, and that fixes them. I tell you what it is, mister—I give you just three years to spend your money and ruin yourself; and then you will become a confirmed drunkard, like the rest."

The first part of her prophecy was only too true. Thank God! the last has never been fulfilled, and never can be.

Perceiving that the old woman was not a little elated with her bargain, Mr. _____ urged upon her the propriety of barring the dower. At first, she was outrageous, and very abusive, and rejected all his proposals with contempt; vowing that she would meet him in a certain place below, before she would sign away her right to the property.

"Listen to reason, Mrs. H_____," said the land speculator. "If you sign the papers before the proper authorities, the next time your son drives you to C_____, I will give you a silk gown."

"Pshaw! Buy a shroud for yourself; you will need it before I want a silk gown," was the ungracious reply.

"Consider, woman; a black silk of the best quality."

"To mourn in for my sins, or for the loss of the farm?"

"Twelve yards," continued Mr. _____, without noticing her rejoinder, "at a dollar a yard. Think what a nice church-going gown it will make."

"To the devil with you! I never go to church."

"I thought as much," said Mr. _____, winking to us. "Well, my dear madam, what will satisfy you?"

"I'll do it for twenty dollars," returned the old woman, rocking herself to and fro in her chair; her eyes twinkling, and her hands moving convulsively, as if she already grasped the money so dear to her soul.

"Agreed," said the land speculator. "When will you be in town?"

"On Tuesday, if I be alive. But, remember, I'll not sign till I have my hand on the money."

"Never fear," said Mr. _____, as we quitted the house; then, turning to me, he added, with a peculiar smile, "That's a devilish smart woman. She would have made a clever lawyer."

Monday came, and with it all the bustle of moving, and, as is generally the case on such occasions, it turned out a very wet day. I left Old Satan's hut without regret, glad, at any rate, to be in a place of my own, however humble. Our new habitation, though small, had a decided advantage over the one we were leaving. It stood on a gentle slope; and a narrow but lovely stream, full of pretty speckled trout, ran murmuring under the little window; the house, also, was surrounded by fine fruit-trees.

I know not how it was, but the sound of that tinkling brook, for ever rolling by, filled my heart with a strange melancholy, which for many nights deprived me of rest. I loved it, too. The voice of waters, in the stillness of night, always had an extraordinary effect upon my mind. Their ceaseless motion and perpetual sound convey to me the idea of life—eternal life; and looking upon them, glancing and flashing on, now in sunshine, now in shade, now hoarsely chiding with the opposing rock, now leaping triumphantly over it,—creates within me a feeling of mysterious awe of which I never could wholly divest myself.

A portion of my own spirit seemed to pass into that little stream. In its deep wailings and fretful sighs, I fancied myself lamenting for the land I had left for ever; and its restless and impetuous rushings against the stones which choked its passage, were mournful types of my own mental struggles against the strange destiny which hemmed me in. Through the day the stream still moaned and travelled on,—but, engaged in my novel and distasteful occupations, I heard it not; but whenever my winged thoughts flew homeward, then the voice of the brook spoke deeply and sadly to my heart, and my tears flowed unchecked to its plaintive and harmonious music.

In a few hours I had my new abode more comfortably arranged than the old one, although its dimensions were much smaller. The location was beautiful, and I was greatly consoled by this circumstance. The aspect of Nature ever did, and I hope ever will continue,

> "To shoot marvellous strength into my heart."

As long as we remain true to the Divine Mother, so long will she remain faithful to her suffering children.

At that period my love for Canada was a feeling very nearly allied to that which the condemned criminal entertains for his cell—his only hope of escape being through the portals of the grave.

The fall rains had commenced. In a few days the cold wintry showers swept all the gorgeous crimson from the trees; and a bleak and desolate waste presented itself to the shuddering spectator. But, in spite of wind and rain, my little tenement was never free from the intrusion of Uncle Joe's wife and children. Their house stood about a stone's-throw from the hut we occupied, in the same meadow, and they seemed to look upon it still as their own, although we had literally paid for it twice over. Fine strapping girls they were, from five years old to fourteen, but rude and unnurtured as so many bears. They would come in without the least ceremony, and, young as they were, ask me a thousand impertinent questions; and when I civilly requested them to leave the room, they would range themselves upon the door-step, watching my motions, with their black eyes gleaming upon me through their tangled, uncombed locks. Their company was a great annoyance, for it obliged me to put a painful restraint upon the thoughtfulness in which it was so delightful to me to indulge. Their visits were not visits of love, but of mere idle curiosity, not unmingled with malicious hatred.

The simplicity, the fond, confiding faith of childhood, is unknown in Canada. There are no children here. The boy is a miniature man—knowing, keen, and wide awake; as able to drive a bargain and take advantage of his juvenile companion as the grown-up, world-hardened man. The girl, a gossiping flirt, full of vanity and affectation, with a premature love of finery, and an acute perception of the advantages to be derived from wealth, and from keeping up a certain appearance in the world.

The flowers, the green grass, the glorious sunshine, the birds of the air, and the young lambs gambolling down the verdant slopes, which fill the heart of a British child with a fond ecstasy, bathing the young spirit in Elysium, would float unnoticed before the vision of a Canadian child; while the sight of a dollar, or a new dress, or a gay bonnet, would swell its proud bosom with self-importance and delight. The glorious blush of modest indifference, the tear of gentle sympathy, are so rare on the cheek, or in the eye of the young, that their appearance creates a feeling of surprise. Such perfect self-reliance in beings so new to the world is painful to a thinking mind. It betrays a great want of sensibility and mental culture, and a melancholy knowledge of the arts of life.

For a week I was alone, my good Scotch girl having left me to visit her father. Some small baby-articles were needed to be washed, and after making a great preparation, I determined to try my unskilled hand upon the operation. The fact is, I knew nothing about the task I had imposed upon myself, and in a few minutes rubbed the skin off my wrists, without getting the clothes clean.

The door was open, as it generally was, even during the coldest winter days, in order to let in more light, and let out the smoke, which otherwise would have enveloped us like a cloud. I was so busy that I did not perceive that I was watched by the cold, heavy, dark eyes of Mrs. Joe, who, with a sneering laugh, exclaimed,

"Well, thank God! I am glad to see you brought to work at last. I hope you may not have to work as hard as I have. I don't see, not I, why you, who are no better than me, should sit there all day, like a lady!"

"Mrs. H_____," said I, not a little annoyed at her presence, "what concern is it of yours whether I work or sit still? I never interfere with you. If you took it into your head to lie in bed all day, I should never trouble myself about it."

"Ah, I guess you don't look upon us as fellow-critters, you are so proud and grand. I s'pose you Britishers are not made of flesh and blood like us. You don't choose to sit down at meat with your helps. Now, I calculate, we think them a great deal better nor you."

"Of course," said I, "they are more suited to you than we are; they are uneducated, and so are you. This is no fault in either; but it might teach you to pay a little more respect to those who are possessed of superior advantages. But, Mrs. H_____, my helps, as you call them, are civil and unobliging, and never make unprovoked and malicious speeches. If they could so far forget themselves, I should order them to leave the house."

"Oh, I see what you are up to," replied the insolent dame; "you mean to say that if I were your help you would turn me out of your house; but I'm a free-born American, and I won't go at your bidding. Don't think I come here out of regard to you. No, I hate you all; and I rejoice to see you at the washtub, and I wish that you may be brought down upon your knees to scrub the floors."

This speech only caused a smile, and yet I felt hurt and astonished that a woman whom I had never done anything to offend should be so gratuitously spiteful.

In the evening she sent two of her brood over to borrow my "long iron," as she called an Italian iron. I was just getting my baby to sleep, sitting upon a low stool by the fire. I pointed to the iron upon the shelf, and told the girl to take it. She did so, but stood beside me, holding it carelessly in her hand, and staring at the baby, who had just sunk to sleep upon my lap.

The next moment the heavy iron fell from her relaxed grasp, giving me a severe blow upon my knee and foot; and glanced so near the child's head that it drew from me a cry of terror.

"I guess that was nigh braining the child," quoth Miss Amanda, with the greatest coolness, and without making the least apology. Master Ammon burst into a loud laugh. "If it had, Mandy, I guess we'd have cotched it." Provoked at their insolence, I told them to leave the house.

The tears were in my eyes, for I felt certain that had they injured the child, it would not have caused them the least regret.

The next day, as we were standing at the door, my husband was greatly amused by seeing fat Uncle Joe chasing the rebellious Ammon over the meadow in front of the house. Joe was out of breath, his face flushed to deep red with excitement and passion. "You _____ young scoundrel!" he cried, half choked with fury, "if I catch up to you, I'll take the skin off you!"

"You _____ old scoundrel, you may have my skin if you can get at me," retorted the precocious child, as he jumped up upon the top of the high fence, and doubled his fist in a menacing manner at his father.

"That boy is growing up too bad," said Uncle Joe, coming up to us out of breath, the perspiration streaming down his face. "It is time to break him in, or he'll get the master of us all."

"You should have begun that before," said Moodie. "He seems a hopeful pupil."

"Oh, as to that, a little swearing is manly," returned the father; "I swear myself, I know, and as the old cock crows, so crows the young one. It is not his swearing that I care a pin for, but he will not do a thing I tell him to."

"Swearing is a dreadful vice," said I, "and, wicked as it is in the mouth of a grown-up person, it is perfectly shocking in a child; it painfully tells he has been brought up without the fear of God."

"Pooh! pooh! that's all cant; there is no harm in a few oaths, and I cannot drive oxen and horses without swearing. I dare say that you can swear too when you are riled, but you are too cunning to let us hear you."

I could not help laughing outright at this supposition, but replied very quietly, "Those who practise such iniquities never take any pains to conceal them. The concealment would infer a feeling of shame; and when people are conscious of their guilt, they are in the road to improvement." The man walked whistling away, and the wicked child returned unpunished to his home.

The next minute the old woman came in. "I guess you can give me a piece of silk for a hood," said she, "the weather is growing considerable cold."

"Surely it cannot well be colder than it is at present," said I, giving her the rocking-chair by the fire.

"Wait a while; you know nothing of a Canadian winter. This is only November; after the Christmas thaw, you'll know something about cold. It is seven-and-thirty years ago since I and my man left the U-ni-ted States. It was called the year of the great winter. I tell you, woman, that the snow lay so deep on the earth, that it blocked up all the roads, and we could drive a sleigh whither we pleased, right over the snake fences. All the cleared land was one wide white level plain; it was a year of scarcity, and we were half starved; but the severe cold was far worse nor the want of provisions. A long and bitter journey we had of it; but I was young then, and pretty well used to trouble and fatigue; my man stuck to the British government. More fool he! I was an American born, and my heart was with the true cause. But his father was English, and, says he, 'I'll live and die under their flag.' So he dragged me from my comfortable fireside to seek a home in the far Canadian wilderness. Trouble! I guess you think you have your troubles; but what are they to mine?" She paused, took a pinch of snuff, offered me the box, sighed painfully, pushed the red handkerchief from her high, narrow, wrinkled brow, and continued:—"Joe was a baby then, and I had another helpless critter in my lap—an adopted child. My sister had died from it, and I was nursing it at the same breast as my boy. Well, we had to perform a journey of four hundred miles in an ox-cart, which carried, besides me and the children, all our household stuff. Our way lay chiefly through the forest, and we made but slow progress. Oh! what a bitter cold night it was when we reached the swampy woods where the city of Rochester now stands. The oxen were covered with icicles, and their breath sent up clouds of steam. 'Nathan,' says I to my man, 'you must stop and kindle a fire; I am dead with cold, and I fear the babes will be frozen.' We began looking about for a good spot to camp in, when I spied a light through the trees. It was a lone shanty, occupied by two French lumberers. The men were kind; they rubbed our frozen limbs with snow, and shared with us their supper and buffalo skins. On that very spot where we camped that night, where we heard nothing but the wind soughing amongst the trees, and the rushing of the river, now stands the great city of Rochester. I went there two years ago, to the funeral of a brother. It seemed to me like a dream. Where we foddered our beasts by the shanty fire now stands the largest hotel in the city; and my husband left this fine growing country to starve here."

I was so much interested in the old woman's narrative—for she was really possessed of no ordinary capacity, and, though rude and uneducated, might have been a very superior person under different circumstances—that I rummaged among my stores, and soon found a piece of black silk, which I gave her for the hood she required.

The old woman examined it carefully over, smiled to herself, but, like all her people, was too proud to return a word of thanks. One gift to the family always involved another.

"Have you any cotton-batting, or black sewing-silk, to give me, to quilt with?"

"No."

"Humph!" returned the old dame, in a tone which seemed to contradict my assertion. She then settled herself in her chair, and, after shaking her foot awhile, and fixing her piercing eyes upon me for some minutes, she commenced the following list of interrogatories:—

"Is your father alive?"

"No; he died many years ago, when I was a young girl."

"Is your mother alive?"

"Yes."

"What is her name?" I satisfied her on this point.

"Did she ever marry again?"

"She might have done so, but she loved her husband too well, and preferred living single."

"Humph! We have no such notions here. What was your father?"

"A gentleman, who lived upon his own estate."

"Did he die rich?"

"He lost the greater part of his property from being surety for another."

"That's a foolish business. My man burnt his fingers with that. And what brought you out to this poor country—you, who are no more fit for it than I am to be a fine lady?"

"The promise of a large grant of land, and the false statements we heard regarding it."

"Do you like the country?"

"No; and I fear I never shall."

"I thought not; for the drop is always on your cheek, the children tell me; and those young ones have keen eyes. Now, take my advice: return while your money lasts; the longer you remain in Canada the less you will like it; and when your money is all spent, you will be like a bird in a cage; you may beat your wings against the bars, but you can't get out." There was a long pause. I hoped that my guest had sufficiently gratified her curiosity, when she again commenced:—

"How do you get your money? Do you draw it from the old country, or have you it with you in cash?"

Provoked by her pertinacity, and seeing no end to her cross-questioning, I replied, very impatiently, "Mrs. H_____, is it the custom in your country to catechise strangers whenever you meet with them?"

"What do you mean?" she said, colouring, I believe, for the first time in her life.

"I mean," quoth I, "an evil habit of asking impertinent questions."

The old woman got up, and left the house without speaking another word.

AN OCEAN OF GRASS

WILLIAM FRANCIS BUTLER

From *The Great Lone Land* (1872)

Today the Prairie West is a familiar, domesticated place of wheat fields and tall silos seen from a car window. In the last century, however, it was a wild frontier. People read about it as they read about darkest Africa, as we would read about a visit to another planet. In 1870 William Francis Butler, a thirty-two-year-old British army officer serving in Canada, was given the job of crossing this vast territory and reporting back to the federal government about conditions there. Travelling mainly on horseback, Butler covered almost 6,000 kilometres from the banks of the Red River to the Rocky Mountains and back again. On his return he wrote a book about his expedition, The Great Lone Land.

With Butler we are back in the realm of the travel writer. Unlike Hearne or Radisson, though, not much happened to Butler and reading his book, which is presented in the form of a daily journal, is often like enduring the slides of your friend's last vacation. Nonetheless, the images which Butler created—images of a boundless land sparsely populated by vanishing tribes of Indians—remained central to thinking about the West for generations. It is this imaginative content which has caused the book to endure long after other examples of expansionist travel literature have been forgotten.

In 1873 Butler left Canada. He served in the British army in Africa and Egypt and in the Boer War before retiring in 1905. He died in 1910.

A nd now let us turn our glance to this great Northwest whither my wandering steps are about to lead me. Fully 900 miles as bird would fly, and 1,200 as horse can travel, west of Red River an immense range of mountains, eternally capped with snow, rises in rugged masses from a vast stream-seared plain. They who first beheld these grand guardians of the central prairies named them the Montagnes des Rochers; a fitting title for such vast accumulation of rugged magnificence. From the glaciers and ice valleys of this great range of mountains innumerable streams descend into the plains. For a time they wander, as if heedless of direction, through groves and glades and green spreading declivities; then, assuming greater fixidity of purpose, they gather up many a wandering rill, and start eastward upon a long journey. At length the many detached streams resolve themselves into two great water systems; through hundreds of miles these two rivers pursue their parallel courses, now approaching, now opening out from each other. Suddenly, the southern river bends towards the north, and at a point some 600 miles from the mountains pours its volume of water into the northern channel. Then the united river rolls in vast majestic curves steadily towards the north-east, turns once more towards the south, opens out into a great reed-covered marsh, sweeps on into a large cedar-lined lake, and finally, rolling over a rocky ledge, casts its waters into the northern end of the great Lake Winnipeg, fully 1,300 miles from the glacier cradle where it took its birth. This river, which has along with it every diversity of hill and vale, meadow-land and forest, treeless plain and fertile hill-side, is called by the wild tribes who dwell along its glorious shores the Kissaskatchewan, or Rapid-flowing River. But this Kissaskatchewan is not the only river which unwaters the great central region lying between Red River and the Rocky Mountains. The Assineboine or Stony River drains the rolling prairie lands 500 miles west from Red River, and many a smaller stream and rushing, bubbling brook carries into its devious channel the waters of that vast country which lies between the American boundary-line and the pine woods of the lower Saskatchewan.

So much for the rivers; and now for the land through which they flow. How shall we picture it? How shall we tell the story of that great, boundless, solitary waste of verdure?

The old, old maps which the navigators of the sixteenth century framed from the discoveries of Cabot and Cartier, of Varrazanno and Hudson, played strange pranks with the geography of the New World. The coast-line, with the estuaries of large rivers, was tolerably accurate; but the centre of America was represented as a vast inland sea whose shores stretched far into the Polar North; a sea through which lay the much-coveted passage to the long sought treasures of the old realms of Cathay. Well, the geographers of that period erred only in the description of ocean which they placed in the central continent, for an ocean there is, and an ocean through which men seek the treasures of Cathay, even in our own times. But the ocean is one of grass, and the shores are the crests of mountain ranges, and the dark pine forests of sub-Arctic regions. The great ocean itself does not present more infinite variety than does this prairie-ocean of which we speak. In winter, a dazzling surface of purest snow; in early summer, a vast expanse of grass and pale pink roses; in autumn too often a wild sea of raging fire. No ocean of water in the world can vie with its gorgeous sunsets; no solitude can equal the loneliness of a night-shadowed prairie: one feels the stillness, and hears the silence, the wail of the prowling wolf makes the voice of solitude audible, the stars look down through infinite silence upon a silence almost as intense. This ocean has no past—time has been nought to it; and men have come and gone, leaving behind them no track, no vestige, of their presence. Some French writer, speaking of these prairies, has said that the sense of this utter negation of life, this complete absence of history, has struck him with a loneliness oppressive and sometimes terrible in its intensity. Perhaps so; but, for my part, the prairies had nothing terrible in their aspect, nothing oppressive in their loneliness. One saw here the world as it had taken shape and form from the hands of the Creator. Nor did the scene look less beautiful because nature alone tilled the earth, and the unaided sun brought forth the flowers.

October had reached its latest week: the wild geese and swans had taken their long flight to the south, and their wailing cry no more descended through the darkness; ice had settled upon the quiet pools and was settling upon the quick-running streams; the horizon glowed at night with the red light of moving prairie fires. It was the close of the Indian summer, and winter was coming quickly down from his far northern home.

On the 24th of October I quitted Fort Garry, at ten o'clock at night, and, turning out into the level prairie, commenced a long journey towards the West. The night was cold and moonless, but a brilliant aurora flashed and trembled in many-coloured shafts across the starry sky. Behind me lay friends and news of friends, civilization, tidings of a terrible war, firesides, and houses; before me lay unknown savage tribes, long days of saddle-travel, long nights of chilling bivouac, silence, separation, and space!

BINGO

ERNEST THOMPSON SETON

From *Wild Animals I Have Known* (1898)

When it appeared in 1898, Wild Animals I Have Known *established its author, Ernest Thompson Seton, as the inventor of the realistic animal story, a genre which portrays events from the animal's point of view.* Wild Animals *has been translated into fifteen languages and ranks among the all-time best-selling books by a Canadian. Seton assured his audiences that he based his stories on his own observations of particular animals and actual situations. Not long after the publication of* Wild Animals, *this claim was disputed in the pages of* Atlantic Monthly *magazine by another leading American naturalist, who accused Seton of mixing fact and fiction for literary effect. The article raised a storm in naturalist circles—even President Theodore Roosevelt got into the act with an attack on "Nature Fakers"—but Seton, adamant that his stories were based on scientific fact, gradually won over the public to his side of the debate.*

Ernest Thompson Seton was born in England in 1860. He moved to Canada with his family when he was six years old and grew up in Ontario. After studying painting at the Ontario College of Art, he turned to wildlife illustration, writing and public speaking and became the leading popularizer of natural history in North America. He published scientific books but is much more famous for his animal stories, of which he published several volumes, and for his children's novel, Two Little Savages *(1903). He is also famous as the founder of The League of the Woodcraft Indians, an outdoor youth movement which predated the Boy Scouts.*

The League promoted the Indian as the best role model for youngsters and taught its members a variety of wilderness survival skills. Seton believed fervently in the superiority of Indian culture, or at least his version of it. In 1930 he moved to New Mexico where he established a study centre at Seton Village outside of Santa Fe. He died there in 1946.

It was early in November, 1882, and the Manitoba winter had just set in. I was tilting back in my chair for a few lazy moments after breakfast, idly alternating my gaze from the one window-pane of our shanty, through which was framed a bit of the prairie and the end of our cowshed, to the old rhyme of the 'Franckelyn's dogge' pinned on the logs near by. But the dreamy mixture of rhyme and view was quickly dispelled by the sight of a large grey animal dashing across the prairie into the cowshed, with a smaller black and white animal in hot pursuit.

"A wolf," I exclaimed, and seizing a rifle dashed out to help the dog. But before I could get there they had left the stable, and after a short run over the snow the wolf again turned at bay, and the dog, our neighbour's collie, circled about watching his chance to snap.

I fired a couple of long shots, which had the effect only of setting them off again over the prairie. After another run this matchless dog closed and seized the wolf by the haunch, but again retreated to avoid the fierce return chop. Then there was another stand at bay, and again a race over the snow. Every few hundred yards this scene was repeated. The dog managing so that each fresh rush should be toward the settlement, while the wolf vainly tried to break back toward the dark belt of trees in the east. At last after a mile of this fighting and running I overtook them, and the dog, seeing that he now had good backing, closed in for the finish.

After a few seconds the whirl of struggling animals resolved itself into a wolf, on his back, with a bleeding collie gripping his throat, and it was now easy for me to step up and end the fight by putting a ball through the wolf's head.

Then, when this dog of marvelous wind saw that his foe was dead, he gave him no second glance, but set out at a lope for a farm four miles across the snow where he had left his master when first the wolf was started. He was a wonderful dog, and even if I had not come he undoubtedly would have killed the wolf alone, as I learned he had already done with others of the kind, in spite of the fact that the wolf, though of the smaller or prairie race, was much larger than himself.

I was filled with admiration for the dog's prowess and at once sought to buy him at any price. The scornful reply of his owner was, "Why don't you try to buy one of the children?"

Since Frank was not in the market I was obliged to content myself with the next best thing, one of his alleged progeny. That is, a son of his wife. This probable offspring of an illustrious sire was a roly-poly ball of black fur that looked more like a long-tailed bear-cub than a puppy. But he had some tan markings like those on Frank's coat, that were, I hoped, guarantees of future greatness, and also a very characteristic ring of white that he always wore on his muzzle.

Having got possession of his person, the next thing was to find him a name. Surely this puzzle was already solved. The rhyme of the 'Franckelyn's dogge' was in-built with the foundation of our acquaintance, so with adequate pomp we 'yclept him little Bingo.'

The rest of that winter Bingo spent in our shanty, living the life of a lubberly, fat, well-meaning, ill-doing puppy; gorging himself with food and growing bigger and clumsier each day. Even sad experience failed to teach him that he must keep his nose out of the rat-trap. His most friendly overtures to the cat were wholly misunderstood and resulted only in an armed neutrality that, varied by occasional reigns of terror, continued to the end; which came when Bingo, who early showed a mind of his own, got a notion for sleeping at the barn and avoiding the shanty altogether.

When the spring came I set about his serious education. After much pains on my behalf and many pains on his, he learned to go at the word in quest of our old yellow cow, that pastured at will on the unfenced prairie.

Once he had learned his business, he became very fond of it and nothing pleased him more than an order to go and fetch the cow. Away he would dash, barking with pleasure and leaping high in the air that he might better scan the plain for his victim. In a short time he would return driving her at full gallop before him, and gave her no peace until, puffing and blowing, she was safely driven into the farthest corner of her stable.

Less energy on his part would have been more satisfactory, but we bore with him until he grew so fond of this semi-daily hunt that he began to bring 'old Dunne' without being told. And at length not once or twice but a dozen times a day this energetic cowherd would sally forth on his own responsibility and drive the cow home to the stable.

At last things came to such a pass that whenever he felt like taking a little exercise, or had a few minutes of spare time, or even happened to think of it, Bingo would sally forth at racing speed over the plain and a few minutes later return, driving the unhappy yellow cow at full gallop before him.

At first this did not seem very bad, as it kept the cow from straying too far; but soon it was seen that it hindered her feeding. She became thin and gave less milk; it seemed to weigh on her mind too, as she was always watching nervously for that hateful dog, and in the mornings would hang around the stable as though afraid to venture off and subject herself at once to an onset.

This was going too far. All attempts to make Bingo more moderate in his pleasure were failures, so he was compelled to give it up altogether. After this, though he dared not bring her home, he continued to show his interest by lying at her stable door while she was being milked.

As the summer came on the mosquitoes became a dreadful plague, and the consequent vicious switching of Dunne's tail at milking-time even more annoying than the mosquitoes.

Fred, the brother who did the milking, was of an inventive as well as an impatient turn of mind, and he devised a simple plan to stop the switching. He fastened a brick to the cow's tail, then set blithely about his work assured of unusual comfort while the rest of us looked on in doubt.

Suddenly through the mist of mosquitoes came a dull whack and an outburst of 'language.' The cow went on placidly chewing till Fred got on his feet and furiously attacked her with the milking-stool. It was bad enough to be whacked on the ear with a brick by a stupid old cow, but the uproarious enjoyment and ridicule of the bystanders made it unendurable.

Bingo, hearing the uproar, and divining that he was needed, rushed in and attacked Dunne on the other side. Before the affair quieted down the milk was spilt, the pail and stool were broken, and the cow and the dog severely beaten.

Poor Bingo could not understand it at all. He had long ago learned to despise that cow, and now in utter disgust he decided to forsake even her stable door, and from that time he attached himself exclusively to the horses and their stable.

The cattle were mine, the horses were my brother's, and in transferring his allegiance from the cow-stable to the horse-stable Bingo seemed to give me up too, and anything like daily companionship ceased, and, yet, whenever any emergency arose Bingo turned to me and I to him, and both seemed to feel that the bond between man and dog is one that lasts as long as life.

The only other occasion on which Bingo acted as cowherd was in the autumn of the same year at the annual Carberry Fair. Among the dazzling inducements to enter one's stock there was, in addition to a prospect of glory, a cash prize of 'two dollars,' for the 'best collie in training.'

Misled by a false friend, I entered Bingo, and early on the day fixed, the cow was driven to the prairie just outside of the village. When the time came she was pointed out to Bingo and the word given—'Go fetch the cow.' It was the intention, of course, that he should bring her to me at the judge's stand.

But the animals knew better. They hadn't rehearsed all summer for nothing. When Dunne saw Bingo's careering form she knew that her only hope for safety was to get into her stable, and Bingo was equally sure that his sole mission in life was to quicken her pace in that direction. So off they raced over the prairie, like a wolf after a deer, and heading straight toward their home two miles away, they disappeared from view.

That was the last that judge or jury ever saw of dog or cow. The prize was awarded to the only other entry.

Bingo's loyalty to the horses was quite remarkable; by day he trotted beside them, and by night he slept at the stable door. Where the team went Bingo went, and nothing kept him away from them. This interesting assumption of ownership lent the greater significance to the following circumstance.

I was not superstitious, and up to this time had had no faith in omens, but was now deeply impressed by a strange occurrence in which Bingo took a leading part. There were but two of us now living on the De Winton Farm. One morning my brother set out for Boggy Creek for a load of hay. It was a long day's journey there and back, and he made an early start. Strange to tell, Bingo for once in his life did not follow the team. My brother called to him, but still he stood at a safe distance, and eyeing the team askance, refused to stir. Suddenly he raised his nose in the air and gave vent to a long, melancholy howl. He watched the wagon out of sight, and even followed for a hundred yards or so, raising his voice from time to time in the most doleful howlings. All that day he stayed about the barn, the only time that he was willingly separated from the horses, and at intervals howled a very death dirge. I was alone, and the dog's behaviour inspired me with an awful foreboding of calamity, and weighed upon me more and more as the hours passed away.

About six o'clock Bingo's howlings became unbearable, so that for lack of a better thought I threw something at him, and ordered him away. But oh, the feeling of horror that filled me! Why did I let my brother go away alone? Should I ever again see him alive? I might have known from the dog's actions that something dreadful was about to happen.

At length the hour for his return arrived, and there was John on his load. I took charge of the horses, vastly relieved, and with an air of assumed unconcern, asked, "All right?"

"Right," was the laconic answer.

Who now can say that there is nothing in omens?

And yet, when long afterward, I told this to one skilled in the occult, he looked grave, and said, "Bingo always turned to you in a crisis?"

"Yes."

"Then do not smile. It was you that were in danger that day; he stayed and saved your life, though you never knew from what."

Early in the spring I had begun Bingo's education. Very shortly afterward he began mine.

Midway on the two-mile stretch of prairie that lay between our shanty and the village of Carberry, was the corner-stake of the farm; it was a stout post in a low mound of earth, and was visible from afar.

I soon noticed that Bingo never passed without minutely examining this mysterious post. Next I learned that it was also visited by prairie wolves as well as by all the dogs in the neighbourhood, and at length, with the aid of a telescope, I made a number of observations that helped me to an understanding of the matter and enabled me to enter more fully into Bingo's private life.

The post was by common agreement a registry of the canine tribes. Their exquisite sense of smell enabled each individual to tell at once by the track and trace what other had recently been at the post. When the snow came much more was revealed. I then discovered that this post was but one of a system that covered the country; that in short, the entire region was laid out in signal stations at convenient intervals. These were marked by any conspicuous post, stone, buffalo skull, or other object that chanced to be in the desired locality, and extensive observation showed that it was a very complete system for getting and giving the news.

Each dog or wolf makes a point of calling at those stations that are near his line of travel to learn who has recently been there, just as a man calls at his club on returning to town and looks up the register.

I have seen Bingo approach the post, sniff, examine the ground about, then growl, and with bristling mane and glowing eyes, scratch fiercely and contemptuously with his hind feet, finally walking off very stiffly, glancing back from time to time. All of which, being interpreted, said:

"*Grrh! woof!* there's that dirty cur of McCarthy's. *Woof!* I'll 'tend to him to–night. *Woof! Woof!*" On another occasion, after the preliminaries, he became keenly interested and studied a coyote's track that came and went, saying to himself, as I afterward learned:

"A coyote track coming from the north, smelling of dead cow. Indeed? Pollworth's old Brindle must be dead at last. This is worth looking into."

At other times he would wag his tail, trot about the vicinity and come again and again to make his own visit more evident, perhaps for the benefit of his brother Bill just back from Brandon! So that it was not by chance that one night Bill turned up at Bingo's home and was taken to the hills where a delicious dead horse afforded a chance to suitably celebrate the reunion.

At other times he would be suddenly aroused by the news, take up the trail, and race to the next station for later information.

Sometimes his inspection produced only an air of grave attention, as though he said to himself, "Dear me, who the deuce is this?" or "It seems to me I met that fellow at the Portage last summer."

One morning on approaching the post Bingo's every hair stood on end, his tail dropped and quivered, and he gave proof that he was suddenly sick at the stomach, sure signs of terror. He showed no desire to follow up or know more of the matter, but returned to the house, and half an hour afterward his mane was still bristling and his expression one of hate or fear.

I studied the dreaded track and learned that in Bingo's language the half-terrified, deep-gurgled *'grrr-wff'* means *'timber wolf.'*

These were among the things that Bingo taught me. And in the after time when I might chance to see him arouse from his frosty nest by the stable door, and after stretching himself and shaking the snow from his shaggy coat, disappear into the gloom at a steady trot, trot, trot, I used to think:

"Aha! old dog, I know where you are off to, and why you eschew the shelter of the shanty. Now I know why your nightly trips over the country are so well timed, and how you know just where to go for what you want, and when and how to seek it."

In the autumn of 1884, the shanty at De Winton Farm was closed and Bingo changed his home to the establishment, that is, to the stable, not the house, of Gordon Wright, our most intimate neighbour.

Since the winter of his puppyhood he had declined to enter a house at any time except during a thunderstorm. Of thunder and guns he had a deep dread—no doubt the fear of the first originated in the second, and that arose from some unpleasant shot-gun experiences, the cause of which will be seen. His nightly couch was outside the stable, even during the coldest weather, and it was easy to see that he enjoyed to the full the complete nocturnal liberty entailed. Bingo's midnight wanderings extended across the plains for miles. There was plenty of proof of this. Some farmers at very remote points sent word to old Gordon, that if he did not keep his dog home nights, they would use the shotgun, and Bingo's terror of firearms would indicate that the threats were not idle. A man living as far away as Petrel, said he saw a large black wolf kill a coyote on the snow one winter evening, but afterward he changed his opinion and 'reckoned it must 'a' been Wright's dog.' Whenever the body of a winter-killed ox or horse was exposed, Bingo was sure to repair to it nightly, and driving away the prairie wolves, feast to repletion.

Sometimes the object of a night foray was merely to maul some distant neighbour's dog, and notwithstanding vengeful threats, there seemed no reason to fear that the Bingo breed would die out. One man even avowed that he had seen a prairie wolf accompanied by three young ones which

resembled the mother, except that they were very large and black and
had a ring of white around the muzzle.

True or not as that may be, I know that late in March, while we were
out in the sleigh with Bingo trotting behind, a prairie wolf was started
from a hollow. Away it went with Bingo in full chase, but the wolf did
not greatly exert itself to escape, and within a short distance Bingo was
close up, yet strange to tell, there was no grappling, no fight!

Bingo trotted amiably alongside and licked the wolf's nose.

We were astounded, and shouted to urge Bingo on. Our shouting and
approach several times started the wolf off at speed and Bingo again
pursued until he had overtaken it, but his gentleness was too obvious.

"It is a she-wolf, he won't harm her," I exclaimed as the truth dawned
on me. And Gordon said: "Well, I be darned."

So we called our unwilling dog and moved on.

For weeks after this we were annoyed by the depredations of a prairie
wolf who killed our chickens, stole pieces of pork from the end of the
house, and several times terrified the children by looking into the window
of the shanty while the men were away.

Against this animal Bingo seemed to be no safeguard. At length the
wolf, a female, was killed, and then Bingo plainly showed his hand by
his lasting enmity toward Oliver, the man who did the deed.

Changes took me far away from Manitoba, and on my return in 1886
Bingo was still a member of Wright's household. I thought he would
have forgotten me after two years absence, but not so. One day early in
the winter, after having been lost for forty-eight hours, he crawled home
to Wright's with a wolf-trap and a heavy log fast to one foot, and the
foot frozen to stony hardness. No one had been able to approach to help
him, he was so savage, when I, the stranger now, stooped down and laid
hold of the trap with one hand and his leg with the other. Instantly he
seized my wrist in his teeth.

Without stirring I said, "Bing, don't you know me?"

He had not broken the skin and at once released his hold and offered
no further resistance, although he whined a good deal during the removal
of the trap. He still acknowledged me his master in spite of his change

of residence and my long absence, and notwithstanding my surrender of ownership I still felt that he was my dog.

Bing was carried into the house much against his will and his frozen foot thawed out. During the rest of the winter he went lame and two of his toes eventually dropped off. But before the return of warm weather his health and strength were fully restored, and to a casual glance he bore no mark of his dreadful experience in the steel trap.

During the same winter I caught many wolves and foxes who did not have Bingo's good luck in escaping the traps, which I kept out right into the spring, for bounties are good even when fur is not.

Kennedy's Plain was always a good trapping ground because it was unfrequented by man and yet lay between the heavy woods and the settlement. I had been fortunate with the fur here, and late in April rode in on one of my regular rounds.

The wolf-traps are made of heavy steel and have two springs, each of one hundred pounds power. They are set in fours around a buried bait, and after being strongly fastened to concealed logs are carefully covered in cotton and in fine sand so as to be quite invisible.

A prairie wolf was caught in one of these. I killed him with a club and throwing him aside proceeded to reset the trap as I had done so many hundred times before. All was quickly done. I threw the trap-wrench over toward the pony, and seeing some fine sand near by, I reached out for a handful of it to add a good finish to the setting.

Oh, unlucky thought! Oh, mad heedlessness born of long immunity! That fine sand was *on the next wolf-trap* and in an instant I was a prisoner. Although not wounded, for the traps have no teeth, and my thick trapping gloves deadened the snap, I was firmly caught across the hand above the knuckles. Not greatly alarmed at this, I tried to reach the trap-wrench with my right foot. Stretching out at full length, face downward, I worked myself toward it, making my imprisoned arm as long and straight as possible. I could not see and reach at the same time, but counted on my toe telling me when I touched the little iron key to my fetters. My first effort was a failure; strain as I might at the chain my toe struck no metal. I swung slowly around my anchor, but still failed. Then a painfully taken observation showed I was much too far to the west. I set about working around, tapping blindly with my toe to discover the key. Thus wildly groping with my right foot I forgot about the other till there was a sharp 'clank' and the iron jaws of trap No. 3 closed tight on my left foot.

The terrors of the situation did not, at first, impress me, but I soon found that all my struggles were in vain. I could not get free from either trap or move the traps together, and there I lay stretched out and firmly staked to the ground.

What would become of me now? There was not much danger of freezing for the cold weather was over, but Kennedy's Plain was never visited excepting by the winter wood-cutters. No one knew where I had gone, and unless I could manage to free myself there was no prospect ahead but to be devoured by wolves, or else die of cold and starvation.

As I lay there the red sun went down over the spruce swamp west of the plain, and a shorelark on a gopher mound a few yards off twittered his evening song, just as one had done the night before at our shanty door, and though the numb pains were creeping up my arm, and a deadly chill possessed me, I noticed how long his little ear-tufts were. Then my thoughts went to the comfortable supper-table at Wright's shanty, and I thought, now they are frying the pork for supper, or just sitting down. My pony still stood as I left him with his bridle on the ground patiently waiting to take me home. He did not understand the long delay, and when I called, he ceased nibbling the grass and looked at me in dumb, helpless inquiry. If he would only go home the empty saddle might tell the tale and bring help. But his very faithfulness kept him waiting hour after hour while I was perishing of cold and hunger.

Then I remembered how old Girou the trapper had been lost, and in the following spring his comrades found his skeleton held by the leg in a bear-trap. I wondered what part of my clothing would show my identity. Then a new thought came to me. This is how a wolf feels when he is trapped. Oh! what misery have I been responsible for! Now I'm to pay for it.

Night came slowly on. A prairie wolf howled, the pony pricked up his ears and walking nearer to me, stood with his head down. Then another prairie wolf howled and another, and I could make out that they were gathering in the neighbourhood. There I lay prone and helpless, wondering if it would not be strictly just that they should come and tear me to pieces. I heard them calling for a long time before I realized that dim, shadowy forms were sneaking near. The horse saw them first, and his terrified snort drove them back at first, but they came nearer next time and sat around me on the prairie. Soon one bolder than the others crawled up and tugged at the body of his dead relative. I shouted and he retreated growling. The pony ran to a distance in terror. Presently the wolf returned, and after two or three of these retreats and returns, the body was dragged off and devoured by the rest in a few minutes.

After this they gathered nearer and sat on their haunches to look at me, and the boldest one smelled the rifle and scratched dirt on it. He retreated when I kicked at him with my free foot and shouted, but growing bolder as I grew weaker he came and snarled right in my face. At this several others snarled and came up closer, and I realized that I was to be devoured by the foe that I most despised, when suddenly out of the gloom with a guttural roar sprang a great black wolf. The prairie wolves scattered like chaff except the bold one, which seized by the black newcomer was in a few moments a draggled corpse, and then, oh horrors! this mighty brute bounded at me and—Bingo—noble Bingo, rubbed his shaggy, panting sides against me and licked my cold face.

"Bingo—Bing—old—boy—Fetch me the trap-wrench!"

Away he went and returned dragging the rifle, for he knew only that I wanted something.

"No—Bing—the trap-wrench." This time it was my sash, but at last he brought the wrench and wagged his tail in joy that it was right. Reaching out with my free hand, after much difficulty I unscrewed the pillar-nut. The trap fell apart and my hand was released, and a minute later I was free. Bing brought the pony up, and after slowly walking to restore the circulation I was able to mount. Then slowly at first but soon at a gallop, with Bingo as herald careering and barking ahead, we set out for home, there to learn that the night before, though never taken on the trapping rounds, the brave dog had acted strangely, whimpering and watching the timber-trail; and at last when night came on, in spite of attempts to detain him he had set out in the gloom and guided by a knowledge that is beyond us had reached the spot in time to avenge me as well as set me free.

Stanch old Bing—he was a strange dog. Though his heart was with me, he passed me next day with scarcely a look, but responded with alacrity when little Gordon called him to a gopher-hunt. And it was so to the end; and to the end also he lived the wolfish life that he loved, and never failed to seek the winter-killed horses and found one again with a poisoned bait, and wolfishly bolted that; then feeling the pang, set out, not for Wright's but to find me, and reached the door of my shanty where I should have been. Next day on returning I found him dead in the snow with his head on the sill of the door—the door of his puppyhood's days; my dog to the last in his heart of hearts—it was my help he sought, and vainly sought, in the hour of his bitter extremity.

BATHED IN BLISS

RICHARD MAURICE BUCKE

From *Cosmic Consciousness* (1901)

Richard Maurice Bucke was a sixty-four-year-old psychiatrist in London, Ontario when he published Cosmic Consciousness, *one of the classic texts of twentieth-century religious mysticism. The book presents Bucke's theory that mankind is evolving toward a higher state of being in which everyone will exist in a state of permanent transcendent bliss, or cosmic consciousness. It is also a collection of case studies of figures in history whom Bucke believed had experienced this ecstatic state. Though its style is cumbersome,* Cosmic Consciousness *has enjoyed huge readership and, remarkably, has been in print virtually without interruption since its publication.*

Richard Maurice Bucke was born in England in 1837 but grew up on a backwoods farm in Ontario. After an adventurous youth wandering the American West, he returned to Canada to enroll in medicine at McGill University (having never been to school before). Following graduation, he continued his studies in England, then set up a medical practice in Sarnia. In 1876 he began a distinguished career as a mental hospital administrator. Bucke was a close friend of the American poet, Walt Whitman, whom he believed to be "the greatest man of my day." He wrote the first biography of Whitman and was one of the poet's literary executors. Their friendship is depicted in the recent movie, Beautiful Dreamers. *Bucke died in 1902 after a fall.*

The following selection from Cosmic Consciousness *summarizes Bucke's theory of psychic evolution.*

What is Cosmic Consciousness? The present volume is an attempt to answer this question; but notwithstanding it seems well to make a short prefatory statement in as plain language as possible so as to open the door, as it were, for the more elaborate exposition to be attempted in the body of the work. Cosmic Consciousness, then, is a higher form of consciousness than that possessed by the ordinary man. This last is called Self Consciousness and is that faculty upon which rests all of our life (both subjective and objective) which is not common to us and the higher animals, except that small part of it which is derived from the few individuals who have had the higher consciousness above named. To make the matter clear it must be understood that there are three forms or grades of consciousness. (1) Simple Consciousness, which is possessed by say the upper half of the animal kingdom. By means of this faculty a dog or a horse is just as conscious of the things about him as a man is; he is also conscious of his own limbs and body and he knows that these are a part of himself. (2) Over and above this Simple Consciousness, which is possessed by man as by animals, man has another which is called Self Consciousness. By virtue of this faculty man is not only conscious of trees, rocks, waters, his own limbs and body, but he becomes conscious of himself as a distinct entity apart from all the rest of the universe. It is as good as certain that no animal can realize himself in that way. Further, by means of self consciousness, man (who knows as the animal knows) becomes capable of treating his own mental states as objects of consciousness. The animal is, as it were, immersed in his consciousness as a fish in the sea; he cannot, even in imagination, get outside of it for one moment so as to realize it. But man by virtue of self consciousness can step aside, as it were, from himself and think: "Yes, that thought that I had about that matter is true; I know it is true and I know that I know it is true." The writer has been asked: "How do you know that animals cannot think in the same manner?" The answer is simple and conclusive—it is: There is no evidence that any animal can so think, but if they could we should soon know it. Between two creatures living together, as dogs or horses and men, and each self conscious, it would be the simplest matter in the world to open up communication. Even as it is, diverse as is our psychology, we do, by watching his acts, enter into the dog's mind pretty freely—we see what is going on there—we know that the dog sees and hears, smells and tastes—we know that he has intelligence—adapts means to ends—that he reasons. If he was self conscious we must have learned it long ago. We have not learned it and it is as good as certain that no dog, horse, elephant or ape ever was self conscious. Another thing: on man's self consciousness is built everything in and about us distinctively human. Language is the objective of which self consciousness is the subjective. Self consciousness and language (two in one, for they are two halves of the same thing) are the sine qua non of human social life, of manners, of institutions, of industries of all kinds, of all arts useful and fine. If any animal possessed self consciousness it seems certain that it would upon that master faculty build (as man has done) a superstructure of language; of reasoned out customs, industries, art. But no animal has done this, therefore we infer that no animal has self consciousness.

The possession of self consciousness and language (its other self) by man creates an enormous gap between him and the highest creature possessing simple consciousness merely.

Cosmic Consciousness is a third form which is as far above Self Consciousness as is that above Simple Consciousness. With this form, of course, both simple and self consciousness persist (as simple consciousness persists when self consciousness is acquired), but added to them is the new faculty so often named and to be named in this volume. The prime characteristic of cosmic consciousness is, as its name implies, a consciousness of the cosmos, that is, of the life and order of the universe. What these words mean cannot be touched upon here; it is the business of this volume to throw some light upon them. There are many elements belonging to the cosmic sense besides the central fact just alluded to. Of these a few may be mentioned. Along with the consciousness of the cosmos there occurs an intellectual enlightenment or illumination which alone would place the individual on a new plane of existence—would make him almost a member of a new species. To this is added a state of moral exaltation, an indescribable feeling of elevation, elation, and joyousness, and a quickening of the moral sense which is fully as striking and more important both to the individual and to the race than is the enhanced intellectual power. With these come, what may be called a sense of immortality, a consciousness of eternal life, not a conviction that he shall have this, but the consciousness that he has it already.

Only a personal experience of it, or a prolonged study of men who have passed into the new life, will enable us to realize what this actually is; but it has seemed to the present writer that to pass in review, even briefly and imperfectly, instances in which the condition in question has existed would be worth while. He expects his work to be useful in two ways: First, in broadening the general view of human life by comprehending in our mental vision this important phase of it, and by enabling us to realize, in some measure, the true status of certain men who, down to the present, are either exalted, by the average self conscious individual, to the rank of gods, or, adopting the other extreme, are adjudged insane. And in the second place he hopes to furnish aid to his fellow men in a far more practical and important sense. The view he takes is that our descendants will sooner or later reach, as a race, the condition of cosmic consciousness, just as, long ago, our ancestors passed from simple to self consciousness. He believes that this step in evolution is even now being made, since it is clear to him both that men with the faculty in question are becoming more and more common and also that as a race we are approaching nearer and nearer to that stage of the self conscious mind from which the transition to the cosmic conscious is effected. He realizes that, granted the necessary heredity, any individual not already beyond the age may enter cosmic consciousness. He knows that intelligent contact with cosmic conscious minds assists self conscious individuals in the ascent to the higher plane. He therefore hopes, by bringing about, or at least facilitating this contact, to aid men and women in making the almost infinitely important step in question.

The immediate future of our race, the writer thinks, is indescribably hopeful. There are at the present moment impending over us three revolutions, the least of which would dwarf the ordinary historic upheaval called by that name into absolute insignificance. They are: (1) The material, economic and social revolution which will depend upon and result from the establishment of aerial navigation. (2) The economic and social revolution which will abolish individual ownership and rid the earth at once of two immense evils—riches and poverty. And (3) The psychical revolution of which there is here question.

Either of the first two would (and will) radically change the conditions of, and greatly uplift, human life; but the third will do more for humanity than both of the former, were their importance multiplied by hundreds or even thousands.

The three operating (as they will) together will literally create a new heaven and a new earth. Old things will be done away and all will become new.

Before aerial navigation national boundaries, tariffs, and perhaps distinctions of language will fade out. Great cities will no longer have reason for being and will melt away. The men who now dwell in cities will inhabit in summer the mountains and the sea shores; building often in airy and beautiful spots, now almost or quite inaccessible, commanding the most extensive and magnificent views. In the winter they will probably dwell in communities of moderate size. As the herding together, as now, in great cities, so the isolation of the worker of the soil will become a thing of the past. Space will be practically annihilated, there will be no crowding together and no enforced solitude.

Before Socialism crushing toil, cruel anxiety, insulting and demoralizing riches, poverty and its ills will become subjects for historical novels.

In contact with the flux of cosmic consciousness all religions known and named to-day will be melted down. The human soul will be revolutionized. Religion will absolutely dominate the race. It will not depend on tradition. It will not be believed and disbelieved. It will not be a part of life, belonging to certain hours, times, occasions. It will not be in sacred books nor in the mouths of priests. It will not dwell in churches and meetings and forms and days. Its life will not be in prayers, hymns nor discourses. It will not depend on special revelations, on the words of gods who came down to teach, nor on any bible or bibles. It will have no mission to save men from their sins or to secure them entrance to heaven. It will not teach a future immortality nor future glories, for immortality and all glory will exist in the here and now. The evidence of immortality will live in every heart as sight in every eye. Doubt of God and of eternal life will be as impossible as is now doubt of existence; the evidence of each will be the same. Religion will govern every minute of every day of all life. Churches, priests, forms, creeds, prayers, all agents, all intermediaries between the individual man and God will be permanently replaced by direct unmistakable intercourse. Sin will no longer exist nor will salvation be desired. Men will not worry about death or a future, about the kingdom of heaven, about what may come with and after the cessation of the life of the present body. Each soul will feel and know itself to be immortal, will feel and know that the entire universe with all its good and with all its beauty is for it and belongs to it forever. The world peopled by men possessing cosmic consciousness will be as far removed from the world of to-day as this is from the world as it was before the advent of self consciousness.

As has been either said or implied already, in order that a man may enter into Cosmic Consciousness he must belong (so to speak) to the top layer of the world of Self Consciousness. Not that he need have an extraordinary intellect (this faculty is rated, usually far above its real value and does not seem nearly so important, from this point of view, as do some others) though he must not be deficient in this respect, either. He must have a good physique, good health, but above all he must have an exalted moral nature, strong sympathies, a warm heart, courage, strong and earnest religious feeling. All these being granted, and the man having reached the age necessary to bring him to the top of the self conscious mental stratum, some day he enters Cosmic Consciousness. What is his experience? Details must be given with diffidence, as they are only known to the writer in a few cases, and doubtless the phenomena are varied and diverse. What is said here, however, may be depended on as far as it goes. It is true of certain cases, and certainly touches upon the full truth in certain other cases, so that it may be looked upon as being provisionally correct.

a. The person, suddenly, without warning, has a sense of being immersed in a flame, or rose-colored cloud, or perhaps rather a sense that the mind is itself filled with such a cloud of haze.

b. At the same instant he is, as it were, bathed in an emotion of joy, assurance, triumph, "salvation." The last word is not strictly correct if taken in its ordinary sense, for the feeling, when fully developed, is not that a particular act of salvation is effected, but that no special "salvation" is needed, the scheme upon which the world is built being itself sufficient. It is this ecstasy, far beyond any that belongs to the merely self conscious life, with which the *poets*, as such, especially occupy themselves: As

Gautama, in his discourses, preserved in the "Suttas"; Jesus in the "Parables"; Paul in the "Epistles"; Dante at the end of the "Purgatorio" and beginning of "Paradiso"; Shakespeare in the "Sonnets"; Balzac in "Seraphita"; Whitman in the "Leaves"; Edward Carpenter in "Towards Democracy"; leaving to the *singers* the pleasures and pains, loves and hates, joys and sorrows, peace and war, life and death, of self conscious man; though the *poets* may treat of these, too, but from the new point of view, as expressed in the "Leaves": "I will never again mention love or death inside a house"—that is, from the old point of view, with the old connotations.

c. Simultaneously or instantly following the above sense and emotional experiences there comes to the person an intellectual illumination quite impossible to describe. Like a flash there is presented to his consciousness a clear conception (a vision) in outline of the meaning and drift of the universe. He does not come to believe merely; but he sees and knows that the cosmos, which to the self conscious mind seems made up of dead matter, is in fact far otherwise—is in very truth a living presence. He sees that instead of men being, as it were, patches of life scattered through an infinite sea of non-living substance, they are in reality specks of relative death in an infinite ocean of life. He sees that the life which is in man is eternal, as all life is eternal; that the soul of man is as immortal as God is; that the universe is so built and ordered that without any peradventure all things work together for the good of each and all; that the foundation principle of the world is what we call love, and that the happiness of every individual is in the long run absolutely certain. The person who passes through this experience will learn in the few minutes, or even moments, of its continuance more than in months or years of study, and he will learn much that no study ever taught or can teach. Especially does he obtain such a conception of THE WHOLE, or at least of an immense WHOLE, as dwarfs all conception, imagination or speculation, springing from and belonging to ordinary self consciousness, such a conception as makes the old attempts to mentally grasp the universe and its meaning petty and even ridiculous.

This awakening of the intellect has been well described by a writer upon Jacob Behmen in these words: "The mysteries of which he discoursed were not reported to him, he BEHELD them. He saw the root of all mysteries, the UNGRUND or URGRUND, whence issue all contrasts and discordant principles, hardness and softness, severity and mildness, sweet and bitter, love and sorrow, heaven and hell. These he SAW in their origin; these he attempted to describe in their issue and to reconcile in their eternal results. He saw into the being of God; whence the birth or going forth of the divine manifestation. Nature lay unveiled to him—he was at home in the heart of things. His own book, which he himself was (so Whitman: 'This is no book; who touches this touches a man'), the microcosm of man, with his three-fold life, was patent to his vision."

d. Along with moral elevation and intellectual illumination comes what must be called, for want of a better term, a sense of immortality. This is not an intellectual conviction, such as comes with the solution of a problem, nor is it an experience such as learning something unknown before. It is far more simple and elementary, and could better be compared to that certainty of distinct individuality, possessed by each one, which comes with and belongs to self consciousness.

e. With illumination the fear of death which haunts so many men and women at times all their lives falls off like an old cloak—not, however, as a result of reasoning—it simply vanishes.

f. The same may be said of the sense of sin. It is not that the person escapes from sin; but he no longer sees that there is any sin in the world from which to escape.

g. The instantaneousness of the illumination is one of its most striking features. It can be compared with nothing so well as with a dazzling flash of lightning in a dark night, bringing the landscape which had been hidden into clear view.

h. The previous character of the man who enters the new life is an important element in the case.

i. So is the age at which illumination occurs. Should we hear of a case of cosmic consciousness occurring at twenty, for instance, we should at first doubt the truth of the account, and if forced to believe it we should expect the man (if he lived) to prove himself, in some way, a veritable spiritual giant.

j. The added charm to the personality of the person who attains to cosmic consciousness is always, it is believed, a feature in the case.

k. There seems to the writer to be sufficient evidence that, with cosmic consciousness, while it is actually present, and lasting (gradually passing away) a short time thereafter, a change takes place in the appearance of the subject of illumination. This change is similar to that caused in a person's appearance by great joy, but at times (that is, in pronounced cases) it seems to be much more marked than that. In these great cases in which illumination is intense the change in question is also intense and may amount to a veritable "transfiguration." Dante says that he was "transhumanized into a God." There seems to be a strong probability that could he have been seen at that moment he would have exhibited what could only have been called "transfiguration." In subsequent chapters of this book several cases will be given in which the change in question, more or less strongly marked, occurred.

WE HAVE NO KNIVES

VILHJALMUR STEFANSSON

From *My Life with the Eskimo* (1913)

In May, 1910, on the frozen ocean north of the Arctic mainland, the thirty-one-year-old Icelandic-Canadian explorer and scientist, Vilhjalmur Stefansson, encountered a party of Inuit from Victoria Island who had never before seen White men. The meeting is described here in an extract from My Life with the Eskimo, *Stefansson's book about his travels in the Arctic between 1908 and 1912. The passage is a wonderful illustration of the excitement, confusion and misunderstanding which surrounded all such encounters. Later during the same expedition, Stefansson met a group of people he called the Blond Eskimos, now known as the Copper Inuit. Because of their fair features, he theorized that these people were descendants of early Europeans. This theory, later disproved, touched off a heated scientific debate; the great Norwegian explorer Roald Amundsen called the idea "palpable nonsense," and other critics were even less kind.*

Vilhjalmur Stefansson was no stranger to controversy; his flair for publicity earned him the suspicion of many scientists who believed that he put self-promotion ahead of scholarship. Stefansson was born near Gimli, Manitoba in 1879. After training as an anthropologist at Harvard University he made three excursions into the Arctic, the last (1913-18) as leader of the Canadian Arctic Expedition. In between expeditions he gave public lectures and wrote a series of books which established him as the reigning Arctic "expert" of his day. Based on his experiences, Stefansson believed strongly in a form of Arctic travel that relied on local resources and local people. He also advocated unusual nutritional theories, heavy on meat and butter, which he developed by observing the Inuit. He was an impassioned proponent of the economic potential of the "friendly Arctic," arguing that the North was not as hostile to human occupation as people believed. By the mid-1920s his ideas and schemes had fallen out of favour in Canada and he spent the rest of his life in the United States, where he died in 1962.

On May 9th, nineteen days out from Langton Bay, we came upon signs that made our hearts beat faster. It was at Point Wise, where the open sea begins to be narrowed into Dolphin and Union straits by the near approach to the mainland of the mountainous shores of Victoria Island. The beach was strewn with pieces of drift-wood, and on one of them we found the marks of recent choppings with a dull adze. A search of the beach for half a mile each way revealed numerous similar choppings. Evidently the men who had made them had been testing the pieces of wood to see if they were sound enough to become the materials for sleds or other things they had wished to make. Those pieces which had but one or two adze marks had been found unsound; in a few places piles of chips showed that a sound piece had been found there and had been roughed down for transportation purposes on the spot. Prepossessed by the idea that Victoria Island was probably inhabited because Rae had seen people on its southwest coast in 1851, and the mainland probably uninhabited because Richardson had failed to find any people on it in 1826 and again in 1848, I decided that the men whose traces we saw were probably Victoria Islanders who had with sleds crossed the frozen straits from the land whose mountains we could faintly see to the north, and had returned to its woodless shores with the drift-wood they had picked up here. We learned later that this supposition was wrong; the people whose traces we found were mainland dwellers whose ancestors must have been hunting inland to the south when Richardson twice passed without seeing them.

The night after this discovery we did not sleep much. The Eskimo were more excited than I was, apparently, and far into the morning they talked and speculated on the meaning of the signs. Had we come upon traces of the Nagyuktogmiut "who kill all strangers"? Fortunately enough, my long-entertained fear that traces of people would cause a panic in my party was not realized. In spite of all their talk, and in spite of the fact that they were seriously afraid, the curiosity as to what these strange people would prove to be like—in fine, the spirit of adventure, which seldom crops out in an Eskimo—was far stronger than their fears. We were therefore up early the next morning, and soon out on the road.

All that day we found along the beach comparatively fresh traces of people, chiefly shavings and chips where the hewing and shaping of wood had taken place. None seen that day were of the present winter, though some seemed to be of the previous summer; but the next morning, just east of Point Young, we found at last human footprints in the crusted snow and sled tracks that were not over three months old. That day at Cape Bexley we came upon a deserted village of over fifty snow houses; their inhabitants had apparently left them about midwinter, and it was now the 12th of May.

The size of the deserted village took our breath away. Tannaumirk, the young man from the Mackenzie River, had never seen an inhabited village among his people of more than twelve or fifteen houses. All his old fears of the Nagyuktogmiut "who kill all strangers" now came to the surface afresh; all the stories that he knew of their peculiar ways and atrocious deeds were retold by him that evening for our common benefit.

A broad but three months' untravelled trail led north from this village site across the ice toward Victoria Island. My intentions were to continue east along the mainland into Coronation Gulf, but I decided nevertheless to stop here long enough to make an attempt to find the people at whose village we had camped. We would leave most of our gear on shore, with Pannigabluk to take care of it, while the two men and myself took the trail across the ice. This was according to Eskimo etiquette—on approach to the country of strange or distrusted people non-combatants are left behind, and only the able men of the party advance to a cautious parley. In this case the Mackenzie River man, Tannaumirk, was frightened enough to let his pride go by the board and to ask that he, too, might stay on shore at the camp. I told him he might, and Natkusiak and I prepared to start alone with a light sled, but at the last moment Tannaumirk decided he preferred to go with us, as the Nagyuktogmiut were likely in our absence to discover our camp, to surprise it by night, and to kill him while he slept. It would be safer, he thought, to go with us. Pannigabluk was much the coolest of the three Eskimo; if she was afraid to be left alone on shore she did not show it; she merely said that she might get lonesome if we were gone more than three or four days. We left her cheerfully engaged in the mending of our worn footgear, and at 2.30 p.m., May 13th, 1910, we took the old but nevertheless plain trail northward into the rough sea ice.

It was only near shore that the ice was rough, and with our light sled we made good progress; it was the first time on the trip that we did not have to pull in harness ourselves; instead we took turns in riding, two sitting on the sled at the same time and one running ahead to cheer the dogs on. We made about six miles per hour, and inside of two hours we arrived at another deserted village, about a month more recent than the one found at Cape Bexley. We were, therefore, on the trail not of a travelling party but of a migratory community.

As we understood dimly then and know definitely now, each village on such a trail should be about ten miles from the next preceding, and should be about a month more recent. The explanation of this is simple. The village of a people who hunt seal on level "bay" ice must not be on shore, for it is not convenient for a hunter to go more than five miles at the most from camp to look for the seal-holes, and naturally there are no seal-holes on land; the inhabitants of a sea village can hunt through an entire circle whose radius is about five miles; the inhabitants of a shore village can hunt through only half a circle of the same radius, for the other half of it will be on land. When the frost overtakes the seals in the fall, each of them, wherever he happens to be, gnaws several holes in the thin ice and rises to these whenever he needs to breathe. As the ice thickens he keeps them open by continuous gnawing, and for the whole of the winter that follows he is kept a prisoner in their neighbourhood because of the fact that if he ever went to a considerable distance he would be unable to find a place to reach the air, and would therefore die of suffocation. By the aid of their dogs the Eskimo find these breathing-holes of the seals underneath the snow that hides them in winter, and spear the animals as they rise for air. In a month or so the hunters of a single village will have killed all the seals within a radius of about five miles; they must then move camp about ten miles, so that a five-mile circle around their next camp shall be tangent to the five-mile circle about their last one; for if the circles overlapped there would be that much waste territory within the new circle of activities. If, then, you are following such a trail and come to a village about four months old, you will expect to find the people who made it not more than forty miles off.

In the present case our task was simplified by the fact that the group we were following had not moved straight ahead north, but had made their fourth camp west of the second. Standing on the roofs of the houses of the second camp, we could see three seal-hunters a few miles to the west, each sitting on his block of snow by a seal-hole waiting for the animal to rise.

The seal-hunters and their camp were up the wind, and our dogs scented them. As we bore swiftly down upon the nearest of the sealers the dogs showed enthusiasm and anticipation as keen as mine, keener by a great deal than did my Eskimo. As the hunter was separated from each of his fellow-huntsmen by a full half-mile, I thought he would probably be frightened if all of us were to rush up to him at the top speed of our dogs. We therefore stopped our sled several hundred yards away. Tannaumirk had become braver now, for the lone stranger did not look formidable, sitting stooped forward as he was on his block of snow beside the seal-hole; he accordingly volunteered to act as our ambassador, saying that the Mackenzie dialect (his own) was probably nearer the stranger's tongue than Natkusiak's. This seemed likely, so I told him to go ahead. The sealer sat motionless as Tannaumirk approached him; I watched him through my glasses and saw that he held his face steadily as if watching the seal-hole, but that he raised his eyes every second or two to the (to him) strange figure of the man approaching. He was evidently tensely ready for action. Tannaumirk by now was thoroughly over his fears, and would have walked right up to the sealer, but when no more than five paces or so intervened between them the sealer suddenly jumped up, grasping a long knife that had lain on the snow beside him, and poising himself as if to receive an attack or to be ready to leap forward suddenly. This scared our man, who stopped abruptly and began excitedly and volubly to assure the sealer that he and all of us were friendly and harmless, men of excellent character and intentions.

I was, of course, too far away to hear, but Tannaumirk told me afterward that on the instant of jumping up the sealer began a monotonous noise which is not a chant nor is it words—it is merely an effort to ward off dumbness, for if a man who is in the presence of a spirit does not make at least one sound each time he draws his breath, he will be stricken permanently dumb. This is a belief common to the Alaska and Coronation Gulf Eskimo. For several minutes Tannaumirk talked excitedly, and the sealer kept up the moaning noise, quite unable to realize, apparently, that he was being spoken to in human speech. It did not occur to him for a long time, he told us afterward, that we might be something other than spirits, for our dogs and dog harness, our sleds and clothes, were such as he had never seen in all his wanderings; besides, we had not, on approaching, used the peace sign of his people, which is holding the hands out to show that one does not carry a knife.

After what may have been anything from five to fifteen minutes of talking and expostulation by Tannaumirk, the man finally began to listen and then to answer. The dialects proved to differ about as much as Norwegian does from Swedish, or Spanish from Portuguese. After Tannaumirk had made him understand the assurance that we were of good intent and character, and had showed by lifting his own coat that he had no knife, the sealer approached him cautiously and felt of him, partly (as he told us later) to assure himself that he was not a spirit, and partly to see if there were not a knife hidden somewhere under his clothes. After a careful examination and some further parley, he told Tannaumirk to tell us that they two would proceed home to the village, and Natkusiak and I might follow as far behind as we were now; when they got to the village we were to remain outside it till the people could be informed that we were visitors with friendly intentions.

As we proceeded toward the village other seal-hunters gradually converged toward us from all over the neighbouring four or five square miles of ice and joined Tannaumirk and his companion, who walked about two hundred yards ahead. As each of these was armed with a long knife and a seal-spear, it may be imagined that the never very brave

Tannaumirk was pretty thoroughly frightened—to which he owned up freely that night and the few days next following, though he had forgotten the circumstance completely by next year, when we returned to his own people in the Mackenzie district, where he is now a drawing-room lion on the strength of his adventures in the far east. When we approached the village every man, woman, and child was outdoors, waiting for us excitedly, for they could tell from afar that we were no ordinary visitors. The man whom we had first approached—who that day acquired a local prominence which still distinguishes him above his fellows—explained to an eagerly silent crowd that we were friends from a distance who had come without evil intent, and immediately the whole crowd (about forty) came running toward us. As each came up he would say: "I am So-and-so. I am well disposed. I have no knife. Who are you?" After being told our names in return, and being assured that we were friendly, and that our knives were packed away in the sled and hidden under our clothing, each would express his satisfaction and stand aside for the next to present himself. Sometimes a man would present his wife, or a woman her husband, according to which came up first. The women were in more hurry to be presented than were the men, for they must, they said, go right back to their houses to cook us something to eat.

After the women were gone the men asked us whether we preferred to have our camp right in the village or a little outside it. On talking it over we agreed it would be better to camp about two hundred yards from the other houses, so as to keep our dogs from fighting with theirs. When this was decided, half a dozen small boys were sent home to as many houses to get their fathers' snow-knives and house-building mittens. We were not allowed to touch a hand to anything in camp-making, but stood idly by, surrounded continually by a crowd who used every means to show how friendly they felt and how welcome we were, while a few of the best house-builders set about erecting for us the house in which we were to live as long as we cared to stay with them. When it had been finished and furnished with the skins, lamp, and the other things that go to make a snow house the coziest and most comfortable of camps, they told us they hoped we would occupy it at least till the last piece of meat in their storehouses had been eaten, and that so long as we stayed in the village no man would hunt seals or do any work until his children began to complain of hunger. It was to be a holiday, they said, for this was the

first time their people had been visited by strangers from so great a distance
that they knew nothing of the land from which they came.

These simple, well-bred, and hospitable people were the savages whom
we had come so far to see. That evening they saw for the first time the
lighting of a sulphur match; the next day I showed them the greater
marvels of my rifle; it was a day later still that they first understood that
I was one of the white men of whom they had heard from other tribes,
under the name *kablunat*.

I asked them: "Couldn't you tell by my blue eyes and the colour of
my beard?"

"But we didn't know," they answered, "what sort of complexions the
kablunat have. Besides, our neighbours to the north have eyes and beards
like yours." That was how they first told us of the people whose discovery
has brought up such important biological and historical problems, the
people who have since become known to newspaper readers as the "Blond
Eskimo."

One of the things that interested me was to see some shooting with the
strong-looking bows and long copper-tipped arrows that we found in the
possession of every man of the tribe. I therefore said that I would like to
have them illustrate to me the manner in which they killed caribou, and
I would in turn show them the weapons and method used by us. Half a
dozen of the men at once sent home for their bows, and a block of snow
to serve as a target was set up in front of our house. The range at which
a target a foot square could be hit with fair regularity turned out to be
about thirty or thirty-five yards, and the extreme range of the bow was
a bit over one hundred yards, while the range at which caribou are
ordinarily shot was shown to be about seventy-five yards. When the
exhibition was over, I set up a stick at about two hundred yards and fired
at it. The people—men, women, and children—who stood around had
no idea as to the character of the thing I was about to do, and when they
heard the loud report of my gun all the women and children made a
scramble for the houses, while the men ran back about fifteen or twenty
yards and stood talking together excitedly behind a snow wall. I at once
went to them and asked them to come with me to the stick and see what

had happened to it. After some persuasion three of them complied, but unfortunately for me it turned out that I had failed to score. At this they seemed much relieved, but when I told them I would try again they protested earnestly, saying that so loud a noise would scare all the seals away from their hunting grounds, and the people would therefore starve.

It seemed to me imperative, however, to show that I could keep my word and perforate the stick at two hundred yards, and in spite of their protests I got ready to shoot again, telling them that we used these weapons in the west for seal-hunting, and that the noise was found not to scare seals away. The second shot happened to hit, but on the whole the mark of the bullet on the stick impressed them far less than the noise. In fact, they did not seem to marvel at it at all. When I explained to them that I could kill a polar bear or a caribou at even twice the distance the stick had been from me they exhibited no surprise, but asked me if I could with my rifle kill a caribou on the other side of a mountain. When I said that I could not, they told me a great shaman in a neighbouring tribe had a magic arrow by which he could kill caribou on the other side of no matter how big a mountain. In other words, much to my surprise, they considered the performance of my rifle nothing wonderful.

I understand the point of view better now than I did then. It is simply this: if you were to show an Eskimo a bow that would in the ordinary way shoot fifty yards farther than any bow he ever saw, the man would never cease marvelling, and he would tell of that bow as long as he lived; he would understand exactly the principle on which it works, would judge it by the standards of the natural, and would find it to excel marvelously. But show him the work of the rifle, which he does not in the least understand, and he is face to face with a miracle; he judges it by the standards of the supernatural instead of by the standards of the natural; he compares it with other miraculous things of which he has heard and which he may even think he has himself seen, and he finds it not at all beyond the average of miracles; for the wonders of our science and the wildest tales of our own mythologies pale beside the marvels which the Eskimo suppose to be happening all around them every day at the behest of their magicians.

Perhaps I might here digress from the chronological order of my story to point out that the Eskimo's refusal to be astonished by the killing at a great distance of caribou or by a bear by a rifle bullet whose flight was unerring and invisible, was not an isolated case. When I showed them later my binoculars that made far-away things seem near and clear, they were of course interested; when I looked to the south or east and saw bands of caribou that were to them invisible, they applauded, and then followed the suggestion: "Now that you have looked for the caribou that are here to-day and found them, will you not also look for the caribou that are coming to-morrow, so that we can tell where to lie in ambush for them?" When they heard that my glasses could not see into the future, they were disappointed and naturally the reverse of well impressed with our powers, for they knew that their own medicine-men had charms and magic paraphernalia that enabled them to see things the morrow was to bring forth.

At another time, in describing to them the skill of our surgeons, I told them they could put a man to sleep and while he slept take out a section of his intestines or one of his kidneys, and the man when he woke up would not even know what had been done to him, except as he was told and as he could see the sewed-up opening through which the part had been removed. Our doctors could even transplant the organs of one man into the body of another. These things had actually never been seen done, but that they were done was a matter of common knowledge in my country. It was similar in their country, one of my listeners told me. He himself had a friend who suffered continually from backache until a great medicine-man undertook to treat him. The next night, while the patient slept, the medicine-man removed the entire spinal column, which had become diseased, and replaced it with a complete new set of vertebrae, and—what was most wonderful—there was not a scratch on the patient's skin or anything to show that the exchange had been made. This thing the narrator had not seen done, but the truth of it was a matter of common knowledge among his people. Another man had had his diseased heart replaced with a new and sound one. In other words the Eskimo believed as thoroughly as I in the truth of what he told; neither of us had seen the things actually done, but that they were done was a matter of common belief among our respective countrymen; and the things he told of his medicine-men were more marvelous than the things I could tell of mine. In fact, I had to admit that the transplanting of spinal columns and hearts was beyond the skill of my countrymen; and as they had the good breeding not to openly doubt any of my stories, it would have been ill-mannered of me to question theirs. Besides, questioning them would have done no good; I could not have changed by an iota their rock-founded faith in their medicine-men and spirit-compelling charms. In spite of any arguments I could have put forth, the net result of our exchange of stories would have been just what it was, anyway—that they considered they had learned from my own lips that in point of skill our doctors are not the equals of theirs.

JELLY ROLL AND ME

GREY OWL

From *Pilgrims of the Wild* (1935)

During the early 1930s a striking figure dressed in buckskin and braids appeared on the lecture circuit in Canada and Great Britain. Claiming to be a backwoods trapper of Indian descent, Grey Owl was an instant media sensation. In speeches, articles, books, and later movies, he told the story of how he had abandoned trapping under the influence of his Iroquois wife, Anahareo, to become a fervent conservationist determined to preserve the wilderness from the depredations of industrial society. Partly because of his exotic background, partly because of his message, the public responded to Grey Owl with enthusiasm. His lectures sold out. His books went into many printings. The rich and the famous clamoured to meet him. The Canadian government made a series of films celebrating his work as a conservationist.

When Grey Owl died in 1938 at the age of fifty-nine, the press almost immediately broke the remarkable story of the man who had for years been passing himself off as an Indian: Grey Owl in fact had been Archie Belaney from Hastings, England. As a youngster he developed a fascination for the North American Indian and when he was seventeen he left home and came to Canada to lead the life of a backwoodsman. In northern Ontario he apprenticed himself to the Ojibway of Lake Temagami, married an Ojibway woman, and turned himself into a skilled trapper and guide. When he underwent his conversion from killing to preserving wildlife, he shrewdly recognized that the public would take his message more

97

seriously if it seemed to come from an Indian, so he claimed for himself an Indian identity.

Grey Owl wrote four books about wilderness life and his efforts at wildlife preservation. To maintain the illusion of native ancestry, he worked hard at cultivating an unsophisticated style which would not give away the fact that he was an educated Englishman. Readers believed that he made up in sincerity and realism for what he lacked in literary polish. Indeed, lack of polish was very much part of his appeal. And there is no doubting that appeal. His books received very positive reviews in Canada, the United States, and Britain;
they remain in print today as eloquent statements of the environmental ethic.

The following extract is from Pilgrims of the Wild, *Grey Owl's "autobiography." It describes a winter he spent in the bush in northern New Brunswick with only Jelly Roll, one of his beaver pets, as company.*

Meanwhile I myself was busy. Hunting season was open and hunters swarmed in the woods. This made it necessary for me to patrol the scene of Jelly's activities all night, and I slept beside her burrow in the day time. I much doubted if there were many of the Cabano men who would have deliberately killed her, but as with McGinnis and McGinty, it would only take one man to turn the trick and I was resolved to take no chances.

I was greatly assisted in this by the trapper who claimed the hunting ground I was occupying. Instead of trying to oust me from his holdings, on finding that I was without a canoe he lent me one, and drew me a map of the district so I could patrol the more effectively.

Hunting season passed and the woods became again deserted and we, this beaver and I, carried on our preparations for the Winter each at his own end of the lake. The outlet, near which my cabin was situated, passed through a muskeg, and the immediate neighbourhood was covered with spindling birch which I was rapidly using up for wood. Jelly had by far the best part of it so far as scenery was concerned, being picturesquely established at the mouth of a small stream that wandered down from the uplands through a well timbered gully. Here she lived in state. She fortified her burrow on the top with mud, sticks, and moss, and inside it had a fine clean bed of shavings (taken from stolen boards), and had a little feed raft she had collected with highly unskilled labour, and that had a very amateurish look about it. But she was socially inclined, and often came down and spent long hours in the camp. When it snowed she failed to show up and I would visit her, and hearing my approach while still at some distance, she would come running to meet me with squeals and wiggles of welcome. We had great company together visiting back and forth this way, and I often sat and smoked and watched her working, and helped in any difficulties that arose. After the ice took her visits ceased altogether, and becoming lonesome for her I sometimes carried her to the cabin on my back in a box. She did not seem to mind these trips, and carried on a conversation with me and made long speeches on the way; I used to tell her she was talking behind my back. She made her own way home under the ice in some mysterious manner and always arrived safely, though I made a practice of following her progress along the shore with a flashlight, to make sure she did. This distance was over half a mile and I much admired the skill with which she negotiated it, though she cheated a little and ran her nose into muskrat burrows here and there to replenish her air supply. One night, however, after going home, she returned again unknown to me, and in the morning I found the door wide open and her lying fast asleep across the pillow. Nor did she ever go outside again, evidently having decided to spend the Winter with me; which she did. So I bought a small galvanised tank for her and sunk it in the floor, and dug out under one of the walls which I considered to be a pretty good imitation of a beaver house interior.

Almost immediately on her entry, a certain independence of spirit began to manifest itself. The tank, after a lengthy inspection was accepted by her as being all right, what there was of it; but the alleged beaver house, on being weighed in the balance was found to be wanting, and was resolutely and efficiently blocked up with some bagging and an old deer skin. She then dug out at great labour, a long tunnel under one corner of the shack, bringing up the dirt in heaps which she pushed ahead of her and painstakingly spread over the floor. This I removed, upon which it was promptly renewed. On my further attempt to clean up, she worked feverishly until a section of the floor within a radius of about six feet was again covered. I removed this several different times with the same results, and at last was obliged to desist for fear that in her continued excavations she would undermine the camp. Eventually she constructed a smooth solid sidewalk of pounded earth clear from her tunnel to the water supply, and she had a well beaten play ground tramped down all around her door. Having thus gained her point, and having established the fact that I was not going to have everything my own way, she let the matter drop, and we were apparently all set for the Winter. But these proceedings were merely preliminaries. She now embarked on a campaign of constructive activities that made necessary the alteration of almost the entire interior arrangements of the camp. Nights of earnest endeavours to empty the woodbox (to supply materials for scaffolds which would afford ready access to the table or windows), alternated with orgies of destruction, during which anything not made of steel or iron was subjected to a trial by ordeal out of which it always came off second best. The bottom of the door which, owing to the slight draught entering there, was a point that attracted much attention, was always kept well banked up with any materials that could be collected, and in more than one instance the blankets were taken from the bunk and utilised for this purpose. Reprimands induced only a temporary cessation of these depradations, and slaps and switchings produced little squeals accompanied by the violent twisting and shaking of the head, and other curious contortions by which these animals evince the spirit of fun by which they seem to be consumed during the first year of their life. On the few occasions I found it necessary to punish her, she would stand up on her hind feet, look me square in the face, and argue the point with me in her querulous treble of annoyance and outrage, slapping back at me right manfully on more than one occasion; yet she never on any account attempted to make use of her terrible teeth. Being in disgrace, she would climb on her box alongside me at the table, and rest her head on my knee, eyeing me and talking meanwhile in her uncanny language, as though to say, "What are a few table legs and axe handles between men?" And she always got forgiven; for after all she was a High Beaver, Highest of All The Beavers, and could get away with things no common beaver could, things that no common beaver would ever even think of.

When I sat on the deer skin rug before the stove, which was often, this chummy creature would come and lie with her head in my lap, and looking up at me, make a series of prolonged wavering sounds in different keys, that could have been construed as some bizarre attempt at singing. She would keep her eyes fixed steadily on my face all during this performance, so I felt obliged to listen to her with the utmost gravity. This pastime soon became a regular feature of her day, and the not unmelodious notes she emitted on these occasions were among the strangest sounds I have ever heard an animal make.

In spite of our difference in point of view on some subjects, we, this beast with the ways of a man and the voice of a child, and I, grew very close during that Winter for we were both, of our kind, alone. More and more as time went on she timed her movements, such as rising and retiring and her mealtimes, by mine. The camp, the fixtures, the bed, the tank, her little den, and myself, these were her whole world. She took me as much for granted as if I had also been a beaver, and it is possible that she thought that I belonged to her, with the rest of the stuff, or figured that she would grow up to be like me and perhaps eat at the table when she got big, or else that I would later have a tail and become like her.

Did I leave the camp on a two day trip for supplies, my entry was the signal for a swift exit from her chamber, and a violent assault on my legs, calculated to upset me. And on my squatting down to ask her how the thing had been going in my absence, she would sit up and wag her head slowly back and forth and roll on her back and gambol clumsily around me. As soon as I unlashed the toboggan, every article and package was minutely examined until the one containing the never-failing apples was discovered. This was immediately torn open, and gathering all the apples she could in her teeth and arms, she would stagger away erect to the edge of her tank, where she would eat one and put the rest in the water. She entered the water but rarely, and after emerging from a bath she had one certain spot where she sat and squeezed all the moisture out of her fur with her forepaws, very hands in function. She did not like to sit in the pool which collected under her at such times, so she took possession of a large square of birch bark for a bath-mat, intended to shed the water, which it sometimes did. It was not long before she discovered that the bed was a very good place for these exercises, as the blankets soaked up the moisture. After considerable inducement, and not without some heartburnings, she later compromised by shredding up the birch bark and spreading on it a layer of moss taken from the chinkings in the walls. Her bed, which consisted of long, very fine shavings which she unravelled, was pushed out at intervals and spread on the floor to air, being later returned to the sleeping quarters. Both these procedures, induced by the requirements of an unnatural environment, were remarkable examples of adaptibility on the part of an animal, especially the latter, as in the natural state the bedding is taken out and discarded entirely, fresh material being sought. The dish out of which she ate, on being emptied she would shove into a corner, and was not satisfied until it was standing up against the wall. This trick seems to be instinctive with all beaver, and can be attributed to their desire to preserve the interior of their habitation clear of any form of debris in the shape of peeled sticks, which are likewise set aside in the angle of the wall until the owner is ready to remove them.

Any branches brought in for feed, if thrown down in an unaccustomed place, were drawn over and neatly piled near the water supply, nor would she suffer any sticks or loose materials to be scattered on the floor; these she always removed and relegated to a junk pile she kept under one of the windows. This I found applied to socks, moccasins, the wash board, and the broom, etc., as well as to sticks. This broom was to her a kind of staff of office which she, as self-appointed janitor, was forever carrying around with her on her tours of inspection, and it also served, when turned end for end, as a quick, if rather dry lunch, or something in the nature of a breakfast food. She would delicately snip the straws off it, one at a time, and holding them with one end in her mouth would push them slowly in, while the teeth, working at great speed, chopped it into tiny portions. This operation resembled the performance of a sword swallower as much as it did anything else, and the sound produced was similar to that of a sewing machine running a little out of control. A considerable dispute raged over this broom, but in the end I found it easier to buy new brooms and keep my mouth shut.

Occasionally she would be indisposed to come out of her apartment, and would hold long-winded conversations with me through the aperture in a sleepy voice, and this with rising and falling inflections, and a rhythm, that made it seem as though she was actually saying something, which perhaps she was. In fact her conversational proclivities were one of the highlights of this association, and her efforts to communicate with me in this manner were most expressive, and any remark addressed to my furry companion seldom failed to elicit a reply of some kind, when she was awake, and sometimes when she was asleep.

To fill her tank required daily five trips of water, and she got to know by the rattle of the pails when her water was to be changed. She would emerge from her seclusion and try to take an active part in the work, getting pretty generally in the way, and she insisted on pushing the door to between my trips, with a view to excluding the much dreaded current of cold air. This was highly inconvenient at times, but she seemed so mightily pleased with her attempts at co-operation that I made no attempt to interfere. Certain things she knew to be forbidden she took a delight in doing, and on my approach her eyes would seem to kindle with a spark of unholy glee and she would scamper off squealing with trepidation, and no doubt well pleased at having put something over on me. Her self-assertive tendencies now began to be very noticeable. She commenced to take charge of the camp. She, so to speak, held the floor, also anything above it that was within her reach, by now a matter of perhaps two feet and more. This, as can be readily seen, included most of the ordinary fixtures. Fortunately, at this late season she had ceased her cutting operations, and was contented with pulling down anything she could lay her hands on, or climb up and get, upon which the article in question was subjected to a critical inspection as to its possibilities for inclusion into the rampart of heterogeneous objects that had been erected across her end of the camp, and behind which she passed from the entrance of her dwelling to the bathing pool. Certain objects such as the poker, a tin can, and a trap she disposed in special places, and if they were moved she would set them back in the positions she originally had for them, and would do this as often as they were removed. When working on some project she laboured with an almost fanatical zeal to the exclusion of all else, laying off at intervals to eat and comb her coat with the flexible double claw provided for that purpose.

She had the mischievous proclivities of a monkey combined with much of the artless whimsicality of a child, and she brightened many a dreary homecoming with her clumsy and frolicsome attempts at welcome. Headstrong past all belief, she had also the proprietary instinct natural to an animal, or a man, that builds houses and surrounds himself with works produced by his own labour. Considering the camp no doubt as her own personal property, she examined closely all visitors that entered it, some of whom on her account had journeyed from afar. Some passed muster, after being looked over in the most arrogant fashion, and were not molested; if not approved of, she would rear up against the legs of others, and try to push them over. This performance sometimes created a mild sensation, and gained for her the title of The Boss. Some ladies thought she should be called The Lady of the Lake, others The Queen. Jelly the Tub I called her, but the royal title stuck and a Queen she was, and ruled her little kingdom with no gentle hand.

There was one change that this lowly animal wrought in my habit of mind that was notable. Human companionship, in spite of, or perhaps on account of my solitary habits, had always meant a lot to me. But before the coming of Anahareo I had enjoyed it only intermittently. Its place had been taken by those familiar objects with which I surrounded myself, which were a part of my life,—a canoe that had been well-tried in calm and storm and had carried me faithfully in good water and bad, a pair of snowshoes that handled especially well, a thin-bladed, well-tempered hunting axe, an extra serviceable tump-line, my guns, a shrewdly balanced throwing knife. All these belongings had seemed like living things, almost, that could be depended on and that I carefully tended, that kept me company and that I was not above addressing on occasion. Now there was this supposedly dumb beast who had, if not entirely supplanted them, at least had relegated them to their normal sphere as useful pieces of equipment only. In this creature there was life and understanding; she moved and talked and did things, and gave me a response of which I had not thought an animal capable. She seemed to supply some need in my life of which I had been only dimly conscious heretofore, which had been growing with the years, and which marriage had for a time provided. And now that I was alone again it had returned, redoubled in intensity, and this sociable and home-loving beast, playful, industrious and articulate, fulfilled my yearning for companionship as no other creature save man, of my own kind especially, could ever have done. A dog, for all his affection and fidelity, had little power of self-expression, and his activities differed greatly from those of a human being; a dog was sometimes too utterly submissive. This creature comported itself as a person, of a kind, and she busied herself at tasks that I could, without loss of dignity, have occupied myself at; she made camp, procured and carried in supplies, could lay plans and carry them out and stood robustly and resolutely on her own hind legs, metaphorically and actually, and had an independence of spirit that measured up well with my own, seeming to look on me as a contemporary, accepting me as an equal and no more. I could in no way see where I was the loser from this association, and would not, if I could, have asserted my superiority, save as was sometimes necessary to avert wilful destruction.

Her attempts at communication with me, sometimes ludicrous, often pitiful, and frequently quite understandable, as I got to know them, placed her, to my mind, high above the plane of ordinary beasts. This, and the community of interest we had of keeping things in shape, of keeping up the home so to speak, strengthened indissolubly the bond between the two of us, both creatures that were never meant to live alone.

D'SONOQUA

EMILY CARR

From *Klee Wyck* (1941)

Emily Carr, British Columbia's most famous painter, came to writing late in her life. Most of the stories and sketches included in her six books (a seventh book, Hundreds and Thousands, *a selection from her journals, was published two decades after her death) were written when she was in her sixties and failing health restricted her ability to paint. She began writing without formal literary education. "I did not know book rules," she admitted in her autobiography,* Growing Pains, *so she made up two of her own: "Get to the point as directly as you can; never use a big word if a little one will do." Following these rules, she produced work in a voice which was fresh, lively, and entirely her own. The form she preferred was the brief sketch and all her books are collections of vignettes, told with charming simplicity and directness. Even her autobiography is more a series of sketches than a sustained narrative.*

Emily Carr was born in Victoria in 1871. She studied art in San Francisco, London and Paris but found her themes much closer to home in the lush rainforest of the Pacific Coast and the Aboriginal people who inhabited it. Her first book, Klee Wyck, *appeared in the fall of 1941 and was an instant critical and popular success in Canada, praised for its sympathetic portrayal of Native people and its evocative descriptions of the West Coast landscape. In 1942 the book won a Governor-General's Award, then presented by the Canadian Authors' Association. The following selection is a chapter from* Klee Wyck.

Carr's success as an author increased in the fall of 1942 with the appearance of her second book, The Book of Small, *about her childhood, followed two years later by* The House of All Sorts, *about her experiences as a boarding-house keeper. She died in 1945; four more books appeared posthumously.*

I was sketching in a remote Indian village when I first saw her. The village was one of those that the Indians use only for a few months in each year; the rest of the time it stands empty and desolate. I went there in one of its empty times, in a drizzling dusk.

When the Indian agent dumped me on the beach in front of the village, he said, "There is not a soul here. I will come back for you in two days." Then he went away.

I had a small griffon dog with me, and also a little Indian girl, 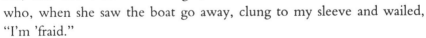 who, when she saw the boat go away, clung to my sleeve and wailed, "I'm 'fraid."

We went up to the old deserted Mission House. At the sound of the key in the rusty lock, rats scuttled away. The stove was broken, the wood wet. I had forgotten to bring candles. We spread our blankets on the floor, and spent a poor night. Perhaps my lack of sleep played its part in the shock that I got, when I saw her for the first time.

Water was in the air, half mist, half rain. The stinging nettles, higher than my head, left their nervy smart on my ears and forehead, as I beat my way through them, trying all the while to keep my feet on the plank walk which they hid. Big yellow slugs crawled on the walk and slimed it. My feet slipped and I shot headlong to her very base, for she had no feet. The nettles that were above my head reached only to her knee.

It was not the fall alone that jerked the "Oh's" out of me, for the great wooden image towering above me was indeed terrifying.

The nettle bed ended a few yards beyond her, and then a rocky bluff jutted out, with waves battering it below. I scrambled up and went out on the bluff, so that I could see the creature above the nettles. The forest was behind her, the sea in front.

Her head and trunk were carved out of, or rather into, the bole of a great red cedar. She seemed to be part of the tree itself, as if she had grown there at its heart, and the carver had only chipped away the outer wood so that you could see her. Her arms were spliced and socketed to the trunk, and were flung wide in a circling, compelling movement. Her breasts were two eagle-heads, fiercely carved. That much, and the column of her great neck, and her strong chin, I had seen when I slithered to the ground beneath her. Now I saw her face.

The eyes were two rounds of black, set in wider rounds of white, and placed in deep sockets under wide, black eyebrows. Their fixed stare bore into me as if the very life of the old cedar looked out, and it seemed that the voice of the tree itself might have burst from that great round cavity, with projecting lips, that was her mouth. Her ears were round, and stuck out to catch all sounds. The salt air had not dimmed the heavy red of her trunk and arms and thighs. Her hands were black, with blunt finger-tips painted a dazzling white. I stood looking at her for a long, long time.

The rain stopped, and white mist came up from the sea, gradually paling her back into the forest. It was as if she belonged there, and the mist were carrying her home. Presently the mist took the forest too, and, wrapping them both together, hid them away.

"Who is that image?" I asked the little Indian girl, when I got back to the house.

She knew which one I meant, but to gain time, she said, "What image?"

"The terrible one, out there on the bluff."

"I dunno," she lied.

I never went to that village again, but the fierce wooden image often came to me, both in my waking and in my sleeping.

Several years passed, and I was once more sketching in an Indian village. There were Indians in this village, and in a mild backward way it was "going modern." That is, the Indians had pushed the forest back a little to let the sun touch the new buildings that were replacing the old community houses. Small houses, primitive enough to a white man's thinking, pushed here and there between the old. When some of the big community houses had been torn down, for the sake of the lumber, the great corner posts and massive roof-beams of the old structure were often left, standing naked against the sky, and the new little house was built inside, on the spot where the old one had been.

It was in one of these empty skeletons that I found her again. She had once been a supporting post for the great centre beam. Her pole-mate, representing the Raven, stood opposite her, but the beam that had rested on their head was gone. The two poles faced in, and one judged the great size of the house by the distance between them. The corner posts were still in place, and the earth floor, once beaten to the hardness of rock by naked feet, was carpeted now with rich lush grass.

I knew her by the stuck-out ears, shouting mouth, and deep eye-sockets. These sockets had no eye-balls, but were empty holes, filled with stare. The stare, though not so fierce as that of the former image, was more intense. The whole figure expressed power, weight, domination, rather than ferocity. Her feet were planted heavily on the head of the squatting bear, carved beneath them. A man could have sat on either huge shoulder. She was unpainted, weather-worn, sun-cracked, and the arms and hands seemed to hang loosely. The fingers were thrust into the carven mouths of two human heads, held crowns down. From behind, the sun made unfathomable shadows in eye, cheek, and mouth. Horror tumbled out of them.

I saw Indian Tom on the beach, and went to him.

"Who is she?"

The Indian's eyes, coming slowly from across the sea, followed my pointing finger. Resentment showed in his face, greeny-brown and wrinkled like a baked apple,—resentment that white folks should pry into matters wholly Indian.

"Who is that big carved woman?" I repeated.

"D'Sonoqua." No white tongue could have fondled the name as he did.

"Who is D'Sonoqua?"

"She is the wild woman of the woods."

"What does she do?"

"She steals children."

"To eat them?"

"No, she carries them to her caves; that," pointing to a purple scar on the mountain across the bay, "is one of her caves. When she cries 'OO-oo-oo-oeo,' Indian mothers are too frightened to move. They stand like trees, and the children go with D'Sonoqua."

"Then she is bad?"

"Sometimes bad . . . sometimes good," Tom replied, glancing furtively at those stuck-out ears. Then he got up and walked away.

I went back, and sitting in front of the image, gave stare for stare. But her stare so over-powered mine, that I could scarcely wrench my eyes away from the clutch of those empty sockets. The power that I felt was not in the thing itself, but in some tremendous force behind it, that the carver believed in.

A shadow passed across her hands and their gruesome holdings. A little bird, with its beak full of nesting material, flew into the cavity of her mouth, right in the pathway of that terrible OO-oo-oo-oeo. Then my eye caught something that I had missed—a tabby cat asleep between her feet.

This was D'Sonoqua, and she was a supernatural being, who belonged to these Indians.

"Of course," I said to myself, "I do not believe in supernatural beings. Still—who understands the mysteries behind the forest? What would one do if one did meet a supernatural being?" Half of me wished that I could meet her, and half of me hoped I would not.

Chug—chug—the little boat had come into the bay to take me to another village, more lonely and deserted than this. Who knew what I should see there? But soon supernatural beings went clean out of my mind, because I was wholly absorbed in being naturally seasick.

When you have been tossed and wracked and chilled, any wharf looks good, even a rickety one, with its crooked legs stockinged in barnacles. Our boat nosed under its clammy darkness, and I crawled up the straight slimy ladder, wondering which was worse, natural sea-sickness, or supernatural "creeps." The trees crowded to the very edge of the water, and the outer ones, hanging over it, shadowed the shoreline into a velvet smudge. D'Sonoqua might walk in places like this. I sat for a long time on the damp, dusky beach, waiting for the stage. One by one dots of light popped from the scattered cabins, and made the dark seem darker. Finally the stage came.

We drove through the forest over a long straight road, with black pine trees marching on both sides. When we came to the wharf the little gas mail-boat was waiting for us. Smell and blurred light oozed thickly out of the engine room, and except for one lantern on the wharf everything else was dark. Clutching my little dog, I sat on the mail sacks which had been tossed on to the deck.

The ropes were loosed, and we slid out into the oily black water. The moon that had gone with us through the forest was away now. Black pine-covered mountains jagged up on both sides of the inlet like teeth. Every gasp of the engine shook us like a great sob. There was no rail round the deck, and the edge of the boat lay level with the black slithering horror below. It was like being swallowed again and again by some terrible monster, but never going down. As we slid through the water, hour after hour, I found myself listening for the OO-oo-oo-oeo.

Midnight brought us to a knob of land, lapped by the water on three sides, with the forest threatening to gobble it up on the fourth. There was a rude landing, a rooming-house, an eating-place, and a store, all for the convenience of fishermen and loggers. I was given a room, but after I had blown out my candle, the stillness and the darkness would not let me sleep.

In the brilliant sparkle of the morning when everything that was not superlatively blue was superlatively green, I dickered with a man who was taking a party up the inlet that he should drop me off at the village I was headed for.

"But," he protested, "there is nobody there."

To myself I said, "There is D'Sonoqua."

From the shore, as we rowed to it, came a thin feminine cry—the mewing of a cat. The keel of the boat had barely grated in the pebbles, when the cat sprang aboard, passed the man shipping his oars, and crouched for a spring into my lap. Leaning forward, the man seized the creature roughly, and with a cry of "Dirty Indian vermin!" flung her out into the sea.

I jumped ashore, refusing his help, and with a curt "Call for me at sun-down," strode up the beach; the cat followed me.

When we had crossed the beach and come to a steep bank, the cat ran ahead. Then I saw that she was no lean, ill-favoured Indian cat, but a sleek aristocratic Persian. My snobbish little griffon dog, who usually refused to let an Indian cat come near me, surprised me by trudging beside her in comradely fashion.

The village was typical of the villages of these Indians. It had only one street, and that had only one side, because all the houses faced the beach. The two community houses were very old, dilapidated, and bleached, and the handful of other shanties seemed never to have been young; they had grown so old before they were finished, that it was then not worth while finishing them.

Rusty padlocks carefully protected the gaping walls. There was the usual broad plank in front of the houses, the general sitting and sunning place for Indians. Little streams ran under it, and weeds poked up through every crack, half hiding the companies of tins, kettles, and rags, which patiently waited for the next gale and their next move.

In front of the Chief's house was a high, carved totem pole, surmounted by a large wooden eagle. Storms had robbed him of both wings, and his head had a resentful twist, as if he blamed somebody. The heavy wooden heads of two squatting bears peered over the nettle-tops. The windows were too high for peeping in or out. "But, save D'Sonoqua, who is there to peep?" I said aloud, just to break the silence. A fierce sun burned down as if it wanted to expose every ugliness and forlorness. It drew the noxious smell out of the skunk cabbages, growing in the rich black ooze of the stream, scummed the water-barrels with green slime, and branded the desolation into my very soul.

The cat kept very close, rubbing and bumping itself and purring ecstatically; and although I had not seen them come, two more cats had joined us. When I sat down they curled into my lap, and then the strangeness of the place did not bite into me so deeply. I got up, determined to look behind the houses.

Nettles grew in the narrow spaces between the houses. I beat them down, and made my way over the bruised dark-smelling mass into a space of low jungle.

Long ago the trees had been felled and left lying. Young forest had burst through the slash, making an impregnable barrier, and sealing up the secrets which lay behind it. An eagle flew out of the forest, circled the village, and flew back again.

Once again I broke silence, calling after him, "Tell D'Sonoqua—" and turning, saw her close, towering above me in the jungle.

Like the D'Sonoqua of the other villages she was carved into the bole of a red cedar tree. Sun and storm had bleached the wood, moss here and there softened the crudeness of the modelling; sincerity underlay every stroke.

She appeared to be neither wooden nor stationary, but a singing spirit, young and fresh, passing through the jungle. No violence coarsened her; no power domineered to wither her. She was graciously feminine. Across her forehead her creator had fashioned the Sistheutl, or mythical two-headed sea-serpent. One of its heads fell to either shoulder, hiding the stuck-out ears, and framing her face from a central parting on her forehead which seemed to increase its womanliness.

She caught your breath, this D'Sonoqua, alive in the dead bole of the cedar. She summed up the depth and charm of the whole forest, driving away its menace.

I sat down to sketch. What was the noise of purring and rubbing going on about my feet? Cats. I rubbed my eyes to make sure I was seeing right, and counted a dozen of them. They jumped into my lap and sprang to my shoulders. They were real—and very feminine.

There we were—D'Sonoqua, the cats, and I—the woman who only a few moments ago had forced herself to come behind the houses in trembling fear of the "wild woman of the woods"—wild in the sense that forest-creatures are wild—shy, untouchable.

JUNE

RODERICK HAIG–BROWN

From *A River Never Sleeps* (1946)

For a quarter of a century, Roderick Haig-Brown produced a steady stream of books about fish and fishing which won him an international reputation in the fraternity of anglers. His writing reflects an intimate knowledge of the wilderness gained from his years as a logger, trapper and guide, as well as the hours he spent in the quiet contemplation of river and tidal pool. Recently, with the rise of the environmental movement, his books have found a new audience for their evocation of a natural world unsullied by human greed.

Roderick Haig-Brown was born in England in 1908 and came to the Pacific Northwest as a teenager to work in a logging camp. He subsequently moved to Vancouver Island where he made his living as a guide and as a writer. His first books were animal stories reminiscent of Ernest Thompson Seton. It was the publication of The Western Angler *in 1939 that established his reputation as a writer about fishing in the tradition of Isaac Walton. He settled in Campbell River where he served as a stipendiary magistrate for thirty-four years. He was a fishing crony of many prominent writers and businessmen and during the 1950s and 1960s became involved in protests against the environmental impact of economic development along B.C.'s rivers. Haig-Brown died in 1976.*

A River Never Sleeps, *from which the following selection comes, is a month-by-month account of some of Haig-Brown's fishing experiences. The*

General Money to whom he refers was Brigadier General Noel Money, a retired British army officer who ran the Qualicum Inn on Vancouver Island.

June is the midsummer month, yet in the temperate latitude of southern England and the British Columbia coast it is not full summer; growth is still fresh and young, and the rivers still have the flow of stored-up winter snow or rain. All the summer months are trout fisher's months, I suppose, wherever trout swim and feed. Yet June is generally a quiet month on the Campbell, and in most of the lakes near sea level the surface water is almost too warm for good fly-fishing. Some of the mountain streams make good fishing, but it is too early for the really cold ones.

In June, were I near enough to it, I would always go into the Kilipi River, which flows into Nimpkish Lake. Once I had a trap line up the valley, and in the winters I used to catch fine trout for food as they lay behind the late-spawning coho salmon. But in June I fished there for fun and caught, not many fish, but always fish that surprised me.

Generally, I had to go there over a short weekend, leaving a logging camp after work on Saturday, walking through to Nimpkish Lake, then rowing six or eight miles up or down the lake to the mouth of the river. That left time to make a quick camp, cook supper and fish through the river's straight swift run from my camp to the lake. Sometimes I caught nothing on that first evening, once I caught two fine cutthroats, each over three pounds, which ran out into the lake so far that I waded almost shoulder deep to hold them and turn them. Once I hooked, on the fly and fairly in the mouth, a five-pound sockeye salmon; this was surprising enough, because properly organized sockeyes are not supposed to take fly or bait of any kind at all readily. It was the more surprising because sockeyes don't run to the Kilipi; but I was reaching well out into the lake at the time, and perhaps a passing school had turned momentarily into the fresh flow of current. I saw no others roll or jump.

On the Sunday I usually fished the canyon and the water below it, but sometimes I walked the five or six miles through to the meadows, to see them in their summer green; the Kilipi meadows are always full of deer as no other place I know, and the deer are bold and calm. It is almost as though, knowing little of the rifle, they place a human being's power of harming them on a par with that of the cougar: they watch cautiously, even suspiciously; they bound away if you come upon them too suddenly or too closely; but generally they stand with heads arrogantly raised, eyes impersonally curious, unless one is within a hundred feet or so—half a dozen easy springs for a hunting cougar. I like the meadows if only for the deer, but there are many birds there too. The snipe nest there, and ruffed grouse drum steadily through the day among the crabapples and cedars. Song sparrows are always there, summer and winter, warblers are quick in the swamp grass, and at different times I have seen goldfinches and vireos, bluebirds, meadowlarks, kinglets, red-winged blackbirds, flickers with the lovely flash of orange under their wings, downy woodpeckers, and the swooping flight and scarlet crests of pileated woodpeckers.

Bears love the meadows in fall, when the salmon are running, but they come there in summer as well, to roll in cool mud wallows and rub themselves against the trunks of big crabapples. The trout, like the bears, are interested mainly in the salmon runs, but a few of them seem to stay there through the year. A small fork of the river runs through the meadows, deep and slow and very clear. Once I came quietly to the deepest pool of all, ten or twelve feet from smooth surface to pale gravel, and saw three good trout lying quite still on the bottom. It seemed almost foolish to fish for them with anything less interesting than a worm, but I tied on a big dry sedge and cast it well above the nearest fish. Three times I floated it over him, and the third time I thought I saw him move. Perhaps it was less than a movement, simply a stiffening of the body, a tightening of the muscles. I cast again, and as the fly touched the water, he started up. He came slowly, his body tilted only a little, with a feathery lightness of flying, up and up and up through brilliant water that seemed lighter and clearer than air. He met the fly perfectly, dropped back under it for a moment, then quietly took it. I fished for the rest of the afternoon but could not move the others.

It is a little like that in the canyon. I have never seen many fish there in June, but the few that are there can be seen; one sees them from above and knows the climb down is worth while. Nearly always they are deep down in the pools, apparently little concerned with feeding, and nearly always they are big cutthroats, beautifully coloured. But they do feed there, and they seem to love best of all the bright, blue-green cedar borer beetles. All trout seem to like these beetles, and I made up my own clumsy imitation long ago—a body of emerald green and blue seal's fur, ribbed with bronze peacock herl and gold thread, wings of green peacock and a light blue hackle tied above them. I fish it drowned, with little movement, and in the Kilip it was often an hour's work to get the fly down to where the trout would take an interest in it. But the take was always worthwhile, the solemn opening and closing of a great mouth, the twist of a wide body against the strike and a strong run, deep down. Once only I hooked a summer steelhead somewhere far below me in a pool that I had not examined from above. I was standing on a little pinnacle of rock from which I could not move, and it was nearly half an hour before I could bring him back to it. Then, as I reached down to slip a finger in his gills, I fell in. For a few moments I floundered about, trying to climb back on the rock without losing my rod, then I gave up with a good grace and swam to the tail of the pool, praying that the line would not tangle my legs. It did not, and when I climbed out again the fish was still hooked.

But for all its surprises and delights, the Kilipi never gave me really good June fishing, though some northwest rivers have. Almost any stream with a real stock of nonmigratory trout should be at its best in June, when there are plentiful hatches of fly and the water is cool and lively enough to keep the fish active. June is transition from spring to summer, a month when everything has its full vigour, before anything is stale or mature. In June May flies may be thick on the water, stone-fly nymphs may still be crawling up the rocks to split their cases and fly away, midges will be dancing in clouds near the water's edge and falling spent on the water to move fish that the angler finds it difficult to tempt with his larger flies; and on June evenings may come the early sedge hatches.

None of these interest the summer steelhead; yet June is perhaps the best steelhead month of all the year. The fish are not so numerous then as later, in September and early October when the fall run is in. But those that have come up from salt water are perfect, bright and clean, still several months from the full maturity and the slowing bulk of developed ovaries and milt sacs. When a June fish takes, he is into his run before you can move to raise the rod, and that run is fierce and long and dangerous. Almost always a June fish is a jumping fish, a bold, wild, jumping fish, and he is little concerned to keep within the limits of the pool in which he has taken the fly.

Good summer steelhead runs are less common than good winter runs. Oregon rivers and northern California rivers draw fine runs. Some rivers in Washington state have good runs, and the North Fork of the Stillaguamish has been set aside by a wise authority for fly-fishing only. In British Columbia there are many rivers with summer-run fish, but most of them are not easily accessible to anglers. For some reason, the rivers on the east coast of Vancouver Island, accessible from the Island Highway, draw few summer fish. The Campbell has no true summer run; the Oyster, the Courtenay, the Qualicum rivers and all the smaller streams between them, in spite of good winter runs, do not draw summer fish. I believe the Cowichan had a fair run at one time, but Indian fishing killed it. North of Seymour Narrows, rivers such as the Nimpkish have runs, and several of the mainland rivers have really fine runs. There is one in particular that I mean to try out now that the war is over; it comes to a river in Ramsay Arm, near the mouth of Bute Inlet.

Nearly all the rivers on the west coast of Vancouver Island have summer runs, but only one of them is easily reached—the Stamp River at Alberni. The Stamp is General Money's river and will always be so far as I am concerned. The General lived at Qualicum until he died in 1941, and there he built the big hotel and golf course. He was the wisest and best fisherman I have ever known in British Columbia, and he was also probably the keenest. A few months before he died, Ann and I stopped at his house on our way up the Island. It was a cold, wet December evening, and we found him just changed after a day of searching for winter fish in one of the Qualicum rivers. All the clothes he had worn during the day were hung to dry in the warmest place in the house. He had been really wet, right to the skin, and his day had given him a move from only a single fish, but the General was happy and satisfied with it and was already making plans for the next day.

When you fished with General Money, you fished as his guest; and never was a host more gracious or better informed on the possibilities of his domain. It was a June day when I first went down to the Stamp with him, a sunny day after rain the night before. We drove to the cottage he had built on the high bank above his favourite pool, put up our rods and walked to the edge of the clifflike bank. General Money's Pool is at a good, wide bend of the river; above it there is a straight reach of fast water as far as the mouth of the Ash and below it a broken rapid that gathers itself through two or three hundred yards to a narrow pool under the far bank. From where we were standing we had a clear view of the pool and its bottom, except when a light breeze ruffled the surface, and after looking for a while we knew that there were fish in it—three together, well down the pool and near the middle, and a fourth a little below them and well over to the far side. The General was pleased. "Water's in fine shape," he said. "I'm glad I got you out today."

We walked down the steep trail to the pool, and he settled himself in his favourite place under the big trees near the head.

"Fish this top part through," he told me, "in case there's something there. You'll cover those three fish from the kidney stones—you'll see them, two light-coloured, kidney-shaped stones on this side. When they're under your feet, you ought to be reaching the fish. Then you might reach the other one with a long cast from the flat rock just below the kidney stones. It won't be much good below that."

I fished carefully down, came to the kidney stones, cast well across and felt a good heavy pull as the fly came round in midstream. The fish ran without hesitation, hard for the tail of the pool. I put on a heavy strain, and he jumped out twice, still going away, tumbling over himself and splashing the shining water high at each fall. The jumps slowed him a little, and he turned and came back up the pool very fast; opposite me, only thirty or forty feet out, he jumped again beautifully, very high out of the water. For a moment after that he was quiet. The General was beside me now.

"You must get him," he said. "It would be too bad to lose the first fish of the day."

"I'd like to keep him away from the others," I said. "We don't want to disturb the pool too much."

"Don't worry about that, man. Make sure of him."

But the fish ran straight across, and I worked upstream a little so that I had a chance to hold him well above the best part of the pool. After five more good minutes the General gaffed him for me.

"Go and catch another one," he said.

"No, sir. You fish now."

"Go on and fish. I like to watch you."

More than anything, I wanted to watch him, but it seemed too late to say that now. I washed my fly and looked over my gut, then started in again well above the stones. When they were under my feet again, I realized that I was a little breathless and anxious. It suddenly occurred to me that the General was watching me, closely and critically. I had done well enough with the first fish, but I began to wonder if I might not bungle something now, and I remembered how I hate to put a man in some good favourite place where I know there are fish and see him spoil it. The fly swung round without a touch, and I cast again. Still nothing, and nothing to a third cast. I felt disappointed, but I moved on down and left them then. It seemed better to do that than chance putting them off altogether. At the flat rock I drew more line off the reel and reached well over toward the far side. It was a good cast, but short of the fish, I felt sure, and I wondered if I could handle two or three more yards of line. I took them out, picked up, measured out an ordinary cast, then picked up and cast again with all the drive I could put into the rod. The last loop of line left my hand and I felt the pull of its leaving come cleanly against the reel. The fly curled over, carrying the gut out to its full length, and began fishing. I saw a brown-backed shape come up to meet it, waited a moment, then tightened on him. He began to jump at once, again and again and again, all across the tail of the pool. The General was coming along the bank behind me.

"Lightly hooked," I said. "He won't stay on long."

"I know, I know," he said. "Try and get him though. Bring him into this side, if you can, and I'll go below you and try to put the gaff in him."

The fish had come up the pool a little, but he started down and began jumping again. At the tail of the pool he was right on the surface, working almost gently against me, and I thought for a moment I could swing him across to where the General was waiting. Then the fly came away.

"Rotten luck," the General said. "If anyone had told me you could get over to that fish with only thigh boots and an eleven-foot rod, I'd never have believed him."

That was the most tactful and graceful remark any man has ever made to me after the loss of a good fish. I went back from the pool with a feeling of merit that was completely without justification but extremely pleasant.

We rested the pool for fifteen or twenty minutes, then the General himself started down it. He was a tall slim man, very straight, with a long, brown face, deeply lined, and blue eyes bright and quick to smile against the brownness. He moved out gracefully and easily until he was in water over his hips; then he began to put out line with his doublehanded thirteen-foot rod. He was spey casting, rolling the line out in a long loop that lifted the fly from the water in front of him and carried it over and out in a straight smooth cast that covered the whole water. He worked his fly across, deep and slow, moved down a step or two and cast again, letting the big shining curve of the rod carry the burden of the work. He had fished this pool a thousand times, made each cast he was making now a thousand times before, but his mind was with his fly, working it down to the fish, bringing it easily into the swifter water near his own bank, holding it with the long rod so that it would not cross too quickly, ready to meet the fierce, quick pull of a taking fish with a tightening of the line at the right moment. I watched him cast again, and judged that he was almost at the kidney stones. The fly came in midstream, a shade too quickly, I thought, and the General lowered his rod point. Then the fish took. I saw the rod lift and bend and saw clearly the delayed boil of the fish's deep turn. The big rod dipped to him, met his runs and his jumps, humoured him away from the rocks and bad water at the tail of the pool, brought him up and held him at last on his side and ready for the gaff. I set the gaff and brought him ashore, and the General looked at him, his eyes and face alight with the pleasure of it. "I thought we could take another," he said.

It was on one of the last days I fished with him, not much over a year before he died, that he caught a fish in his pool by a new method. It was an August day, and the river was very low—too low, the General said, for someone had closed the gate at the dam and made a drop of a foot or more during the night. I was almost glad because I had planned to fish the greased line anyway; the low water and the hot bright day were perfect for it. The General said he just wanted to sit in the shade and watch; his doctor had warned him a few days earlier that he must show his heart a little consideration.

So I started down with the greased line and a tiny silver-bodied fly that I had tied the night before. I fished carefully, by the book, casting a slack line well across, lifting the belly of the line each time before the current could draw on it, holding the fly right up under the surface in a slow, easy drift all the way across. The fish came again as I reached the kidney stones and came as a good fish sometimes does to the greased line, with a long slashing rise that threw water a foot into the air. For once I did the rest of it right—pointed my rod straight downstream, held it well into my own bank and let the delayed pull on the belly of the line set the hook. When the General gaffed him, he said with something like awe in his voice, "Look at that fly. Right in the back corner of the mouth, exactly the way it's supposed to be."

That was the best of all the days we had together. We ate our lunch in the shade and drank bottles of cool stout. Then I went upstream with the General's big rod and left him to fish his pool with the greased line. Something told me to fish the heavy white water, and I was hardly getting the fly well out before I hooked a fish. He started downstream, and I glanced quickly along the river to pick a place to gaff him, then looked down to the pool where the General was fishing. I saw his rod come up and knew that he was into one as well. Suddenly I was afraid. I thought of the sharp stab of excitement that comes with the surface rise to the greased line, of the long strain of the fight with a small fly and light gut, of those last anxious moments as the fish comes within reach of the gaff. I began to run downstream, caring nothing about my own fish, which tumbled on ahead of me. I wondered if I could break him in—it's not always so easy when you want to. Then I saw he was close to shore, and I reached for my gaff almost without thinking. He started out as I came up to him, but I made a lucky stroke and caught him just above the tail. In a moment I had him on the bank, tapped him on the head, dropped the rod and started on again.

As I came down to the big pool, I saw the General was getting his gaff ready. I shouted, "I'll do that, sir," but he looked back and smiled and shook his head. Then I saw him lean forward and gaff his fish with an easy, gentle stroke. He waded ashore and I met him.

"That's a wonderful sport," he said. "We should have tried it long ago." He knelt beside his fish and freed the fly from the corner of the jaw. "I'm going to send away for a light rod as soon as we get home. You must help me pick one out of the catalogue."

We took the fish back in the shade and sat down. "That's my day's fishing," the General said. "I'm getting old. But we've found something new for the river after all these years."

THE FIRST OF JULY, 1867

DONALD CREIGHTON

From *John A. Macdonald:The Young Politician* (1952)

Donald Creighton's two-volume biography of John A. Macdonald—The Young Politician (1952) and The Old Chieftain *(1955)—is considered by historians to be a model of political biography. Written in clear, vivid prose, it dissolves the distinction between popular and academic history. Creighton believed that history was a literary art, not a social science. He combined the research and analytic skills of an academic with the imaginative sweep of a novelist. Macdonald emerges from the biography as an heroic figure, his career symbolic of the development of Canada as a nation. Both volumes of the biography won Governor-General's awards, and the book is credited with sparking a revival of political biography within the historical profession. Unhappily, few of his emulators match Creighton's flair for dramatic presentation.*

Donald Creighton (1902-1979) joined the history department at the University of Toronto when he was twenty-five years old and remained affiliated with the university for the rest of his life. He wrote many books and articles and is perhaps best known academically for his first book, The Commercial Empire of the St. Lawrence *(1937), in which he developed the Laurentian thesis, the argument that Canadian historical development has been based on trade and communication flowing along an east-west corridor roughly analogous to the Great Lakes-St. Lawrence River system.*

The following selection is from the epilogue to Volume One of the biography,

John A. Macdonald: The Young Politician. *It describes events on July 1, 1867, the day on which the Dominion of Canada was proclaimed.*

The day was his, if it was anybody's. He, above all others, had ensured its coming, and he had prescribed the order of its celebration. But the actual day—July 1—was not his first choice. For simple and practical reasons—he did not believe the preparations could be completed earlier—he would have preferred a date a fortnight later. But he was far away from London when the matter was finally settled; and on May 22 a royal proclamation announced that the union of British North America was to come into effect two weeks before his chosen date. "So you see," he wrote off to Fisher of New Brunswick, "we are to be united in Holy Matrimony on 1st July—just a fortnight too soon." There was certainly not a great deal of time to make the necessary arrangements. "Much has to be done before then—," he told Tilley, "the members of the cabinet are to be determined, the offices distributed, the policy considered, and the whole machinery set in motion." But even with the weight of all these practical, political matters, he found time to give some attention to the day itself. Others would expatiate eloquently upon its significance— after he had done the work of bringing it about. He was neither an orator nor a prophet. And it was characteristic of him to speak of what was so largely his own creation with jocular understatement rather than with rhetorical hyperbole. "By the exercise of common sense and a limited amount of that patriotism which goes by the name of self-interest," he wrote frankly to Shea of Newfoundland, "I have no doubt that the Union will be for the common weal." He would never exaggerate any occasion or glorify any future; but he had the conservative's feeling for historical continuity, for the stages in the process of national growth; and from the first he had determined that the day of the Dominion's beginning should have its appropriate celebration. "On the 1st July, as you know," he wrote Denis Godley, Monck's secretary, "Confederation will be a fixed fact and we think it well that some ceremony should be used in inaugurating the new system." It was decided to make the day a general holiday. The volunteers were to turn out; and Sir John Michel, the Commander of the Forces, was requested to make sure that, in the various garrisons throughout the country, "Royal salutes shall be fired, and the Royal standard hoisted, with such other military show as is usual on festive occasions."

He could prescribe the order of the day; but he could not determine the weather. Yet it did not disappoint him. Officially the northern hemisphere was ten days away from the summer solstice; but in the Maritime Provinces and along the St. Lawrence River valley there was as yet almost no signs that this long six-months' period, in which the sun's power had daily and majestically increased, had ended at last in its appointed fashion. The first of July belonged, by natural right, to the little group of the richest days of the year; and in 1867 no accident occurred to rob it of its birthright. On the previous night certain Canadians, watching the sky anxiously, had been disturbed by the appearance of a few ominous clouds; but by the morning these threats had vanished completely. All through the federation, the day dawned fair and warm, with a clear, cobalt-blue sky, and a little breeze that took the hottest edge off the brightest sun. Everybody noticed the beauty of the day; everybody observed how auspicious was its splendour. "On aimera à se rappeler," declared the editor of the *Journal des Trois Rivières*, "quand la Confédération aura subi l'épreuve du temps, combien a été beau le jour de son inauguration."

The day began long before Macdonald was up; in Ottawa it probably began even before he had gone to bed. Just after midnight struck, a long salute of 101 guns was fired, while all the church bells pealed, and a huge bonfire was kindled. Then, presumably, the people of Ottawa went to bed; but neither they nor Her Majesty's loyal subjects in other parts of the new Dominion were permitted to enjoy too long a rest on that short summer night. Early in the morning, when the sky was hardly yet paling with the approach of sunrise, the royal salutes began. At Saint John, New Brunswick, the twenty-one guns in "honour of this greatest of all modern marriages" were fired off at four o'clock. At six, they sounded out from Fort Henry, just across the river from Kingston. And at eight, when it was now full day, the Volunteer Artillery of Halifax discharged a long salvo from the Grand Parade, which came back, as if in booming echoes, from the guns of the naval brigade on the Dartmouth side of the harbour. The bells were ringing also, in town halls, and clock towers, and church steeples. High Mass was sung in the cathedral at Three Rivers at seven o'clock in the morning; and all over the country, people dressed in their

Sunday best were walking soberly along the streets to pray, in early church services, for the welfare of the Dominion.

By nine o'clock, the sun was already high. The air was warm; the sky's benignant promise was unqualified. People thronged the streets of their own cities and towns, or crowded into excursion trains and steamers to join in the celebrations of their neighbours. The steamer *America* brought nearly 300 visitors across the lake from St. Catharines to swell the crowds in Toronto. And down in the Eastern Townships, the little villages of Missisquoi—Philipsburg, Bedford, Dunham, and Frelighsburg—arranged a common celebration to which people flocked from all over the county. All the shops were shut; the streets were bright with flags and bunting. "Bientôt," wrote one correspondent of a French-Canadian town, "St. Jean disparut dans les drapeaux et les pavillons." Down in the Maritime Provinces, where the anti-Confederates watched the bright day with sullen disapproval, a few shops stayed ostentatiously open; a few doors were hung with bunches of funereal black crepe; and in Saint John, New Brunswick, a certain doctor defiantly flew his flag at half-mast until a party of volunteers happened to come along, offered politely to assist him in raising it, and, on receiving a furious refusal, raised it anyway and went on their way rejoicing. But there were few enough such incidents; and everywhere it was a good-humoured crowd that pressed along, on foot and in carriages, under the banners, and triumphal arches and the great inscriptions and transparencies which, in English and French, offered "success to the Confederacy" and "Bienvenue à la nouvelle puissance."

It was mid-morning—nearly eleven o'clock. The crowds were thicker now, and they pushed their way along more purposefully, as if towards an important objective. The day marked the greatest state occasion in the history of British North America, and now its solemn, official climax was at hand. The Grand Parade at Halifax, Barrack Square at Saint John, Queen's Park at Toronto, and Victoria Square and the Place d'Armes in Montreal were rapidly filling up with waiting citizens. And all over the country, in scores of market squares, parks, and parade grounds, the little officials of Canada, the mayors, and town clerks, and reeves, and wardens, were about to read the Queen's proclamation, bringing the new federation into official existence. In Kingston, the mayor and committee stood on a great scaffolding which workmen had been busily erecting in the market square since early morning. The town clerk of Sarnia carried the proclamation honourably in a carriage, while the Sarnia band and the volunteers paraded proudly in front, and behind came another carriage and four, with four young girls, all in white, representing the four provinces of the new Dominion. At the parade ground in Montreal, the troops, regulars and militia, formed the three sides of a great square. Sir John Michel, the Commander of the Forces, waited with his officers in its centre; and then the Mayor and the Recorder, bearing the proclamation, arrived resplendently in a fine carriage drawn by six white horses. The proclamation was read; the bands crashed into "God Save the Queen"; there were cheers for the Queen and the new Dominion. Then the Volunteer Field Battery began another royal salute; down on the river the guns of the *Wolverine* boomed their response. And, at every seventh explosion, the *feu de joie* "cracked deafeningly along, up and down the lines, from the new breach-loaders."

As eleven o'clock drew close, they were all waiting—all except Edward Kenny, of course, who had hardly had time to collect his senses and his luggage, let alone make the long journey between Nova Scotia and Ottawa. A crowd of Ottawa citizens had gathered outside the Eastern Departmental Building, and people had even pushed their way along the corridors to the doors of the Privy Council chamber. Monck was expected at almost any minute. The Governor-General, in his characteristic easy-going fashion, had not sailed from England until the last possible moment, and had reached Quebec on June 25. "I bring out with me," he wrote assuringly to Macdonald, "my new commission and the Great Seal of Canada, Ontario, and Quebec, so that everything is ready to start the new coach on Monday next." The new coach was indeed ready; but Monck was apparently unaware that he should contribute anything special to the pomp and circumstance of its send-off. "I hope the people of Ottawa," he wrote anxiously to Macdonald, "will be satisfied to postpone any *demonstration* until I come to remain at Rideau Hall as I should like that my present visit should be considered one for business only." To be told that the inauguration of Confederation was "business only" was a little depressing to the spirit. Yet Monck had some justification for looking rather coolly upon the visit to Ottawa that he was about to undertake. It was nearly three years ago that George Brown had described Rideau Hall as a "miserable little house." "To patch up that building," he had insisted to Macdonald, "will cost more than a new one . . . " But, despite this advice, the government had decided to "patch up" instead of building anew, and even after three years the "patching up" process was not complete. Monck could camp out for a night or two at Rideau Hall; but permanent residence would certainly have to be deferred till later. He may have been slightly annoyed. He would hardly have been human if he had not been. But there was more than a little temporary irritation back of his casual attitude to July first. He had believed firmly in Confederation, and had done all in his power to strengthen it and forward its progress. But Carnarvon's visions would have been quickly dissipated in his practical, workaday mind. A "good man," Macdonald described him later, but quite unable, from the constitution of his mind, "to rise to the occasion."

Along with a large crowd of people, Macdonald had waited on the dock for the steamer *Queen Victoria*, which had borne Monck up to Ottawa on Friday, June 28. He would have liked to see Lord Monck, as head now of the new state, in a role more imposing than his former one. In April, after the British North America Act had been passed, he had suggested that it would be gratifying to the people of Canada if the Governor-General could be styled Viceroy as in India. But such touches of purple had not been applied; if Canada could not be a kingdom, presumably she could not have a viceroy. And it was simply a very typical mid-Victorian gentleman, in civilian clothes, and with only his private secretary, Godley, as an attendant, who had landed at Ottawa and driven away in a carriage to Rideau Hall. There had been no reception on Friday night, and no ceremony; and now, as he waited anxiously for the Governor on the morning of July 1, Macdonald knew very well that he could expect a repetition of the same kind of gentlemanly informality. He was not disappointed. Monck drove up to the East Block in plain clothes and with Godley as his only companion. The crowd of waiting people was hardly aware of his arrival, and there was no demonstration. He walked along the corridors to the Privy Council chamber. The prospective councillors, the judges, and a few officers in uniform were waiting for him there; and after he had entered the room, the doors were thrown open to the public.

The brief, business-like ceremony began. Godley read Monck's new commission; and the judges—Chief Justice Draper, Chief Justice Richards, and Justices Mondelet, Hagarty, and Wilson—administered the oaths. The Governor, his hand resting on the Bible, spoke the solemn words in a clear, firm voice; and then, having shaken hands with the judges, he seated himself in the chair of state. Up to this point the proceedings had been unremarkable, and could easily have been anticipated; but now came an announcement which Macdonald could have foretold only in the most general fashion. Monck had determined that the coming of Confederation should be marked by the distribution of honours; and, in comformity with a custom which up to that time had been invariable, he and the Colonial Office officials had among them decided what the honours were to be. Cartier, Galt, Tupper, Tilley, McDougall, and Howland were to be made Companions of the Bath—there was no doubt about that. There was equally no doubt that Macdonald should be given a superior honour, for in Monck's opinion he had unquestionably been the principal architect of federal union. But what form should this special royal favour take? At first Monck thought of a Baronetcy; but in the end he agreed with the new Colonial Secretary, the Duke of Buckingham and Chandos, that Macdonald should be made a Knight Commander of the Bath. It was a sharp distinction between the new Prime Minister and his colleagues; and, as Macdonald heard Monck make the announcement that morning, he must have realized instantly that it would be regarded as an invidious distinction as well. In one minute a grave political mistake had been made. But the public session was over; the onlookers withdrew from the Privy Council chamber—the newspaper correspondents among them; and in a few minutes the news of the awards would be speeding over the telegraph wires. The thing had been done; and a little while later Monck and his new councillors, including his new Knight, adjourned their meeting to review the troops on Parliament Hill.

It was high noon now, and for the last hour and a half, all through the four provinces, the military parades and reviews had been going on. At an early hour in the morning the citizens of Kingston had been streaming across the Cataraqui Bridge and up to the Barriefield Common to secure the choicest positions for the spectacle; and before half-past ten, when the review began in Toronto, the Torontonians had gathered in an "immense circle" round the reviewing grounds to the north-west of the city. In little places like Cayuga, where the 37th Battalion of Haldimand Rifles paraded—"the 37th cannot be surpassed by any Battalion in Canada"—it was the volunteers, of course, who made up the review. But in the larger towns of Halifax, Quebec, and Montreal, where there were imperial garrisons, the regular soldiers gave a smart professional air to the exercises; and at Toronto the most romantic feature of the whole day's entertainment was the presence of the 13th Hussars, the "Noble Six Hundred" of Balaclava, who had newly arrived in town. For a couple of hours, while the bright day grew rapidly warmer, and the vendors of soda water, ice cream and confectionery did a roaring trade, the troops marched, and drilled and fought mimic battles. Cavalry crashed against hollow squares and "thin red lines"; the Hussars went by at the gallop in a blur of blue and silver; and everybody admired the wonders of the new Snider-Enfield breech-loading rifle. Then came the grand march past, and the general salute, and the review was over.

In Ottawa, the last of the troops marched down Parliament Hill and away, and the crowd, in search of its midday meal, began slowly to disperse. The square, with the fountain playing in the middle, was nearly empty. But Monck, Macdonald, and the other ministers, after only a brief interval, returned to the Privy Council chamber to complete the list of essential actions, without which government in Canada and its provinces could not have functioned at all. It was early afternoon—the climax of the long summer's day. In the height of the sky, the sun seemed scarcely to have moved; and the whole earth sunned itself luxuriously in the careless assurance of the long hours of warmth that lay ahead. From the windows of the Privy Council chamber, one could watch the river, all splashed with sunshine, flowing smoothly away past the high cliffs of Major Hill Park towards the north-east. Beyond the far bank stretched the pale green river flats, and beyond them, rising abruptly in wave after long, low wave of pine trees, were the Laurentian hills. In that far country where all the colours seemed to darken so swiftly into sombre blues, there was, on most days and in most lights, the harsh suggestion of something vast and gnarled and forbiddingly inhospitable. But on this day of brilliant sunshine, the colours of the whole ragged landscape had mysteriously lightened and freshened; the dull blue had narrowed to a thin line at the horizon, and it was possible to distinguish clearings, and perhaps a village or a winding road—the signs of indomitable human life. It was warmer now—the heat of an unruffled summer's day. And they must have felt it in the Privy Council office as they worked away, swearing in the ministers to their respective offices, appointing the Lieutenant-Governors of the different provinces, setting the coach in motion, in Monck's own phrase.

In the meantime, most of the population of Canada had gone on holiday. The parades were over; the proclamation had been read; everything official—civil or military—was finished. And the people had packed up, left their houses, and gone off to sports, games, and picnics. At Three Rivers, a large crowd of spectators watched the Union Club and the Canadian Club play "une partie de cricket." There were games in the cricket grounds at Kingston, while the band of the Royal Canadian Rifles played faithfully on during the long afternoon; and out on the waters of the bay the competing sailboats moved gracefully along the course round Garden Island and back. The citizens of Barrie turned out to Kempenfelt Bay to watch the sailing and sculling races, and to amuse themselves at the comic efforts of successive competitors to "walk the greasy pole" which extended thirty feet beyond the railway wharf, with a small flag fluttering at its end. At Dunnville, down in the Niagara peninsula, a new race-course had just been laid out. People came from all around "to witness the birthday of the course as well as that of the nation"; and while "the Dunnville and Wellandport brass bands discoursed sweet music to the multitude," the spectators watched the exciting harness race between Black Bess and Jenny Lind.

In dozens of small villages, where there were no bands or race-courses, and where there could be no water sports, the farmers and their wives and children thronged out early in the afternoon to the local fair grounds or picnic place. Sometimes this common occupied a piece of high ground just outside the village, where a great grove of maple trees gave a pleasant shelter from the heat; and sometimes it lay a mile or two away—a broad, flat stretch of meadowland, through which a shallow river ran. The waggons and buggies stood together in a row; the unharnessed horses were tethered in the shade of a group of tall elm trees; and out in the sunshine the young people and the children played their games and ran off their sports. For an hour or two the small boys who were later to drive the Canadian Pacific Railway across their country and who were to found the first homesteads in the remote prairies, jumped across bars and ran races. The long shadows were creeping rapidly across the turf when they all sat down to a substantial supper at the trestle tables underneath the trees. Afterwards they gossiped and chattered idly in the still calm evening. Then it grew slowly darker, and the children became sleepy; and they drove home over the dusty summer roads.

By nine o'clock, the public buildings and many large houses were illuminated all across Canada. And in Toronto the Queen's Park and the grounds of the private houses surrounding it were transformed by hundreds of Chinese lanterns hung through the trees. When the true darkness had at last fallen, the firework displays began; and simultaneously throughout the four provinces, the night was assaulted by minute explosions of coloured light, as the roman candles popped away, and the rockets raced up into the sky. In the cities and large towns, the spectacle always concluded with elaborate set pieces. The Montrealers arranged an intricate design with emblems representing the three uniting provinces—a beaver for Canada, a mayflower for Nova Scotia, and a pine for New Brunswick. At Toronto the words "God Save the Queen" were surrounded by a twined wreath of roses, thistles, shamrocks, and *fleur-de-lys*; and at Hamilton, while the last set pieces were blazing, four huge bonfires were kindled on the crest of the mountain. In Ottawa, long before this, Monck and Macdonald and the other ministers had quitted the Privy Council chamber; and Parliament Hill was crowded once again with people who had come to watch the last spectacle of the day. The parliament buildings were illuminated. They stood out boldly against the sky; and far behind them, hidden in darkness, were the ridges of the Laurentians, stretching away, mile after mile, towards the north-west.

A NIGHT CRAWL IN WINNIPEG

NORMAN LEVINE

From *Canada Made Me* (1958)

Canada Made Me, *Norman Levine's memoir about his trip across Canada in the 1950s, belongs to a small sub-genre of Canadian literature motivated by an intense dislike of the country. Other examples of Anti-Canlit include Susanna Moodie's* Roughing It in the Bush, *Wyndham Lewis's autobiographical novel* Self Condemned, *and, more recently, Eva Hoffman's* Lost in Translation. *Levine joined the group in 1958 when* Canada Made Me *was published in England. It did not appear in Canada for another twenty years, probably because of its unflattering portrait of the country. In the book Levine records the details of his progress from city to city. He usually stayed in the poorer sections of town and it is this view of life from the other side of the tracks which gives* Canada Made Me *its uniqueness, as well as its sour tone. Aside from Vancouver, which comes off rather well, Levine has little good to say about his native land, which he seems to find drab, low-brow and squalid. The extract below describes a night out in Winnipeg.*

Norman Levine grew up in Ottawa and served in the RCAF during the Second World War. After graduating from McGill University in 1949, he moved to England, finding like other writers of his generation that it was impossible to sustain the literary life in post-war Canada. He has published poetry collections and two novels, but he is best known for his short stories, which have been translated into several languages and published in several collections. Apparently reconciled to his homeland, he returned here to live in 1980.

I was to meet Bobbie, the newspaper reporter, at the Press Club. We had arranged over the telephone that he would show me around the night spots of the city. When I arrived at the club the place was empty. A large room with comfortable leather easy-chairs and chesterfields. I went into a small adjoining room: a few wooden tables and chairs and a bar with a hotplate for snacks. The bartender was sitting on a high stool. We had a drink. He spoke English badly. He was thin, small sharp features, a bald head, thin lips. He said he had come eight months ago from Hamburg, but he didn't like the licensing laws in Manitoba. "It is ridiculous, hypocritical. You buy bottles in liquor-commission and you go home or to the hotel room and you booze. Drink like civilized people? No." He had been in London for a visit. He liked the pubs. "That is proper way to drink; Germany is even better." He judged all countries by their licensing laws. "It is good money here, true. But . . . " He wiped a glass absent-mindedly. "*Garnichts.* We have plenty of snow, cold, wind and sand in Hamburg, but there is something warm inside when you walk the streets. There is people like yourself, maybe more poorer people like yourself, who make you feel good, important as a person. Not like here. Nobody care here about you. Dog eat dog. You work. Good. Then you drive home. Good. And finished. This is centre of a big city. It should be exciting, *ja.* It is dead, like a cemetery." But after a few more drinks we stopped discussing Canada, the cold, the licensing laws. And he taught me the German words to "Falling in Love Again." And I taught him the words to "Ain't We Got Fun." Then Bobbie arrived with two others.

Bobbie at first looked deceptively young. Then one noticed that the blond hair was thinning, dandruff on jacket-shoulders, the layers of fat on the back of the neck, the belly pushed out, and the sweat continually appearing on his forehead soon after he wiped it off. He apologized for being late and as he had no car he had asked another person, a New Zealander, to come along. The New Zealander had asked a Nova Scotian who was at a loose end. They were also reporters. The New Zealander went to school in England and spoke a mixture of American with an affected English accent. The Nova Scotian was the dullest person I remember meeting. He looked as if he was ready to fall asleep. A square face, bad skin, a dull brown suit, a scraggy moustache on the top lip, and black hairs sticking out of his nose and ears. He said nothing except "Yeah, yeah" to whatever someone else had said. Neither did he contribute towards the drinks. His jaw kept falling open, his shoulders hung down. I wondered if it would be possible to get rid of him quickly.

We got in the New Zealander's car; Bobbie suggested that we drive down Main Street, not far from the hotel where I was staying. We parked the car by the city hall, the large front sign, KEEP WINNIPEG BEAUTIFUL AND CLEAN. Walked along the side-streets. They were empty, dark, and cold. The mud had frozen and it was easier to walk now than in the daytime.

Bobbie said he had been a crime reporter and knew this part of the city well. He wouldn't say where we were going. He crossed over the street, and we all stopped outside a small Chinese laundry. An old wooden shack, a thin opening cut out in the door and the opening was covered by a wire screen. He knocked. A pair of eyes came to the screen then the door opened.

The Chinaman was old, hunched, with a bald head, and his face was eaten away in places from some disease. He could hardly speak English. He went behind a curtain in the room and reappeared by a wooden counter.

"Have you any Rubbee?" Bobbie said.

"Beeg bottle?" the old man said.

"Let's see beeg bottle."

The old man stooped down behind the counter and brought up a large bottle the size of a milk bottle with a colourless liquid inside.

"One dollar," the Chinaman said.

Bobbie opened the cork, smelled the liquid and pretended he was interested in buying it. A few bundles of laundry were wrapped in brown paper on a wooden table by a window. The window had the green blind down. There was an opening in the back wall behind the counter leading into a room with a rocking chair by an oil-drum stove.

"Have you anything smaller?" Bobbie said.

The old man became suspicious. He bent down again behind the counter and brought out a small bottle that said "Rubbing Alcohol." I recognized it as a standard brand from one of the drugstores.

"Dirty-five cents," the Chinaman said.

We looked at it. There was certainly more value in the big bottle. A knock on the door. The old man slowly went to the door, looked through the screen-slot, then opened the door. A bum came in, large, unshaven, an old coat, heavy boots, and thick woolen socks. He had a paper bag full of empty dollar bottles. The Chinaman took the bag, counted the number of empty bottles and gave the old man one full dollar bottle. The old man put it inside his coat and went out. Bobbie noticed the small bottle was three-quarters full. "Someone has had a drink out of it," he said to the old man. The old man appeared not to understand. We went out.

From there Bobbie led us to the next side-street to the Lighthouse Mission. A large sign said JESUS SAVES. Inside was a long classroom with benches, a stage, and a man in a dapper suit near a microphone. Bobbie said that the man was a politician, but so far he had been unsuccessful. On the benches there were about twenty people. Down-and-outs, panhandlers, bums, unshaven old men and women, dressed in tattered odds and ends. One Indian woman sat by herself against the wall in a fur coat with large holes in it. Then the slick man said, "Now let's not cough or make too much noise because we are going to be on the air in three minutes." The clock on the wall moved to eight. He pointed to a man sitting in the front row who stood up and tiptoed to the microphone. "Now we will have the blessing by Brother Wolfe." The man thundered out rapidly. While he was talking two girls crept on to the stage, one carried a guitar. As soon as the blessing ended they immediately began to sing "I Wonder Where My Wandering Boy Is Tonight," yodelling at the end of each verse. A woman came next to the stage and, as soon as the duet stopped, she began to read out letters and the answers to them. They were all read in the same hurried over-the-fence-gossip voice, without a pause, as if her entire contribution was one long sentence. The letters enclosed donations and they said how wonderful it was to hear the Lighthouse Mission every Saturday night living out in the prairie. And immediately she went on. "Thank you Brother MacDonald and for your good news that you can hear us so well we all join you in prayer and hope you will get better soon and we here are praying for your recovery and everyone who is listening to us tonight I want you to pray for Brother MacDonald's recovery and we are all pleased that you will be sending your donation on. Everybody's little bit helps and it is all the same in the eyes of the Lord and the next letter is from Sister Emerick from Dauphin and Sister I'm glad to say is also a regular listener of ours and I know how trying. . . . " So it went on. Then more hymns from the hill-billy duet; another short booming blessing from Brother Wolfe; while the audience waited patiently for it to be over and for the doughnuts and the coffee to be served.

We came out of the mission. The Nova Scotian had fallen asleep. He woke up in the cold air and said he was thirsty and where were we going to get a drink. It was too late for the beer parlours. A pretty Indian-looking girl with a white streak in her black hair stood in front of a bare window of a small dilapidated house. She beckoned us to come over. We went across the street.

She was a fortune teller. The small empty front room was curtained off and behind it I could hear children speaking Italian and a man shouting. We haggled about the price. She was firm. "One dollar. If you are not satisfied, no need to pay."

She took me to a curtained-off room on the other side of the door. Only a bare wooden table and two chairs. We sat by the table and she looked at my palm. "You will live a long time. You will make lots of money. Someone loves you, but she is far away. You will be big success, but you must do it yourself. Do not wait for others to do it for you. Only by hard work will you get to your success. And you will have lots of money if you work hard." Then she asked me to stand up and take out what I had in my left trouser pocket. There were two quarters, a nickel, and a few coppers. She took a quarter and stood facing me and very solemnly she touched one shoulder with the quarter then the other, then opened my left trouser pocket and pretended to throw the quarter inside. All the time chanting in a Welsh accent. "Bless this pocket, may it always have lots of money." Then the other pocket. "Bless this pocket, may it always have lots of money." She asked me to take out what I had in my back pocket. I brought out my wallet. She asked for some paper money. I took out a dollar bill. She did the same with the dollar bill as she did with the quarter, touching both shoulders, then opening my back pocket and pretending to throw it in. "Bless this wallet, may it always have some money."

Now she said, "Have you any questions you want answered?"

I hesitated. What does one say? This was a game and like all games there are certain rules one doesn't break.

"When will my journey end?"

She too hesitated. But not for long, for it was her rules we were using. With the same rhythm that she used in blessing my pockets she said, "When you make lots of money."

I paid her the dollar and she put it inside her brassière.

Outside it was cold. In the dark passages, between the houses, tramps sat on newspapers and drank out of those dollar bottles of rubbing alcohol. Some were lying on their side, their hands and the bottle between their legs, as if asleep.

From there Bobbie took us to Moon's café. We all wanted a drink. He knew the woman behind the counter. She gave him the address of two bootleggers. We drove first to an address on Schultz Street. The house was difficult to find. The roads were frozen mud, snow and slush and the residential street was dark, only one street light at the corner. Then we walked along the dark side of the street to where several cars were parked.

It was small like an outdoor toilet away from a wooden house. The snow on the lawn had melted during the day, and the earth in places was muddy, and planks led across the frozen mud to a door. Bobbie knocked several times in the dark. Finally a light flickered through a slot. The door opened. A young boy stood at the door. Behind him a huge fat woman squatted in a chair, a bottle of beer dangled from her hand. "Never saw you boys. I'm sorry. I don't let anybody in I don't know."

The second address was easy. Bobbie said it would be easy. He remembered he had come here before and they weren't fussy. Again the slot, the light, and a woman, larger than the other one, opened the door. She was grotesque. She must have been close to seven feet and well over three hundred pounds. Hanging breasts, fat legs, a lot of loose flesh, lifeless, and exaggerated by a torn green sweater that was many sizes too small and a short skirt. She looked deflated as if she had just had a baby.

The first room was dark. A man sat on a chesterfield, and after the woman let us in she went back beside the man on the chesterfield. The next room was dark except for the light that came from a huge jukebox in the corner. It was light enough to see another chesterfield, old and battered, and two chairs. We sat there and waited until there was no place in the final room, the kitchen.

An oil stove, two shabby chesterfields against the walls, a door to the toilet, a plain sink with one tap high above it, the pipe to the tap covered in rust. The walls were bare. A single light, very bright, hung down in the middle of the kitchen. A tall young boy with bad teeth was serving the drinks. There was a man in a post-office jacket, an older man in a suede windbreaker and ski-cap, and a short fat man in a suit. The tall young boy was dressed all in black. Black shirt, black trousers. The shirt had white colonel stars on the epaulets. He asked us.

"You all want a nip?"

We said we did.

He asked the others to drink up. He took their small glasses, rinsed them, and gave each of us a brown-coloured liquid that smelled of methylated spirits. I had only taken one sip when he came around. "O.K., boys, knock it back." He needed the glasses for the others. There were only two glasses for the entire room, in case of a raid.

Men kept coming in. Some with their lunchpails, others dressed in sport suits, overcoats, windbreakers. A young boy, his face covered with lipstick, brought out a hip-flask. "A dollar's worth." A girl came in drunk. She was very thin and wore a light fawn coat, high black shoes. She looked haggard. She drank the alcohol down in one gulp, screwed up her face, then it hit her. She doubled up and quickly went into the toilet where we could hear her vomiting.

Strangers bought each other drinks. They were cheap, twenty-five cents a glass, and after the initial raw burning sensation in the throat, they did not seem to have a great deal of effect. The flavour was that of the Kik that the boy used to colour the alcohol. He kept rinsing and filling the same two glasses and passing them around and collecting his money. He took out a thick bundle of dollar bills and transferred the bundle to his back pocket. His shift was finishing, he said, and someone else was due to come on in five minutes. He said they were open twenty-four hours a day.

The drink had made the Nova Scotian even more morose. He kept on grumbling that he was hungry. We drove to another dark street to a tall undecorated house. There was a light on in a top room. Bobbie was sweating. He went out and knocked loudly on the door. But there was no answer. He knocked several times and still no reply. He threw a snowball up, but couldn't hit a window. He shouted out and threw more snowballs; but no one opened the door. "I guess the girls are all shacked up for the night," he said.

And suddenly I became impatient with all this tomfoolery and I wanted the evening to end. Perhaps Bobbie misunderstood me, or perhaps I misunderstood him, or perhaps Winnipeg didn't have "night spots"; but I had no enjoyment out of this slumming, the kind of pretence that treats poverty as something picturesque. Poverty is always picturesque for those who nip in, have a quick naughty look, then go back to their safe places. Perhaps this evening was for them a kind of joke, an excuse to get away from the wife, the kids, the routine. The New Zealander and the Nova Scotian kept getting more solemn and dull as the evening went on. And Bobbie more of a salesman, selling me the sights of the down-and-outs. He told the New Zealander to stop the car outside a flophouse and in we went. Bobbie went straight to the desk and, confident as anything, asked the attendant for a fictitious Mr. Miller. The attendant looked through the book, to see if Mr. Miller was there for the night. The excuse of this performance was to get us inside to have a look at the husks of men sitting dumbly and patiently around the room by the walls. It was intended as entertainment. And I was fed up and disgusted with them and with myself. I left the three of them and walked back along Main Street. Cold freezing night. Desolate. No dogs, no cats, not even a person. The closed cafés, secondhand stores, looked even shabbier in the darkness and the frost. I passed the town hall, KEEP WINNIPEG BEAUTIFUL AND CLEAN, woke the old man who was dozing behind the desk in the hotel to get my room key. The cheap room had the welcome of something familiar; it felt like home. And I slept in until after ten next morning, when the woman came around to make the beds, and to sew a button on my winter coat which she saw was loose.

IN SEARCH OF WHITEMUD

WALLACE STEGNER

From *Wolf Willow* (1962)

In Wolf Willow, *Wallace Stegner effaces the border between fiction, memoir, and history, combining all three in a moving evocation of the prairie landscape and an unsentimental meditation on the importance of place. His book is sometimes classified as fiction, chiefly because in two long chapters recreating the winter of 1906-07, when the cattle ranches of southern Alberta and Saskatchewan were devastated by extreme cold, he imagines characters and invents incidents. However, the rest of the book is a mixture of history and personal memoir which takes the author back to the hometown of his boyhood in an attempt to understand how his own character, his own destiny, was shaped by the place in which he grew up. It is appropriate that Stegner mixes genres because one of the book's main themes is the process by which we turn memory into myth—fact into fiction and back again—and how the two intersect to shape personal identity.*

Wallace Stegner (1909-1993) was born in Iowa and is best known, in the United States at least, for his writings about the American West. When he was a youngster, in 1914, his family moved across the border to the Cypress Hills country of southwestern Saskatchewan where his parents tried unsuccessfully to homestead. Beaten down by weather and circumstances, the Stegners returned to the U.S. in 1920. It took Wallace Stegner forty years to transmute that childhood experience into prose. Wolf Willow *is more than just another memoir about*

pioneering on the Canadian Plains. It is a book about memory itself: how it is
created and how it endures.

In Wolf Willow Stegner calls his town Whitemud. It is actually Eastend,
Saskatchewan, where the house the Stegners lived in has been restored as an arts
centre.

In the fall it was always a moment of pure excitement, after a whole
day on the trail, to come to the rim of the South Bench. More likely
than not I would be riding with my mother in the wagon while my father
had my brother with him in the Ford. The horses would be plodding
with their noses nearly to their knees, the colt would be dropping tiredly
behind. We would be choked with dust, cranky and headachy with heat,
our joints loosened with fifty miles of jolting. Then miraculously the land
fell away below us, I would lift my head from my mother's lap and push
aside the straw hat that had been protecting my face from the glare, and
there below, looped in its green coils of river, snug and protected in its
sanctuary valley, lay town.

The land falls below me now, the suddenness of my childhood town
is the old familiar surprise. But I stop, looking, for adult perception has
in ten seconds clarified a childhood error. I have always thought of the
Whitemud as running its whole course in a deeply sunken valley. Instead,
I see that the river has cut deeply only through the uplift of the hills; that
off to the southeast, out on the prairie, it crawls disconsolately flat across
the land. It is a lesson in how peculiarly limited a child's sight is: he sees
only what he can see. Only later does he learn to link what he sees with
what he already knows, or has imagined or heard or read, and so come
to make perception service inference. During my childhood I kept hearing
about the Cypress Hills, and knew that they were somewhere nearby.
Now I see that I grew up in them. Without destroying the intense
familiarity, the flooding recognition of the moment, that grown-up
understanding throws things a little out of line, and so it is with mixed
feelings of intimacy and strangeness that I start down the dug-way grade.
Things look the same, surprisingly the same, and yet obscurely different.
I tick them off, easing watchfully back into the past.

There is the Frenchman's stone barn, westward up the river valley a
couple of miles. It looks exactly as it did when we used to go through
the farmyard in wagon or buckboard and see the startled kids disappearing

around every corner, and peeking out at us from hayloft door and cowshed after we passed. Probably they were *métis*, halfbreeds; to us, who had never heard the word *métis*, they were simply Frenchmen, part of the vague and unknown past that had given our river one of its names. I bless them for their permanence, and creep on past the cemetery, somewhat larger and somewhat better kept than I remember it, but without disconcerting changes. Down below me is the dam, with its wide lake behind it. It takes me a minute to recollect that by the time we left Whitemud Pop Martin's dam had long since washed out. This is a new one, therefore, but in approximately the old place. So far, so good.

The road I bump along is still a dirt road, and it runs where it used to run, but the wildcat oil derrick that used to be visible from the turn at the foot of the grade is not there any longer. I note, coming in toward the edge of the town, that the river has changed its course somewhat, swinging closer to the southern hills and pinching the road space. I see a black iron bridge, new, that evidently leads some new road off into the willow bottoms westward, toward the old Carpenter ranch. I cannot see the river, masked in willows and alders, and anyway my attention is taken by the town ahead of me, which all at once reveals one element of the obscure strangeness that has been making me watchful. Trees.

My town used to be as bare as a picked bone, with no tree anywhere around it larger than a ten-foot willow or alder. Now it is a grove. My memory gropes uneasily, trying to establish itself among fifty-foot cottonwoods, lilac and honeysuckle hedges, and flower gardens. Searched for, plenty of familiarities are there: the Pastime Theatre, identical with the one that sits across Main Street from the firehouse in my mind; the lumber yard where we used to get cloth caps advertising De Laval Cream Separators; two or three hardware stores (a prairie wheat town specializes in hardware stores), though each one now has a lot full of farm machinery next to it; the hotel, just as it was rebuilt after the fire; the bank, now remodelled into the post office; the Presbyterian church, now United, and the *Leader* office, and the square brick prison of the old school, now with three smaller prisons added to it. These are old acquaintances that I can check against their replicas in my head and take satisfaction from. But among them are the evidences of Progress—hospital, Masonic Lodge, at least one new elevator, a big quonset-like skating rink—and all tree-shaded, altered and distorted and made vaguely disturbing by greenery. In the old days we all used to try to grow trees, transplanting them from the Hills or getting them free with any two-dollar purchase from one of the stores, but they always dried up and died. To me, who came expecting a dusty hamlet, the change is charming, but memory has been fixed by time as photographs fix the faces of the dead, and this reality is dreamlike. I cannot find myself or my family or my companions in it.

My progress up Main Street, as wide and empty and dusty as I remember it, has taken me to another iron bridge across the eastern loop of the river, where the flume of Martin's irrigation ditch used to cross, and from the bridge I get a good view of the river. It is disappointing, a quiet creek twenty yards wide, the colour of strong tea, its banks a tangle of willow and wild rose. How could adventure ever have inhabited those willows, or wonder, or fear, or other remembered emotions? Was it along here I shot at the lynx with my brother's .25-.20? And out of what log (there is no possibility of a log in these brakes, but I distinctly remember a log) did my bullet knock chips just under the lynx's bobtail?

A muddy little stream, a village grown unfamiliar with time and trees. I turn around and retrace my way up Main Street and park and have a Coke in the confectionery store. It is run by a Greek, as it used to be, but whether the same Greek or another I would not know. He does not recognize me, nor I him. Only the smell of his place is familiar, syrupy with old delights, as if the ghost of my first banana split had come close to breathe on me. Still in search of something or someone to make the town fully real to me, I get the telephone book off its nail by the wall telephone and run through it, sitting at the counter. There are no more than seventy or eighty names in the Whitemud section. I look for Huffman—none. Bickerton—none. Fetter—none. Orullian—none. Stenhouse—none. Young—one, but not by a first name I remember. There are a few names I do remember—Harold Jones and William Christenson and Nels Sieverud and Jules LaPlante. (That last one startles me. I always thought his name was Jewell.) But all of the names I recognize are those of old-timers, pioneers of the town. Not a name that I went to school with, not a single person who would have shared as a contemporary my own experience of this town in its earliest years, when the river still ran clear and beaver swam in it in the evenings. Who in town remembers Phil Lott, who used to run coyotes with wolfhounds out on the South Bench? Who remembers in the way I do the day he drove up before

Leaf's store in his democrat wagon and unloaded from it two dead hounds and the lynx that had killed them when they caught him unwarily exposed out on the flats? Who remembers in *my* way the stiff, half-disemboweled bodies of the hounds and the bloody grin of the lynx? Who feels it or felt it, as I did and do, as a parable, a moral lesson for the pursuer to respect the pursued?

Because it is not shared, the memory seems fictitious, and so do other memories: the blizzard of 1916 that marooned us in the schoolhouse for a night and a day, the time the ice went out and brought both Martin's dam and the CPR bridge in kindling to our doors, the games of fox-and-geese in the untracked snow of a field that is now a grove, the nights of skating with a great fire leaping from the river ice and reflecting red from the cutbanks. I have used those memories for years as if they really happened, have made stories and novels of them. Now they seem uncorroborated and delusive. Some of the pioneers still in the telephone book would remember, but pioneers' memories are no good to me. Pioneers would remember the making of the town; to me, it was made, complete, timeless. A pioneer's child is what I need now, and in this town the pioneers' children did not stay, but went on, generally to bigger places farther west, where there was more opportunity.

Sitting in the sticky-smelling, nostalgic air of the Greek's confectionery store, I am afflicted with the sense of how many whom I have known are dead, and how little evidence I have that I myself have lived what I remember. It is not quite the same feeling I imagined when I contemplated driving out to the homestead. That would have been absolute denial. This, with its tantalizing glimpses, its hints and survivals, is not denial but only doubt. There is enough left to disturb me, but not to satisfy me. So I will go a little closer. I will walk on down into the west bend and take a look at our house.

In the strange forest of the school yard the boys are friendly, and their universal air of health, openness, and curiosity reassures me. This is still a good town to be a boy in. To see a couple of them on the prowl with air rifles (in my time we would have been carrying .22's or shotguns, but we would have been of the same tribe) forces me to readjust my disappointed estimate of the scrub growth. When one is four feet high, ten-foot willows are a sufficient cover, and ten acres are a wilderness.

By now, circling and more than half unwilling, I have come into the

west end of town, have passed Corky Jones's house (put off till later that
meeting) and the open field beside Downs's where we used to play
run-sheep-run in the evenings, and I stand facing the four-gabled white
frame house that my father built. It ought to be explosive with nostalgias
and bright with recollections, for this is where we lived for five or six of
my most impressionable years, where we all nearly died with the flu in
1918, where my grandmother "went crazy" and had to be taken away
by a Mountie to the Provincial asylum because she took to standing
silently in the door of the room where my brother and I slept—just
hovered there for heaven knows how long before someone discovered
her watching and listening in the dark. I try to remember my
grandmother's face and cannot; only her stale old-woman's smell after she
became incontinent. I can summon up other smells, too—it is the smells
that seem to have stayed with me: painting paint and hot tin and lignite
smoke behind the parlour heater; frying scrapple, which we called
headcheese, on chilly fall mornings after the slaughtering was done; the
rich thick odour of doughnuts frying in a kettle of boiling lard (I always
got to eat the "holes"). With effort, I can bring back Christmases,
birthdays, Sunday School parties in that house, and I have not forgotten
the licking I got when, aged about six, I was caught playing with my
father's loaded .30-.30 that hung above the mantel just under the Rosa
Bonheur painting of three white horses in a storm. After that licking I
lay out behind the chopping block all one afternoon watching my big
dark heavy father as he worked at one thing and another, and all the time
I lay there I kept aiming an empty cartridge case at him and dreaming
murder.

Even the dreams of murder, which were bright enough at the time,
have faded; he is long dead, and if not forgiven, at least propitiated. My
mother, too, who saved me from him so many times, and once missed
saving me when he clouted me with a chunk of stove wood and knocked
me over the wood box and broke my collarbone: she too has faded.
Standing there looking at the house where our lives entangled themselves
in one another, I am infuriated that of that episode I remember less her
love and protection and anger than my father's inept contrition. And
walking all around the house trying to pump up recollection, I notice
principally that the old barn is gone. What I see, though less changed

than the town in general, still has power to disturb me; it is all dreamlike, less real than memory, less convincing than the recollected odors.

Whoever lives in the house now is a tidy housekeeper; the yard is neat, the porch swept. The corner where I used to pasture my broken-legged colt is a bed of flowers, the yard where we hopefully watered our baby spruces is a lawn enclosed by a green hedge. The old well with the hand pump is still in the side yard. For an instant my teeth are on edge with the memory of the dry screech of that pump before a dipperful of priming water took hold, and an instant later I feel the old stitch in my side from an even earlier time, the time when we still carried water from the river, and I dipped a bucket down into the hole in the ice and toted it, staggering and with the other arm stuck stiffly out, up the dugway to the kitchen door.

Those instants of memory are persuasive. I wonder if I should knock on the door and ask the housewife to let me look around, go upstairs to our old room in the west gable, examine the ceiling to see if the stains from the fire department's chemicals are still there. My brother and I used to lie in bed and imagine scenes and faces among the blotches, giving ourselves inadvertent Rorschach tests. I have a vivid memory, too, of the night the stains were made, when we came out into the hard cold from the Pastime Theatre and heard the firehouse bell going and saw the volunteer fire department already on the run, and followed them up the ditch toward the glow of the fire, wondering whose house, until we got close and it was ours.

It is there, and yet it does not flow as it should, it is all a pumping operation. I half suspect that I am remembering not what happened but something I have written. I find that I am as unwilling to go inside that house as I was to try to find the old homestead in its ocean of grass. All the people who once shared the house with me are dead; strangers who would have effaced or made doubtful the things that might restore them in my mind.

Behind our house there used to be a footbridge across the river, used by the Carpenters and others who lived in the bottoms, and by summer swimmers from town. I pass by the opaque and troubling house to the cutbank. The twin shanties that through all the town's life have served as men's and women's bath houses are still there. In winter we used to hang our frozen beef in one of them. I remember iron evenings when I went out with a lantern and sawed and haggled steaks from a rocklike hind quarter. But it is still an academic exercise; I only remember it, I do not feel the numb fingers and the fear that used to move just beyond the lantern's glow.

Then I walk to the cutbank edge and look down, and in one step the past comes closer than it has yet been. There is the grey curving cutbank, not much lower than I remember it when we dug cave holes in it or tunnelled down its drifted cliff on our sleds. The bar is there at the inner curve of the bend, and kids are wallowing in a quicksandy mudhole and shrieking on an otter slide. They chase each other into the river and change magically from black to white. The water has its old quiet, its whirlpools spin lazily into deep water. On the footbridge, nearly exactly where it used to be, two little girls lie staring down into the water a foot below their noses. Probably they are watching suckers that lie just as quietly against the bottom. In my time we used to snare them from the bridge with nooses of copper wire.

It is with me all at once, what I came hoping to re-establish, an ancient, unbearable recognition, and it comes partly from the children and the footbridge and the river's quiet curve, but much more from the smell. For here, pungent and pervasive, is the smell that has always meant my childhood. I have never smelled it anywhere else, and it is as evocative as Proust's madeleine and tea.

But what is it? Somehow I have always associated it with the bath house, with wet bathing suits and damp board benches, heaps of clothing, perhaps even the seldom rinsed corners where desperate boys had made water. I go into the men's bath house, and the smell is there, but it does not seem to come from any single thing. The whole air smells of it, outside as well as in. Perhaps it is the river water, or the mud, or something about the float and footbridge. It is the way the old burlap-tipped diving board used to smell; it used to remain in the head after a sinus-flooding dive.

I pick up a handful of mud and sniff it. I step over the little girls and bend my nose to the wet rail of the bridge. I stand above the water and sniff. On the other side I strip leaves off wild rose and dogwood. Nothing doing. And yet all around me is that odour that I have not smelled since I was eleven, but have never forgotten—have *dreamed*, more than once. Then I pull myself up the bank by a grey-leafed bush, and I have it. The tantalizing and ambiguous and wholly native smell is no more than the shrub we called wolf willow, now blooming with small yellow flowers.

It is wolf willow, and not the town or anyone in it, that brings me home. For a few minutes, with a handful of leaves to my nose, I look across at the clay bank and the hills beyond where the river loops back on itself, enclosing the old sports and picnic ground, and the present and all the years between are shed like a boy's clothes dumped on the bath house bench. The perspective is what it used to be, the dimensions are restored, the senses are as clear as if they had not been battered with sensation for forty alien years. And the queer adult compulsion to return to one's beginnings is assuaged. A contact has been made, a mystery touched. For the moment, reality is made exactly equivalent with memory, and a hunger is satisfied. The sensuous little savage that I once was is still intact inside me.

AN EVENING WITH JAMES JOYCE

MORLEY CALLAGHAN

From *That Summer in Paris* (1963)

The suicide of the American novelist, Ernest Hemingway, in 1961 led to the publication in Canada of two important memoirs about Paris in the 1920s: That Summer in Paris *and* Memoirs of Montparnasse. *That Summer in Paris is Morley Callaghan's account of his triangular relationship with Hemingway and F. Scott Fitzgerald, and of the months he and his wife lived in France in 1929. Callaghan and Hemingway used to box regularly for exercise, and Callaghan organized his memoir around a sparring session in which he knocked Hemingway to the mat while Fitzgerald was supposed to be keeping track of the time. The incident has lost whatever interest it may have had, but Callaghan's book remains a wonderful evocation of expatriate literary life in the French capital before everyone became famous and the Depression arrived to spoil it all.*

Morley Callaghan was born in Toronto in 1903. He began publishing stories in the "little magazines" in 1926 and his first novel appeared in 1928. He went on to a career which spanned six decades. That Summer in Paris *is Callaghan's only book of non-fiction. The following selection from it describes his meeting with James Joyce.*

On the boulevard one night at the *apéritif* hour we encountered McAlmon. "What are you doing tonight?" he asked.

"Nothing, as usual."

"I'm having dinner with Jimmy Joyce and his wife at the Trianon. Why don't you join us?"

150

Jimmy Joyce! "No," I said quickly. "I understand he hates being with strangers and won't talk about anybody's work."

"Who told you all this?"

"Hemingway."

"Oh nuts," he said, curling his lip. "Don't you want to see Jimmy? You'll like him. You'll like Nora, too."

"Well, of course we want to meet Joyce."

"See you in about an hour and a half at the Trianon," and he went on his way.

He had made it sound as if anyone could drop in on the Joyces at any time. Jimmy, he had called him. Yet Sylvia Beach kept on throwing up her protective screen as dozens of English and American scholars tried to get close to the Irish master. What kind of magic touch did McAlmon have? Was it possible that Joyce had the same sneaking respect for McAlmon that I had myself and liked drinking with him? We'd soon see. At twilight we approached the Trianon just as casually as we might approach a bus stop.

It was a restaurant near the Gare Montparnasse, where the food was notably good. Just to the right as you go in we saw McAlmon sitting with the Joyces. The Irishman's picture was as familiar to us as any movie star's. He was a small-boned, dark Irishman with fine features. He had thick glasses and was wearing a neat dark suit. His courtly manner made it easy for us to sit down, and his wife, large bosomed with a good-natured face, offered us a massive northerly ease. They were both so unpretentious it became impossible for me to resort to Homeric formalities. I couldn't even say, "Sir, you are the greatest writer of our time," for Joyce immediately became too chatty, too full of little bits of conversation, altogether unlike the impression we had been given of him. His voice was soft and pleasant. His humour, to my surprise, depended on puns. Even in the little snips of conversation, he played with words lightly. However, none of his jokes made his wife laugh out loud, and I was reminded of McAlmon's story that she had once asked the author of the comic masterpiece *Ulysses*, "Jimmy, have we a book of Irish humour in the house?"

No matter what was being said, I remained aware of the deep-bosomed Nora Joyce. The food on the table, the white tablecloths, our own voices, everything in the restaurant seemed to tell me Joyce had got all the stuff of Molly Bloom's great and beautiful soliloquy at the close of *Ulysses* from this woman sitting across from me; all her secret, dark night thoughts and yearning. Becoming a little shy, I could hardly look at her. But the quiet handsome motherly woman's manner soon drove all this nonsense out of my head. She was as neighbourly and sympathetic as Joyce himself. They both gossiped with a pleasant ease.

The sound of Joyce's voice suddenly touched a memory of home which moved me. My father, as I have said, didn't read modern prose, just poetry. Fond of music as he was, he wouldn't listen to jazz. He wouldn't read Anderson. I had assumed he would have no interest in experimental prose. When that copy of *This Quarter* carrying my first story, along with the work of Joyce, Pound, Stein, Hemingway and others, had come to our house, my father sat one night at the end of the kitchen table reading it. Soon he began to chuckle to himself. The assured little smirk on his face irritated me. Passing behind his shoulder, I glanced down at the page to see what he was reading. "Work in Progress," by James Joyce, which was a section from *Finnegan's Wake*. Imagining he was getting ready to make some sarcastic and belittling remark, I said grimly, "All right. What's so funny?"

But he looked up mildly; he had untroubled blue eyes; and he said with genuine pleasure, "I think I understand this. Read it like Irish brogue. . . . Shem is short for Shemus just as Jem is joky for Jacob. A few toughnecks are gettable. . . . It's like listening to someone talking in a broad Irish brogue, isn't it, Son?" "Yeah," I said. But I felt apologetic.

And now, after listening to Joyce in our general gossiping, I blurted out that my father had said the new Joyce work should be read aloud in an Irish brogue. Whether it was Joyce or McAlmon who cut in quickly, agreeing, I forget. It came out that Joyce had made some phonograph records of the work; in the way he used his voice it had been his intention to make you feel you were listening to the brogue; much of the music and meaning was in the sound of the brogue. So my father helped me; I wanted to go on: had Joyce read those proofs of *A Farewell to Arms* which I knew Hemingway had taken to him? Why not ask him? But there had been that warning from Hemingway, "He doesn't like to talk about the work of other writers." I felt handcuffed, exasperated, and therefore was silent. So Joyce had to make most of the conversation. Were we going to London? Sooner or later? He wrote down the name of an inexpensive hotel near the Euston Station.

McAlmon, who had been drinking a lot as usual, suddenly got up, excused himself and went toward the washroom. And then, almost as soon as McAlmon's back was turned, Joyce, leaning across the table, asked quietly, "What do you think of McAlmon's work?"

Surprised, I couldn't answer for a moment. Joyce? Someone else's work? Finally I said that McAlmon simply wouldn't take time with his work; he had hypnotized himself into believing the main thing was to get down the record.

"He has talent," Joyce said. "A real talent; but it is a disorganized talent." And as he whispered quickly about this disorganized talent, trying to get it all in before McAlmon could return, I wanted to laugh. How had the story got around that the man wouldn't talk about another writer? Then Joyce suddenly paused, his eyes shifting away. McAlmon was on his way back from the washroom and like a conspirator Joyce quickly changed the subject.

As McAlmon came sauntering over to us with his superior air, I noticed a change in his appearance. He looked as if he had just washed his face and combed his hair. From past experience I knew what it meant. When with people he respected he would not let himself get incoherently drunk; he would go to the washroom; there he would put his finger down his throat, vomit, then wash his face, comb his hair, and return sober as an undertaker.

It was now about ten o'clock. Turning to his wife, Joyce used the words I remember so well. "Have we still got that bottle of whiskey in the house, Nora?"

"Yes, we have," she said.

"Perhaps Mr. and Mrs. Callaghan would like to drink it with us."

Would we? My wife said we would indeed and I hid my excitement and elation. An evening at home with the Joyces, and Joyce willing to talk and gossip about other writers while we killed a bottle! Stories about Yeats, opinions about Proust! What would he say about Lawrence? Of Hemingway? Did he know Fitzgerald's work? It all danced wildly in my head as we left the restaurant.

Looking for a taxi, McAlmon had gone ahead with Mrs. Joyce and Loretto. Joyce and I were trailing them. The street was not lighted very brightly. Carried away by the excitement I felt at having him walking beside me, I began to talk rapidly. Not a word came from him. I thought he was absorbed in what I was saying. Then far back of me I heard the anxious pounding of his cane on the cobblestones and turned. In the shadows he was groping his way toward me. I had forgotten he could hardly see. Then headlights of an approaching taxi picked him up, and in the glaring light he waved his stick wildly. Conscience-stricken, I wanted to cry out. Rushing back, I grabbed him by the arm as the taxi swerved around us. I stammered out an apology. He made some pun on one of the words I used. I don't remember the pun, but since I was trembling the poor quick pun seemed to make the situation Joycean and ridiculous.

The Joyces lived in a solid apartment house, and in the entrance hall Mrs. Joyce explained we would have to use the lift in shifts; it was not supposed to carry more than two people at one time. For the first ascension my wife and Mrs. Joyce got into the lift. When it returned, McAlmon offered to wait while Joyce and I ascended. No, said Joyce, the three of us would get in. The lift rose so slowly I held my breath. No one spoke. Out of the long silence, with the three of us jammed together, came a little snicker from Joyce. "Think what a loss to English literature if the lift falls and the three of us are killed," he said dryly.

The Joyce apartment, at least the living room in which we sat, upset me. Nothing looked right. In the whole world there wasn't a more original writer than Joyce, the exotic in the English language. In the work he had on hand he was exploring the language of the dream world. In this room where he led his daily life I must have expected to see some of the marks of his wild imagination. Yet the place was conservatively respectable. I was too young to have discovered then that men with the most daringly original minds are rarely eccentric in their clothes and their living quarters. This room was all in a conventional middle-class pattern with, if I remember, a brown-patterned wallpaper, a mantel, and a painting of Joyce's father hanging over the fireplace. Mrs. Joyce had promptly brought out the bottle of Scotch. As we began to drink, we joked and laughed and Joyce got talking about the movies. A number of times a week he went to the movies. Movies interested him. As he talked, I seemed to see him in a darkened theatre, the great prose master absorbed in camera technique, so like the dream technique, one picture then another flashing in the mind. Did it all add to his knowledge of the logic of the dream world?

As the conversation began to trail off, I got ready. At the right moment I would plunge in and question him about his contemporaries. But damn it all, I was too slow. Something said about the movies had reminded McAlmon of his grandmother. In a warm, genial, expansive mood, and as much at home with the Joyces as he was with us, he talked about his dear old grandmother, with a happy nostalgic smile. The rich pleasure he got out of his boyhood recollections was so pure that neither the Joyces nor my wife nor I could bear to interrupt. At least not at first. But he kept it up. For half an hour he went on and on. Under my breath I cursed him again and again. Instead of listening to Joyce, I was listening to McAlmon chuckling away about his grandmother. Quivering with impatience I looked at Joyce, who had an amused little smile. No one could interrupt McAlmon. Mrs. Joyce seemed to have an extraordinary capacity for sitting motionless and looking interested. The day would come, I thought bitterly, when I would be able to tell my children I had sat one night with Joyce listening to McAlmon talking about his grandmother.

But when McAlmon paused to take another drink, Joyce caught him off balance. "Do you think Mr. and Mrs. Callaghan would like to hear the record?" he asked his wife.

"What record?" asked McAlmon, blinking suspiciously, and for a moment I, too, thought Joyce had been referring to him. Now Mrs. Joyce was regarding my wife and me very gravely. "Yes," she said. "I think it might interest them."

"What record?" McAlmon repeated uneasily.

Mrs. Joyce rose, got a record out of a cabinet and put it on the machine. After a moment my wife and I looked at each other in astonishment. Aimee Semple McPherson was preaching a sermon! At that time everyone in Europe and America had heard of Mrs. McPherson, the attractive, seductive blond evangelist from California. But why should Joyce be interested in the woman evangelist? and us? and McAlmon? Cut off, and therefore crestfallen, he, too, waited, mystified. Joyce had nodded to me, inviting my scholarly attention. And Mrs. Joyce, having sat down, was watching my wife with a kind of saintly concern.

The evangelist had an extraordinary voice, warm, low, throaty, and imploring. But what was she asking for? As we listened, my wife and I exchanging glances, we became aware that the Joyces were watching us intently, while Mrs. McPherson's voice rose and fell. The voice, in a tone of ecstatic abandonment, took on an ancient familiar rhythm. It became like a woman's urgent love moan as she begged, "Come, come on to me. Come, come on to me. And I will give you rest . . . and I will give you rest . . . Come, come. . . . " My wife, her eyebrows raised, caught my glance, then we averted our eyes, as if afraid the Joyces would know what we were thinking. But Joyce, who had been watching us so attentively, had caught our glance. It was enough. He brightened and chuckled. Then Mrs. Joyce, who had also kept her eyes on us, burst out laughing herself. Nothing had to be explained. Grinning mischievously, in enormous satisfaction with his small success, Joyce poured us another drink.

Before we could comment his daughter, a pretty, dark young woman, came in. And a few minutes later, his son too joined us. It was time for us to leave.

When we had taken Robert McAlmon, publisher of the city of Paris, home, we wandered over to the Coupole. That night we shared an extraordinary elation at being in Paris. We didn't want to go back to the apartment. In the Coupole bar we met some friends. One of them asked Loretto if she could do the Charleston. There in the bar she gave a fine solo performance. A young, fair man, a Servian count, who had been sitting at the bar holding a single long-stemmed red rose in his hand, had been watching her appreciatively. But one of our friends told him the dancing girl was my wife. With a shy, yet gallant bow to me from a distance, he asked if he had permission to give Loretto the rose. It was a good night.

THE DIEFENBAKER PHILOSOPHY

PETER C. NEWMAN

From *Renegade in Power* (1963)

Peter C. Newman's account of John Diefenbaker ushered in a new era in political writing in Canada. Never before had anyone written so critically about a leading politician with the benefit of so much inside information. Donald Creighton's biography of John A. Macdonald, for example, praises its subject, whereas Newman attempts to bury his. When Renegade in Power *appeared in October 1963, just a few months after Diefenbaker's electoral defeat, it created an instant sensation for what it revealed about the failings of the Conservative government and the frank way it described the world of Ottawa politics. It was featured in news stories as well as the book pages and quickly sold 50,000 copies, unprecedented for a book of its type. Diefenbaker himself hated it. Claiming to have no interest in reading the book, he nonetheless never spoke to its author again, characterizing Newman as a Liberal hack and a "literary scavenger of trash."*

*Peter C. Newman was thirty-four years old and the Ottawa editor of*Maclean's *magazine when he published* Renegade in Power. *Following the success of the book, he wrote a similar, though less successful, account of the Lester Pearson administration, then began chronicling the lifestyles of the rich and famous in a series of books. His most recent work is a three-volume history of the Hudson's Bay Company.*

The following selection from Renegade in Power *describes Diefenbaker's brand of Conservative philosophy.*

157

Almost everything that happened during the Diefenbaker years—from the small triumph of the Bill of Rights to the bald fiasco of the Coyne affair—reflected the attitudes and motives of the man from Prince Albert.

Because his nominally Conservative administration was concerned with short-run objectives rather than any logical progression of long-term priorities, most Canadians who worried about such things believed that John Diefenbaker had no political philosophy of his own. This was neither fair nor convincing.

There was, of course, an underlying opportunism to his politics, as there must be in the professional make-up of every democratic leader, but Diefenbaker was also driven by more noble concepts. For the few men and women who caught a glimpse of them, it became possible to admire his ideals, without respecting his performance.

By picking John Diefenbaker as their leader in 1956, Canada's Conservatives had committed themselves to an ideological and emotional upheaval. But the transfiguration that Diefenbaker brought about in his Party, once he attained office, was more distinct than even his own supporters had anticipated.

The trappings of true Tory philosophy were swept away as the man from Prince Albert laid down his personal testament of what Canadian Conservatism meant to *him*.

By instinct, Diefenbaker was a humanitarian and, to that extent, a liberal. By temperament, he was a high Tory. This unique combination produced a political philosophy that defied simple classification as either Liberal or Conservative.

The philosophy of John Diefenbaker was by no means a consciously contrived creed. It was a cast of mind, lacking coherent and continuing expression even in his own speeches. But occasionally, its governing precepts could be winnowed out of his rhetorical torrent. And even more important clues could be gained from analyzing his background and the conditions of the times in which he formed his remarkably enduring political theories.

The philosophy that has to be called "Diefenbakerism" amounted, in essence, to a distrust of the great power groupings in contemporary Canada and the belief that broadly based citizen participation, speaking through a strong political leader, can reconcile the opposing economic interests of individual citizens.

Nearly all Diefenbaker's principles were based on this assumption. From it flowed his positive identification with minority groups, his demands for a more egalitarian society, and his hostility toward the men of power whose ambitions were too broad for the nation he sought to build.

Historically, he was influenced by three men: Sir John A. Macdonald, in his political psychology; Mackenzie King, in his political tactics and strategy; and Franklin Delano Roosevelt, in his policies.

The personal roots of his political dogma stretched back to the grain-growing West of the twenties and thirties. He came to maturity among men who cursed their isolation and damned their unavoidable dependence on the goods and services of Toronto manufacturing interests. He felt—and was profoundly influenced by—the economic carnage of the Depression, which hit no part of Canada more severely than Saskatchewan. World demand for wheat had dropped so low by 1931 that the province's agricultural income totalled only $8 million, compared with $228 million for 1928.

Diefenbaker forged his liberalism out of day-to-day experiences rather than abstract contemplation. To prevent the recurrence of the misery wrought by the Depression seemed a high calling. Like many others of his generation and upbringing, he realized there was only one way for Prairie farmers to help themselves: through collective political action. That was the foundation of Diefenbaker's deep-seated faith in politics as a means for furthering individual welfare. A typical exposition of this belief was his impromptu oration to a group of Tory M.P.s who crowded into his parliamentary office on March 26, 1960, to celebrate the twentieth anniversary of his first election to the Commons: "I would remind you," he told them, "of all the discoveries made in medicine, science, sociology, and economics that must be translated in this House of Commons through legislation, before they can be put to use and work for the public good. Every advance in human welfare that is achieved must come through this translation, by the parliamentarian."

Diefenbaker was convinced that politics was the highest form of human activity. In an address to the 1952 convocation of McMaster University, in Hamilton, Ontario, he had advocated the establishment of academic courses for professional politicians. "One or more Canadian universities," he said, "might consider the establishment of a Chair of Politics, so that young men and women imbued with a desire to enter parliament or a legislature might take postgraduate courses, where practical politics would be studied."

In politics, more than in any other field of endeavour, men are changed by their positions. But Diefenbaker was remarkably consistent in his crusades. Many of his legislative achievements were based on ideas he had been propounding on the hustings for decades.

When Diefenbaker first came to Ottawa, after the 1940 election, he was shocked by the reactionary Toryism of his eastern colleagues. He regarded most of the Ontario members as men who believed that the function of government was to create the conditions in which big business can flourish. This, to him, amounted to a deliberate repeal of the twentieth century.

In three general elections Diefenbaker had watched his party being denied power because of its espousal of a philosophy which to him appeared hopelessly dated. He waged a sixteen-year battle to reorient the economic, social, and racial principles of his party, then finally smashed the hurdle himself in the 1957 campaign, by adopting liberal policies and ignoring Tory philosophy altogether.

Once in power, he transcended the most sacred of Tory tenets: that it is wrong for citizens to cast the responsibility for their personal prosperity onto the state. He thus shattered the basic belief of Canadian Conservatives, who had always opposed undue government interference with the capacities of the individual.

Diefenbaker's brand of Conservatism continued to stress his party's traditionally "unshakable belief" in the preservation and strengthening of the family, the community, and small business. But in a marked departure from Tory philosophy, he attempted to encourage the welfare of these social institutions through multiplying government handouts.

In the process, Diefenbaker committed his party to bringing the nation closer to a welfare state than any previous government of Canada. "We socialists," Douglas Fisher, the outspoken CCF/NDP member from Port Arthur, Ontario, remarked during the 24th Parliament, "find it quite simple in many cases to cast our vote for most of the measures that are brought in here. I have not been able to recognize in that monster party that flows around the sides of this chamber any clear-cut exposition of what I thought they were directly concerned with, that is free enterprise, private enterprise, and all that."

Diefenbaker's overriding consideration was to avoid the identification with Bay Street that had brought about the ruin of R.B. Bennett and hurled the Conservative Party into the political wilderness for twenty-two years.

It was obvious very early in the Diefenbaker Years that his was a Conservative government in name only. Instead of moving to promote and strengthen the country's financial community, Diefenbaker rushed in the opposite direction—harassing, curbing, and discouraging free enterprise at every turn. In the privacy of their clubs, dismayed executives clucked their disapproval of Diefenbaker and all his works as a fundamentally disruptive force. The right-wing Fort Erie *Letter Review* condemned Diefenbaker's concept of social justice for being "as revolutionary as Marxism, but perhaps a better name for it would be Robin Hoodism."

Diefenbaker was not swayed by these attacks. He never lost the conviction that he was fulfilling the historical purpose of his concept of Conservatism. He realized that some form of the welfare state would eventually come to Canada. By putting into effect his version of that welfare state, he thought he could crush the Liberal Party between his own group and the socialists. He tried to trap the Liberals into opposing his leftist legislation, to isolate them on his right.

This was difficult enough to do while trying at the same time to govern the country, but it also meant that Diefenbaker had to reorient the thinking and feeling within his own ranks. This struggle with the reactionaries in the Conservative Party—who made up the majority of its senior and most censorious element—was one of his ugliest problems while in office.

To outsiders the landslide proportions of his 1958 victory seemed to indicate that Diefenbaker could mould his party as he wished, but this was not the case. The Conservative parliamentary caucus was a motley crew ranging in the political spectrum from two former lieutenants of Adrien Arcand, the leader of the prewar fascist National Unity Party, to a left-wing Quebec M.P. who campaigned on a platform of state medicine, against "the evil power of the doctors."

Diefenbaker's main campaign to reform his party was directed over the heads of both his cabinet and his political organization, to the man he thought he understood best of all: "the average Canadian." He had a moral proclivity to be at one with this mythical creature and in nearly every speech repeated an incantation for his benefit. "My abiding interest is your interest; my guiding principle is the welfare of the average Canadian," he characteristically declared in the opening telecast of the 1962 election. In his final telecast of that campaign, broadcast on June 14, he tried to invoke his rapport with "the average Canadian" to support his stand on devaluation. He leaned into the camera, and earnestly asked his unseen audience: "Do you really think that the Government and I would bring in anything that would harm you—the average Canadian?"

Throughout his term of office, Diefenbaker catered to "the average Canadian" in almost everything he did. On November 15, 1961, for instance, he participated in a realistic civil defence exercise which called for him and six ministers to huddle in the basement of his official residence, and go through the motions of invoking the War Measures Act. Since it was obvious that if the practice alert had been real, the Prime Minister would have been killed, reporters asked him whether he really intended to remain at 24 Sussex Drive, if war came. "This is one of those decisions not subject to change," was the reply. "I would not take any more precaution than is available to the average Canadian."

Because "average Canadians" don't ride around in Cadillacs, Diefenbaker refused to use the luxury automobiles while campaigning. In Edmonton, during the 1962 election, he passed up four shiny limousines offered by the local Conservative committee, before climbing into a nondescript Chevrolet. (His aversion to Cadillacs dated from the 1957 campaign. While riding in one in Nanaimo, British Columbia, he noticed a butcher come out of his shop, cup his hands, and shout: "Here comes the Tories in their Caddies.")

To identify not only his office but himself with the aspirations of the legendary "average Canadian," Diefenbaker always attempted to ally his past personally with the area where he was speaking. This was an old habit. It never sounded more preposterous than in a speech he made in Halifax on July 11, 1947. Trying to establish his family contact with the Atlantic port, he earnestly proclaimed: "Had it not been for the trade winds between here and Newfoundland, my great-great-grandmother would have been born in Halifax."

Despite such absurdities, there was no doubt that he cared passionately for the large land he governed. He never revealed his patriotism more openly than on Dominion Day of 1961, when he rose in his parliamentary seat and declared: "I know there are some who feel a sense of embarrassment in expressing pride in their nation, perhaps because of the fear that they might be considered old-fashioned or parochial. I do not belong to that group. I realize that a warped and twisted nationalism is productive of tyranny. But a healthy loyalty and devotion to one's country constitutes a most fruitful inspiration in life." In a raspy tenor, Diefenbaker then led the House of Commons in the singing of "O Canada" and "God Save the Queen."

Although there was a strong strain of nationalism inherent in Diefenbaker's appeal and personality, it did not show up very clearly in his legislative efforts. Aside from establishing the Royal Commission on Publications, whose recommendations to save Canadian magazines he ignored, and calling federal-provincial meetings on Canadianizing the constitution and the adoption of a distinctive Canadian flag, he did nothing significant to further the cause of Canadian nationalism. Still, he believed in the need to build on the upper half of the continent a northern nationality that would become powerful enough to withstand absorption attempts by the United States, and it was in this passion that Diefenbaker saw his place in history.

Out of his personal analysis of Canadian history—particularly that of the Conservative Party—came Diefenbaker's conviction that instead of rallying behind contemporary leaders, Canada's Tories had, for generations, been expending their energies in an obsessive, unrequited quest for a reincarnation of Sir John A. Macdonald, the Party's founder and most successful prime minister.

While their beatification of him might have prompted little more than a thigh-slapping guffaw from the irreverent Sir John A., Canadian Conservatives had always been deadly earnest about exalting Macdonald's memory. At the Party's 1942 leadership convention, for instance, speaker after speaker supporting John Bracken's candidacy gravely reminded the delegates that Bracken's father had been one of the mourners at Sir John

A. Macdonald's funeral. Nobody mentioned that this, in fact, was the only previous connection that Bracken, a Progressive who had governed Manitoba for twenty years with Liberal support, actually had with the Conservative Party.

Once Diefenbaker had recognized the unquenchable longing of Canadian Conservatives for another Macdonald, he resolutely set about to cast himself in the role.

By fostering the myth that he was the twentieth-century embodiment of Sir John A.'s sober virtues, Diefenbaker was at first merely accommodating his ambitions to the collective dream of his followers. But gradually he inspired himself into thinking that Macdonald's magic mantle had indeed come to rest on his shoulders. Like most self-made men, he became adept at worshipping his creator.

To substitute for Macdonald's self-imposed destiny of giving Canada its nationhood, Diefenbaker chose as *his* destiny the economic emancipation of the North. "Just as Sir John A. led in the securing of the West," he repeatedly asserted during the 1958 campaign, "so we must win the new Northern Frontier."

The Party faithful across the country not unnaturally interpreted Diefenbaker's impressive electoral victories in 1957 and 1958 as proof that their patiently preserved fantasy of the day when another Macdonald would lead them out of the political wilderness had finally come to pass. Only a politician with some sort of hereditary link to Macdonald, they reasoned, could have succeeded so magnificently in basing his assumption of power on a direct appeal to the people.

Loyal Conservatives responded by sending Diefenbaker the many souvenirs of their Party founder that they and their fathers had collected and cherished. It was as though these well-intentioned donors hoped that, by surrounding the Prime Minister with physical reminders of his illustrious predecessor, some of Macdonald's flair for leadership might rub off.

That the expected alchemy failed to take place was certainly not due to any shortage of totems.

At his office in Parliament Hill's East Block, Diefenbaker worked under a portrait and beside a full-figure statuette of Macdonald. His inkwell had once belonged to Sir John A. In the Privy Council chamber, Diefenbaker sat in Macdonald's original chair, and dried the signature on his instructions with Sir John's spring blotter. One of Macdonald's mantel clocks timed his movements and had to be carted to whichever of his three Parliament Hill offices Diefenbaker was occupying. In his official residence, at 24 Sussex Drive, Diefenbaker encircled himself even more liberally with Macdonald relics, including parts of his library, many portraits of him, his easy chair, another clock, and a medallion given to a barber who had once shaved Sir John. The most valuable item in the collection was a copy, in Macdonald's own handwriting, of the original National Policy, drawn up on January 16, 1878, at a political meeting in Toronto's Shaftesbury Hall.[1]

During his years in office, Diefenbaker was surrounded by these trappings of another age, but his homage to Macdonald went far beyond the accumulation of physical objects. Every January 11 he commemorated Sir John A.'s death by leading a pilgrimage of Tory parliamentarians to lay a wreath at the foot of Macdonald's statue on Parliament Hill.

Allister Grosart's party machine capitalized on the Diefenbaker-Macdonald myth by issuing large, Tory-blue posters during the 1958 election which showed the Prime Minister standing before a framed portrait of Macdonald. The only text on the poster was:

TWO GREAT CONSERVATIVES:
SIR JOHN A. — RT. HON. JOHN D.

Diefenbaker's Macdonald cult probably reached its climax during a small election meeting at St. Boniface, Manitoba, in the 1962 campaign. Laurier Regnier, a local lawyer who had been elected as the Tory M.P. in 1958 after five previous defeats at the polls (he lost again in 1962), introduced Diefenbaker as the man who put Macdonald in the shade. "When history is written and the new generations read it, it probably will say that Sir John A. Macdonald was only the precursor of the Rt. Hon. John G. Diefenbaker," he told the audience of 150.

A much more praiseworthy and realistic historical concern of John Diefenbaker was his view of Canada not as a bi-racial, but as a multi-racial, nation. As the first Canadian prime minister who was not of purely British or French stock, Diefenbaker was genuinely sympathetic to the welfare of the two million immigrants who had crossed the Atlantic in the postwar years. "Being of mixed origin myself, I knew something, in my boyhood

days in Saskatchewan, of the feeling that was all too apparent in many
parts of Canada, that citizenship depended upon surnames, or even upon
blood counts," he told a meeting of eighty-five ethnic editors in Ottawa,
in the winter of 1961. "It was then, as a boy on the empty Prairies, that
I made the initial determination to eliminate this feeling that being a
Canadian was a matter of name and blood."

It was little wonder that Diefenbaker was sensitive and bitter about the
Canadian attitude to non-Anglo-Saxon names. His own was not infre-
quently abused. As late as February 1943, at a meeting of the Women's
Conservative Association of Toronto, Diefenbaker was urged to change
his name for the sake of his own political career. But he refused. "It's
'Dief' as in 'chief,'" he explained, "followed by 'en,' and then 'baker.'"

Before he became well known, Diefenbaker would tell speakers whose
job it was to introduce him that all they had to remember was that his
name rhymed with "Studebaker." Inevitably, in August 1953, at a Tory
rally in Vancouver, he was presented as "Mr. John Studebaker." Curiously
enough, he was dogged by such mistakes even after he became a national
figure. At St. Leon, Quebec, during the 1957 election campaign, he was
introduced to local Conservatives, by a Conservative, as "*Monsieur
Diefenburger.*" On March 15, 1958, at a small ceremony in West
Vancouver's Park Royal, an Indian chief called Mathias Joe presented an
Indian walking-stick to him, with the tribute: "John Diefenbacon, you
are the thunderbird of our country."

Diefenbaker was inordinately proud of the fact that in the 24th
Parliament, his Conservative contingent included representatives of eighteen different racial origins, including a Chinese Canadian (Douglas Jung,
Vancouver Centre) and a Lebanese (Ed Nasserden, Rosthern). One of
his chief accomplishments within the Conqervative Party was to open its
hierarchy to all races and religions—a state of affairs that had not always
been true.

Diefenbaker enjoyed speaking to audiences of varied ethnic origin,
always stressing his sympathy with their aims, and underlining his fervent
anti-communism. In a typical utterance, on July 9, 1961, at a commem-
orative rally marking the hundredth anniversary of the death of nineteenth-century anti-Czarist Ukrainian poet Taras Shevchenko,
Diefenbaker, quivering with emotion, intoned this tribute: "As I read this
thrilling and often heart-rending story, I wonder how the Ukrainian race

and nation . . . survived. There is no simple answer. But . . . there is the hand of a Divine Providence preserving an amazing people for eventual deliverance. . . . If I did not believe that, I would not believe in the establishment of Ukrainian nationhood . . . in God's good time."

The emotional impact of such appeals was difficult to exaggerate. Petro Wolyniak, editor of *New Days*, a Ukrainian monthly published in Toronto, described the scene in this moving eulogy: "The Prime Minister stood as if cast in bronze. I wondered if he would shed a tear. I saw that he was moved no less than I, that he felt as each of us that this was no ordinary singing, that this was a people's prayer to the great martyr of the Ukrainian earth. . . . Well, I thought to myself, praise be to God that we have as a leader of Canada a human being not only of great political wisdom, able to foresee many things, but a person of great heart and soul as well."

Diefenbaker's speeches raised the hopes of Canada's Ukrainian community to such a pitch that the editor of *Ukrainsky Visti* (Ukrainian News) suggested that Ottawa should immediately begin negotiations for the establishment of diplomatic recognition of an independent Ukraine.

One of the unfortunate side-effects of Diefenbaker's presentation of himself as the only Canadian political leader with the courage and the ideological stamina to stand up to the Kremlin was the Conservative Party's attempt to smear Lester Pearson as being "soft on communism." It was an undercover campaign that generally took the form of snide insinuations which, because they were not open accusations, could not effectively be contradicted.

The defamation of Pearson dated back to the 1958 campaign. One curious incident was a letter written by Dr. Joseph A. Sullivan, a long-time friend of Diefenbaker, who was named to the Senate early in the Conservative regime. The letter was sent to Father William Muckle, pastor of Our Lady of Lourdes Church in the Toronto constituency of Rosedale, where David Walker was running as the Conservative candidate. Dated February 24, 1958, it read:

> Dear Father Muckle,
> I am writing you on behalf of the Conservative candidate in the coming election on March 31, 1958. I have no hesitancy in endorsing Mr. David Walker.

It is my considered and firm belief that as a result of that distinguished statesman and Christian gentleman, the Rt. Hon. Louis St. Laurent, that the enclosed clipping reveals my own thinking.

I can assure you that with the Catholic minister of justice we have in the Hon. E. David [sic] Fulton and the other members of the party, to which I heartily subscribe, that you can rest assured that there will be no possibility of any left-wing tendencies in this present government.

I trust that you will accept these remarks in sincerity and a true Christian belief.

> Yours sincerely,
> Senator Sir Joseph A. Sullivan,[2]
> M.D., FRCS *ENG.*, QHS, KCSG.

With the letter, written on official Senate stationery but mailed from the Senator's St. George Street office in Toronto, was enclosed a transcript of an editorial in the Rightist American publication *National Review*, which claimed that Pearson had been running "the Soviet Union's errands" and that only the restraints of Mr. St. Laurent had kept him in line.

Despite such excesses, the Conservative Party under Diefenbaker's leadership was genuinely concerned with the rights of ethnic minorities. The man from Prince Albert undoubtedly was the first Canadian prime minister to understand the urgent problems of the immigrants.

This understanding flowed from his concept of "social justice"—one of the pillars of Diefenbaker's political philosophy. He believed passionately that it is the duty of the undeserving rich to support the deserving poor, of whom he elected himself the articulate representative. He defined "social justice" as "the concept of fairness to each and fairness to all," and came closest to clarifying what he meant during a House of Commons debate on March 4, 1960, when he broke into a routine agricultural supply motion to attack the deficiency payment demands of western farm leaders. "We recognize," he said, "the principle that public money should be used to relieve distress on the basis of need, and any scheme which gives no help, or very little, to those who are most in need, is socially indefensible."

The idea of "social justice," which Diefenbaker never really managed to interpret meaningfully to the voters, was at the very root of his political persuasion. He tried to appropriate to himself the cry from every underdeveloped sector of the country's population—a cry not for charity or special privileges, but for an equalization of opportunity within the Canadian confederation.

It was Diefenbaker's privately held conviction that neither Christian charity nor free enterprise is adequate to rescue the underprivileged. The gap between the two seemed to him to require a comprehensive contributory system covering the aged, the unemployed, the sick, the injured, and the otherwise underprivileged, with the state guaranteeing assistance where adequate facilities were not available.

Diefenbaker seemed to believe that such a system would by no means rob the individual of the chance to become a proud, participating member of a self-reliant society. His insistence that no government had the right to interfere with the sanctity of the family unit had its basis in the Judaic rather than Christian tradition.

This was an important, if subtle, departure from the social welfare policies of Mackenzie King. While King's social welfare measures were designed as handouts to fill demonstrated needs, Diefenbaker claimed to be giving Canadians help that it was their right to expect. It was social *welfare* to get emergency protection against the hazards of modern life; but it was social *justice* to get help that brought the individual citizen to the same economic level as his fellow Canadians.

While Diefenbaker was never able to raise government transfer payments to the astronomical proportions required to implement fully his concept of social justice, his administration did increase welfare payments by 100 percent—from $885 million in 1957 to $1,970 millions in 1962. (Roughly $160 millions of this jump, however, was accounted for by benefits paid under the Hospital and Diagnostic Act, given royal assent on April 1, 1957, two months before the Conservatives took office. Another $100 millions was directly attributable to population increases during the Diefenbaker Years.)

Under Diefenbaker, Canada surpassed even the welfare statism of the United Kingdom in the proportion of individual incomes accounted for by government transfer payments in the form of unemployment insurance, family allowances, veterans' pensions, and the like. By the time Diefenbaker had been in power three years some 14,800,000 Canadians—about 80 percent of the population—were receiving direct government aid in one of its many forms.

Notes

1. The recording secretary at the meeting was a young reporter for the Guelph *Herald* called Acton Burrows, later Manitoba's first Deputy Minister of Agriculture. He willed the document to his son Aubrey, a Toronto publisher who, just before he died in 1957, sent it to Diefenbaker. The statuette in Diefenbaker's office, the work of Louis Hébert, was donated by Major E.G. Cahoon, a retired road engineer living at Alymer, Quebec, who inherited it from his father, a Toronto painting contractor who had been the local manager of Macdonald's election campaigns. The clock in Diefenbaker's office came from Sir Joseph Pope's descendants. The easy chair was a present from Mrs. Walter Evans of Waterloo, Ontario, whose father had been Macdonald's law partner. The medallion was sent in by Frank Pethick of Bowmanville, Ontario, who got it in 1891, when, as an apprentice barber in Toronto, he shaved Sir John. He recalled that when he took hold of the Prime Minister's nose to scrape his upper lip, Macdonald quipped: "You're the only man who can lead me by the nose that way."

2. The "Sir" is a papal knighthood.

BEFORE WE WERE FAMOUS

JOHN GLASSCO

From *Memoirs of Montparnasse* (1970)

Memoirs of Montparnasse *is Canada's other Lost Generation memoir. Like* That Summer in Paris, *it apparently was stimulated by the suicide of Ernest Hemingway in 1961. When* Memoirs *appeared in 1970 the author, John Glassco, claimed that the manuscript had been written in 1932-33 when he was hospitalized with tuberculosis, set aside, and then discovered in the 1960s and published almost without changes. Indeed, one of the stylistic devices of the book is that it purports to be written by an author on the verge of premature death looking back at his youth. Thanks to some scholarly detective work by Philip Kokotailo, we now know that* Memoirs *was written for the most part in the 1960s, probably in response to Morley Callaghan's memoir. The people and events which appear in the book are only "based on" life as Glassco lived it in Paris. As a result, some critics have called the book fiction, while others prefer "non-fiction novel." No matter how undependable the chronology or the dialogue or the incidents described, Glassco's book remains an engrossing evocation of an actual place and time, literary Paris in the 1920s, and an actual personality, his own.*

John Glassco was born in Montreal in 1909. His family belonged to the city's English-speaking business elite and he was educated at fashionable private schools and at McGill University. Early in 1928 Glassco went to Paris with his close friend Graeme Taylor to escape his family and to pursue the literary life. He remained in Europe until 1932 when he returned to Montreal to get treatment for a serious case of tuberculosis. A poet, essayist, pseudonymous pornographer, translator, and editor, he was an integral part of Montreal's English-language literary community until his death in 1981.

The following selection from Memoirs of Montparnasse *describes Glassco's meeting with the American writer Robert McAlmon.*

Spring was laving the city in warmth and pale gold.

"I have sad news for you two gentlemen," said the proprietor of the Hotel Jules-César. "I must raise the price of your room. This cuts me to the heart, for I understand you are men of letters and I am a great admirer of literature in any language. From now on your room will cost you an extra ten francs a day—to cover my increased expenses."

"But surely," said Graeme, "your expenses will not be so high now, with no heating?"

"Put it in a new way, then. We are all caught up in the inexorable law of supply and demand. It is the month of May, you see, and the Americans are coming."

Making a survey of hotel prices in the neighbourhood, we found they had all been raised for the same reason. This was discouraging. We saw ourselves forced to spend much less on food or drink, and perhaps on both. That evening we met Daphne Berners at the Dôme. She was looking as handsome as ever in the tailored suit and fedora hat.

"Angela and I are going tomorrow to live with an old hake in Marly," she said. "She wants me to paint her portrait—in renaissance costume. I can stretch the job out for two or three months because we both love the green grass and the birds, not to mention all the good country food and the nice fresh milk and cheese. Do you want to sublet our studio?"

We agreed immediately and moved our trunks there the next day.

The place looked even better by daylight. The little strip of garden facing the row of studios now turned out to be filled with friezes and sculptures discarded by former tenants who had either left them in payment of rent or found them too heavy to move. They were of many styles and periods. There was a portrait-bust of a man in a frock-coat with his palm supporting his chin in a fine, melting, bourgeois-romantic attitude; a bas-relief of the Three Graces in which, contrary to custom, they were all seen from behind; and an astonishing sculpture representing a pair of standing Eskimos locked in the act of coitus, like a double peanut, and giving a powerful impression of unity. Opposite the studio was a ramshackle booth housing three stand-up toilets.

The studio itself combined beauty and inconvenience. There was no electricity, only a cold-water wash-basin, and the roof leaked badly though fortunately not on the beds. But it was about 40 feet by 60, 20 feet high at least, with a full skylight and a whole north wall made up of waist-high windows. To us, who had been cooped up in the windowless little room in the Jules-César all winter, it brought a message of physical freedom. For furniture there was a big battered desk with a leather top, a round table to eat at, four comfortable swaybacked chairs, some tattered tapestry curtains flanking the alcove, and two double beds stuffed with straw. There were a few unfinished portraits still in canvas stretchers on the roughly plastered walls—all of them, Daphne told us, by Lady Duff Twisden, who later figured as the insufferable heroine of *The Sun Also Rises*. The only complication, it turned out when we signed the inventory, was that everything in the studio belonged to different people—most of the furniture to Janet Flanner, the hangings to Dr. Maloney, and the beds to a man called Boomhower, whom we never met; the only things Daphne owned were the collection of half-broken dishes, the pots and pans, the gramophone, and a great adjustable cheval-glass. We never knew who owned the lease, and merely paid the rent to a concierge, an old woman called Madame Hernie who lived across the street and spent all her time illuminating the entries in a folio-sized album devoted to the records of her family funerals.

This place was to be our home on and off for the next year and a half. It was here that I tried seriously to write for the first time, here I brought my two or three girls, and here I met the woman with whom I at last fell in love and whom, however miserable the outcome of that love, I shall always remember in this setting as she undressed one night in a luminous haze of gaslight and moonbeams before we threw ourselves in ecstasy on one of Mr. Boomhower's straw-stuffed beds. It was the theatre of my youth.

The rue Broca was a great deal farther from Montparnasse than the Jules-César, but the studio was cheaper and more comfortable than the hotel-room, and the exercise of walking a mile to the quarter every evening did us both good. We had already had quite enough of the Right Bank and had long since given up the luxury of taxis. We now explored the working quarter to the east, the network of streets running off in all directions from the rue de la Glacière, the home of unusual occupations and trades: of the producers of catskin waistcoats, fake antiques, glass eyes, woodworking machinery, and martinets for punishing children. We learned the elements of cookery, bought a shopping-basket, and came home weighed down with wine and cheese. Waking at eleven o'clock we had a view of sunstruck steeples, chimney-pots, and the greenery of the neighbouring Ursuline Convent, and every day on our way to Montparnasse we passed the handsome medieval walls of the city madhouse and the Santé prison. Graeme had resumed planning *The Flying Carpet* and I was writing the third chapter of this book when I received another letter from my father.

"You have now been almost two months in Paris," he wrote, "and after further consideration of your project of a literary career I must once again express my disapproval. As you well know, I altogether disapprove of literature as a futile and unmanly pursuit and one that cannot but lead to poverty and unhappiness. I accordingly advise you that your allowance from now on will be halved."

This was a blow. However, fifty dollars a month was enough for us to get along for a while, and the rent was paid for three months.

"Perhaps," said Graeme, "one of us should get some kind of work. I'll go to the *Chicago Tribune* and see if they need a proofreader."

But they did not. In the evening we decided to go to the counter of the Dôme and drink until things looked rosier.

Diana Tree was there. She had by now severed her connection with her surrealist lover and was living alone. She was talking of Raymond Duncan, a walking absurdity who dressed in an ancient handwoven Greek costume and wore his hair in long braids reaching to his waist, adding, on ceremonial occasions, a fillet of bay-leaves.

"He's really not a bad kind of person," she said. "He has a heart of gold and some of his designs for weaving are very chaste. Damn it all, he is sincere."

"Rats," said a small, handsome, carelessly dressed man standing beside her. "He's an exhibitionist with nothing to show. He's trying to prove he's something besides being Isadora's brother, and he's not. His milieu is the bourgeoisie. Yah!"

"Have you met Robert McAlmon?" said Diana. "Bob, these are the boys from Montreal."

He looked at us with humorous contempt. "Have a drink," he said. "Di has been telling me about you. You're Canadians. I was in the Canadian army for a while during the war but I deserted."

I had heard of him only as a minor legend, as a man saddled with the nickname of "Robber McAlimony," which he had gained by marrying a wealthy woman and then living alone and magnificently on an allowance from her multimillionaire father. I was at once impressed by his charm, loneliness, and bitterness, touched by his vanity and refreshed by his rudeness; even at this first meeting he was impressive through a total absence of attitude or artifice. I had not yet read anything he had written.

After a few more drinks he proposed going to the bar of the Coupole. "I've a charge account there," he said. "Paying for drinks is depressing. Come on, kids!"

At the Coupole we switched from vermouth to brandy. McAlmon's own capacity for alcohol was astounding; within the next half-hour he drank half a dozen double whiskies with no apparent effect. His conversation, consisting of disjointed expletives and explosions of scorn, was fascinating in its anarchy. He admired no writing of any kind, either ancient or modern; all government was a farce; people were fools or snobs. He spoke of his friends with utter contempt, insulted Diana and laughed at Graeme and me—but all with such an absence of conviction that one could not take him seriously. He was obviously enjoying himself. I soon became hungry—for Graeme and I, following our new plan of saving money, had gone without lunch.

"We'll have dinner here," Bob said, and at once ordered a *canard pressé* and two bottles of Moselle.

The duck arrived half an hour later and there was barely enough for three. Diana, however, had made a point of ordering three double ice-cream sodas from the American soda-fountain to finish off with. "The boys," she said, "have good appetites. That duck, McAlmon, is just a snob dish. You always order it. Will you tell me for God's sake why?"

He threw back his head. "It makes no demands on me. It has an elegant quality and I can face eating it and seeing other people eating it. Now let's all have another drink."

"Not for me," she said. "I have to get back to my love-child in St. Cloud, bless his black little heart." She turned to me as she went out:

"Good night, don't drink too much, and watch out for the Great White Father."

McAlmon now turned his wit against Graeme and me. I had already noticed his small thin mouth and piercing stare, but it was clear he was far from being the kind of invert whose predilection shapes his whole personality.

"What did Diana say to you?" he said, drawing his chair up.

"Not to drink too much."

"Rats, what you two need is a good drunk." He pushed between us, putting his arms around our shoulders. "Come out of yourselves. Be extrovert. You especially," he pinched my ear. "Forget all this turd about the literary life for a while. It doesn't suit you at all."

I nodded. He was rich, famous, and extremely amusing, and moreover I liked him enormously.

It soon appeared that his chosen role was to be the fatherly or avuncular, and I began to hope he was more vain of being seen with young men than actually covetous of their favours. This hope was dispelled by a burly, moonfaced man, dressed in baggy tweeds with his necktie clewed by a gold pin, who came noisily into the bar and greeted our table with a loud, "Well, Bob, up to your old tricks again?"

McAlmon's sallow face turned pink. "If it isn't Ernest, the fabulous phony! How are the bulls?"

"And how is North America McAlmon, the unfinished Poem?" He leaned over and pummelled McAlmon in the ribs, grinning and blowing every beery breath over the table. "Room for me here, boys?"

"It's only Hemingway," said Bob loudly to both of us. "Pay no attention and he may go away."

Hemingway gave a lopsided grin and moved into a seat at the next table. He was better looking than his pictures, but his eyes were curiously small, shrewd and reticent, like a politician's, and he had a moustache that was plainly designed to counteract the fleshy roundness of his jowls, though it did not. I found him almost as unattractive as his short stories—those studies in tight-lipped emotionalism and volcanic senti-mentality that, with their absurd plots and dialogue, give me the effect of a gutless Prometheus who has tied himself up with string.

"See anything of Sylvia these days?" he asked diffidently.

"The Beach? Rats, no! We had a row last year. I don't like old women anyway."

"No one could accuse you of that, Bob."

"Leave my friends out of this."

"Me? You brought them in. Anyway, go to hell." Hemingway got up and moved heavily to the bar.

"Watch," said Bob. "Pretty soon he'll be twisting wrists with some guy at the bar. Trying to establish contact. Ah ha ha ha! and he never will. Just a poor bugger from the sticks. But believe me, he's going places, he's got a natural talent for the public eye, has that boy. He's the original Limelight Kid, just you watch him for a few months. Wherever the limelight is, you'll find Ernest with his big lovable boyish grin, making hay. Balls. We'd better go to the rue de Lappe. I crave genuine depravity."

He herded us outside and into an open taxi. The night was like velvet, the spring sky full of stars, the air soft and humid and full of the exciting smell of city dust laid by sprinklers. My stomach, at last assimilating the mixture of vermouth, brandy, duck, wine, and ice-cream soda, was soon settled by the motion of the wheels. We went down the boulevard Raspail, along St. Germain, crossed the Pont Sully to reach the Bastille, and then slid into a mysterious, sinister street lit here and there by the lights of little *dancings*. We stopped outside the Bal des Chiffoniers.

"Now watch out, boys," said Bob in a conspiratorial tone. "Don't get high-hat with anyone. If they want to dance with you, go ahead. But don't let them steer you into the can or you'll get raped."

I liked the Bal des Chiffoniers. Unlike the Petite Chaumière it was brilliantly lit and the atmosphere was genuine. These pale weedy youths in shabby tight-fitting suits, sporting so many rings and bracelets, these heavy men with the muscles of coal-heavers, rouged, powdered, and lipsticked, these quiet white-haired elders with quivering hands and heads and the unwinking stare of the obsessed—all conveyed the message of an indomitable vitality, a quenchless psychic urge. Never had I felt the force of human desire projected with such vigour as by these single-minded devotees of the male; and I felt at the same time that this very desire, barely tolerated and so often persecuted by society, had already made its tragic marriage of convenience with the forces of a stupid criminality simply because both were equally proscribed and hunted down. These profound thoughts were interrupted by Bob calling for champagne.

Even before it arrived Graeme had been seized upon as dance partner by an odd creature in a silver-laced black velvet doublet and shoulder-length ringlets, who spoke in a strange archaic French because, as he said, he was reproducing the graces, at once virile and baroque, of the age of Louis XIII. For my own part I was soon waltzed around the floor by a coal-black Negro of ferocious appearance who never uttered a word but danced so well that I even began to enjoy myself. The vertigo of the French waltz, whoever one's partner, is always superior to that induced by alcohol.

When the band stopped the Negro led me back silently to our table, where Bob was sitting and drinking a magnum of *mousseux*. He was about to leave when Bob told him to sit down.

"I'll bet you're an American," he said in English. "Come on. Aren't you?"

The Negro grinned shyly. "Sure I am, you guessed it. Name of Jack Relief, but trying to pass for a foreigner. I thank you kindly and I *will* join you for a few minutes, being solitary here. My, but don't your friend here dance good! A petal, a feather, a regular pussycat on his footsies. Can I offer you a genuine Cuban cigarillo?" He presented a silver case. Bob did not smoke, but Graeme and I took the thin brown cigarettes and lit them. The aroma was delicious but the smoke was curiously perfumed.

"This is a nice place," I said. "Do you come here often?"

"Sure, I admire the atmosphere. It has colour. I'm a great lover of colour in any form. The colour of this place is, to speak right out of my imagination, a kind of yellow-green."

"No," said Bob. "It's mauve, a turd-brown mauve."

"Perhaps you are speaking, sir, in a popular or accepted way of verbiage. When I identified it as yellow-green I was employing the subjective spectrum of Mallarmé or possibly Rimbaud. In that acception, I would beg to differ, though such impressions are always differential and a matter of dispute."

"I see you're literary," said Bob. "Who is your favourite author?"

"Shakespeare," said Jack Relief without hesitation. "And after him Thomas Hardy."

"Hardy? No, no. Too grim, too rustic. He goes around blowing out the candles of the human spirit."

"Perhaps he is too Protestant a Jansenist," said Relief. "But what breezes blow through his books! Reading Hardy, I feel the wind of Egdon Heath blowing against my poor cheeks. It is the breath of fate, which is also the breath of freedom. We are all involved in that wind."

I suddenly realized I was nauseated. The room seemed to be whirling and dipping in its blaze of lights. The Negro's cigarette must have been fortified. I managed to get to the door. Graeme followed me, wearing a worried look. I was aware of Bob paying for the *mousseux* and hurrying out to join us.

"He should have some coffee," he said, pushing me out of the Bal des Chiffoniers and leading the way to a corner café. We stood at the zinc counter and drank boiling coffee laced with chicory. I began to feel better at once.

"You made a hit with the dinge," Bob was saying.

"I'm sorry I broke the party up. You never managed to dance. And we didn't even finish the champagne."

"Don't let that worry you. Come on, Graeme. A whisky, you and me. I'll bet we're both Presbyterians. My old man was a minister."

"So is mine," said Graeme. "He never had a church though, he went out on horseback converting the Indians in the Yukon."

"Rats! They were all converted long ago."

"No, not from paganism. He was converting them from Catholicism."

"How did he make out?"

"I think he re-baptized about a hundred. But of course they all went back to Rome eventually."

"You should tell Ernest about that, Graeme. He's a Catholic and an Indian lover. Christ, I bet he'd make a story out of it. Another of his constipated stories. To hell with literature. Let's go to Bricktop's. How about you, sweetie-pie?"

"I'm fine," I said. "Let's go to Bricktop's. Where is it?"

"It's a long, long way, but the night is young." Holding on to the bar with both hands, he began to dance with his feet. "A long, long way to the Place Pigalle, where the pimps are playing, the whores are swaying, the fairies saying, 'Won't you dance with me, prance with me, be my pal on the Place Pigalle.'" He kicked his legs in a wild splay-footed shuffle. "Come on, where's a cab?"

We found another open taxi at the Bastille and drove along the wide bright boulevards—Beaumarchais, Magenta, and Rochechouart—until we arrived in the blaze of lights of the spider-web of tourist traps, clip-joints and dives around the Place Pigalle. I had never been here before, and though the way the lights staggered up and down the steep hill was attractive I found the atmosphere of the whole district depressing, with the pimps slouching at every corner, the touts outside the boîtes yelling at the passing groups of soldiers and tourists, and every now and then a passing busload of middle-aged American women peeping out from the sectioned windows. We stood at the counter of the Café Pigalle and had some brandy while Bob snuffed the air like a hound.

"God, what a wonderful smell this quarter has!" he said. "Just like a county fair back home. It's got a special quality too, so phony you can hardly believe it. The triumph of the fake, the old come-on, the swindle—it's marvellous, it's just like life."

After being skillfully short-changed for our drinks we went down the hill, fighting off the whores who came flapping out of the darkness at us like birds, until we reached a leather-covered door studded with brass nails and with a small round *vasistdas* at eye-level.

"Why, Mistah Bob!" cried a big Negro in a scarlet-and-gold uniform who threw open the door at once. "Come in, Mistah Bob! And how you feelin'? Bricktop baby! Come! Here's the big spendin' man himself."

A small, plump, glowing Negress with a bush of dyed red hair ran up and embraced Bob, twittering, "Bob, honey, so *good* to see you! Just so *good*. You and your young friends want to sit at the bar, huh? Hey you, Houston, get off that stool and give some room to the clients, you hear me? Get behind that bar where you belong!"

A small grinning black man in a white jacket slipped under the bar and came up on the other side.

"First round is on the house, Houston," said Bricktop. "Anything the boys desire, except the champagne."

We had three of Houston's specials. This was a long drink of such potency that the first sip seemed to blow the top of my head off.

Bob, already restive in familiar surroundings, began eyeing the people at the tables with his usual air of challenge and hostility. Bricktop slid up beside Graeme and whispered to him, "You make Bob behave till I'm done singing, eh baby? I can tell he primed for mischief. I got some very prominent people here tonight, real big folks from show business, and I don't want Bob to insult them right off."

"Right," said Graeme. He was always impressive in any situation calling for firmness and quick thinking, and I admired his way of distracting Bob, who already seemed prepared to launch from his stool and accost a party in ball-gowns and tail-coats, among whom I recognized Beatrice Lillie.

"Listen, McAlmon," he said, "just why do you run down every book written in the last thirty years? I agree with you about Hemingway, he's not even a serious writer, but what about Fitzgerald? Now isn't *Gatsby* a good book, perhaps a great book?"

"*Great? Great?* Jesus, what is all that snob-crap compared to *War and Peace*?"

"*War and Peace*? A movie by DeMille. A blown-up mural full of characters from a comic strip. An epic for morons."

Bob gave his lipless smile. "You know, Graeme, you're right eloquent. You may even have something there. I thought you were just another Presbyterian from the sticks, but I'm changing my mind as of now. Anyway, the only people I don't like are the bankers. Are you with me there, Graeme?"

"All the way. My brother's a banker. Ssh . . . "

Bricktop had begun to sing. Her voice, small but beautifully true, tracing a vague pattern between song and speech, fitting itself to the sprung rhythms of a piano playing by an old and dilapidated Negro, seemed to compose all by itself a sentiment at once nostalgic and fleeting, anonymous and personal, inside the song itself; her voice followed rather than obeyed the music, wreathing an audible arabesque around her; the melody, something banal by Berlin or Porter, was transformed and carried into a region where the heard became the overheard and the message one of enchanting sweetness and intimacy.

The polite ripple of applause seemed to infuriate Bob. "Christ, you'd think it was some leached-out phony like Alice Faye singing," he said. "These bastards don't know what it's all about. Balls, balls!" he suddenly yelled. "Ladies and gentlemen, did you know you were dead? I'm speaking to *you*—yes, you collection of pukes and poops right over there. Just listen for a moment. I'm part of the show here. You're getting my act for nothing."

Someone began to laugh. This put Bob in a good humour. He stood up and bowed with extraordinary grace. "You, my friends, have the luck to be listening to an old-fashioned sot. I speak to you out of my subconscious. Some of you seem to be English: I hate the English. Some of you look like Americans: I hate you too. And if there are any Canadians among you, let me say that I hate all Canadians, only not quite so much as Yanks and limeys."

"Hear, hear!" said Beatrice Lillie. "The maple leaf forever."

"Down with the maple leaf!" cried Bob in a sudden fury. "Bugger the American eagle! This is the age of the rat and the weed, get that through your thick skulls! You're being pushed out, boys, and I'm glad to see it. You're nice and decorative, sure, you've got a nice way of brushing your hair, but you've got to go. It's in the stars. The writing is on the outhouse wall—"

"Now Bob," said Bricktop, sliding up to him. "Please Bob, you keep this clean. Come dance with me, honey, and we give all these people time to study out what you just said. Baby, that was a real message! Walter—music now, please. *Shlo*, huh?"

She pulled him onto the dance floor as the old Negro played the opening bars of *Chloë*. Bob, holding Bricktop at arm's length in country style, flapped his feet awkwardly; the alcohol seemed to be at last affecting his balance. But when the music stopped he jumped back nimbly onto his stool, drained his glass and called for a whisky. Bricktop signed to Houston.

Bob downed half the fresh drink and stood up again. "I'm going to sing! This is an aria from my Chinese opera." He raised his arms, opened his mouth wide and began a hideous, wordless, toneless screaming. The effect was both absurd and painful; a dead silence fell over the room. Reeling against his stool, his head raised to the ceiling like a dog, yowling, he suddenly seemed to be no longer a drunken nuisance but a man who had gone mad; he was, I thought, actually either out of his mind or trying to become so. Suddenly he turned white, staggered, looked around wildly, and fell back into the arms of the big dinner-coated Negro who had appeared at the bar.

"Gentlemen, you give me a hand with Mistah Bob, huh?" said the bouncer jovially.

"The taxi's outside," said Bricktop. "Boys, we just done give him a little quietener. Nothing to hurt. He be all right in a half an hour. You give him my love when he wakes up."

Bob was carefully carried out and lifted into the taxi.

"Where'll we go now?" I asked Graeme.

"We might get something to eat at the Coupole."

Bob was still unconscious when we reached the Coupole. Lifting him out we saw a two-man bicycle patrol coming along the street. These police, whose job is to survey the city's night life, are the oldest and most brutal of their kind, a different kind from the smirking, bowing, multilingual traffic police on the Right Bank. Remembering that neither Graeme nor I had identity cards, I felt my stomach turning over.

"Ho, ho, what's this?" said the first policeman, stopping his bicycle.

"It's our friend," said Graeme quickly in English, gesturing. "An American, he's a drunk, *eever. Americain, eever.*"

"Oh ho! A drunken American, eh?" He got off his bicycle, stepped up to Bob whom we were holding up, slapped his cheeks, felt his pulse, and fingered his clothes. "It's an American, all right. They're all Americans. This is not our affair. Good night, gentlemen."

"My God," I said. "Suppose we'd answered in French."

"I thought you were going to. That settles it, we're going down to the Préfecture tomorrow and get identity cards. Now let's get Mistah Bob into the bar."

He was remarkably light and it was no trouble getting him through the double doors and onto one of the banquettes. I was arranging his hands over his chest when Gaston came running.

"What have you done to him? Good God, he is not dead? He owes me three thousand francs!"

Bob began snoring loudly.

"Thanks be to heaven," said Gaston. "What would you like to drink?"

"Two orders of scrambled eggs and two large white coffees."

When the food came Bob was still snoring, but his sleep was broken by the occasional groan or curse; the Mickey Finn was wearing off. His eyes, cavernous under the ragged eyebrows, began to open and close, his mouth to twitch. I put my hand on his forehead and found it covered with cold sweat.

"Let's try to get some brandy into him," said Graeme. "It can't do any harm."

"He's been drinking whisky for the last six hours, perhaps he shouldn't change."

He was already trying to sit up when Graeme put a glass of neat whisky under his long Barrymore nose. The reaction was immediate: his hand came up and knocked it to the floor.

"Poison!" he yelled. "No more poison! Give me some mother's milk."

Supported by Graeme's arm around his shoulder he drank deeply from our jug of hot milk, shook his head like a dog, and then began to weep quietly.

"Come on, Bob," I said. "We'll take you home."

"I have no home. No home."

"Well, then, where are you staying?"

"I wouldn't have a home if you paid me. Where's my sister?"

"Look, haven't you got a hotel or something?"

"I'm an exile." The tears were streaming down his cheeks.

They began turning out the lights in the bar.

"We'd better take him back to the studio," said Graeme. "If we leave him here they'll just put him out in the street."

"Come on, Bob," I said. "Let's all go to our place."

"No, no," he muttered. "Take me to the Fitzroy Tavern—Fitzroy Square, just around the corner."

But he made no resistance when we supported him into a taxi. On the way to the rue Broca he seemed to fall asleep again and we carried him through the garden and into the studio. The first cold light of dawn was coming through the windows as we laid him on my bed, took off his shoes, jacket and tie and covered him with a blanket. Waking uncomfortably a few hours later, however, I found he had made his way between Graeme and me and I began to wonder if he had been quite as helpless as he appeared to be in the Coupole bar.

NORWAY HOUSE

HEATHER ROBERTSON

From *Reservations Are for Indians* (1970)

The late 1960s was a turning point for the administration of Indian affairs in Canada. In June, 1969, the Liberal government of Pierre Elliot Trudeau released its infamous White Paper on Indian policy. Among other things, this document proposed to assimilate Native people once and for all. The White Paper elicited furious opposition from most Aboriginal people, who strongly objected to losing their traditional rights and privileges. It sparked a flurry of political activism by both Aboriginals and White reformers. For a while, at least, Indians jumped to the top of the political agenda in the country.

It was in this context that twenty-seven-year-old journalist, Heather Robertson, published her account of life on Western Canadian reserves, Reservations Are for Indians. *For many readers the book was their first exposure to the Third World conditions in which many Aboriginal people lived. The book presents the view of an engaged outsider who has visited "Indian Country" and has returned with an eyewitness report of conditions there. An example of the "new journalism" of the period, it eschews cool objectivity in favour of a passionate, first-person narrative.*

Heather Robertson was, in her own words, "a recent university graduate steeped in the academic social analysis of the New Left and a rookie reporter with The Winnipeg Tribune" *when she began her research for* Reservations *in 1965. Since that time she has become one of Canada's leading writers of popular history.*

185

Her trilogy of historical novels—Willy, Lily, *and* Igor—*fabricates a version of the Mackenzie King years.*

The following selection from Reservations Are for Indians *describes the reserve at Norway House in northern Manitoba.*

The River

Lake Winnipeg spills over, at its northeastern tip, to form the Nelson River which flows, with increasing momentum, through a series of lakes, until it empties into Hudson Bay at York Factory.

The lake is messy about dying. Much of it just oozes away for miles on either side of the Nelson's banks, forming great stretches of muskeg covered with scraggly spruce, scrub and coarse grass. A few rocky promontories jut out from the squishy morass. A man can sink up to his waist or, in fact, out of sight in this bog when it is wet in the spring. It can grow grass, but is almost always too wet to allow cattle to eat it or men to mow it. In the summer, the muskeg produces clouds of mosquitoes which rise like a pestilence from stagnant pools.

Here, the Nelson is filled with islands, large and small. On these islands, for hundreds, perhaps thousands, of years, Indians camped. On one of the rocky promontories, just downstream from where the lake empties into the Nelson, the Hudson's Bay Company built a fort and, shortly after, James Evans, Methodist, built a church. Around these two foreign objects, these two intruders, the tissues of a community formed—a school, log cabins, frame houses.

Until the coming of the railroad to western Canada, Norway House was the heart and head of the western fur trade. All water routes to Hudson Bay from Alberta and Saskatchewan led to Norway House.

Norway House (called that because The Bay post was built by a couple of Norwegian carpenters) was a booming frontier town, a crossroads. Settlers and supplies were channelled south down the lake to Red River. Explorers and traders went west. Furs were shipped north. The community, if it could be called that, was based on the principle of transience. Since everyone, except for a small handful of executives, clergymen, and Indians, was going somewhere. Norway House made sense only as a junction, a refuelling stop, a jumping-off place. It produced nothing itself.

Some of these people dropped off to form a kind of scum, sediment, which clung to the river's banks and islands. Bay men married Indian women, built houses and raised families. The Indians came to depend more and more on the post and settled more closely around it. Boat men and traders would retire and settle down or form casual liaisons and raise children. Illegitimate children, products of brief encounters, grew up and stayed in Norway House, the only home they knew. In 1873, the treaty with the Indians gave them a stretch of land along the south shore of the river, including the fort's point of Rossville, and solidified their community.

Fur began to get scarce, prices dropped and, by the time the railway went through in the south, the Hudson's Bay Company was beginning to close out its operation at Norway House. After the railway came, supplies and people no longer passed through Lake Winnipeg, York boats rotted on the shore, and the economy receded rapidly. The transients left for good, leaving Norway House to fend for itself as best it could, a few hundred people scattered in log shacks through the rocks and muskeg, a couple of churches, a school.

Norway House is a dank and dark place. The air is heavy and damp even in winter. The lowness, flatness of Norway House are sensible, tangible, immediately—a shallow bowl with slippery sides. Seen from the airplane window, Norway House is a blot. Four hundred miles north of the blank whiteness and scrubby wilderness of the Interlake, it may be anticipated as a relief; instead, it gathers up and intensifies the desolation, and provides the human counterpart of wilderness.

The first glimpse of Norway House is of a large black and white jail-like structure with a huge blackened chimney belching smoke which befouls the snow around the barracks for several hundred yards in every direction. The barracks, dirty white with black trim, is the center of a black puddle it has spewed over itself while, for miles around, the snow is white.

The community grows like mould along the shores of the river. A few solid core growths are connected by filaments of houses. It creeps for almost ten miles south from Rossville, down both sides of the river and covering, with a loose network, two large islands, Fort Island and Mission Island.

The community floats on the surface of the water in suspended animation, as if it had, like green scum, grown out of the river. The grass and dark scraggly trees creep out of the river. The slime on the bottom has solidified—it is difficult to know where water ends and land begins. The river shore is vague, fuzzy, shifting as it were floating, heaving with the undulations of the water. The river itself is huge and sprawling, dwarfing the dull, monotonous trees. Near Rossville, two miles across, it is almost a lake. It flows everywhere, forming channels, streams, bays, and inlets. The land is an excrescence of no value. The river is everything. It is made on a different scale.

The river reduces the human to insignificance. In the winter, the glare of its expanses of white ice makes the white-painted buildings of the settlement look grey, dirty, false. Square, neat, painted buildings are an absurdity in this fluidity. They look like toys, silly child's blocks, yellow, red, and white. Every building, house, school, hospital, church, is built to face the river. Men do not look at one another but rather gaze at the water or at the ice, separately, all in a row, entranced by the space, the brightness.

The river has all the light. Even in winter when the water is buried under ten feet of solid ice, the river flows with blinding, reverberating, roaring light, and in the summer too, the light on the water, not the water itself, gives a sense of continual motion. In summer, because of the break and sweep of the waves, the light moves faster, flickers, while in winter it is solid, steady, heavy.

When the river is frozen, the pinks, yellows, blues, and purples which bounce off the ice are so clear and brilliant that even fresh paint looks drab and faded. Only the river reflects light; everything else absorbs it. The new yellow, turquoise, and brown government buildings look old and ugly; white paint is grey, and the drab brown and grey wood Indian homes are not seen at all.

The land has no light, no colour at all. The trees are dark: murky green-brown-black, an indeterminate colour. The shore is simply a dark shape, a place where the light ends, filled with hidden quagmires. It is shadow. The land has no colour. Everything is black and white. The people too.

White people live in white or coloured buildings on the rocky promontories at Norway House—the bright, light places jutting into the river. The promontories are also the highest points of land.

Brown people live in brown or grey buildings in the bush—in the dark, brown, shadowy places, hidden by trees. These places are lower than the rocky points, and marshy.

Clearings

Rossville is the largest and most organized of the white clearings in the bush at Norway House. The Hudson's Bay Company built its fort on the outermost tip of granite on a large peninsula extending into the river from the south shore.

The Methodist church is beside it, on the highest windy crag in the area with a splendid view downriver. Behind the church and fort on their desolate promontory cluster the Indian Affairs complex of buildings, the United Church residential school and, farther back behind the school barn where the trees begin, several dozen Indian homes.

A Roman Catholic church and school occupy another large rock south on the peninsula. The Indians' homes are scattered along the river banks. At the very tip of the point stands a stone cairn in memory of James Evans. The residential school surrounded by a wire fence is the building which, from the air, looks like jail. From the ground, the ashes from the chimney are more noticeable. The hospital used to be here until it was moved to Fort Island, on its own promontory.

The Indian Affairs buildings are white with green trim, as is the Roman Catholic school. The United Church school is white and black. The old fort was white, but only its main gate remains. The new Bay store is yellow and jaundiced green, the church on the point is cream and brown and all the buildings are frame.

Behind the school barn, out of use since the policy of making Indian school children raise hogs has gone out of fashion, two rows of Indian homes straggle off towards the trees. Most are whitewashed log cabins with unpainted shingle roofs, the whitewash turned a pleasant weathered grey. Most have woodpiles as high as the roof, so the visual impression is of a great heap of logs, out of which a tumbledown, sagging cottage takes form. Chips and sawdust cover the ground in front. Some of the houses are covered with artificial-black tarpaper, a few new ones are pre-fab plywood and one is painted bright pink. A similar group of homes clusters around the Roman Catholic complex to the south. The white men's churches and government buildings look stiff and incongruous perched on the rocks, as though dropped helter-skelter by some giant gull. Their drab cream and bilious yellow colour is visible for miles, each unique in shape, colour, style.

The Indians' homes seem to have grown out of the ground, even the pink one. They are not a healthy, natural, or beautiful growth, but like fungus, and have the same vague monotony as the trees. Each log shack looks like every other log shack. They have been built to an Indian Affairs plan—same size, same whitewash, same shingles, same windows, same people. This monotony makes them nearly invisible.

The second white community, and the most important, lies a mile directly upriver from Rossville, on Fort Island, a swampy island which takes up most of the river, leaving a narrow channel on each side. This community is built around the hospital, a low brown and yellow building flanked by white clapboard nurses' residences and the yellow building of the administrator which, like the yellow church in Rossville, is high on a rocky point, commanding a broad view of the river. The airplanes land and take off in front of the hospital, and around it are the hydro plant, the telephone building, and the community development officer's house-office. Along the northern shore of the island are a second Hudson's Bay store, a post office, school, airline office, and the only hotel. Just as at Rossville, the institutions stand out in the landscape, while Metis homes are scattered and hidden for miles along the river shore. Indian and Metis homes are located on the opposite side of the island at its other end. Across the channel from the hospital, Metis homes struggle for miles along the shore. The only institutions on the northern shore are a Pentacostal church and a school. Farther upriver, past Fort Island, the darkness increases. Three small clearings have been made in the bush, for a Roman Catholic Mission and school, an Anglican mission and school across from it on Mission Island, and, upriver, a second Anglican school and a United Church building. Indian and Metis homes are located on Mission Island and on both shores.

The community of Norway House stretches, all told, about ten miles upriver from Rossville. Within that ten miles live 2,700 people. Treaty Indians number 1,700; Metis 700 and whites 250, and all these people form a community of great interdependence. These people are served by nine schools. Many people are illiterate and speak almost no English. They are cared for by six churches representing four denominations. Few people attend church. The white people provide services for the Indian people. The Indians permit themselves to be serviced by the white people. Allowing themselves to be cared for is the daily occupation of 2,400 people at Norway House.

There are no other occupations. The fish to be caught will feed only a handful of families, and too few animals are left to make trapping a source of livelihood. There is no industry or agriculture. A few years ago, Indian Affairs shipped up some cattle by barge but they have since disappeared. Some drowned, some starved, some froze, many were eaten. Some were shot: "This guy from the government came in one day to my place and shot all my cattle with a gun. He said they weren't good. I never got any more." Some were probably diseased.

(One bull, which had apparently gored someone to death, was put ashore on a small island off Rossville point. The bull was covered with tar and ignited, according to local legend. Its agonized bellows could be heard throughout the community. For a long time the island was called Bull Island. It is now called Drunken Island, for different reasons.)

An Indian agent who had either seen or heard about the luxuriant grass at Norway House was not apprised of the fact that the grass grows in water, and is, in most years, impossible to harvest. The cattle starved in the winter for want of hay. An attempt to grow potatoes and other vegetables suffered similar inundation.

Occasionally, odd construction jobs will come up or men will leave their families in the community to work outside. The rest work for the white people who are there to work for them. Or they don't work at all and allow themselves to be serviced to the maximum by unemployment insurance, welfare, and Family Allowance.

Tracks

The way a community functions internally can be seen best in the winter when everything is thrown into relief by the snow, and the tracks that people make are visible. The widest and most worn trails lead to the important places, the school, the stores, and the hospital.

In the summer, the river is the road at Norway House. It is a chaos of speeding motor boats, big, ponderous scows, powerful RCMP boats, little canoes almost vertical in the air with the thrust of a heavy outboard. The air is filled with an incessant roar, even at night when the Indians steer by landmarks in total darkness, gauging the speed and distance of other boats by the sounds of their engines.

In the winter, the river is still the road (Norway House has no real roads) but the only vehicles are some bombardiers and a few skidoos.

These are owned by important government people (Indian Affairs has a bombardier; so does the hospital) except for a few Indians who run a bombardier taxi service around the community at fifty cents a trip. Five dollars to charter. Everyone else travels on foot.

The most important tracks are made by the airplane from Winnipeg which comes in and goes out three days a week. It is the only contact with the outside besides radio-telephone. The outside, where all decisions are made, controls Norway House and that is why the plane is so important. It brings inspectors, agitators, writers, visitors, politicians who might have an important effect on the settlement's life. It takes away sick people, important people, lucky people. The plane brings all the mail, newspapers, and gossip. Everybody's pay cheque comes in on that plane, and it brings food and clothing from the mail orders.

The hospital gives the airline a lot of business by sending sick people to Winnipeg. The plane lands in front of the hospital to be close to the patients, and a hospital staff person is usually on the plane or meeting it. The hospital is, therefore, the first to get any news. It knows everything sooner than anyone else in Norway House. This liaison with the airline, TransAir, is an important source of power in Norway House, for the hospital personnel can easily give the impression of having information they do not in fact possess. They know, at least, who gets off every flight, what that person is doing in Norway House, and whether he is likely to be a threat to the hospital.

The Un-working Class

A window in the boys' recreation room on the second floor of the United Church residential school in Rossville overlooks the school's backyard with its unused barn, trampled playground, and sheds. To the left are the two scraggly rows of Indian shacks. Straight ahead hidden in the bush, blocked off by a wing of the school, are more Indian homes. Near the barn, a thin metal pipe about three feet high sticks straight out of the ground. On the end is a tap. A man comes from behind the barn, walking slowly and deliberately across the open space. He carries an aluminum pail in each hand, goes to the tap, sets one pail underneath, fills it, sets the other in its place, and fills it too. He turns the tap off, picks up both his pails, turns, and walks even more slowly and deliberately back in the direction from which he came, slopping a little of the water on the snow as he goes. He appears again on the other side of the barn, heading between two rows of log shacks, and finally disappears behind a house. By this time another man is at the tap, with one pail. He had come from the opposite direction. He fills it and carries it out of sight. In a few moments, a woman comes along, pulling two pails on a toboggan, accompanied by two small children. All these people move at a leisurely, methodical, deliberate pace. Looking more closely at the tap, a well-worn trail can be seen leading up to it and away. The snow around it is trampled into mud.

That tap is the water supply for the 109 Indian homes of Rossville. The path that leads to it is the most important in the community. If someone were to stand at the window in the school for a whole day, he would probably see a person from every household come to that tap with a pail. It is a new path, three years old. The people used to take their water from the river, hauling it out more or less in front of their houses. The river was found to be polluted in 1964. Now they use the school water supply, which is chlorinated.

Water-getting is an extremely important ritual in Rossville. A large number of men come to that tap, young, able-bodied men carrying pails a child could handle. These men have no other jobs, so they make water-getting into a job, a symbol of their ability to provide at least that much for their families. Water carrying consumes a lot of hours in a day, particularly if small pails are used. It can take up as much as three hours of a day.

You look at these men, coming one after the other, each with his silly little pail and you think: How stupid! If that man carried two large pails and walked at twice the speed, he could carry four times as much water in half the time. Or better still, why don't they get together, all these individual men, and pay one man with a large water wagon or barrels to deliver water to the entire community? With the time they'd save, they'd be able to work more, make more money.

Work at what? There is no work. That's why these men carry water. They are not stupid. Save time for what? To sit around?

If these men were too busy to carry water, they'd *have* to hire someone.

This path tells many things about Norway House—the slow, deliberate round of daily chores performed for the sake of having something to do, every day almost exactly the same as the one before it. By the time a man has been carrying water 200 yards three times a day every day for three

years, it is an important routine in his life. He depends on it. His family
depends on him. What if he is offered a job? How can he take it? Who
will provide water for his family? He will turn the job down or will take
it and quit after two weeks in order to go back to hauling water. He has
turned into a housekeeper. In order to survive the idleness of having no
job at all, he magnified the importance of basic family chores until he
equates them with work. What was, in a tougher age, women's work, is
now man's work. He feels insulted if anyone suggests he should stir himself
to find a job. He is already working. Instinctively, he makes it as slow,
inefficient, and time-consuming as possible so he will be able to convince
himself that it is really laborious.

Ritualized inactivity is hard to destroy. It is difficult for a man accustomed
to the ritual of fishing or trapping to adjust to a world where there are no
fish and no fur-bearing animals. He simply applies his skills to something
else—meaningless work, and, by doing so, makes it meaningful to himself.
The biggest mistake that any vocational counsellor or job-placement advisor
could make is to assume that these men are unemployed. They aren't. They
are working very hard at not working. A counsellor, to tempt them into
something more productive than carrying water, has to redirect all the energy
which is being poured into the un-work.

By ordering the Indians to use the water out of the tap, the white
community at Norway House provided an excellent alternative for the
genuine work which is not available. The water has to come from the
tap because the river is polluted. The white men polluted the river.
Therefore, the white men have provided work for the Indians, just as
they promised. No one is unemployed at Norway House.

The Bay is the only building in Rossville which faces inland, its back
to the river, its door towards the people. It is the only building you don't
have to walk half way around to get in the front door. From this door a
well-worn path leads across the mile or more of open ice to the second
white community, the hospital community, and past it down Fort Island
to the Anglican mission at the bottom of Mission Island. This path, invisible
in the summer, in the winter is the most obvious route in the community.

From the Rossville point, a procession of little black figures can be
seen wending its way across that blank stretch of open ice, exposed to
the north wind in the full, intense cold.

Most of these pilgrims make the trip on foot, although a skidoo will occasionally scoot across, or a blue bombardier lumber along, shooing people out of its way. These people are Indian or Metis, old and young, men and women, going to, or coming from, The Bay. For many, it is a two or three mile walk each way. Some older women in cotton stockings, print cotton skirts, and black nylon windbreakers, pull toboggans with bags of groceries but many of them carry nothing. All walk at the same unhurried pace, feeling neither the wind nor the cold.

These people too are working. They are going to The Bay. On this particular day, that is the most important thing they have to do. The people of Norway House, scattered up and down ten miles, have no news medium which tells them what is happening in Norway House. So news is carried by people. In summer, it is easy to do by boat, but in winter news must be carried by foot.

For the Indians and Metis, The Bay is the newspaper and the radio station of the community. Half an hour of standing around at The Bay brings a resident up to date on all the latest developments—who has arrived or left, a birth or death, a bit of scandal, prospects of jobs. The women cluster inside the store, near the door where they can see who comes in and who goes out. Everyone's purchases are also closely evaluated, since income can be estimated very accurately from a bag of groceries. The men stand outside in a row along the wall. From this point looking in towards the community, they can see everyone, where he is going, who he is talking to.

Going to The Bay is, like water-getting, an inactivity which, by nature of repetition, turns into work. It symbolizes the acquisition of food and clothing even though, in nine trips out of ten, nothing may be purchased. Or the money will be spun out so some little item can be bought each day. The long walk is also time consuming. If the weather is cold, the person has an excuse to stay longer in the store to get warm.

The Hospital

The hospital is the principal institution at Norway House. It is the main employer. Sickness is the primary industry.

The hospital, as in African communities, gives Norway House what structure and meaning it has. It is a northern Lambarene. The hospital or the hospital mentality, controls the entire community, Indian, Metis, and white, and the hospital administrator, as the highest ranking civil servant, is, in effect, the Administrator of the community. Everyone depends on the hospital. It is today what the Hudson's Bay was a century ago.

1963—In Rossville, the children are vomiting. Children with poisoned bowels are admitted to the hospital daily. They are its most frequent users. Not infrequently, a small child or baby, untreated, will starve to death from rejecting all his food or, weakened with malnutrition, will fall sick with pneumonia. Filth causes this diarrhea and vomiting. Doctors despair of the slovenly housekeeping of the Indian women in Rossville: "They just will not learn to keep things clean. They can't see the connection between a dirty privy, a fly, and a sick child. Then they blame the hospital. They leave food out uncovered until it goes bad or all kinds of flies and dogs and things get into it. You should see some of their water pails, all scum. Haven't been washed for years. With those kind of homes, what can you do? Mice and lice and God knows what running through everything. At least the kids get clean at the hospital."

A public health nurse is employed to make home visits, checking up on sick children and attempting to teach the women the importance of cleanliness. She doesn't make much headway, and the children continue to get sick.

"My kids were sick all the time, throwing up. I couldn't get a job. I had to stay home all the time, getting water, chopping wood to keep them warm. I couldn't leave them. As soon as one would get better, another would be sick."

Sam Anderson got a job as assistant to the health nurse. He was hard-working, anxious to learn and it would keep him close enough to home to help his family. He had been raised in Norway House, knew everyone, and spoke Cree better than English. It was his job to interpret to the Indian women the importance of cleanliness. Sam and the health nurse spent a lot of time looking into outdoor privies in Rossville, most of them filthy. "Dirt," Sam lectured the Indian women in Cree, "makes little animals like lice, only much, much smaller, so small you can't see them. These are called germs. When the germs in this dirt get on food or into water, they make it bad. Your children get sick from eating these germs." The women giggled. Imagine not being able to see an animal.

Sam, they thought, must have got converted to some new white man's religion (the Pentecostals had been active in the area). Disinfectant was, however, issued free to the women and some of them sloshed it around with a will. The children continued to get sick.

Every day, someone from each of the 109 families in Rossville would walk to the river bank a few yards in front of his house, pail in either hand, and scoop out buckets of clear, cold water. Norway House people had always taken their water from the river. There is nowhere else; inland water is brackish from the muskeg.

> I learned how to test the water to see if it is pure. One day, I tested our drinking water from the pail. It was poisoned. Then I went to the river and took a sample from there. It was poisoned. I took a lot of samples from the river—everywhere the water was not good. —Sam Anderson

In the hospital, two miles upriver from Rossville, a patient flushed a shiny white disinfected toilet. In a rush of water, the excrement disappeared like magic, proceeded along a network of hidden pipes and, minutes later, was excreted into the Nelson River, raw, untreated, unprocessed. It proceeded on its way downriver to Rossville. Patients, nurses, doctors, cooks, janitors—130 people—used that sparkling running water system at the hospital every day. What happened to all the blood, the dirty dishwater, the contents of bedpans, the vomit? It was pumped into the river. Two miles later, the people of Rossville dipped out what was left and drank it. Their children got sick. They went to the hospital. There, they produced sewage which went into the river.

"How could I tell them? They are powerful white people. I'm just an Indian."

Sam sent away his water samples to experts in Winnipeg. They verified his findings. Armed with his letters, Sam broke the news to the administrator. "The hospital is making the children of Rossville sick."

Sewage still goes into the river but it is treated first. Even so, the people of Rossville have to carry their water in pails from the residential school.

Sickness has been good business at Norway House since the hospital was first built at Rossville in 1923. Almost as soon as it opened, it was overcrowded. It was a pathetic venture. A puny white clapboard two-storey structure with one doctor was expected to treat all the sick Indians of northeastern Manitoba. Moreover, the doctor had to recruit his own patients, flying little monoplanes into isolated lakes and bringing his sick people out to Norway House.

The Indians were very sick, sicker even than the outside doctors suspected. Tuberculosis and malnutrition were almost universal, starvation was frequent, and epidemics of measles, diphtheria, and whooping cough carried off hundreds of children every year. Pneumonia and venereal disease were commonplace, and smallpox was a recent memory.

To the idealists, the hospital, perched on its barren rock, was a beacon of hope. To the cynics, it was a fortress. The hospital has never lost its military connotations as a bastion in the war against disease, and against sick people.

> The hospital is death. The doctors there killed the Indian people. Some say they tortured them to death, cut them open alive. Nobody who went to the hospital came back. We knew that as soon as the doctor said a man had to go to the hospital, he was a dead man. Many sick people would hide in the woods when the doctor came. They wanted to die at home, in their own place. —[Unidentified] Indian

Because the hospital was so small, only the sickest people could be taken there, and many of them were on the verge of death. The hospital became a kind on terminal care institution. The Indian could see no point in going to a strange building to die. Facilities were inadequate at the hospital and, as in any hospital, some people died who shouldn't have died or who would have lived with better care. The white man promised life and produced death. Those patients who were not so seriously ill would be treated on the spot in the community, and their recovery was usually attributed to natural causes rather than to the doctor.

Hospitals do not normally recruit patients. Teams of interns do not patrol the streets, pouncing on unsuspecting passers-by, punching needles in them, stripping them and subjecting them to an instant physical examination. Those diagnosed as sick are not apprehended and locked up until cured or dead in a strange institution in a state of quarantine, away from friends and relatives. Doctors do not canvass from house to house, banging on doors, demanding to examine all the people inside. They do not make threats about the terrible fate awaiting those who refuse to be examined. Hospitals and doctors expect people who feel ill to seek them out.

In times of crisis and extreme emergency, however, hospitals become authoritarian and aggressive—if for instance a community is stricken with the plague, typhoid, or polio. Then the hospital takes over the whole community. Norway House has been in a state of crisis and epidemic since the hospital opened. The alert is always sounding. Nurses patrol the community, searching for the slightest sign of incipient disease. Northern Manitoba is an epidemic area. Disease must be sought out and eradicated. Pain involved in the cure is secondary. The hospital is doing battle with death itself.

The panic which is felt by the staff of a small, understaffed, and inadequate hospital in the middle of a plague has never decreased. Every Indian is seen as a potential patient, a source of infection, and Indians are bodies to examine, treat, cure.

Patients are actively recruited, sometimes impressed. Almost every pregnant Indian woman in its region is flown into the hospital at least a month before delivery time (at public expense) and boarded in the community until the baby is born. She is then flown home with the baby. This kind of red-carpet treatment certainly provides an incentive for the women, married or not, to have children—one month's paid holiday by air. All this fuss and expense could be virtually eliminated except in problem births if there were enough nurses and trained midwives in the communities. Children, accessible to the hospital when at school, are watched even more closely. They are examined for everything and popped into the hospital at the drop of a hat.

There is a strong element of religious crusade to the hospital's zealous battle against disease. The public health nurse is the knight in the field. Cleanliness is her doctrine. Illustrated tracts under her arm, she travels from house to house, keeping a sharp eye open for lice, impetigo, coughs, and rickets in the children while she talks about disinfectant and toothbrushes. She hopes to be able to apprehend any people who are already sick, and to prevent future sickness from occurring by giving sound advice. The attack has recently become more discreet. Because health units have been set up in many isolated areas, doctors no longer drop out of the sky in airplanes. The bombardier service, which was operated in winter to pick up sick people and bring them in, has been discontinued because the Indians use it as a free taxi. Because the emphasis has lately shifted from cure to prevention, the doctors are no longer in direct touch with so many people, and the war against disease has taken on some of the appearance of an intelligence operation, in which the Indians serve as the spies.

CRAIGELLACHIE

PIERRE BERTON

From *The Last Spike* (1971)

Since the publication of his two books on the construction of the Canadian Pacific Railway—The National Dream *(1970) and its sequel* The Last Spike—*Pierre Berton has enjoyed immense success as a popularizer of Canadian history. His well-paced narrative style relies on the liberal deployment of colourful characters and dramatic incidents. As well, his stories are usually supported by a patriotic subtext celebrating Canadian nationality. In the CPR books, for example, the railway becomes an exercise in nation-building, a symbol of unity without which Canada would not exist. In less skilled hands Berton's approach might become formulaic; however, no other Canadian historian has managed to interest such a large audience in its own past.*

Pierre Berton was already a media celebrity when he turned his hand to writing history. He was born in the Yukon in 1920 and began a career in newspaper journalism in Vancouver before moving to Toronto where he worked at Maclean's *and then as a columnist for the* Star. *He is known to television viewers as a panelist on* Front Page Challenge, *the longest-running game show on North American television. Berton followed his CPR books with a succession of popular histories about a variety of subjects, including the War of 1812, the Great Depression, the First World War, the settling of the West, and Niagara Falls. He has won the Governor-General's award for non-fiction three times.*

The following selection describes the driving of the Last Spike at Craigellachie in 1885. It is the conclusion to the CPR set.

E dward Mallandaine wanted to fight the Indians. When the news of their rebellion reached Victoria, where he lived and went to school, there was no holding him; and his father, a pioneer architect and engineer, did not try to hold him. He booked passage to New Westminster, got aboard the new CPR line out of Port Moody, and took it as far as Eagle Pass Landing. He was just seventeen years old, small for his age with a thin, alert face, half-hidden by a black cap. He trudged over the line of the partly finished road until he reached Golden, at the foot of the Kicking Horse, and there he learned, to his intense disappointment, that the rebellion was over and that the troops from eastern Canada, which had had all the adventure and all the glory, were already on their way home.

He was disappointed and disgusted. He headed west again, through the Rogers Pass and into Farwell, with its single street lined with log and frame shacks. There was a feeling of excitement in Farwell that summer of 1885. The town was the half-way point between the two Ends of Track: freight outfits bustled in from the Rogers and the Eagle Passes; boats puffed into the new docks from the mines at the Big Bend of the Columbia; a new post office was opening. Young Mallandaine decided to stay for a while in Farwell and go into business for himself. He opened a freighting service between the town and Eagle Pass Landing, taking a pony through the Gold Range twice each week along the tote road carved out by the railway contractors and soliciting orders for newspapers and supplies from the navvies along the way. It was hard going but it made a profit.

For a teenage boy it was an exciting time in which to live and an exciting place in which to be. Mallandaine was bright enough to realize that history was being made all around him and he noted it all in his mind for later reference: the spectacle of fifty men hanging over the face of the cliffs at Summit Lake, drilling holes in the rock; the sound of thunder in the pass as hundreds of tons of rock hurtled through the air; the sight of a hundred-foot Howe truss put together in a single day; the long, low huts where the navvies, mostly Swedes and Italians, slept "huddled in like bees in a hive with little light and ventilation"; the accidents, brawls, drinking, and gambling in the camps, "with men of all nationalities throwing away their hard-earned pay at faro, stud poker, and other games of chance"; a gunbattle with two men shot in a gambling den not far from the Farwell post office; and, towards the end of the season, the rough pageantry of the Governor General, Lord Lansdowne himself, riding on horseback through the gap between the two lines of steel on his way to the coast.

Each time Mallandaine made his way through Eagle Pass that gap was shorter. He noted "day by day the thousands of feet of earth removed and . . . the swarms of men slaving away like ants for the good of the gigantic enterprise." By October it became clear that the road would be finished by first snow. The mushroom towns began to lose their inhabitants and a general exodus took place as the contractors discharged more and more men. Now, as the boy moved through the mountains, he noticed the way-side houses shut up and deserted, contractors' equipment being shifted and carted away, and hundreds of men travelling on foot with all their belongings to the east or to the west. Some of the rougher characters, who had operated saloons and gambling dens, became road agents, "and many a poor man who had been toiling all summer, was obliged to deliver up his earnings."

All the activity that had excited Edward Mallandaine on his arrival began to die away, and an oppressive silence settled on the pass—a silence broken only by the hideous shrieking of the construction locomotives echoing through the hills, as they rattled by with flat cars loaded with steel rails. Mallandaine felt a kind of chill creeping into his bones—not just the chill of the late October winds, sweeping down through the empty bunkhouses, but the chill of loneliness that comes to a man walking through a graveyard in the gloom.

"It seemed as though some scourge had swept this mountain pass. How ghostly the deserted camps would look at night! How quiet it all seemed!" The pass became so lonely that Mallandaine almost began to dread the ride between Farwell and the Landing. There was something eerie about the sight of boarded-up buildings, dump cars left by the wayside, and portions of contractors' outfits cast aside along the line of the tote road. And the silence! Not since the days of the survey parties had the mountains seemed so still. Mallandaine decided to pack it in; there was no business left to speak of anyway. He made plans to return to his parents' home in Victoria. There was, however, one final piece of business, which he did not want to miss. He was determined to be on hand when the last spike on the Canadian Pacific Railway was driven.

On the afternoon of November 6, the last construction train to load rails—an engine, a tender, and three flat cars—left Farwell for Eagle Pass. Mallandaine was one of several who climbed aboard and endured the "cold, cheerless, rough ride" that followed. A few miles out of Farwell, it began to snow. The rails became so slippery that when one gumbo grade was reached the locomotive could not creep over it and, after three attempts in which the train slid backwards down the incline, one car had to be abandoned.

Far into the darkness of the night the little train puffed, its passengers shivering with cold. Mallandaine, lying directly upon the piled-up rails and unable to sleep, was almost shaken to pieces as the train rattled over the unballasted roadbed. Finally it came to a stop. The youth tumbled off the flat car in the pitch dark, found an abandoned box car, and managed a short sleep. At six that morning the track crews were on the job. By the time Mallandaine awoke, the rails had almost come together.

At nine o'clock, the last two rails were brought forward and measured for cutting, with wagers being laid on the exact length that would be needed: it came to twenty-five feet, five inches. A peppery little man with long whiskers, wearing a vest with a heavy watch chain, cut the final rail with a series of hard blows. This was the legendary Major Rogers. One of the short rails was then laid in place and spiked; the second was left loose for the ceremony. The crowd, which included Al Rogers, Tom Wilson, Sam Steele, and Henry Cambie, waited for the official party to appear.

It is perhaps natural that the tale of the driving of the last spike on the CPR should have become a legend in which fancy often outweighs fact; it was, after all, the great symbolic act of Canada's first century, a moment of solemn ritual enacted in a fairyland setting at the end of a harrowing year. Two days before the spike was driven, George Stephen had cabled in cipher from England: "Railway now out of danger." The bonds had risen to 99, the stock to $52\frac{1}{2}$. Nine days after the spike was driven, Louis Riel kept his rendezvous with the hangman at Regina. In more ways than one the completion of the railway signalled the end of the small, confined, comfortable nation that had been pieced together in 1867.

It is not surprising, then, that some who were present that day in the mountains—a construction boss named George Munro was one—should have recalled half a century later that the spike was made of gold. Munro claimed that it was pulled out and taken east. The Perthshire *Advertiser* of Scotland, in a special issue honouring Alexander Mackenzie, "a Perthshire lad who rose to eminence," stated that the former prime minister's widow drove the spike, which was "of 18 carat gold with the word Craigellachie in diamonds. It was replaced almost immediately with a serviceable one of steel and the first presented to Mrs. Mackenzie who afterward wore it as a brooch." But Mrs. Mackenzie was not a widow in 1885 and there was no golden spike. The Governor General had had a silver spike prepared for the occasion; it was not used, and His Excellency, who had expected to be present, had been forced to return to Ottawa from British Columbia when weather conditions caused a delay in the completion of the line.

"The last spike," said Van Horne, in his blunt way, "will be just as good an iron one as there is between Montreal and Vancouver, and anyone who wants to see it driven will have to pay full fare." He had toyed with the idea of an elaborate celebration and excursion but found it impossible to fix limits on the necessary invitations. It would have resulted "in a vast deal of disappointment and ill feeling"—not to mention expense.

The truth was that the CPR could not afford a fancy ceremony. It had cost the Northern Pacific somewhere between $175,000 and $250,000 to drive its golden spike. The CPR might be out of danger, but it had enormous expenditures facing it. Stephen proposed paying off the five-million-dollar temporary loan almost immediately. Van Horne's whole purpose was to get a through line operating to the Pacific so that he could tap the Asian trade. There would be time for ceremonies later on.

The very simplicity and near spontaneity of the scene at Eagle Pass—the lack of pomp, the absence of oratory, the plainness of the crowd, the presence of the workmen in the foreground of the picture—made the spectacle an oddly memorable one. Van Horne and a distinguished party had come out from Ottawa, Montreal, and Winnipeg for the occasion. The big names, lounging at their ease in the two parlour cars "Saskatch-ewan" and "Matapedia," included Donald A. Smith, Sandford Fleming, John Egan, John McTavish, the land commissioner, and George Harris, a Boston financier who was a company director. Because of the incessant rains the party was held up for several days at Farwell until the work was completed.

Meanwhile, on the far side of the mountains, Andrew Onderdonk's private car "Eva" came up from Port Moody with Michael Haney aboard, pulling the final load of rails to the damp crevice in the mountains which the general manager, with a fine sense of drama, had decided years before to name Craigellachie. The decision predated Stephen's memorable telegram to Donald A. Smith. When Van Horne first joined the company the word was in common use because of an incident in 1880, when the Syndicate was being formed out of the original group that had put the St. Paul railway together. One of the members had demurred at the idea of another railway adventure and suggested to Stephen that they might only be courting trouble. Stephen had replied with that one word, a reference to a Scottish poem which began with the phrase: "Not until Craigellachie shall move from his firm base. . . . " Van Horne, hearing of the incident, decided that if he was still with the CPR when the last spike was driven, the spot would be marked by a station called Craigellachie.

It was a dull, murky November morning, the tall mountain sheathed in clouds, the dark firs and cedars dripping in a coverlet of wet snow. Up puffed the quaint engine with its polished brass boiler, its cordwood tender, its diamond-shaped smokestack, and the great square box in front containing the acetylene headlight on whose glass was painted the number 148. The ceremonial party descended and walked through the clearing of stumps and debris to the spot where Major Rogers was standing, holding the tie bar under the final rail. By common consent the honour of driving the connecting spike was assigned to the eldest of the four directors present—to Donald A. Smith, whose hair in five years of railway construction had turned a frosty white. As Fleming noted, the old fur trader represented much more than the CPR. His presence recalled that long line of Highlanders—the Mackenzies and McTavishes, Stuarts and McGillivrays, Frasers, Finlaysons, McLeods, and McLaughlins—who had first penetrated these mountains and set the transcontinental pattern of communication that the railway would continue.

Now that moment had arrived which so many Canadians had believed would never come—a moment that Fleming had been waiting for since 1862, when he placed before the government the first practical outline for a highway to the Pacific. The workmen and the officials crowded around Smith as he was handed the spike hammer. Young Edward Mallandaine was determined to be as close to the old man as possible. He squeezed in directly behind him, right next to Harris, the Boston financier, and directly in front of Cambie, McTavish, and Egan. As the little hunchbacked photographer, Ross of Winnipeg, raised his camera, Mallandaine craned forward so as to see and be seen. Fifty-nine years later, when all the rest of that great company were in their graves, Colonel Edward Mallandaine, stipendiary magistrate and reeve of the Kootenay town of Creston, would be on hand when the citizens of Revelstoke, in false beards and borrowed frock-coats, re-enacted the famous photograph on that very spot.

The spike had been hammered half-way home. Smith's first blow bent it badly. Frank Brothers, the roadmaster, expecting just such an emergency, pulled it out and replaced it with another. Smith posed with the uplifted hammer. The assembly froze. The shutter clicked. Smith lowered the hammer unto the spike. The shutter clicked again. Smith raised the hammer and began to drive the spike home. Save for the blows of the hammer and the sound of a small mountain stream gushing down a few feet away, there was absolute silence. Even after the spike was driven home, the stillness persisted. "It seemed," Sanford Fleming recalled, "as if the act now performed had worked its spell on all present. Each one appeared absorbed in his own reflections." The spell was broken by a cheer, "and it was no ordinary cheer. The subdued enthusiasm, the pent-up feeling of men familiar with hard work, now found vent." More cheers followed, enhanced by the shrill whistle of the locomotives.

All this time, Van Horne had stood impassively beside Fleming, his hands thrust into the side pockets of his overcoat. Though this was his crowning moment, his face remained a mask. In less than four years, through a miracle of organization and drive, he had managed to complete a new North West Passage, as the English press would call it. Did any memories surface in that retentive mind as the echoes of Smith's hammer blows rang down the corridor of Eagle Pass? Did he think back on the previous year when, half-starved and soaking wet, he had come this way with Reed and Rogers? Did he reflect, with passing triumph, on those early days in Winnipeg when the unfriendly press had attacked him as an idle boaster and discussed his rumoured dismissal? Did he recall those desperate moments in Ottawa and Montreal when the CPR seemed about to collapse like a house of cards? Probably not, for Van Horne was not a man to brood or to gloat over the past. It is likelier that his mind was fixed on more immediate problems: the Vancouver terminus, the Pacific postal subsidy, and the Atlantic steamship service. He could not predict the future but he would help to control it, and some of the new symbols of his adopted country would be of his making: the fleet of white Empresses flying the familiar checked flag, the turreted hotels with their green château roofs, boldly perched on promontory and lakefront; and the international slogan that would proclaim in Arabic, Hindi, Chinese, and a dozen other languages that the CPR spanned the world.

As the cheering died the crowd turned to Van Horne. "Speech! Speech!" they cried. Van Horne was not much of a speechmaker; he was, in fact, a little shy in crowds. What he said was characteristically terse, but it went into the history books: "All I can say is that the work has been done well in every way."

Major Rogers was more emotional. This was his moment of triumph too, and he was savouring it. In spite of all the taunts of his Canadian colleagues, in spite of the skepticism of the newspapers, in spite of his own gloomy forebodings and the second thoughts of his superiors, his pass had been chosen and the rails ran directly through it to Craigellachie. For once, the stoic Major did not trouble to conceal his feelings. He was "so gleeful," Edward Mallandaine observed, "that he upended a huge tie and tried to mark the spot by the side of the track by sticking it in the ground."

There were more cheers, some mutual congratulations, and a rush for souvenirs—chips from the tie, pieces of the sawn rail. Young Arthur Piers, Van Horne's secretary, spotted the first twisted spike lying on the track and tried to pocket it. Smith, however, told him to hand it over; he wanted it as a souvenir. Smith had also tossed the sledge aside after the spike was driven but, before he left, one of the track crew, Mike Sullivan, remembered to hand it to him as a keepsake. Then the locomotive whistle sounded again and a voice was heard to cry: "All aboard for the Pacific." It was the first time that phrase had been used by a conductor from the East, but Fleming noted that it was uttered "in the most prosaic tones, as of constant daily occurrence." The official party obediently boarded the cars and a few moments later the little train was in motion again, clattering over the newly laid rail and over the last spike and down the long incline of the mountains, off towards the dark canyon of the Fraser, off to the broad meadows beyond, off to the blue Pacific and into history.

BREAKING PRAIRIE SOD

JAMES M. MINIFIE

From *Homesteader* (1972)

Memoirs of a Prairie boyhood, or girlhood, are a staple item of Canadian non-fiction. For the most part they are written in workmanlike prose; one is reminded of the faithful team of oxen, heads down, broad shoulders straining against the traces, plowing each sentence like a straight furrow through the tough prairie sod. In some instances, however, the "sod-hut memoir" manages to engage our attention as literature. Wallace Stegner is one example; James M. Minifie is another. Stegner is the more ambitious writer of the two. His book, Wolf Willow, *not only remembers the pioneer experience but attempts to understand the connection between remembering and writing. Minifie is unaware that this is an issue. He is more practical and down to earth. As the selection below illustrates, his book pays a great deal of attention to the everyday details of how things got done. At the same time, he conveys an almost mythic sense of his father's battle against the indifferent elements.*

James M. Minifie left Saskatchewan in 1923 to attend Oxford University as a Rhodes scholar. He did not return to reside in Canada for forty-five years, but as a correspondent for the CBC in post-war Washington he became familiar to millions of Canadians as one of the leading journalists of his generation. Retiring to Victoria in 1968, he began work on the memoirs which appeared as Homesteader *and its sequel,* Expatriate, *published posthumously. Minifie died in 1974.*

His land! My father looked around. To the north the land fell away in a gentle slope to the grassy verges of the Big Slough. Beyond it, a slow rise took the khaki-coloured grasslands to the horizon, marked by a low range of hills over which he had driven yesterday. Westwards there was a flat, possibly wet, but showing no signs of the dangerous white alkali which destroyed fertility. As far as he could see, there was neither tree nor bush—nothing to clear away before you start to plough, my father reflected. He was already plotting out his farm. A little cluster of low hills suggested a site for house and barn, if only because it was good for nothing else.

First, however, it would be necessary to find water. Slough water could not do for household use, and wells were tricky. There was no spring, nor any obvious depression which might indicate an underground water-course. However, at the foot of one of the small hills there was a heavy growth of buffalo-willow and plenty of waterweed, a low plant of the genus glycerrhizia, or wild licorice, whose roots were supposed to go down to water within fifteen feet. There were in addition a couple of ant-hills, which was also a good sign. Like the badgers, ants were supposed to go down to water not too far below the surface. My father built another small cairn to mark his trial well-site, and then realized that he was very hungry, and that his wagon and the food were half a mile away. Even as he headed back north-east, however, he noted the little ponds scattered among the hills, and determined to make this his pasture—good forage and water, and with luck, a well.

He headed for the stone cairn he had built at the corner of his half-section and then struck east, figuring he would find his wagon easily enough. He hoped so, for the mosquitoes arose from the grass-like smoke, and while he slapped at them the enormity of his task began to overwhelm him. He tried to marshal his work in order of importance: prairie to be broken, crop seeded, well dug, barn built, cellar dug, house built, pasture fenced.

As he walked he collected horse-dung for his cook-fire. Weathered "prairie coal" makes a quick, hot fire, soon ablaze, soon dead; on it he put a pot of water for the inevitable porridge, and grilled a couple of rashers of bacon on the tines of a pitchfork. Between layers of toast these tasted good, but the porridge was lifeless—he had forgotten to put salt in it. However, the water in the double-boiler was good for tea once the duck-feathers and mosquito larvae were strained out. Porridge and bread were dull and my father noted: Should have bought some jam—or corn syrup would perhaps be better; it would go on porridge as well as bread. He began to realize that porridge would be his staple diet for some time. He had no disposition to linger over the meal, even had the mosquitoes permitted.

As soon as the porridge was consumed, he hitched up and drove back to the well-site. Taking a handful of laths, he strode west from the boundary cairn, driving in a lath every fifty yards. These would be markers for his plough; without them he would have little chance of ploughing a straight furrow to the west end of his land; dog's leg furrows made a man a laughing-stock and the land unfriendly. Anxious to run a straight furrow at the start, my father chose the single-share sulky rather than the gang-plough, as easier to handle for the first trip. He hitched up four of the oxen, Buck and Bright, Blackie, and Jerry. Oxen were preferable to horses for the heavy task of breaking the prairie. They were slow, but when they felt an obstacle they stopped, where horses would jump into the collar and strain until something gave, either the harness, the evener to which they were hitched, or the plough. This could be expensive to repair and put the rig out of action until it was done.

At the top of the little rise where he had placed the marker, my father let the blade down. It scraped the gravel for a few feet, then bit in, furrowing the three-inch sod bound together with the roots and remains of grasses, flowering plants—roses, yellow bean, and prairie crocus. This sod had kept the surface intact for ten thousand years of wind and rain, frost and sun and snow, since the retreating ice-sheet abandoned its hundreds of feet of debris shorn from rocks of the northern shield to form the happy hunting ground of a succession of nomad wanderers until the farmers came, intent on destroying that millennial ground-cover to produce a year or two of intensive crops until the exhausted fabric began to unravel and fall into ruins before the incessant beating of the wind.

There was no hint of all this in the brisk north-west breeze which rippled the Big Slough and drove the mosquitoes away from the straining oxen. There was no ominous flight of birds, no thunder on the left to suggest caution in disturbing the stable life-pattern of the short-grass prairie. The plough bit into the turf and turned it over in a long dark ribbon. At the foot of the hill the share struck a boulder buried in the turf. The eveners creaked, the oxen stopped in their tracks and allowed their chains to go slack. My father struggled to keep his seat and tripped the share out of the ground. The obstacle was an ice-borne intruder of grey granite which had lain there from time immemorial, almost invisible, with only a rounded tip protruding among the grasses. Fortunately for him the oxen had halted when they felt the extra weight. It would not be wise to risk another encounter between plough and boulder. He took the crowbar from the wagon and walked along the line of laths, watching carefully for other half-hidden impediments. He was learning the first prairie lesson, picking stone. All along the line he had marked for ploughing the unearthed small boulders, less than a foot across, weighing ten to twenty pounds each and showing great variety: limestone, pink, grey, and blue granite, an occasional piece of slate, and even old basic brown trap rock. He left them in a line, to be moved away on a stone-boat—whenever he found time to build one. That was another priority beating remorselessly on him—a stone-boat: two runners under a two-by-six platform, and a two-horse hitch.

He began to be aware of the ruthless pressure of time that bears down on the shoulders of every farmer and particularly of every new farmer. There is never enough time on the prairie. Ploughing cannot start until the frost is out of the ground, for the prairies freeze a foot or more deep during the long winter. Once the land is ploughed, seed must be thrown in as fast as possible at what the farmer guesses or senses is the optimum soil condition. Planted too early the seedlings can be damaged by late frost, frequent in May. Planted too late they risk frost damage before the grain has matured in August. Then the crop must be cut and stooked, again in a wild rush to secure optimum conditions, and threshed as soon as possible to get a good price before the new crop deluges the market and sends the price sliding downwards. In between seeding and binding, hay must be cut, cured, and stored against winter; summer-fallow must be worked, granaries and bins built, harness and machinery repaired, seed cleaned for next year, fences built and repaired, and all the thousand and six daily chores performed—cows milked, stables cleaned out, eggs collected, chickens feathered, peas picked and shelled, gardens weeded, leaks in the roof mended, wells cleaned out, potatoes dug and stored, hogs butchered, sausage ground, bacon cured, horses shod, shares sharpened, cream skinned and churned, outhouse moved to a new pit and last season's Eaton's mail-order catalogue hung on the wall.

The farmer, and particularly the ploughman, is the poetical symbol of fruitful toil, celebrated in two thousand years of bucolic verse. The ploughman has been almost as romanticized as the good shepherd. It is time to look at the facts. There is not much poetry in ploughing. For the first trip the ploughman's mind is occupied in trying to keep the furrow straight and even. He notes for future reference the dry or sodden patches, the half-buried boulders which should be removed; he notes and avoids the killdeer's nest while the mother tries to draw his attention away by feigning a broken wing. After the first hour, the monotonous tearing of the turf numbs his senses. Nests and boulders appear under the share before they can be avoided. If the ploughman walks behind his implement, he is soon too weary to do more than set one foot in front of the other and too tired to think. If he rides the plough, the more common practice on the prairies, it is still no bed of roses. After the first trip or two (the trip is out and back, usually half a mile each way on the standard half-section farm) physical discomfort appears. The incessant joggling of the seat pulls at the posterior muscles. Ploughman's piles are a common occupational hazard. So much for the poetry of the plough: mind numb, tail sore, all the ploughman wants at the end of his day is a meal and a night's sleep. There were no such boons for my father at the end of his first half-day's breaking—two acres turned over.

In some ways the oxen looked after themselves better than their drivers did. Towards noon, after a hard morning's breaking, their patience began to wear thin. They were thirsty after hours in the hot sun, drooling long ropy saliva. There was a beautiful rippling slough just beyond the end of the furrow, but instead of slaking their thirst they were required to turn around for another trip. At noon the oxen revolted. With one accord they refused to turn at the end of the trip; they headed straight for that beautiful, shining water. My father set the plough deeper; the oxen put their weight into the collars and plunged on, cutting a six-inch furrow straight into the slough. There the team stopped, dipped their muzzles thankfully into the water, and drank their fill; then they moved quietly out, ready for another trip. The deep furrow persisted for years, a testimony to bovine determination to be their own master. My father cherished this memorial of his pioneer days, and refused to allow it to be obliterated. He had much in common with the oxen, he felt. At the time he was amused and thankful that the oxen had slaked their thirst and then moved on, instead of lying down, as horses were apt to do when they felt put upon.

My father was glad enough to make the oxen an excuse to quit. At the end of the next trip, he unhitched, gave them some hay and a bundle of straw, and left them to their ruminations until it was time to start the afternoon's breaking. He might have been wise to take a leaf from the oxen's book, but he submitted instead to the ruthless pressure of his calendar.

At the end of his day's ploughing, as the sun neared the horizon, he gouged holes with the crowbar into the tough prairie; then he hammered in the willow stakes he had brought from Sintaluta for fence posts. It was essential to be able to turn the oxen into pasture in the evening. After two hours of this, and little enough to show for it, he was too tired to do anything but spoon up the cold remains of the morning's porridge, and wash it down with slough-water, regardless of the wigglers and the feathers. He had no time or strength for refinements such as tea or a fire for himself—just something filling to eat; for the oxen hay and straw. Then he would roll up in his blankets under the wagon—a shelter against the dew. It is not hard to rise at sun-up from such a bed.

Fence posts in, barbed wire had to be strung. Barbed wire is diabolical.

It cuts and tears, trips and slips, tangles in knots, and breaks with a savage backlash. My father unrolled a length of fifty yards, wound one end to a solid corner post, and tied the other end to the wagon. Then he drove ahead until the wire was taut, but not so strained as to break. Then, as quickly as if he were securing some wild beast, he stapled it to the posts, always careful to keep his head turned away, lest the wire snap and lacerate him. It is like trying to tie up a tiger with bare hands.

One strand would have to do for the time being; enough to discourage wanderers. There were no tempting fields of oats or alfalfa on the other side, against which three strands would have been needed to retain cattle. Horses are more timid, but if they do break through they are apt to panic and cut themselves badly.

Priorities had to be revised as experience demanded. No matter that he rose at daybreak, there were never enough hours in the day for any but the most pressing tasks. He moved up to top priority the stringing of a fence around the pasture where the horses and oxen could be turned to graze with some assurance that they would be there when wanted for the day's work. The little sloughs gave them water, but these would not last forever. They would dry up before the end of summer; those that escaped would freeze solid in winter. A well was essential. No house should be built until nearby water was assured. But the fearful labour and the uncertainty deterred him. There were no post-hole borers, no well-drilling equipment on that frontier. The homesteader had to dig his well with a crowbar and a spade.

After putting it off for three days my father took the fateful decision to start on the well, there where the buffalo-willow, water-weed, badger holes, an ant-hill augured for success. Using the crowbar and spade alternately, he removed the turf from a circle six feet in diameter. This was a generous width, but he knew that, once he got down to his own level, he would need a wide hole in order to have room to throw the earth up over the lip. But it meant that for each foot he sank the hole, he would have to move 28.26 cubic feet of earth. He could not expect to strike water short of twelve feet down—lucky if he did then—which meant moving very nearly 340 cubic feet of soil. The tough glacial clay, studded with stones like plums in a pound of cake, challenged his strength and endurance. It was too much after a day's ploughing, so he limited himself to one hour every evening, reserving his major effort for Saturday and Sunday. As a Lord's Day occupation it was not in the same class with St. Modwen's or reading W.G. Grace on cricket.

As he excavated deeper, the stones began to thin out, and the earth became more closely packed. At four feet it occurred to him like a thunderbolt that he was digging himself in with no way of getting out. But using his spade as a stepladder, and grasping desperately at the buffalo-willow growing near the lip, he pulled himself out and collapsed on the grass, sweating in panic at having so nearly buried himself.

To prevent any repetition, he built a ladder of two-by-fours with cross slats for rungs, and let this down into the pit. It was comforting, but it took up so much space that he found it difficult to toss the earth up over the lip. At length he was forced to the wearisome and time-consuming alternative of hauling up a bucketful of earth, then descending the ladder to fill it up again. It was back-breaking toil.

At ten feet he was encouraged by the appearance of sand, moist sand, which might indicate that he was reaching an aquifer. Another foot, and the crowbar sank easily into the sandy stratum. When he pulled it out, water welled up in the hole. That was it! He had found water! He hastily scooped a hole and watched, fascinated, as the trickle of sand and water oozed in from the south, very cold, as if it had just melted from eternal snows. "You and I, Water," he said, "came a long way to meet here. You look after me," he went on, addressing the water as if it were a living sentient thing, "and I'll look after you, give you a good roof over your head, and a strong cribbing so there will be no cave-in on top of you." You have to dig a well, he said to himself, and find your own water, to know why men used to worship at wells.

He filled a bucket with the muddy sand and dragged it to the top. In half an hour the sediment had settled, leaving half a bucket of clear water. He tried it. It was so cold it made his mouth ache; but it was sweet water, not saline, not alkaline, a little earthy still, but good for man and beast. He took a long draught of his water—his water! His mind went back to his youth, and a cold spring bubbling out at the foot of the Malvern Hills from which he had once drunk on a walking tour. He would call this Malvern Link, after that cold spring found on a sunny day so long ago. He consecrated it then and there, pouring a little onto the ground, like a tithe. He looked down into the pit and rejoiced at the gleam of water at the bottom.

Building a crib and well-head was almost as demanding a one-man task as digging the well itself. But it was essential and immediate, both to prevent the sides from caving in and to guard against cattle falling into the hole, as well as to permit water to be drawn up, which cannot be done without standing out over the lip. Like most operations on the raw prairie, crib-making was more difficult in the performance than in the conception. My father threw down four two-by-fours and some common boarding, of varied widths, one inch thick. He followed them down on the ladder. Then, up to the knees in perishing cold water and quicksand, he nailed the boards to the lower studs. The last six feet he put together above ground and lowered by rope to be fitted on to the bottom half. The meeting was none too exact, but it held. Then he boarded over the top of the cribbing, fitted a lid with a hand-grip, and hung bucket and rope over a dowel post. Building a winch was beyond him. He would be content to lower a bucket by hand and swing it expertly so that its lip scooped into the water with little or no disturbance of the sand and silt at the bottom, to be drawn up, brimming, hand over hand. By this method an expert with the bucket could bring up the mice, voles, or even gophers which had fallen into the well, to die either of shock, drowning, or chill.

I subsequently became skillful at this feat, and could capture, without stirring up the mud, any of the minor fauna which had found release there. When this came to my mother's attention, she renewed her pressure for a pump. The well came just within the working depth of a simple suction valve. The rejoicing when it was installed died away as soon as it was discovered that instead of entire mice coming up in the bucket, the pump brought up bits and pieces of mice which had got jammed in the valves and disintegrated. On one occasion I caught a small grass snake which had fallen into the water. He was a difficult catch, as he did not keep still long enough to get the bucket squarely under him. His water-speed slowed as the cold took possession, and he was a very subdued snake when I fished him out of the bucket and restored him to the warm prairie grass. Despite the disadvantage of morselled mice, the pump had these advantages: it brought up water in quantity without stirring up the sand and mud, and it eliminated the danger of my falling into the well, which was not negligible in winter when the cap and lid were sheathed in ice, and the rope itself was frozen so stiff it was like using a pole.

My father might not have dared to flout against the odds on getting water had he known how heavy they were against him. We learned afterwards that Jones, who had come from water-rich Vermont to take up the adjoining section 3, dug five dry holes before getting water, only to find that his successful well was squarely on the road allowance and had to be filled in. For years he had to exist on a barrel a day drawn from the creek four miles away and none too good at that. By and large, however, with some unlucky exceptions, this was a good district for water. A stratum of sand and gravel underlay the surface cover at about twelve feet. It was not, however, fed entirely by surface water, for it survived years of drought. Geologists have since theorized that this aquifer was the bed of a prehistoric river, fed by the retreating icecap. Below it lay a band of heavy blue clay, twenty feet thick. Below this again was abundant water, but always so alkaline as to be undrinkable, scouring both cattle and men.

His own well completed, my father knocked together a trough against the day the sloughs dried up. He had difficulty making it watertight. In theory, if two-by-sixes are laid side by side, the contiguous edges bruised by a hammer will swell and effect a watertight joint. In practice this does not happen. Father's trough leaked like a sieve, and held water hardly long enough to give oxen their fill. He patched up the joint with tar-paper and lath so that it was reasonably watertight. Once winter came, the moisture in the joint froze and effectively sealed it for long enough to satisfy the oxen.

It was always a marvel to me how much water an ox would drink. In the dead of winter, with icicles hanging from the trough, the water about to congeal, an ox would take a mouthful, warm it for a moment over his tongue before downing it, then put his muzzle into the trough and slop up more and more and more. I counted them on a cold winter morning drinking eight buckets each. Hauling forty buckets to satisfy five of the brutes at twenty below zero was agonizing. Unlike horses they stubbornly refused to nibble snow, no matter how thirsty they were; they would die of dehydration first. For watering these brutes, the pump was a great boon. These, however, were solutions for the distant future.

SHELTER FROM THE STORM

CASSIE BROWN

From *Death on the Ice* (1972)

Disaster, whether natural or man-made, has been a staple of non-fiction writing in Canada, and one of the best examples of the disaster story is Death on the Ice, *an account of the 1914 misadventures of the Newfoundland sealing fleet. A large party of sealers became separated from their ship that season and had to remain out on the ice overnight in a howling storm. Before rescuers arrived, seventy-seven men froze to death. Cassie Brown based the details of her tension-filled narrative on the evidence given at a subsequent public inquiry. The tragic events are skillfully embedded in a thorough account of the seal hunt and its importance to Newfoundland culture.* Death on the Ice *sold nearly 100,000 copies, a phenomenal number for a book of "local history." It is one of those rare books which seem to speak for an entire community.*

Cassie Brown was born in Newfoundland in 1919. She has been a prolific writer since she was a teenager. Along with Death on the Ice, *which she wrote with the editorial assistance of the novelist Harold Horwood, she has written two other books about notable shipwrecks. Her skills as a writer of fast-paced narrative may well owe something to the fact that she is also the author of many dramatized scripts for radio and has been involved in amateur theatrics.*

The following selection describes the terrible suffering endured by the men on the ice as they attempt to find their way back to the ship.

The men on the ice were lost, unutterably weary, their reserves of strength low after hours of rough travel. Wet feet and damp clothes added to their misery. The wind whistled through the night, tearing at them. A few voices gloomed: "We'm never gonna see home again." And who could honestly deny the danger? Weren't they already on their last legs through fatigue?

"We'm gonna die." The whisper went here and there throughout the crowd.

Cecil Mouland said to his cousin Ralph: "*I'm* not gonna die." In his mind's eye he could see Jessie's serious young face, and the faces of half a dozen other young men who had an eye on her. No sir, none of them fellers were going to get Jessie! "I don't know about you fellers, but *I'm* not gonna die," he said grimly.

Most of them took it gamely enough, and answered the call as Dawson, Mouland, and Bungay gave orders to the men of their watches. Jones's watch hung around waiting for orders, but he gave none, so they distributed themselves among the other watches, mostly those of Dawson and Mouland. Now they formed three groups on three pans within hailing distance of one another. Jones himself went to Dawson's pan. Howlett, with William Pear in tow, went with Dawson, whom he had been with all day. Benjamin Piercey attached himself to Mouland's watch since that was where most of the New Perlican men were.

A check proved that the pans offered little protection in the form of pinnacles or rafters under which they could take shelter, but the edges were rough and hummocky, with many loose cakes of ice piled up around them. Beyond their floes, lesser pans rose and fell steeply, confirming their fear that they were dangerously close to the edge of the ice-field. Pans had been known to scatter, the men on them driven off to sea. . . .

"All hands set to and build shelters," was the order.

To build even simple shelters was a monumental chore for the exhausted men. It meant chopping at the ice hummocks with their gaffs until they had enough loose blocks of ice to build a crude wall, then plastering it with snow until it would serve as a wind break. They simply didn't have the strength.

In Arthur Mouland's watch only a handful of men made half-hearted attempts to find and bring ice blocks to the place he indicated, and his voice crackled with annoyance.

"*All* hands will bring ice to build a gaze," he snapped. And since many still stood around, shivering and drooping, he said brusquely, "I don't mean one or two hands build a gaze, *I mean all of you*. Get busy."

The "gaze" took its name from its use in hunting, but it would serve a different end tonight. Since the chill factor of the wind might be equal to thirty or forty degrees of temperature, the gaze might well mean the difference between life and death.

Mouland drove them on relentlessly as they dragged the ice into place with their weary limbs, stabbing with their gaffs, ready at every move to fall on their faces. After a long time they had a wall, thirty feet long, running across the pan so as to break the wind from the east-south-east. They had built near enough to the edge to use the hummocky ice as part of the wall, and Mouland had made them keep at it until it was a foot higher than their heads. All the holes were liberally plastered with wet snow. Soon they were protected from everything except the drift that broke over the top and sifted softly down upon them.

But Mouland still was not satisfied.

"All right," he said. "Now I want the ends turned in."

They grumbled that it was good enough, but he drove them on. They plodded back and forth, bringing more ice, packing more snow, until they had lost all feeling in their arms and all sense of time—it was a labour that would never end. But at last the two wings were built, and he was satisfied.

"If the wind shifts we'll *need* them ends," he said.

They huddled in the shelter while the wind keened over their heads. Huddled with them were some men from Sidney Jones's watch, men who had taken no part in the building and who, Mouland thought, were dangerously overcrowding the pan. Mouland ordered them off. "Go find your own master watch," he said. "You're not stayin' with us."

His voice brooked no argument, and the leaderless men slunk away, all except Benjamin Piercey. "Can I stay, Mr. Mouland?"

"You're not in my watch."

"No, sir, but I'm from New Perlican, and all the New Perlican men are with you. They're my chums. I don't know them other fellers." While Mouland considered this, Piercey added, "They're all gone now, sir, and it's too dark and dangerous for a man to go wanderin' around the ice alone."

"Stay then," Mouland agreed. He did not like ordering men out of his shelter, but it was the men of his watch he had set himself to save.

On his pan, Dawson ordered: "Stick yer gaffs in the snow, men. Line 'em up against the wind. . . . Now, get blocks of ice an' lay 'em along the gaffs."

They did so, slowly, clumsily, their bodies aching with weariness. Jones, who had hovered around Dawson, now melted into the crowd and disappeared. His men hung around the fringes of Dawson's watch. They did not offer to help build the shelter. Noting this, Dawson snapped, "What are *ye* standin' around fer? Get to work."

Some of them did, but others refused to budge. "We don't take orders from you, Tom Dawson."

"If ye stay on this pan ye do," Dawson threatened, but he was too physically exhausted to make good any kind of threat, and most of them knew it.

His wall grew slowly, extending across the floe. At last it was shoulder-high, and they stopped.

"That's not high enough, men, get on with it," he ordered.

"Skipper, we can't lift our arms no higher; we got no strength left," they protested.

"Besides, it's mild, Skipper Tom; it's gonna turn to rain," another said.

Dawson knew just how they felt, and he, too, expected it to rain and then clear off.

"It should be higher," he said, "but I guess it'll do."

Already some of his men were crouching beneath the wall, shredding their tow ropes, cutting shavings from their gaff stems. A match flared in cupped hands, and in a few minutes flames were licking upwards, crackling around the greasy wood as gaff handles and flagpoles were sacrificed. Three men removed their boots and dried their wet socks. Now, if only they had a seal or two. They thought lovingly of the panned seals they had left, several hours back, under the *Stephano*'s flag. They got out their hard tack, and began chewing it.

On Bungay's pan the situation was much the same. The men had laboured to erect a shelter, but had balked at building it higher than arm level: "Skipper, we'm tired."

Tuff did not insist, so Bungay didn't.

In the shelter of the ice walls little fires flickered and glowed as the men dug into their meagre rations—hard tack for most, rolled oats and raisins for a few, here and there a tin of molasses mixed with Radway's Ready Relief. They had no regular utensils, but here and there a tin, containing snow, was held over a fire to be heated. Hot water mixed with Radway's really warmed your insides.

The ice walls gave the lost sealers only partial shelter. Although it hardly seemed possible, the weather was getting worse. The wind backed from the east to the north and back to the east again, but kept backing farther northward, whistling across the ice-field to lash at the men with the stinging rawness that made their flesh ache. The wet snow clung to their clothes, their hair, their eyebrows, their beards; it trickled icily down their necks. Cecil Mouland thought longingly of the oilskins back in his bunk. If he'd brought 'em along, they would not only keep out the wet snow, but protect him from the wind, too.

Wet, cold, and miserable as they were, the prolonged mildness still convinced them that the weather wouldn't get any worse. They clustered around flickering fires made from their poles, trying to magically draw a little warmth from them. When some of Jones's men, who had done nothing to assist in the building of the shelter, pushed themselves forward to share what little warmth the fires gave, there were howls of indignation. "Get the hell outa here, you . . . ! "

But despite their howls and even kicks, the interlopers doggedly remained.

John Howlett had taken great pains to light a fire and nurse it with shavings from his gaff stem. Now, with contributions from other sealers, he had a fine fire going, generating warmth and cheer in the blackness. To this fire Jones's men also crowded, edging away sealers who stretched chilled hands for warmth. There were indignant mutterings from Dawson's men, and a small amount of shoving, but most of their energies had gone into the building of the shelter; they had nothing left over to enable them to assert their rightful places at the fire.

Howlett put an end to it. "You bloody well want a fire, you bloody well build a fire," he yelled, and kicked the blazing sticks to the four winds. They sputtered, smoked, and died.

At this point they made a disconcerting discovery. Those who had been closest to the fire now found the cold more chilling than before; it was as if the heat had "opened their pores" and allowed the wind to burrow in through their skin. They had been numb before, but now their very bones felt naked. They could not stand much more of this, they told one another through chattering teeth; and thereafter they kept a respectable distance from other fires.

Still, some did not heed the wisdom of the few, and snatched the comfort of a blazing fire, happily roasting hands and faces, ignoring the warnings of others not to get too close or stay too long.

"Don't burn all yer gaffs," Dawson warned. "Ye'll need 'em to get back to the ship."

Gradually the hard-won fuel ran out and the fires dwindled. One by one they went out. The wind and the cold and the all-enveloping darkness returned.

Newfoundland log:
  10 p.m. Strong gale and drifting snow. Ship burned down. Wind force 6.

It was nearly midnight when the warm air generating all the fury of the storm finally condensed its moisture, and torrential rain replaced the wet snow. Down it came, a cold cloudburst, soaking them to the skin.

The men huddled close to give each other protection and warmth. The two shoulder-high walls couldn't keep them even partially dry. Only those in Arthur Mouland's watch had any real shelter. Their wall was snug and tight. The rain beat against it but could find no loophole. When the wind backed to the north, they crowded to the north corner, which gave them some protection. But beneath their feet the snow turned to slush that soaked through their boots. If they had felt cold and miserable before, they were indescribably wretched now, some of them too wretched to care about living. But so far only one man was missing, and in the rain at least they would not freeze to death.

There was a stir in the crowd. "Get a move on, fellers. Can't stand around. Gotta exercise and kape warm."

There was pushing and prodding as they got on the move, shuffling round and round, so weary they barely realized they were moving, so exhausted that each foot seemed to weigh a ton.

William Pear was too ill to move about. He was not a seaman. He did not have the stamina of his hardier companions, nor did anyone else at this stage have the stamina to haul a sick man around. They helped him until they could help no more, then they left him alone. Pear sprawled on the ice.

Now they were all soaked to the skin. But the old hands knew that as long as the rain kept up, they were safe. But if it started to freeze. . . . They squinted miserably up into the rain, and prayed that it would continue.

For more than an hour the rain beat down in a deluge. Then the storm moved eastward into the Atlantic. Icy air from the north rushed in behind it. Without a lull or a warning, the wind chopped around to the north-north-east, the temperature dropped rapidly to sixteen above zero, and the rain froze into pellets of sleet.

The wind chill factor now created conditions equivalent to twenty degrees below zero. Men, wet through, crouched on the ice, had little hope.

About twenty miles north of the *Newfoundland*, the *Nascopie*, all by herself, was burned down snugly. Coaker had written:

> The early morning was clear at 10 a.m. indications of weather observable. At noon it looked as if we would have snow storm, weather mild. At 1 p.m. snow thick, lost sight of men on ice near ship; snow cleared a little and all men taken on board. Captain kept men close to ship all morning. Snowing and blowing bitterly all evening. At nightfall the wind was blowing a gale from the north with snow. Real wintry night. Our men all on board at 1 p.m. when weather came on, considerable swell all day. A stowaway on board ill with mumps and is confined to hospital.

"Real wintry night." On the ice the men were transfixed as the bitter, snow-laden wind, screaming from the north, quickly turned their sodden clothing to ice. An east wind was one thing, a north wind was quite another. Within moments, ice was clinging to their faces.

"Lard Jaysus!" muttered one.

"I knowed it," Jesse Collins said without any satisfaction. "I tell you, the *Greenland* disaster won't be nothin' to this one."

"Whadda we do, Jesse?" a fledging sealer asked the older man.

"We *move*, tha's what we do." He stamped his feet. "We move and kape movin', we don't stop fer a minute. Gotta kape warm; kape the blood movin' so it won't freeze in yer veins."

Some followed his example, others stood around as though they were rooted to the ice. Jesse, a vigorous man, walked among them, pushing, prodding: "Move," he ordered roughly.

The ice shelters had given some protection from the east wind, but the sudden shift had left all except Mouland's men exposed to the frosty north wind and driving snow. Since they had built the walls on the edges of their pans, they could not seek shelter on the lee side.

The men of Jones's watch, congregating with Dawson's men, had grossly overcrowded his pan, leaving little space for exercise. Their wall was useless so they devised their own method of protection by standing four deep with their backs to the wind, the men on the windward side running to leeward to take their place at the front until they had worked back to the windward again.

Here and there, from the three different groups, a few voices rose bravely in song. Soon others joined in. But the bitter wind from Labrador buffeted their ill-clad bodies, and snatched their voices, dispersing them raggedly into the night. Others danced lively jigs to halt the freezing numbness creeping insidiously through their limbs. The huskiest sky-larked and even wrestled with each other.

But there were many who by now were too ill with cold and exhaustion to do more than creep feebly about. They lay on the ice to rest.

"*Move!* Kape moving!" was the order, as those with more vitality forced them back to their feet, trying to shock life into them, to make them walk. But Tom Jordan, brother of Stephen, wandered too near the edge of the pan and, unable to distinguish the slush from the solid ice, fell through. His cry of fright brought two men who hauled him back to the floe. There, trembling with shock, he collapsed and died. He was the first man in Dawson's watch to die.

Ice crusted their clothing, their eyebrows and lashes, even the stubble that bearded their faces; their mittens were unwieldy lumps of ice covering hands that had lost all feeling. To keep on the move took teeth-gritting determination. It was much easier to let the numbness creep up their limbs and into their brain, easier to rest.

"Can't see," one man muttered. Ice on his brow and lashes shuttered his eyes like blinds, and his fingers were too stiff to remove it. In any case, the ice was frozen to the roots of his hair. Many sealers suffered in the same way and stumbled around, blind, until Jesse Collins went from one to the other, biting off the lumps of ice with his teeth. He froze his lips doing it.

In the disaster, Jesse had emerged as leader. It was to him the young men turned, rather than to Tuff and Bungay. The officers were somewhere on the pan, but lost in the crowd and the black night.

"Don't give up, fellers, kape on the move," Collins commanded.

"You're the boss, Jesse."

"Awful tired, can't we take a spell?"

"Can't take a spell, b'ys, but we'll bide a while and go fishin'." His voice rose. "Gather round now."

They gathered round, calling to one anther in wonder, "Jesse says we're goin' fishin'."

"Get yer jiggers ready, b'ys," he bellowed.

They caught on. Everyone went through the motion of preparing lines and jiggers.

"Ready, Jesse."

Then Jesse commanded them to throw their imaginary lines over the sides of their imaginary boats, then to haul in their lines, hand over hand. With great seriousness they obeyed.

"Catch anything, fellers?"

"Naw, Jesse," they chorused.

"We'll kape tryin' then."

They went through the motions time and again.

"There's not much on the jigger today, b'ys," Jesse roared.

They chorused in agreement, "Naw, nothin' on the jigger."

"Then we'll go with hook and line. Bait up yer hooks."

They obediently baited their imaginary hooks with imaginary squid and threw them into the imaginary sea, pulling in, and throwing out until they had the blood coursing through their veins once more.

But even that became wearying after a while, and Jesse roared above the biting wind, "Time to go on parade, b'ys."

They lined up single file and marched round and round the pan, hitting one another on the shoulders, where they felt the cold most of all. Round and round they went, not so fast as to sap their vitality; just a slow, shuffling movement to keep the blood circulating.

Jesse Collins seemed to be everywhere, keeping a sharp eye for malingerers; punching, shaking those who were willing to give in: "*Up, b'y, up!*" he would roar with great ferocity, and the men would struggle to their feet to make one more effort to survive.

Numb with cold and exhaustion, young Cecil Mouland still remembered his grandfather's advice about frost-burn. All the while he was obediently "chawing" his tobacco—it would never do to go home to Jesse with a frost-burned face. His new woolen mitts, knitted by his mother, had extended almost to the elbow when he had put them on that morning. But the wet snow and sleet had shrunk them so that now they failed to cover his wrists. Rawhide boots, heavy-soled and hobnailed, encased his legs snugly to the knees; but in conditions like these they were obviously not wet proof. He remembered, ruefully, that he had skin cuffs aboard ship, as well as oilskins. "What would I give t'have them oilskins now," he told his cousin Ralph.

"Yah!" Ralph mumbled, and eased himself to the ice. "I'm tired, Cec, gotta take a spell."

Cecil let him rest for a minute only. "That's enough, Ralph." He felt a responsibility for Ralph, since he had persuaded the young man to come to the ice-field with him.

On this same pan, Edward Tippett gathered his two young sons, Norman and Abel, to him. With an arm protectively around each, he did his best to shield them from the cold. Near them Alfred and Bob Maidment, who had earlier that day predicted a record disaster, kept determinedly on the move. Both were married and had children; both were determined to see their families again.

The blizzard of the afternoon was a tea party compared to the one now screaming at them from the north; frost seemed to take their breath, stabbed into their lungs, cut their flesh; there was no facing into that wind.

Numbness gripped even the liveliest, and two strapping young men who laughingly had wrestled strenuously earlier were now reeling from exhaustion. They finally fell to the ice, unable to keep going. But Jesse Collins roused them, forced them to their feet. When they again fell in an exhausted stupor, he kindled a small fire with his greasy rope, cut the top off the molasses can he carried on his belt, and, using snow, made a hot, sweet drink which he shared between the two young men. They revived miraculously, apparently with new life in their bodies. But an hour later their strength gave out again. They fell to the ice and died. The heroic Jesse Collins turned to saving others.

The men, deeply religious, comforted themselves with prayers and hymns. Voices rose quaveringly, singing "Lead, Kindly Light" and "Abide With Me." With great feeling they sang, "Does Jesus Care?"

The savage whine of the wind mocked them.

In Arthur Mouland's shelter, the men fared much better. Thanks to the wing he had forced them to build, they had partial protection in one corner. There they huddled while Mouland, barking above the howling wind, kept them moving their feet, constantly marking time. As they huddled together, numbly marching on the same spot, their body heat did not dissipate and they suffered less discomfort than their unfortunate mates out in the open.

Newfoundland log:
   1 a.m. Wind direction North. Wind force 7.
Begins with strong gale from north and drifting snow. Ice packed close, and ship jammed.

The wind backed west of north, and finally held from a point about north by west. All the ice shelters were now completely useless.

The bitter night seemed unending. Each moment was a living hell that dragged interminably on; biting frost and snow rode the gale and the men who could still feel anything suffered unspeakable agony. At some point during the night the snow thinned and finally stopped, but the wind continued to blow with gale force, and ground drift was as blinding as the blizzard had been before.

Great courage was shown on those three ice pans during the dark hours before dawn. Men almost too exhausted to help themselves helped each other. They danced, boxed, and wrestled; they coaxed, wheedled, and rough-housed those who lay on the ice to die. But despite their best efforts, the first grey light revealed many still bodies. Among them were those of William Pear, Bernard and Henry Jordan, Edward Tippett and his two sons, Norman and Abel. Partially covered by snowdrifts, Tippett's arms were frozen around his sons' bodies. They still huddled close to him in death.

CANLIT CRASH COURSE

MARGARET ATWOOD

From *Survival* (1972)

For a new generation of readers, it is difficult to realize how much excitement and controversy accompanied the 1972 publication of Survival: A Thematic Guide to Canadian Literature. *At that time the whole notion that Canada had a literature worth taking seriously was still a new one. "Canlit" courses at universities were struggling to find a place beside their more mature English and American cousins. Margaret Atwood herself was an award-winning poet, but she had not yet emerged as the extremely popular novelist she would become. And her technique, to read back into the national character a pathology she found evident in the literature, seemed confrontational, if not ill-mannered. All in all, then,* Survival *was for its time a daring and quite unprecedented book: a book about literature which was at the same time highly political. And it remains so: a leading Canadian writer, addressing herself to a broad, popular audience, thinking out loud about our national literature.*

In Survival, *Atwood adopts a conventional critical method; she seeks to identify the common themes which preoccupy Canadian writers. It is a book of literary criticism, but its content is aggressively non-academic. Atwood employs the first person throughout, along with a chatty, colloquial style. The selection that follows sets out the main argument of the book.*

Margaret Atwood was born in Ottawa in 1939. Her collection of poetry, The Circle Game, *won a Governor-General's award in 1966 and since then she has*

231

enjoyed consistent critical acclaim, for her poetry and also for a series of novels which
have gained her a large audience worldwide. Probably the country's first celebrity
highbrow novelist, she has used her notoriety to speak out on issues of Canadian
nationalism, feminism, and international human rights.

I'd like to begin with a sweeping generalization and argue that every
country or culture has a single unifying and informing symbol at its
core. (Please don't take any of my oversimplifications as articles of dogma
which allow of no exceptions; they are proposed simply to create vantage
points from which the literature may be viewed.) The symbol, then—be
it word, phrase, idea, image, or all of these—functions like a system of
beliefs (it *is* a system of beliefs, though not always a formal one) which
holds the country together and helps the people in it to co-operate for
common ends. Possibly the symbol for America is The Frontier, a flexible
idea that contains many elements dear to the American heart: it suggests
a place that is *new*, where the old order can be discarded (as it was when
America was instituted by a crop of disaffected Protestants, and later at
the time of the Revolution); a line that is always expanding, taking in or
"conquering" ever-fresh virgin territory (be it The West, the rest of the
world, outer space, Poverty or The Regions of the Mind); it holds out
a hope, never fulfilled but always promised, of Utopia, the perfect human
society. Most twentieth-century American literature is about the gap
between the promise and the actuality, between the imagined ideal
Golden West or City Upon a Hill, the model for all the world postulated
by the Puritans, and the actual squalid materialism, dotty small town, nasty
city, or redneck-filled outback. Some Americans have even confused the
actuality with the promise: in that case Heaven is a Hilton hotel with a
Coke machine in it.

The corresponding symbol for England is perhaps The Island, convenient for obvious reasons. In the seventeenth century a poet called Phineas
Fletcher wrote a long poem called *The Purple Island*, which is based on
an extended body-as-island metaphor, and, dreadful though the poem
is, that's the kind of island I mean: island-as-body, self-contained, a
Body Politic, evolving organically, with a hierarchical structure in
which the King is the Head, the statesmen the hands, the peasants or
farmers or workers the feet, and so on. The Englishman's home as his
castle is the popular form of this symbol, the feudal castle being not only

an insular structure but a self-contained microcosm of the entire Body Politic.

The central symbol for Canada—and this is based on numerous instances of its occurrence in both English and French Canadian literature—is undoubtedly Survival, *la Survivance*. Like The Frontier and The Island, it is a multi-faceted and adaptable idea. For early explorers and settlers, it meant bare survival in the face of "hostile" elements and/or natives: carving out a place and a way of keeping alive. But the word can also suggest survival of a crisis or disaster, like a hurricane or a wreck, and many Canadian poems have this kind of survival as a theme; what you might call "grim" survival as opposed to "bare" survival. For French Canada after the English took over it became cultural survival, hanging on as a people, retaining a religion and a language under an alien government. And in English Canada now while the Americans are taking over it is acquiring a similar meaning. There is another use of the word as well: a survival can be a vestige of a vanished order which has managed to persist after its time is past, like a primitive reptile. This version crops up in Canadian thinking too, usually among those who believe that Canada is obsolete.

But the main idea is the first one: hanging on, staying alive. Canadians are forever taking the national pulse like doctors at a sickbed: the aim is not to see whether the patient will live well but simply whether he will live at all. Our central idea is one which generates, not the excitement and sense of adventure or danger which The Frontier holds out, not the smugness and/or sense of security, of everything in its place, which The Island can offer, but an almost intolerable anxiety. Our stories are likely to be tales not of those who made it but of those who made it back, from the awful experience—the North, the snowstorm, the sinking ship—that killed everyone else. The survivor has no triumph of victory but the fact of his survival; he has little after his ordeal that he did not have before, except gratitude for having escaped with his life.

A preoccupation with one's survival is necessarily also a preoccupation with the obstacles to that survival. In earlier writers these obstacles are external—the land, the climate, and so forth. In later writers the obstacles tend to become both harder to identify and more internal; they are no longer obstacles to physical survival but obstacles to what we may call spiritual survival, to life as anything more than a minimally human being.

Sometimes fear of these obstacles becomes itself the obstacle, and a character is paralyzed by terror (either of what he thinks is threatening him from the outside, or of elements in his nature that threaten him from within). It may even be life itself that he fears; and when life becomes a threat to life, you have a moderately vicious circle. If a man feels he can survive only by amputating himself, turning himself into a cripple or a eunuch, what price survival?

Just to give you a quick sample of what I'm talking about, here are a few capsule Canadian plots. Some contain attempts to survive which fail. Some contain bare survivals. Some contain crippled successes (the character does more than survive, but is mutilated in the process).

Pratt: *The Titanic:* Ship crashes into iceberg. Lost passengers drown.

Pratt: *Brébeuf and His Brethren:* After crushing ordeals, priests survive briefly and are massacred by Indians.

Laurence: *The Stone Angel:* Old woman hangs on grimly to life and dies at the end.

Carrier: *Is It The Sun, Philibert?:* Hero escapes incredible rural poverty and horrid urban conditions, almost makes it financially, dies when he wrecks his car.

Marlyn: *Under the Ribs of Death:* Hero amputates himself spiritually in order to make it financially, fails anyway.

Ross: *As for Me and My House:* Prairie minister who hates his job and has crippled himself artistically by sticking with it is offered a dubious chance of escape at the end.

Buckler: *The Mountain and the Valley:* Writer who has been unable to write has vision of possibility at the end but dies before he can implement it.

Gibson: *Communion:* Man who can no longer make human contact tries to save sick dog, fails, and is burned up at the end.

And just to round things out, we might add that the two English Canadian feature films (apart from Allan King's documentaries) to have had much success so far, *Goin' Down the Road* and *The Rowdyman,* are both dramatizations of failure. The heroes survive, but just barely; they are born losers, and their failure to do anything but keep alive has nothing to do with the Maritime Provinces or "regionalism." It's pure Canadian, from sea to sea.

My sample plots are taken from both prose and poetry, and from regions all across Canada; they span four decades, from the thirties to the early seventies. And they hint at another facet of Survivalism: at some point the failure to survive, or the failure to achieve anything beyond survival, becomes not a necessity imposed by a hostile outside world but a choice made from within. Pushed far enough, the obsession with surviving can become the will *not* to survive.

Certainly Canadian authors spend a disproportionate amount of time making sure that their heroes die or fail. Much Canadian writing suggests that failure is required because it is felt—consciously or unconsciously—to be the only "right" ending, the only thing that will support the characters' (or their authors') view of the universe. When such endings are well-handled and consistent with the whole book, one can't quarrel with them on aesthetic grounds. But when Canadian writers are writing clumsy or manipulated endings, they are much less likely to manipulate in a positive than they are in a negative direction: that is, the author is less likely to produce a sudden inheritance from a rich old uncle or the surprising news that his hero is really the son of a Count than he is to conjure up an unexpected natural disaster or an out-of-control car, tree or minor character so that the protagonist may achieve a satisfactory *failure*. Why should this be so? Could it be that Canadians have a will to lose which is as strong and pervasive as the Americans' will to win?

It might be argued that, since most Canlit has been written in the twentieth century and since the twentieth century has produced a generally pessimistic or "ironic" literature, Canada has simply been reflecting a trend. Also, though it's possible to write a short lyric poem about joy and glee, no novel of any length can exclude all but these elements. A novel about unalloyed happiness would have to be either very short or very boring: "Once upon a time John and Mary lived happily ever after, The End." Both of these arguments have some validity, but surely the Canadian gloom is more unrelieved than most and the death and failure toll out of proportion. Given a choice of the negative or positive aspects of any symbol—sea as life-giving Mother, sea as what your ship goes down in; tree as symbol of growth, tree as what falls on your head—Canadians show a marked preference for the negative.

You might decide at this point that most Canadian authors with any pretensions to seriousness are neurotic or morbid, and settle down instead

for a good read with *Anne of Green Gables* (though it's about an orphan
. . .). But if the coincidence intrigues you—so many writers in such a
small country, and *all with the same neurosis*—then I will offer you a theory.
Like any theory it won't explain everything, but it may give you some
points of departure.

Let us suppose, for the sake of argument, that Canada as a whole is a
victim, or an "oppressed minority," or "exploited." Let us suppose in
short that Canada is a colony. A partial definition of a colony is that it is
a place from which a profit is made, but *not by the people who live there:*
the major profit from a colony is made in the centre of the empire.
That's what colonies are for, to make money for the "mother country,"
and that's what—since the days of Rome and, more recently, of the
Thirteen Colonies—they have always been for. Of course there are
cultural side-effects which are often identified as "the colonial mentality,"
and it is these which are examined here; but the root cause for them is
economic.

   If Canada is a collective victim, it should pay some attention to the
Basic Victim Positions. These are like the basic positions in ballet or the
scales on the piano: they are primary, though all kinds of song-and-dance
variations on them are possible.

   The positions are the same whether you are a victimized country, a
victimized minority group or a victimized individual.

Basic Victim Positions
Position One: To deny the fact that you are a victim.

   This uses up a lot of energy, as you must spend much time explaining
away the obvious, suppressing anger, and pretending that certain visible
facts do not exist. The position is usually taken by those in a Victim group
who are a little better off than the others in that group. They are afraid
to recognize they are victims for fear of losing the privileges they possess,
and they are forced to account somehow for the disadvantages suffered
by the rest of the people in the group by disparaging them. As in: "*I*
made it, therefore it's obvious we aren't victims. The rest are just lazy (or
neurotic, or stupid); anyway it's their own fault if they aren't happy, look
at all the opportunities available for them!"

   If anger is felt by Victims in Position One, it is likely to be directed against one's fellow-victims, particularly those who try to talk about their victimization.

The basic game in Position One is "Deny your victim-experience."

Position Two: To acknowledge the fact that you are a victim, but to explain this as an act of Fate, the Will of God, the dictates of Biology (in the case of women, for instance), the necessity decreed by History, or Economics, or the Unconscious, or any other large general powerful idea.

In any case, since it is the fault of this large *thing* and not your own fault, you can neither be blamed for your position nor be expected to do anything about it. You can be resigned and long-suffering, or you can kick against the pricks and make a fuss; in the latter case your rebellion will be deemed foolish or evil even by you, and you will expect to lose and be punished, for who can fight Fate (or the Will of God, or Biology)? Notice that:

1. The explanation *displaces* the cause from the real source of oppression to something else.

2. Because the fake cause is so vast, nebulous and unchangeable, you are permanently excused from changing it, *and also* from deciding how much of your situation (e.g. the climate) is unchangeable, how much can be changed, and how much is caused by habit or tradition or your own need to be a victim.

3. Anger, when present—or scorn, since everyone in the category is defined as inferior—is directed against both fellow-victims and oneself.

The basic game in Position Two is Victor/Victim.

Position Three: To acknowledge the fact that you are a victim but to refuse to accept the assumption that the role is inevitable.

As in: "Look what's being done to me, and it isn't Fate, it isn't the Will of God. Therefore I can stop seeing myself as a *fated* Victim." To put it differently: you can distinguish between the *role* of Victim (which probably leads you to seek victimization even when there's no call for it) and the *objective experience* that is making you a victim. And you can probably go further and decide how much of the objective experience could be changed if you made the effort.

This is a dynamic position, rather than a static one; from it you can move on to Position Four, but if you become locked into your anger and fail to change your situation, you might well find yourself back in Position Two.

Notice that:

1. In this position the real cause of oppression is for the first time identified.

2. Anger can be directed against the real source of oppression, and energy channelled into constructive action.

3. You can make real decisions about how much of your position can be changed and how much can't (you can't make it stop snowing; you can stop blaming the snow for everything that's wrong).

The basic game of Position Three is repudiating the Victim role.

Position Four: To be a creative non-victim.

Strictly speaking, Position Four is a position not for victims but for those who have never been victims at all, or for ex-victims: those who have been able to move into it from Position Three because the external and/or the internal causes of victimization have been removed. (In an oppressed society, of course, you can't become an ex-victim—insofar as you are connected with your society—until the entire society's position has been changed.)

In Position Four, creative energy of all kinds becomes possible. Energy is no longer being suppressed (as in Position One) or used up for displacement of the cause, or for passing your victimization along to others (Man kicks Child, Child kicks Dog) as in Position Two; nor is it being used for the dynamic anger of Position Three. And you are able to accept your own experience for what it is, rather than having to distort it to make it correspond with others' versions of it (particularly those of your oppressors).

In Position Four, Victor/Victim games are obsolete. You don't even have to concentrate on rejecting the role of Victim, because the role is no longer a temptation for you.

(There may be a Position Five, for mystics; I postulate it but will not explore it here, since mystics do not as a rule write books.)

I devised this model not as the Secret of Life or the answer to everything (though you can apply it to world politics or your friends if you like), but as a helpful method of approaching our literature. It's a model about Victims for the simple reason that I found a superabundance of victims in Canadian literature. If I'd been looking at the nineteenth century English novel I'd have devised a table called Characteristics of Gentlemen; or if I'd been investigating American literature I would have found myself thinking about picaresque anti-heroes; or if I'd been examining German Romantic literature the result would probably have been a diagram of Doppelgängers. But stick a pin in Canadian literature at random, and nine times out of ten you'll hit a victim. My model, then, is a product of my Canadian literary experiences, not a Procrustean bed dreamed up in advance on which Canlit is about to be stretched. Now that I've traced its main outlines, I'll indicate briefly how I intend to use—and not to use—the model.

First, three general points about the model:

·   As I said, this is a verbal diagram; it is intended to be suggestive rather than totally accurate. But experience is never linear: you're rarely in any Position in its pure form for very long—and you may have a foot, as it were, in more than one Position at once.

·   What happens to an individual who has reached Position Three in a society which is still in Positions One and Two? (Not very nice things, usually.) Or, what happens to an individual who is a victim—like a Black in America—in a society which as a whole is *not* being oppressed by another society? (Again, not very nice things.) If, for instance, your society is in Position Two, perhaps you can't move through Position Three into Position Four except by repudiating your society, or at least its assumptions about the nature of life and proper behaviour. This may eventually make Position Four unreal for you: can you fiddle happily while Rome groans?

·   I've presented the model as though it were based on individual rather than social experience. Perhaps the terms would shift slightly if you were to substitute "we" or "our class" or "our country" for "I," and you'd then get a more complicated analysis of Canadian colonialism. My approach is more modest: it sketches a perspective from which Canadian *Literature* makes a surprising amount of sense.

Now, the model as it applies to writing:

·   I assume that *by definition* (mine, and you don't have to believe me) an author is in Position Four at the moment of writing, that is, the moment of creation—though the subject of his book may be Position Two, and the energy for it may come from Position Three. In the rest of his life he shifts around, like everyone else. (The analogous Position Four moment for the reader is not the time it takes to read a book, but the moment of insight—the time when the book makes sense or comes clear). And apart from that comment, I don't want to speculate about the state of authors' souls. Instead, just as in the Preface I proposed the fiction that the literature was being written by Canada, I here propose to regard novels and poems as though they were expressions of Positions, not of authors.

· This method will, I hope, articulate the skeleton of Canadian literature. It will let you see how the bones fit together, but it won't put flesh on them. That is, the method provides a static dissection, rather than a dynamic examination of a process-in-motion. (A "static" model facilitates classification. Trying out a dynamic model would also be interesting.)

· Because I'm not handing out gold stars, I'll try not to do much evaluating—praising or censuring—of books according to this model. Although in real life Position Four may be preferable to Position Two, I do find a consistent and tough-minded Position Two poem preferable to a sloppy and unearned Position Four one. But I'll let you do that kind of evaluation for yourself.

You might try to decide whether, in any given work, the actual conditions of the characters' lives are sufficient to account for the doom and gloom meted out to them. Bare Survival isn't a central theme by accident, and neither is the victim motif; the land *was* hard, and we have been (and are) an exploited colony; our literature is rooted in those facts. But you might wonder, in a snowstorm-kills-man story, whether the snowstorm is an adequate explanation for the misery of the characters, or whether the author has displaced the source of the misery in their world and is blaming the snowstorm when he ought to be blaming something else. If so, it is a Position Two story: quite apart from the subject matter, it expresses a premature resignation and a misplaced willingness to see one's victimization as unchangeable.

And I'll point out too that a book can be a symptom or reflection of a Position (though not necessarily a bad book); or it can be a *conscious examination* of it (though not necessarily a good one). The latter seems less fatalistic; a conscious examination of victim experience—including the *need* to be a victim—suggests a more realistic desire to transcend the experience, even if that is not made explicit in the book.

THE IMPULSE OF SAVAGERY

FARLEY MOWAT

From *A Whale for the Killing* (1972)

Farley Mowat has written more than two dozen books, most of them autobiographical and most of them about the destruction of the natural world by modern, technological society. His work combines forceful polemic—he seems to be in a constant state of indignation—with exciting narrative which usually places the author at the centre of the action.

In January, 1967, while Mowat and his wife Claire were living in Burgeo on the south coast of Newfoundland, a large fin whale blundered into a small cove on the outskirts of town and could not get out again. A handful of local people used the animal for target practice and harrassed it with boats before Mowat could mount a crusade to save it. A Whale for the Killing *is an account of that episode. It is both a dramatic story about a trapped whale and a tragic allegory about man's destruction of the animal kingdom.*

Farley Mowat was born in Belleville, Ontario in 1921 and began writing for a living following the Second World War. His love of animals and of travel are evident in most of his books, which cover a wide range of topics.

Burgeo winter weather often seemed to consist of six days of storm followed by a seventh when all was forgiven, and the seventh day was almost always a Sunday. I once discussed this interesting phenomenon with the Anglican minister but he decently refused to take any credit for it.

Sunday, January 29th, was no exception. It almost seemed as if spring had come. The sun flared in a cloudless sky; there was not a breath of wind; the sea was still and the temperature soared.

Early in the morning Onie Stickland and I went off to Aldridges in his dory. We took grub and a tea kettle since I expected to spend the entire day observing the whale and noting her behaviour for the record. I hoped Onie and I would be alone with her, but there were already a number of boats moored to the rocks at the outer end of the channel when we arrived, and two or three dozen people were clustered on the ridge overlooking the Pond. I saw with relief that nobody was carrying a rifle.

We joined the watchers, among whom were several fishermen I knew, and found them seemingly content just to stand and watch the slow, steady circling of the whale. I used the opportunity to spread some propaganda about Burgeo's good luck in being host to such a beast, and how its continued well-being would help in drawing the attention of faraway government officials to a community which had been resolutely neglected for many years.

The men listened politely but they were skeptical. It was hard for them to believe that anyone outside Burgeo would have much interest in a whale. Nevertheless, there did seem to be a feeling that the whale should not be further tormented.

"They's no call for that sort of foolishness," said Harvey Ingram, a lanky, sharp-featured fisherman, originally from Red Island. "Lave it be, says I. 'Tis doing harm to none."

Some of the others nodded in agreement and I began to wonder whether—if no help came from outside—it might be possible to rouse sufficient interest in the whale, yes, and sympathy for her, so we could take care of her ourselves.

"Poor creature has trouble enough," said one of the men who fished The Ha Ha. But then he took me down again by adding:

"Pond was full of herring first day she come in. Now we sees hardly none at all. When we first see the whale, 'twas some fat, some sleek. Now it looks poorly. Getting razor-backed, I'd say."

We were interrupted by the arrival, in a flurry of spray and whining power, of a big outboard speedboat, purchased through the catalogue by one of the young men who spent their summers on the Great Lakes freighters. He was accompanied by several of his pals, all of them sporting colourful nylon windbreakers of the sort that are almost uniforms for the habitués of small-town poolrooms on the mainland. They came ashore, but stood apart from our soberly dressed group, talking among themselves in tones deliberately pitched high enough to reach our ears.

"We'd a had it kilt by now," said one narrow-faced youth, with a sidelong glance in my direction, "only for someone putting the Mountie onto we!"

"And that's the truth!" replied one of his companions. "Them people from away better 'tend their own business. Got no call to interfere with we." He spat in the snow to emphasize his remark.

"What are we standing here for?" another asked loudly. "We's not afeared of nay goddamn whale. Let's take a run onto the pond. Might have some sport into it yet."

They ambled back to their powerboat and when the youths had clambered aboard, one of the men standing near me said quietly:

"Don't pay no heed, skipper. They's muck floats up in every place. Floats to the top and stinks, but don't mean nothin'."

It was kindly sad, and I appreciated it.

By this time a steady stream of boats was converging on the Pond from Short Reach, The Harbour, and from further west. There were power dories, skiffs, longliners, and even a few rowboats with youngsters at the oars. Burgeo was making the most of the fine weather to come and see its whale.

The majority of the newcomers seemed content to moor their boats with the growing armada out in the entrance cove but several came through the channel into the pond, following the lead of the mail-order speedboat. At first the boats which entered the Pond kept close to shore, leaving the open water to the whale. Their occupants were obviously awed by the immense bulk of the creature, and were timid about approaching anywhere near her. But by noon, by which time some thirty boats, bearing at least a hundred people, had arrived, the mood began to change.

There was now a big crowd around the south and southwest shore of the Pond. In full awareness of this audience, and fortified by lots of beer, a number of young men (and some not so young) now felt ready to show their mettle. The powerful boat which had been the first to enter suddenly accelerated to full speed and roared directly across the Pond only a few yards behind the whale as she submerged. Some of the people standing along the shore raised a kind of ragged cheer, and within minutes the atmosphere had completely—and frighteningly—altered.

More and more boats started up their engines and nosed into the Pond. Five or six of the fastest left the security of the shores and darted out into the middle. The reverberation of many engines began to merge into a sustained roar, a baleful and ferocious sound, intensified by the echoes from the surrounding cliffs. The leading powerboat became more daring and snarled across the whale's wake at close to twenty knots, dragging a high rooster-tail of spray.

The whale was now no longer moving leisurely in great circles, coming up to breathe at intervals of five or ten minutes. She had begun to swim much faster and more erratically as she attempted to avoid the several boats which were chivvying her. The swirls of water from her flukes became much more agitated as she veered sharply from side to side. She was no longer able to clear her lungs with the usual two or three blows after every dive, but barely had time to suck in a single breath before being driven down again. Her hurried surfacings consequently became more and more frequent even as the sportsmen, gathering courage because the whale showed no sign of retaliation, grew braver and braver. Two of the fastest boats began to circle her at full throttle, like a pair of malevolent water beetles.

Meanwhile, something rather terrible was taking place in the emotions of many of the watchers ringing the Pond. The mood of passive curiosity had dissipated, to be replaced by one of hungry anticipation. Looking into the faces around me, I recognized the same avid air of expectation which contorts the faces of a prizefight audience into primal masks.

At this juncture the blue hull of the RCMP launch appeared in the entrance cove. Onie and I jumped aboard the dory and intercepted her. I pleaded with Constable Murdoch for help.

"Some of these people have gone wild! They're going to drive the whale ashore if they don't drown her first. You have to put a stop to it . . . order them out of the Pond!"

The constable shook his head apologetically.

"Sorry. I can't do that. They aren't breaking any law, you know. I can't do anything unless the local authorities ask me to. But we'll take the launch inside and anchor in the middle of the Pond. Maybe that'll discourage them a bit."

He was a nice young man but out of his element and determined not to do anything which wasn't "in the book." He was well within his rights; and I certainly overstepped mine when, in my distress, I intimated that he was acting like a coward. He made no reply, but quietly told Danny to take the police boat in.

Onie and I followed them through the channel, then we turned along the southwest shore where I hailed several men in boats, pleading with them to leave the whale alone. Some made no response. One of them, a middle-aged merchant, gave me a derisive grin and deliberately accelerated his engine to drown out my voice. Even the elder fishermen standing on shore now seemed more embarrassed by my attitude than sympathetic. I was slow to realize it but the people gathered at Aldridges Pond had sensed that a moment of high drama was approaching and, if it was to be a tragic drama, so much the better.

Having discovered that there was nothing to fear either from the whale or from the police, the speedboat sportsmen began to make concerted efforts to herd the great beast into the shallow easterly portion of the Pond. Three boats succeeded in cornering her in a small bight, and when she turned violently to avoid them, she grounded for half her length on a shelf of rock.

There followed a stupendous flurry of white water as her immense flukes lifted clear and beat upon the surface. She reared forward, raising her whole head into view, then turned on her side so that one huge flipper pointed skyward. I had my binoculars on her and for a moment could see all her lower belly, and the certain proof that she was female. Then slowly and, it seemed, painfully, she rolled clear of the rock.

As she slid free there was a hubbub from the crowd on shore, a sound amounting almost to a roar, that was audible even over the snarl of engines. It held a note of insensate fury that seemed to inflame the boatmen to even more vicious attacks upon the now panic-stricken whale.

Making no attempt to submerge, she fled straight across the Pond in the direction of the eastern shallows where there were, at that moment, no boats or people. The speedboats raced close beside her, preventing her from changing course. She seemed to make a supreme effort to outrun them and then, with horrifying suddenness, she hit the muddy shoals and drove over them until she was aground for her whole length.

The Pond erupted in pandemonium. Running and yelling people leapt into boats of all shapes and sizes and these began converging on the stranded animal. I recognized the doctor team—the deputy mayor of Burgeo and his councillor wife—aboard one small longliner. I told Onie to lay the dory alongside them and I scrambled over the longliner's rail while she was still under way. By this time I was so enraged as to be almost inarticulate. Furiously I *ordered* the deputy mayor to tell the constable to clear the Pond.

He was a man with a very small endowment of personal dignity. I had outraged what dignity he did possess. He pursed his soft, red lips and replied:

"What would be the use of that? The whale is going to die anyway. Why should I interfere?" He turned his back and busied himself recording the whale's "last moments" with his expensive movie camera.

The exchange had been overheard, for the boats were now packed tightly into the cul-de-sac and people were scrambling from boat to boat, or along the shore itself, to gain a better view. There was a murmur of approval for the doctor and then someone yelled, gloatingly:

"Dat whale is finished, byes! It be ashore for certain now! Good riddance is what I says!"

Indeed, the whale's case looked hopeless. She was aground in less than twelve feet of water; and the whole incredible length of her, from the small of the tail almost to her nose, was exposed to view. The tide was on the ebb and if she remained where she was for even as little as half an hour, she would be doomed to die where she lay. Yet she was not struggling. Now that no boats were tormenting her, she seemed to ignore the human beings who fringed the shore not twenty feet away. I had the sickening conviction that she had given up; that the struggle for survival had become too much.

My anguish was so profound that when I saw three men step out into the shallows and begin heaving rocks at her half-submerged head, I went berserk. Scrambling to the top of the longliner's deckhouse, I screamed imprecations at them. Faces turned toward me and, having temporarily focused attention on myself, I launched into a wild tirade.

This was a *female* whale, I cried. She might be and probably was pregnant. This attack on her was a monstrous, despicable act of cruelty. If, I threatened, everyone did not instantly get to hell out of Aldridges

Pond and leave the whale be, I would make it my business to blacken Burgeo's name from one end of Canada to the other.

Calming down a little, I went on to promise that if the whale survived she would make Burgeo famous. "You'll get your damned highway!" I remember yelling. "Television and all the rest of it . . . " God knows what else I might have said or promised if the whale had not herself intervened.

Somebody shouted in surprise; and we all looked. She was moving.

She was turning—infinitely slowly—sculling with her flippers and gently agitating her flukes. We Lilliputians watched silent and incredulous as the vast Gulliver inched around until she was facing out into the Pond. Then slowly, slowly, almost imperceptibly, she drifted off the shoals and slid from sight beneath the glittering surface.

I now realize that she had not been in danger of stranding herself permanently. On the contrary, she had taken the one course open to her and had deliberately sought out the shallows where she could quite literally catch her breath, free from the harassment of the motorboats. But, at the time, her escape from what appeared to be mortal danger almost seemed to savour of the miraculous. Also, as if by another miracle, it radically altered the attitude of the crowd, suddenly subduing the mood of feverish excitement. People began to climb quietly back into their boats. One by one the boats moved off toward the south channel, and within twenty minutes Aldridges Pond was empty of all human beings except for Onie and me.

It was an extraordinary exodus. Nobody seemed to be speaking to anybody else . . . and not one word was said to me. Some people averted their eyes as they passed our dory. I do not think this was because of any guilt they may have felt—and many of them *did* feel guilty—it was because *I* had shamed *them*, as a group, as a community, as a people . . . and had done so publicly. The stranger in their midst had spoken his heart and displayed his rage and scorn. We could no longer pretend we understood each other. We had become strangers, one to the other.

My journal notes, written late that night, reflect my bewilderment and my sense of loss.

" . . . they are essentially good people. I know that, but what sickens me is their simple failure to resist the impulse of savagery . . . they seem to be just as capable of being utterly loathsome as the bastards from the cities with their high-powered rifles and telescopic sights and their mindless compulsion to slaughter everything alive, from squirrels to elephants . . . I admired them so much because I saw them as a natural people, living in at least some degree of harmony with the natural world. Now they seem nauseatingly anxious to renounce all that and throw themselves into the stinking quagmire of our society which has perverted everything natural within itself, and is now busy destroying everything natural outside itself. How can they be so bloody stupid? How could *I* have been so bloody stupid?"

Bitter words . . . bitter, and unfair; but I had lost my capacity for objectivity and was ruled, now, by irrational emotions. I was no longer willing, or perhaps not able, to understand the people of Burgeo; to comprehend them as they really were, as men and women who were victims of forces and circumstances of whose effects they remained unconscious. I had withdrawn my compassion from them, in hurt and ignorance. Now I bestowed it all upon the whale.

TWO SOLITUDES

MARIA CAMPBELL

From *Halfbreed* (1973)

Maria Campbell was born in 1940 at Park Valley, Saskatchewan, a northern Métis community. Halfbreed appeared when she was thirty-three years old. It tells the story of growing up on the margins of White society, a victim of racism and poverty, but it is also a powerful story of community and cultural survival. It is similar to Heather Robertson's Reservations Are for Indians, *but it is written inside out from the Native point of view. When it appeared, Halfbreed marked a widening of Canadian non-fiction to include voices outside the Euro-Canadian mainstream. Its publication by a major national publisher, McClelland & Stewart, makes it something of a landmark in the history of non-fiction writing in this country.*

Halfbreed was Maria Campbell's first book; she has gone on to write several others. The following selection recalls everyday life in her Métis community.

The school was built in Spring River when I was nine. It was three miles away, and on opening all the parents had to bring their children for registration. Because it was a mixed school, whites and Halfbreeds were gathered together officially for the first time, but the whites sat down on one side of the room while the Halfbreeds sat on the other. We were also to be inoculated. We didn't know this of course because the teacher felt that if she told our parents we might not come. So there we were, all scrubbed and shining, our fathers and mothers looking proudly on.

The teacher called the roll and parents were to stand in front of her and answer questions. Alex Vandal, the village joker, was at his best that day. He had told Daddy that he was going to act retarded because the whites thought we were anyway, so when his son's name was called he shuffled over. The teacher asked for the first name. Alex replied, "Boy." Then he looked dumbly around and finally yelled at his wife in French and Cree. "Oh, the name is Paul." The teacher then asked whether Paul knew his ABC's? "No." "Does he count?" "No." "Does he know his prayers?" "No." "Does your son believe in Jesus Christ?" "No." "Don't you believe in Jesus?" "I don't know, I never saw the god." Our people looked straight ahead trying not to laugh and the whites were tittering. Alex and Paul returned to their seats all smiles.

When registration was finished, the nurse came in and told the parents what she had to do. She began on our side first, but we didn't realize what was happening until we saw her stick a needle in my brother's arm. Then we started screaming and crying. The parents became excited as well. Dad had to hold me while I kicked and fought with all my might. Then the needle went in and Daddy fainted dead away. We arrived home late in the afternoon, a bedraggled bunch, everyone sniffling and red-eyed with sore arms—our parents completely exhausted. They laughed about it later and Daddy was teased for a long time.

School wasn't too bad—Heaven compared to the Residential School. We had a lot of fights with the white kids, but finally, after beating them soundly, we were left alone. There were many remarks made but we learned to ignore or accept them as time went on. Daddy was concerned with the distance we had to go to school, so one day he came home with a mule. What a horrible, ugly animal, especially when we had our hearts set on a good saddle horse! Dad made a saddle for us and in spite of my pleas we had to climb on one morning and start for school. We went a few yards and the mule stopped. Dad hit it and petted it, but nothing worked, so finally we got off and walked, happy that we did not have to disgrace ourselves by riding that old thing. Our happiness was short-lived however. When we came home, my aunt Ellen, Daddy's youngest sister, was riding Mule around the yard at a good clip. She was leaning over, dangling a pole with grass tied to it in front of his nose. Naturally he was never able to catch it, but he certainly tried. And that's how we went to school during that fall and part of the winter. In January it got too cold for us to hold the pole, and Mule, getting smart, started to balk again. Dad finally sold him and we got our horse, not the beautiful, graceful animal of our dreams, but an old quiet Clydesdale mare. Each day we stopped for three cousins, and all five of us rode Nelly to school. We had her until she was unable to move without discomfort from old age, and Dad put her out of her misery.

We Halfbreeds always played by ourselves unless there was rugby or a ball game, when we played against the whites. It was the same in class; we stayed in two separate groups. Lunch hours were really rough when we started school because we had not realized, until then, the difference in our diets. They had white or brown bread, boiled eggs, apples, cakes, cookies, and jars of milk. We were lucky to have these even at Christmas. We took bannock for lunch, spread with lard and filled with wild meat, and if there was no meat we had cold potatoes and salt and pepper, or else whole roasted gophers with sage dressing. No apples or fruit, but if we were lucky there was a jam sandwich for dessert. The first few days the whites were speechless when they saw Alex's children with gophers and the rest of us trading a sandwich, a leg, or dressing. They would tease and call, "Gophers, gophers, Road Allowance people eat gophers." We fought back of course but we were terribly hurt and above all ashamed. I remember coming home and saying ugly things to Mom. She took me in her arms and tried to hold me, but I kicked her and said that I hated her, Daddy, and "all of you no-good Halfbreeds." She turned away and went outside and a few minutes later Daddy came in and tried to talk to me. When I said the same things to him he just sat there while I cried and shouted that the other kids had oranges, apples, cakes, and nice clothes and that all we had were gophers, moose meat, ugly dresses, and patchy pants. Cheechum was sitting on her pallet listening through all this and when Dad said nothing, she got up and led me outside. She didn't speak for the longest time, just walked. When we were about half a mile from the house she told me to get her a long willow stick and bring it to her. Then she told me to sit beside her and listen.

Many years ago, she said, when she was only a little girl, the Halfbreeds came west. They left good homes behind in their search for a place where they could live as they wished. Later a leader arose from these people who said that if they worked hard and fought for what they believed in they would win against all odds. Despite the hardships, they gave all they had for this one desperate chance of being free, but because some of them said, "I want good clothes and horses and you no-good Halfbreeds are ruining it for me," they lost their dream. She continued: "They fought each other just as you are fighting your mother and father today. The white man saw that that was a more powerful weapon than anything else with which to beat the Halfbreeds, and he used it and still does today. Already they are using it on you. They try to make you hate your people." She stood up then and said, "I will beat you each time I hear you talk as you did. If you don't like what you have, then stop fighting your parents and do something about it yourself." With that, she beat me until my legs and arms were swollen with welts. After she was finished she sat with me till I had stopped crying, and then we walked home. Nothing more was ever said about clothes or food. My first real lesson had been learnt. I always tried to keep my head up and defend my friends and cousins in front of those white kids, even when I knew we were wrong. Sometimes it was very hard to control my disappointment and frustration, and many hours were spent with Cheechum telling her how I felt, and she in turn would try to make me understand.

A family of Seventh-Day Adventists lived a couple of miles from our house on the same road. Their two children, a boy and a girl, were very pale, sickly, and timid-looking, but they acted very authoritarian and superior towards us. On the way home from school we often chased and tormented them. In the winter they drove to school in a small caboose warmed by a wood heater. A caboose is a square wooden box with a door at the back. It has runners and a peephole in front to see and to put the reins through. We would hide by the side of the road and scare their old horse so badly it would run away, tipping over the caboose. It's a wonder they weren't burned alive. Next morning the teacher would receive a letter from the parents and we would be whipped in front of the class, but in the afternoon we would make it just as bad for them until they learned to shut up. After a while they decided it was safer to be on our side and so they tried to be friendly. They gave us their lunches as bribes. They could have had ours but they never did develop a taste for gophers and lard.

Our first teacher was a sad-looking English woman in her late forties. She had never taught Halfbreeds before and we soon realized that she didn't like us. I remember her long straight skirts, her black woven stockings, and ugly black shoes. She had very little hair, and what little she had she scraped back into a bun. She loved to sing and her favourite song was "O Canada." I can still see her whenever I hear that song, waving her arms up and down, completely off key and getting all red in the face from the effort. We had many different teachers during those years; some got the girls pregnant and had to leave; others were alcoholic; and because our school attracted everybody else's rejects, we had a constant stream of teachers. We had one good teacher, Mrs. Park, who was stern but fair. Maybe it was because she treated us as equals that I liked her and did well in school.

When I started school my hair was waist-length and so curly it was almost impossible to comb without pain for me and frustration for Mom. She wanted to cut it but Dad forbade her and threatened anyone who even mentioned scissors and Maria in one breath. Mom combed my hair and wrapped it around her fingers to make long, fat ringlets that fell down around my shoulders. She liked to put a bow on top, and that was even worse than the combing. I knew it looked ridiculous because I was always in short pants, boy's shirts, and bare feet. With warts on my hands and with such dark skin, I knew that ringlets and me did not belong together. Poor Momma, she wanted to have a feminine little girl so badly.

My hair was one of Cheechum's pet grievances and she would attack it with the same patience and determination that she revealed whenever she decided to change something. It was fine with me whenever she braided my hair since I wouldn't have to comb it as often. She would spend an hour rubbing bear grease into it and then braid it. The grease was to keep the curls from popping out of the braids and to give me a shiny, tidy look.

My hair, so thick and so full of bear grease, was a perfect place for head lice, and I was deloused at least twice a month. We never had lice at home but some of the kids with whom I played had them. Daddy laughed while Momma sighed, as she washed my hair in coal oil, muttering all the while about Cheechum whom she knew would rub the bear grease in again. Cheechum would say, "Just wait my girl, your Cheechum will make your hair straight yet." And today at thirty-three, my hair is as straight as a poker.

Our days were spent at school, the evenings doing our chores. Daddy was away trapping from early October until Christmas, and again during the beaver season in spring. How we missed him! It was as if part of us was gone with him, and we were not complete until he had returned. I remember the times he came home, always on Christmas Eve. The food supply in our settlement would be very low at that time of year as the men were all gone on the traplines. However Grannie Campbell and my aunts would bring food they had been saving for a long time to our house. They made cakes with frosty icing, sprinkled with coloured sugar, and baked blueberry, cranberry, and saskatoon pies. The smells would be heavenly, because at that time of year our sole diet was wild meat and potatoes. There was no bannock as the flour was being saved for holiday baking. On Christmas Eve, Grannie, Mom, Jamie, and I always went into the bush for a tree. We decorated it with red and green crêpe paper. There was an angel for the top branch, but no one put it there for that was Daddy's job. Then Mom laid out our best clothes while we all bathed in a washtub, and then put us to bed. At ten-thirty we got up and dressed for midnight Mass. It was a thrilling time—outside we could hear sleigh bells ringing and people laughing and calling back and forth as they drove to church.

Right in the middle of all this Daddy would always walk in, with a full-grown beard and a sack full of fur on his back. First he swung Mom off her feet and kissed her, and then we climbed all over him. I remember that he always smelled like wild mink. He washed himself while Mom and Grannie put his packs away, then we all dressed warmly and walked to church with Grannie Campbell. Cheechum stayed home and kept the fire going.

After Mass we talked around the big heater in the church, and friends and relatives all kissed each other. Then we'd all go home, for that was the one night families spent together at home. Daddy would tell us all the things that had happened to him while he was on the trapline. While Mom tidied up and my grannies smoked their pipes, he put the angel on the tree, and we would say our prayers and go to bed.

Jamie and I always woke up everyone at five o'clock. In the living room our stockings were plumb full and overflowing with nuts and candy canes, oranges and apples—the only ones we ate all year. Under the tree there were gifts for everyone. Mom got a comb and mirror from Daddy; he got shaving lotion; and our grannies got cloth for new dresses. We were given blocks made and painted by Dad and Mom, home-made dolls which looked like the modern day "Raggedy Anns," and shoes from our grannies. Then Daddy made pancakes. That was the only meal he ever cooked while Mom was still alive. He made huge pancakes, and while we all stood around, wide-eyed and breathless, he would toss them in the air and catch them right back in the pan.

Christmas dinner was the highlight of the day. It consisted of meat balls rolled in flour, stewed moose meat, all covered with moose fat, mashed potatoes, gravy, baked squash, and pemmican made of fried meat ground to a powder and mixed with raisins, smashed chokeberries and sugar. After that we filled ourselves with the pudding and cakes until we could hardly move.

All the families visited back and forth during the holidays. After supper, furniture was moved against the wall or put outside while the fiddlers tuned their fiddles. Soon they were sawing out a mean hoedown or a Red River jig, and everyone was dancing. Each family held a dance each evening and we never missed any of them. The hostess baked a nickel inside her cake and whoever got it in his piece held the dance the next night. We stuffed ourselves during those holidays until we hurt, because it would be a year before we would eat like that again. One thing about our people is that they never hoard. If they have something they share all of it with each other, regardless of good or bad fortune. Maybe that's why we're so damn poor.

Old Yes-Sant Arcand put on a dance at his house once a year and invited everyone. He lived on top of a very steep hill with a lake at the bottom. His grandchildren used the hill for a slide in winter and poured water down it so that it was really icy, and with a sled you could go almost to the middle of the lake. I remember one party he had in particular. We all came—Campbells and Vandals together from our area, as well as Arcands from the other area and the Sandy Lake Indians too. As we arrived Mom said, "There's going to be a fight for sure with those Sandy Lake people here," but I paid little attention because there was never a good dance unless there was a good fight. Yes-Sant's cabin was a very long one-room log house with a big stove and heater, and four beds on one side. He had dragged all the furniture outside so there was plenty of room to dance. He was also the proud owner of the largest cellar in the country with a huge trap-door on the floor.

Everybody was enjoying themselves, dancing and eating, when suddenly a fight broke out. The mothers chased all the little kids under the beds and we big ones climbed up to the beams to watch. Soon everyone was fighting and no one knew who was hitting who—Dad even punched out his brother. The heater pipes were knocked over and there was smoke everywhere; then the kitchen stove pipes went down. Dad finally made it to the door and threw it open. Whenever someone came near the door Daddy would slug him and he would go sliding head first or backwards down the slippery hill to the lake. The lights went out and it was pitch black inside, mothers were yelling, kids screaming—a total mass of confusion! Cheechum got Mom and another lady to help her open the trap-door and some of the men fell in. Finally, everyone was either down the hill or in the cellar. (When they tired to climb out Cheechum would hit them on the head with her cane). When everything had settled down, the women lit the lamps and laughed as they set the place to order and got us kids back to bed. Cheechum shut the trap-door and said, "Let them all stay in the cellar and by the time the others climb the hill they'll all be sober." So furniture was hauled back in while some women made tea and everyone sat down to laugh and eat. The men outside weren't able to climb the hill, so they went into the barn with the horses to keep warm. When daylight came they found the path leading to the house. Cheechum scolded them well and then she opened the trap-door and let the others out. What a sight they were with black eyes and smashed noses, nearly frozen and feeling foolish! She scolded them too, and hit a few. We never had a dance without a good fight and we enjoyed and looked forward to it as much as the dancing.

Next to the Christmas festivities, our people looked forward to weddings. Weddings were something special, and were gay and gala affairs, in which everyone in our area and other communities participated. Flowers were made from bright crêpe paper; yards and yards of decorations were made for the houses and the horses. The best-matched team was used for the bride and groom, with a bright red cutter in winter and a red buggie in summer. The horses would have their manes and tails braided the previous day, then they would be brushed and curried until their coats shone and their manes and tails hung in waves. The harness was oiled and strung with bells, and from a long wire hung braided coloured ribbons that fluttered as the horses pranced.

Everyone lined up in the procession with their horse decorated as well. The bride wore a white satin dress which had been worn by many other brides and was altered so many times you could see all the different stitches. The bottom of the dress was trimmed with rows and rows of bright satin ribbons and on the bride's head was a long veil made from cheese cloth, with a halo of little crêpe paper rosettes. The groom was dressed in dark pants and a white or blue satin shirt embroidered with bright floral designs. He wore a band on his arm trimmed with bright ribbons. The horses never galloped or ran—they must have known it was a special occasion as they would arch their heads and prance all the way to church. After the ceremony we would all go to the biggest house in the community where the women would have the food all ready. For two days there would be feasting and dancing and laughter.

The bride and groom would then move into their new home built by the men in the community. On their first night together the rest of us would collect pans, whistles, drums, anything—and sneak over. Then we would all yell and scream and bang pots and pans together till the couple would both come out and make a speech. We loved weddings and our women could hardly wait until they were rested up from one to start match-making again.

OSSIFICATION OF
NATIVE SOCIETY

HOWARD ADAMS

From *Prison of Grass* (1975)

Prison of Grass is a history of Canada told for the first time by an Aboriginal person. The author, Howard Adams, blends his own autobiography with a history of his Métis forebears. His account of the Northwest Rebellion in particular gives an alternative version of past events. The style of the book—its leftist perspective, its engaged tone, and its unapologetic use of Marxist rhetoric —is typical of the 1970s. Adams writes himself into the book and as a result he is able to describe the psychological impact of racism along with its economic and social consequences.

Howard Adams was born in the Métis settlement of St. Louis, Saskatchewan, south of Prince Albert. He completed a PhD at the University of California, where he taught for several years. He recently retired from teaching to write full-time. Prison of Grass was reissued in a revised edition in 1989.

After the political and economic subjugation of a native people comes the final stage of colonialism, the cultural takeover. Once prairie native society was arrested and ossified at the pre-industrial stage after 1885 by being prevented from developing along with the nation's advancing technology and economy, emphasis was placed on its archaic features. Traditional and ritualistic customs, black magic, and other superstitions were retained as long as they served to increase the colonizer's power over the native people. For instance, the position of chief, even though he was powerless, was kept for purely ornamental reasons. All real power and authority was removed from the chief's position and from the other institutions of native society and placed in the hands of white authorities. Consequently, decisions affecting native life were made by the white power structure.

After the Métis and Indians were confined to reserves, colonies, and ghettos during the latter part of the 19th century they were geographically and culturally isolated from mainstream society. Under these conditions it was easy for white authorities to propagate suspicions and beliefs among native communities that served to ossify their culture. Each Indian reserve and halfbreed colony was encouraged to think that it was alone in its struggle, that problems were unique to each community and of their own creation. Primitive beliefs were reactivated so that all political thought and discussion would be smothered or excluded. Powwows and other rituals were allowed or discouraged according to the functions they originally performed in the native society. If they served the original political or religious purposes, they were discouraged because that tended to strengthen the native culture; if they were regarded by the whites as simply colourful, primitive performances, they were permitted and even encouraged. Because there was no basic economy and no work force in native communities, it was impossible for people to interact with one another or with outside workers on this basis. As a result of the witchcraft ideology and the absence of political power on the reserve, politics became irrelevant or non-existent. The cultural and political strength of the native community was destroyed once the meaningful components had been extracted. But the establishment of an archaic, caricature culture did not kill the native culture; on the contrary, it was forced to continue in agony in a limbo existence. The Indian and halfbreed culture that was once open and dynamic became closed and static.

Indians and Métis collaborate with their white oppressors by portraying archaic culture through such public spectacles as the Calgary Stampede. They present themselves as aboriginal people with a primitive culture, although they are performing in the 20th-century space age. Teepees are exhibited, tomahawks and primitive tools displayed, as if they were current implements and customs in Indian society. They dress in traditional Indian garments, sit around and smoke the peace pipe. To make the display more authentic for whites, Indians live in the teepees during the exhibition.

The Indian spectacle has no historical significance because the Calgary Stampede display is not a historical exhibition. Whites insist upon seeing Indians in this primitive way because it corresponds to their stereotypes.

This display is highly amusing to white people, especially to children, who, being easily impressed, come to regard Indians as quaint barbarians. It is a cruel mockery of the true native civilization and a grim misrepresentation of present native customs. The most pitiful part of these spectacles is the dancing, a humiliating experience for other native people because it has no cultural, religious, or artistic quality. These public performances are exclusively for the entertainment of whites. Officials of the Saskatoon Exhibition argued that its Indian show must be staged in this aboriginal manner and in no other way, claiming that the public would not pay to see an Indian show unless it was in this archaic style. These officials cater to the racist mentality of the Canadian people and even make a profit from it.

In the early stages of ossification, social institutions become mere caricatures patterned after the original fertile ones. For instance, the Indian councils used to have the full support of the people to govern their communities. However, the imperial rulers extracted the legitimacy and authority from such councils and left them as mere shells; their powers have been reduced to such matters as "the destruction of noxious weeds," and "the construction and maintenance of boundary fences."[1] Nevertheless, the form of the institution was allowed to remain. These caricature forms embodied a pseudo-respect, but they actually institutionalized contempt for the former traditions to the point of mockery and sadism. At the same time, Indians and halfbreeds were allowed to indulge in all kinds of alien and sterile rituals, such as religious pilgrimages in which council members organized families into groups for long treks to Christian shrines. Since their political power had been reduced, their energy was directed towards trivial matters.

All activities of the native community were completely under the control of the colonizing officials, who made all the decisions affecting the daily operations of native people. Farming was an example of this extreme colonial control. The decision-making authority over farming operations was complete, down to the most trivial detail. Marketing of grain and farm produce could not be carried on without the official permission of the white agent; natives could be imprisoned and deprived of their machinery and stock for breaking the smallest rules. Such were the farming "opportunities" allowed Indians on reserves. This grinding paternalism and prison-like authority has persisted to this day. Of course, each reserve has one or two "show farms" on which a couple of Indians are given special favours in order to develop "successful" farms. These are intended to give the impression that "every Indian could be a successful farmer, if he only tried," and the scheme is effective in degrading the reputations of all other Indians who are not successful farmers. Information showing the number of Indians who have been refused assistance is not made public. In any event, for a native person, farming has become an artificial operation since it was originally intended as "busy work" for the Indians who were forced onto reserves.

With the native population hidden from mainstream society, the philosophy was popularized that the natives would soon die out. The whites generally believed that Indians were horse stealers and ritual sadists who burned missionaries at the stake, collected scalps, and ate human flesh:

> Coupled with his barbarous instincts . . . was his natural inclination to cruelty. It has been truly said that all savage races are like children, in that they have no adequate conception of suffering or pain suffered by others. They were entirely devoid of sympathy. The controlling instinct of the Indian was to kill.
>
> . . . He was animal in his instincts, and he neither knew nor cared about anything not connected with his material wants . . . In conversation . . . all Indians were obscene to a degree unknown to any other people. They seemed to have no conception of vulgarity, obscenity, or decency.
>
> . . . All Indians are lazy and thievish, work being considered degrading . . . vindictiveness and ferocity . . . is a part of Indian nature.[2]

Newspaper reporters would casually refer to Indians as "vile and vicious aborigines."[3] Of course, it was easy for colonizers to standardize and propagate these distorted myths because they had control of the communications media. Perverted images were paraded before the public to help justify and legitimize the incarceration of the entire population of native people. There was nothing sacred in this historical process of colonization; the most intimate and sensitive aspects of native peoples' lives were debased in the most ruthless way. Mockery and ridicule were brutally employed and still are today. It is not uncommon to hear children cry in agony simply because they are Indians or halfbreeds—their misery is the direct result of colonization and white supremacy.

The fall that I was eighteen, I went to work for a farmer fifteen miles from home. Not having any transportation, I was obliged to walk to his farm that day. On the highway I was lucky enough to be given a ride, or so I thought. A couple of Mounties in their car stopped and offered me a ride. It frightened me momentarily because I thought they were going to run me in. Mounties don't ordinarily give this kind of help, especially to the Métis. I had heard many stories about how brutally the police treated Métis and how they pinned false charges on them. But a ride was very welcome at this point. As we started up, the driver asked if I was from St. Louis, and before I even had a chance to answer, the other cop remarked, "There's a lot of smoked meat around that town." I had heard that expression many times before and I knew what it meant. The comment really burned me but I was too scared to argue. As far as I was concerned the girls in St. Louis were very decent. The Mountie continued, "I hear that those halfbreed babes like to have their fun lying down." I tried to change the subject, but the police were interested in pursuing it to the end. The driver asked in a mocking manner, "Is it true they like it better from a white man?" I was getting really angry, while at the same time trying to explain that Métis are just as nice as white girls. They drove on with comments about "redskin hotboxes who didn't wear any pants at all," and kept calling me "chief" in a sneering manner. Although they seemed to have an obsessive interest in native girls, they were also implying that Métis girls were little more than sluts and too dirty for Mounties. One asked, "Is it true that they'll go to bed with anyone for a beer?"

I was relieved when we reached the crossroads where I was to get off, but they drove on slowly and ignored my request to be let out. The driver said to his partner, "The chief probably has some little redskin heifer waiting for him in the bush." They joked together about "horny bucks" and "red peasoups always in heat." One wanted to bet me there wasn't a virgin in St. Louis. I began to think about jumping out since we weren't going very fast. They offered to let me out as soon as I would tell them the secret of "no knock-ups." At that point I said I was going to jump off, and they immediately burst out laughing. Between their fits of laughter they were half shouting, "Jump off, so that's it." They roared on about jump on, jump off, breed games, up and down, in and out, and halfbreed fun. Finally they let me out and drove away in a thunder of laughter. I turned and ran down the road with their mockery ringing in my ears. Shame was burning in my mind like a hot iron. I ran as if I was trying to outrun the Mounties' image of the Métis. I ran till I was exhausted, swearing, spitting, and half crying. That is how the famous redcoats of law and order respect the native people and their society.

According to racial stereotypes, Indians and Métis are naturally shy and withdrawn; they are born that way. Incidents such as the one I have described apparently have nothing to do with it. This notion is pounded into the heads of native children by teachers, priests, white functionaries. Because the children are rarely free from this myth, they don't get opportunities to develop confident and assertive attitudes about themselves. It is a very effective way of preventing the development of bold and articulate leaders, and the absence of such native leaders over the last century shows the success of this inferiorization scheme.

Coupled with the destruction of self-esteem is the suppression and mockery of native languages. In racist institutions such as schools and churches, Indians are discouraged as much as possible from using their native tongues, and Indian names are anglicized and mocked. For example, a child's Indian name may be incorrectly translated; a name which means something like "Fearless-of-his-horses" (referring to a warrior fierce in battle who has many fast horses), may be given in English as "Afraid-of-his-horses." The rough, incorrect translation made by white people is ridiculous and in some cases, as above, virtually the opposite of the original. However, whites take only the surface meaning of the anglicized version and mock the Indian as if he were, in fact, afraid of horses. This is a powerful means of degrading native people. Of course, white men's names are never reinterpreted in the same way for the convenience of native speakers.

Another example of how language is used to degrade the native people is provided by official government pronouncements regarding natives. As part of the program of national and cultural destruction, the government treats Indians and Métis as wards or children. Such attitudes, typical of the colonial mentality, were clearly revealed during the treaty negotiations and the relocation of Indians to reserves after 1885. In the negotiations of Treaty Six, Governor Morris addressed the masses of Indians saying, "Indian children of the Queen . . . I am glad to learn that they [Crees] are looking forward to having their children civilized."[4] The reason for this language is to convey the idea that natives are incapable of governing themselves, and that this justifies absolute government over them. In this way governments encourage their functionaries to look after the "children" in an authoritarian manner.

After reserves were established and Indians had developed a conscience of obedience, police were replaced by bureaucrats, priests, and teachers. The change to new wardens was made possible because Indians and Métis had internalized the myths of inferiority and become placid and subservient. The church was one of the most powerful and effective instruments in destroying native strength, and indoctrination leading to supplicant behaviour was done largely by the clergy. Church and school determine much of the ideology of the native communities by teaching native children to believe in white supremacy, and thus in their own inferiority; this paternalism is effective in keeping Indians and Métis in "child" roles and "in their place." Although these non-military authorities give the appearance of being liberal and democratic, their teaching and administration only continues the work of police.

The results of this mentality can be seen clearly in any reserve village whose population comprises both natives and whites. There are always two distinct communities. The native section has no gas or running water, no paved streets or sidewalks, only trails and dirt roads. Many of the houses are one- or two-room shacks. The differences are more than economic and cultural, they are vividly racial. According to the whites, the native section is a place of lazy, diseased, and evil people incapable of doing anything for themselves, a breeding ground for violence. The whites claim that natives have no culture, no ethics, no sensibility to morality, and no appreciation of law and order. To these colonizers, Indians and Métis destroy and disfigure beauty. The whites speak of their native neighbours in bestial terms, complaining that "they breed like rabbits." They speak of the sinful and depraved behaviour of natives, of shacking-up, of common-law marriages, of sleeping around. The fact is that the native villagers are hungry—hungry for food, for houses, for clothes, for power, and for whatever the whites take for granted. They are crouching villagers, listening to the gossip of the shacks, listening to what the white man wants them to hear, think, and fear. Because the native villagers experience frustration, hostility, and envy, they are always on the defensive and rarely able to progress.

In contrast, the colonizers' section is clean and beautiful. It has electricity, plumbing, paved streets, and garbage collection. It has beautiful modern houses with central heating and all public utilities. It has white authorities who draw handsome salaries because of the native people. These colonizers are privileged because they belong to the power structure and they have physical comfort and luxury because they are white. They have opportunities and unlimited horizons because they are part of mainstream society. The law is on their side because they are administrators. They are able to talk about the native world in rational and objective terms because all the evidence is on their side.

Until fairly recently, the Indian agent managed the reserve people's personal business as official business, and had the right to open their personal mail. In this way, he emphasized that Indians were not individuals in their own right, with their personal, intimate existences, and that white agents had full power over them. The only other place where such extreme dehumanization exists is in prisons—perhaps there is a basis for claiming that Indians and Métis make ideal prisoners. By the same token, whites consider native people as objects and not as persons. This is reflected in phrases such as "our Indians," implying possession of objects, such as toys or pets. Indians and Métis are not allowed to take action on their own, action that would be completely independent from whites. To colonizers, natives are to be controlled; they are not human beings who can engage in normal social relationships and organizations. Natives have to be managed and programmed.

Notes

1. *The Indian Act*, Queen's Printer, Ottawa, 1970, Section 83, p. 4287.
2. J.L. Humfreville, *Twenty Years among our Savage Indians*, Hartford Publishing Company, Hartford, Conn., 1897, pp. 52-53.
3. Saskatchewan *Herald*, North Battleford, May 12, 1883.
4. "The Treaties of Forts Carlton and Pitt," *The Treaties between Her Majesty, Queen Victoria, and the Indians of British North America*, Part II, Queen's Printer, Regina, March 1961, p. 5.

HUNGER MARCH TO EDMONTON

MYRNA KOSTASH

From *All of Baba's Children* (1978)

In 1975 Myrna Kostash, a magazine writer in Toronto, decided to return to her native Alberta to explore her own cultural roots by researching the history of Ukrainian-Canadians. More specifically, she sought to discover how children of the original immigrants made a place for themselves in Canada. The result was All of Baba's Children. *It is a book which is unusual for being a personal account of an ethnic community by a member of that community who was at the same time a successful writer in the mainstream culture. Based on recorded interviews and documentary research,* All of Baba's Children *represents a doubly revisionist approach to Canadian history. First of all, Kostash puts the immigrant at the centre of the story, which in the 1970s was almost unheard of. Secondly, she seeks to replace the Ukrainian community's own "rags-to-riches" view of ethnic history with a more complicated understanding of what it has meant to be "not Anglo" in Canada.*

Recently reprinted, All of Baba's Children *has become a classic of "ethnic" writing in Canada. The following selection describes a farmers' protest during the Depression. Two Hills is a village east of Edmonton where Kostash focussed much of her research.*

Myrna Kostash was born in Edmonton and has been a freelance writer since the early 1970s. All of Baba's Children *was her first book. In 1993-94 she was president of the Writers' Union of Canada.*

A "Communist" in those days was not necessarily a member of the Communist party (if not, they preferred to call themselves "progressives") but someone associated with a range of activity from simple picket lines at the railroad crossing, to campaign work for the Communist (later, the Progressive Labour) party or CCF candidate in an election, to membership in a hall affiliated with the Ukrainian Labour and Farm Temple Association. Memories are long and today these people are still referred to, more or less slyly, as "Reds" or if they have rejoined the church, as "former Reds." The serenity and orderliness of life in Two Hills in 1976 belie the fact that the district was once a scene of tumultuous, not to say violent, political activity, some of it more anarchic and spontaneous than that associated with election campaigns, invited lecturers and May Day concerts. Some people still carry the disgust and passion of the thirties with them, relating their experiences with a conviction more appropriate to past conditions of gross economic privation and of the sense of outrage than to present security and mollification; some speak of those days with nostalgic indulgence; and others with sour disapproval. But no one has forgotten how it was and what happened and no one has grown indifferent to their younger selves who were touched and moved and prodded and jolted by events that almost severed their generation's attachment to the national conceits of peace and good government.

Not that mass protest was an entirely revolutionary idea to the Ukrainian-Canadian community in the thirties; back in 1910, a mass meeting in Winnipeg protested the murder of a Ukrainian student killed in a scuffle between Polish and Ukrainian students in Lviv; in 1914, a cross-section of the community organized spontaneously to protest Bishop Budka's pastoral letter (urging Ukrainian-Canadians to join the Austrian army); and in 1915-16, various organizations struggled around the question of bilingual schooling. But it was the Depression, with its unusual effects and commonality of shared (unhappy) experience, its time-span across the youth of the Canadian-born generation and their identity as natives and citizens by birth ("How dare this happen to us?") and its arrival on the heels of political agitation following the world war and the Winnipeg General Strike, that for the first time provoked Ukrainian-Canadians en masse into prolonged and thoughtful protest against their general condition as working people in Canada. This was hardly a single-issue campaign or a denunciation of some distant calamity in Western Ukraine or even just a series of instances of bloody-mindedness. Mass protest during the Depression was the result of Ukrainian-Canadians finally seeing themselves as part of a class whose function and purpose were explicit: always to be the scapegoat for the vagaries of capitalism and to bear the responsibility of economic and political change.

Only the theoreticians among them explained the situation in such terms but when thousands of farmers and their sympathizers organized marches, drew up demands, organized boycotts and made speeches, they amounted to the same thing: analysts of the Canadian political economy. From their own lives they knew what was going on. Twenty-five cents a bushel for wheat in 1932. Wages and mothers' allowances cut. Foreclosures, evictions and tax sales. Pictures in the newspapers of the jobless in the cities marching with banners down Main Street. Pictures of policemen on horseback and policemen with batons charging into the crowd. Name-calling: "Communist stooges," "savages." Publicity, favourable and otherwise, given the progressive point of view:

> The capitalists were heartless men, only too eager to order the use of truncheons and tear gas on people who, through no fault of their own, had no jobs and no prospects of getting any in the foreseeable future. Brute force decided the outcome of riots, while "class justice" prevailed in the courtroom where rioters were fined or sentenced to short terms of imprisonment. Canada, the argument went on, was becoming a fascist state.[12]

For the people near and in Two Hills, the chance to take direct action against these provocations came in December 1932, with the organization of a Hunger March to Edmonton. Farmers from Myrnam, Slawa, Spedden, Mundare, Vegreville and other towns had announced their intention of joining the march, great quantities of food were donated and "for days on end, women cooked, baked and prepared food, expecting to feed upwards of 3,000 for several days if necessary."[13] The Farmer's Unity League, responsible for organizing all this along with the Workers' Unity League, was distributing pamphlets which demanded, on behalf of all farmers, a minimum income of $1,000 for every farmer, free education and medical care for the poor, old age pensions at sixty years of age and—for good measure—workers' control of the state.[14] The idea behind the march was to present Premier Brownlee with a set of minimal demands—he was, after all, head of the United Farmers of Alberta party—and a display of collective strength. As a brother farmer, how could he not but accept the justice of cancellation of debts, exemption from taxation of small farmers, cessation of sheriff's sales and grain seizures for tax arrears and cash relief? The excitement around these preparations was palpable.

Unfortunately, everything went wrong. A heavy snowfall a week before the set date, December 20, made many roads impassable to out-of-town marchers. Many didn't have enough money or warm clothes for the trip. Application for the right to march to the Legislative Building was turned down by the premier although permission was given for a mass assembly in the market square. The media were hostile.

> Groups of "Hunger Marchers" left on Monday for Edmonton to invade the offices of Prime Minister Brownlee and lay before him their preposterous "demands." At the moment of writing, we do not know what the outcome has been, but we surmise that the Hunger Marchers will find themselves in the same predicament as the King of Spain "who marched right up a hill and marched right down again."[15]

Special squads of police were detailed to prevent the march and

> It was learned via the grapevine that RCMP would be posted at certain country points to turn back, on any excuse whatsoever, groups of people obviously heading for the Hunger March in Edmonton. The word soon spread around. A truckful of farmers from Lavoy fell into the police trap four miles west of Mundare. After they were threatened with arrest unless they turned back, they back-tracked, then learning of a safer route, continued on their way.[16]

In spite of these obstacles, people kept coming in, from Willingdon, Two Hills, Mundare, Smoky Lake, Radway and gathered at the Labour Temple ready to start marching on the afternoon of the 20th. Just before noon, adding insult to injury, the hall was raided by seventy policemen, ostensibly searching for the firearms such a grisly group of revolutionaries must be hiding. "No arms were found. What they did find was a group of women cooking turkey."[17]

Finally, at 2:30 p.m., about 10,000 people had gathered in the market square, some ready to march, some waiting to see what would happen next. It was obvious that a confrontation between marchers and police was inevitable. Machine guns were posted on the roof of the post office building, a phalanx of mounted police were lined up across the street and behind them police on foot, including 150 RCMP brought in from Regina, were poised with batons. It was scary, but no marcher worth his or her salt would retreat now. The order was given to begin marching.

> Carrying slogans and banners, the demonstrators surged forward with loud cheers. Immediately, the foot policemen, swinging their clubs, barred the way. They grabbed at the banners and tore them down but the crowd closed in around them and passed on. The Mounted Police who had been waiting on the sidelines then came galloping into the milling crowd, trampling all those who stood in their way. Reinforcements of foot police rushed in after them, their batons cracking against skulls and bones, drawing blood as they went.
>
> Caught in the police rush, many of the injured screamed. The mood of the crowd changed suddenly. Curses and loud shouts escaped from a thousand throats. A roar of anger swept across the square as unarmed demonstrators near a bunch of Christmas trees, tore off the branches and rushed towards their attackers. But few could withstand the organized attack by the police. In the confusion that followed, the ranks broke. The marchers had advanced only a half block before they were forced to disperse. At 3:05 the Hunger March was over.[18]

Of thirty marchers originally arrested, only seven were ultimately convicted of unlawful assembly. Along the way to trial, cases had been dismissed for lack of evidence, technical errors, poor health, hearsay evidence and a judgment that merely being at a meeting did not constitute unlawful assembly. Not a very spectacular denouement to a police riot. It was assumed, however, that the state's case had been made. Mass displays of popular dissent would not be tolerated. "It was impossible. Some of the things we asked was impossible to expect." Two years later the farmers were at it again.

> There was a grain strike that started at Myrnam (which had a very strong progressive movement). Wheat was eighteen cents a bushel and when the

idea of a strike was proposed the idea spread like wildfire. I was on the picket line with lots of my neighbours right on the road near Lavoy and Vegreville. There was the odd fellow who tried to break through and I understand that there were picketers who took in their grain late at night, after the pickets were down, but we proved ourselves. We showed that people had to fights for their rights.

The picket lines had been thrown up on the roads to prevent farmers from delivering grain to the elevator: the local elevator agent had been grading everybody's shipment at "tough." It took several weeks of picketing (it could have been shorter, had everyone respected the pickets and turned back) to win but win they did, at least technically.

> The Myrnam farmers who have been on strike against their local elevators for several weeks tallied a win last week when one of their main contentions was granted, this being the removal of the present elevator agents there and their replacements by a new set of agents. Whether this will bring about any change in the grading of their wheat is something for the future to tell.[19]

It would have been longer had farmers in other districts not gone out on "sympathy strikes" and thus tied up deliveries to branch elevators along the line. Mass meetings in Ranfurly and Stubno passed strike resolutions with "100 percent unanimity" in support of the actions in Myrnam.

Later that same year, a number of Mundare farmers decided to mount a strike against conditions at local elevators: they were angry about the lack of cleaning equipment which meant they were being docked unnecessarily severely for weeds and were paid for artificially low grades. They issued a set of demands that were considerably more far-reaching than those of the Myrnam farmers: immediate installation of cleaners, more definite and equitable grading and establishment of a minimum price for grain equivalent to cost of production.[20] A picket committee was organized and delegates from other districts committed themselves to organize their own localities in sympathy. A day later, it was obvious this was not going to be a tea-party of a strike. Ten picketers from Mundare overturned a wagon of grain that was on its way to the elevator—under police escort—and were summarily arrested and charged with intimidation with violence, wilful destruction of property and obstruction of police. The trial was set for November 19. The community was appalled.

While the first uproar created by the farm strike at Mundare has subsided, the farmers in various other districts have also threatened to go on strike and it is possible, or probable, that the movement has already extended or will extend in the near future, to Warwick, Fitzallen, Hairy Hill, Two Hills and other points north. At the south, at Inland, Haight, Holden, a policy of watchful, but sympathetic, waiting seems to prevail.

It is not likely that any serious clashes will arise hereafter with the non-striking farmers or with the RCMP. The return of the Grain Commissioners within a week or ten days is being awaited with anxiety, although no one expects the Commissioners to meet all the demands made by the Strike Committee.[21]

It all depends on what one means by "clash." Murder and mayhem, no. Self-defense against scabs and assorted other adversaries, yes. Success, however, was equivocal.

On November 19, 1934, the "Mundare Ten" went to trial. Three had charges against them dropped, leaving seven as defendants: Peter Kleparchuk (a Communist and secretary of the strike committee), William Zaseybida, Metro Ulan, Sam Ulan, Peter Beresiuk, Fred Yaniw, and Joe Osinchuk. The prosecution was conducted by an RCMP sergeant, himself a defendant in another case brought by a Mundare striker, alleging he was struck by the sergeant while being questioned. Lawyers for the defendants were from Edmonton and soundly respectable: Fred C. Jackson and W.R. Howson, MLA. Examination and cross-examination revolved around the question of the overturned wagon. The police presented evidence that "the grain wagon had been pushed, sideways, bit by bit, into the ditch, and cited ridges in the gravel surface to support this view." This evidence was confirmed by an engineering graduate. All of the defendants, however, "denied having touched the wagon or the horses. . . . It went into the ditch, they claimed, because Const. Graves drove it too close to the shoulder of the road." The judge's summation, however, situated the act where it belonged: in the provocative area of civil disobedience.

"In Canada," the bench said, "every citizen has the right to work out his own salvation in his own way. John Lamash had the right to market the products of his labour, and no one had any right to interfere with him by use of violence of threats.

"Picketing itself is no crime, provided it is carried out in an orderly manner, without force. Under our law there is nothing wrong in asking a man not to go to work, or not to deliver grain. But where force enters, the law steps in.

"Violence of this kind will beget violence. It is serious to start violence because no one knows where it will lead, and it is up to this court to prevent it. . . ."[22]

Guilty as charged. The back of the strike was broken. The same evening as the trial, a meeting of Vegreville farmers, organized by Hairy Hill strikers, failed even to move a resolution that district farmers go on strike. The arguments supporting the idea were among the more political and sophisticated of the whole campaign but they fell on deaf (frightened? suspicious?) ears. "If the strike is to be effective it must embrace all farmers." "Farmers are unable to obtain a proper return for our labour. The only way to obtain redress is by direct action for ourselves." "Big companies and corporations stick together. So should the farmers." "We must get our own rights. Others won't do it for us." "Farmers crossing our lines should be completely ostracized." "People in town understand our interests are their interests. Why shouldn't they back us?" Even the presence of George Palmer, a Communist organizer tarred and feathered in Innisfree a week earlier, even his denunciation of "police scab-herders and strike breakers," could not change the mood of resignation. "The chairman then called for a resolution from a Vegreville farmer that the Vegreville district should go on strike. None was forthcoming."[23] On December 12, the *Observer* noted that "Mike Dedinski's truck is once more engaged in hauling grain to Two Hills."

The Vegreville farmers' reluctance to associate themselves with the strike (and hostile neighbours and police and court appearances and fines) is not so mysterious, given that this was 1934 and the "anti-progressive" elements of the area were themselves well organized by this time. Given, too, that many erstwhile sympathizers were exhausted. Carrying on a strike in the middle of winter, standing frozen to the bones at railroad crossings, feeling betrayed and dishonoured by neighbours crossing the picket line and realizing that dumping a can of cream into a ditch was only an irritating prick in the hide of the "system" forced many to withdraw their support. Many who sympathized with the idea of a strike distrusted the Communist leadership. There were those, of course, who bore ill-will towards the strikers but there were others who just couldn't sustain a fever pitch of indignation and excitement months on end. Besides, they were scared.

Back in 1931, the Vegreville Chamber of Commerce had passed a resolution which revived memories of abuse at the hands of the Anglo-Canadian establishment only fourteen years earlier. Given "existing conditions," they recommended deportation of people not Canadian citizens who were in jail, who "have been, *or may become* [italics mine], convicted of criminal offences" and who "may be guilty of making seditious utterances, or who are engaged in attempting to create distrust in, or disrespect for Canadian institutions."[24] This point of view may have been merely tedious if it weren't for the fact that once again immigrants were being singled out, in a time of social crisis, and in an ill-defined manner, as partly responsible for the problem, and for the fact it was seriously debated. An editorial in the *Observer*, for instance, managed simultaneously to disapprove and encourage the Chamber in its resolution. On the one hand, "deportation of undesirable aliens" is a "drastic remedy and not always effective" and "even if all the undesirable aliens are rounded up and deported, our troubles are not over. There are quite as many naturalized Canadians who are agitators and general nuisances." On the other hand, "Canada is now paying, more or less, the penalty of its own folly in encouraging, or at least permitting, certain classes of immigrants to enter the country. . . . The policy of deportation should be carried out much more vigorously by the Dominion Government. . . . Possibly the only thing wrong with [the resolution] is that it requires re-drafting in some particulars. . . ."[25]

This argument would have been merely sophistical, and exclusive to the faint-hearted who imagined hordes of Ukrainian-Canadians brandishing fists, if it weren't for the personalities with more clout and a bigger audience who were saying the same thing. Charlotte Whitton, in 1932 a social worker, presented a report to the Prime Minister's Office on "Unemployment and Relief in Western Canada"; on the face of it, she wrote objectively and merely descriptively.

> The number of single men, foreigners on relief, is unduly large, and in several centres, officials reported them as among their troublesome clients. Language differences, their tendency to segregate, their corporate loyalties,

their susceptibility to seditious propaganda, their known proclivity to hoard money, and the consequent difficulty of ascertaining their actual need of relief, all greatly complicate an already difficult problem in these cities.[26]

Between the lines she is confirming what a lot of Anglo-Canadians believed to be true: that foreigners were unreliable and devious, disloyal and lazy; and that if there weren't any around, there wouldn't be a Depression or Bolshevism or government handouts.

By the thirties, however, it wasn't just Anglo-Canadians who responded with misgivings and animosity to the "troublesome" foreigner; by this time there was among the Ukrainian-Canadians themselves a class of people whose interests were closer to those of the non-Ukrainian establishment than to those of the agitators, the unemployed, the striking farmers. The Ukrainian-Canadian merchant, lawyer, doctor, and large farmer formed an economic and social elite which, although not so wealthy and powerful as its Anglo-Saxon counterpart, was manifestly better off and more influential than Ukrainian-Canadian teachers, tinsmiths, and debtor farmers. Influential in two ways: within their own community and in relationship to the outside establishment. They now "spoke for" the Ukrainian-Canadians as a group, explained and inter- preted them and, in a crunch, assumed the responsibility for defusing the "troublemakers" who caused the Anglo-Canadian establishment such anxiety. There was also a group, popularly called the "nationalists," who were ideologically committed to anti-Communism and pro-Ukrainian- ism (the notion of strength through ethnic pride), and who found themselves very often in agreement with the economic elite in its confrontations with the "progressives," even though they may have been as poor and disdained as any Ukrainian-Canadian on relief. The "nationalists" and the "bourgeoisie" had a common cause, the repression of political dissent from the left; the former were motivated by their repugnance towards any idea or activity that suggested sympathy with Bolshevist ideals, the latter by their vested interest in the status quo of private enterprise. Backed by the church, the school board and the mainstream media, they were an impressive force respected and deferred to by most other Ukrainian-Canadians. To challenge them would take a large measure of confidence, boldness and group support, not to mention the willingness to run the risk of being "Red-baited" and ostracized. To many "ordinary" Ukrainian-Canadians outside the charmed circle, it just wasn't worth it.

While the church spoke for the virtues of humility and piety, the nationalist intelligentsia spoke for the values of patriotism and political conformity. By 1933, there was already established in Two Hills a group of Ukrainian-Canadians known as the "United Loyalists of Canada" (Defenders of Canada and the British Empire) who assumed the responsibility of propagandizing in the community the government's case against the "Reds."

> By the forties, Father had citations from Prime Minister R.B. Bennett for having fought the Communist-inspired farmers' strike. My father was in a bad position. He agreed that they should strike, but he was afraid, because people came to him and said, "We'll have to get something organized against the Ukrainian Communist farmers in your area because it could go very badly for Ukrainians." They wanted to deport a lot of them before World War II, for being Communists. "And if you don't do something to oppose this Communism, it's going to go very badly for your people, we'll still deport them." And my father felt a little bit ashamed that they were getting a bad name with the authorities so he went around organizing meetings against the Communists who were encouraging the farmers' strike. And he was a paid government agent for the federal government of Canada to go around as a strike fighter.

Unsurprisingly, then, by the time of the hunger marches and farmers' strikes, the community was divided in its politics and the marchers' and strikers' failure to sustain a long campaign of protest was as much the result of resistance within the Ukrainian-Canadian community as opposition from without. In one issue of the *Observer* alone four news items recorded the extent of anti-strike sentiment. The mayor of Mundare, Harry White, knowing "full well the parties responsible for [the Mundare strike] and how little they represent the real feeling of the farmers" called a public meeting of "citizens" to discuss ways of handling the situation. (There is no indication in the report of just how broadly representative these "citizens" were.) The meeting determined to swear in special police and to send a request for assistance to the RCMP in Vegreville.

> The strike has been effective at Mundare for a month and has paralysed

business men to such an extent that the merchants of the town, together
with the farmers who oppose the strike, resolved to put an end to it.[27]

In the Willingdon National Hall, a group of district farmers discussed
how best to conduct the strike along "legitimate lines" and without relying
on present "Communistic leadership." They resolved "that the farmers of
the Willingdon district form a farmers' union to be absolutely non-Com-
munistic and non-political, to act in cooperation with all recognized farm
unions in parts of Canada not affiliated with any political party."[28] An
editorial in the *Observer* interpreted this example of farmers' caution as a
sign that the "strike is not by any means approved by the majority of
farmers." It seems to me that they did not so much oppose the idea of a
strike as support the pipedream of a gentlemanly one. If it was true—and
it was—that some farmers, after "whooping it up" at a meeting "went
home and delivered their own grain as fast as they could to elevators at
points where there was no strike but where conditions were exactly the
same as at picketed points," this does not "prove" that the tactic of striking
was misconceived. It shows rather that the organizers had not done their
political education work very well. Otherwise, how could the "bulk of
the farmers decide that they intend to market their own grain in their own
way at their own time"[29] and believe anything would ever change for
them? And in Myrnam, where it had all started a few weeks earlier,

> several loads of grain brought through picket lines Thursday were greeted
> in town by a parade of Nationalists with the Union Jack flying and the
> marchers singing *God Save the King* while several hundred Nationalists and
> Communists gathered in town for an auction looked on.
>
> Only one load was held up but constables were on hand and no trouble
> ensued.[30]

In 1935, six months after the strikes but still inside the vortex of the
Depression, a farmer from Innisfree wrote a letter to the editor summing
it all up. Unlike many farmers, strikers and non-strikers alike, he was able
to see beyond the end of his own bloody nose to the complex
configuration of economics, politics and police power that stood between
the farmers' grievances and their transfiguration into a cohesive resistance
movement. Unlike them, he was not despairing. Angry, yes, caustic and

impassioned, but also serene in his confidence that critical lessons had been learned and, who knows, a revolution of sorts underway.

In 1932 the farmers throughout this province were badly hit by the Depression; 90 percent of them were down and out. They decided to organize and march into Edmonton—our Capital City—and there stage a peaceful demonstration. They considered this would be the best way to present their grievances before the government.

What happened to these farmers upon their arrival in Edmonton? Yes, indeed, the Brownlee farmer government got right behind these poor farmers—but they did it with RCMP. The reception these poverty stricken victims of the Depression received was that of swinging police clubs. . . .

As a result of the grain strike last November at Mundare, some farmers were arrested. They were imprisoned for seven months, in Fort Saskatchewan Jail. When I was in Edmonton early in Feb. this year, I visited the Farmers' Unity League office, and there I saw a delegation that had been sent to visit these imprisoned strikers. They reported that the Warden at the Jail would not, at first, give them permission to see the jailed farmers, but after a long argument he had very sharply and gruffly said that they would be allowed fifteen minutes only. When they did let these visitors in they placed benches between them and the prisoners so that they could not come closer than ten feet. What the farmers would like to ask Mr. Reid [UFA minister of Agriculture] is whether he was elected by farmers or jail wardens?

The farmers' struggle for better grades and against excessive dockage was fought by the "farmer" government. They sent in the RCMP Police to break the struggle. After putting the farmers in jail they set up an "investigation" by the Grain Commissioner, and he turns in the type of report one would expect from a servant of such a government—"the strike was groundless." In the rottenest display of discrimination ever pulled on farmers this government ranked itself alongside the profit-making elevator companies. They know their kind.

However the farmers have learned that organized struggle does benefit them—for it can be proved that grain graded No. 5 tough, before the strike, graded No. 4 dry afterwards. Does that look as though the strike were groundless and that the elevator companies were in the right?

These thoughts are well to keep in mind as election nears. Fortunately we farmers also have memories.[31]

Notes

12. Ivan Avakumovic, *The Communist Party in Canada* (Toronto: McClelland & Stewart, 1975), p. 77.

13. Anne B. Woywitka, "Recollections of a Union Man," *Alberta History*, Vol. 23, No. 4 (Autumn 1975), p. 17.

14. Helen Potrebenko, *No Streets of Gold* (Vancouver: New Star, 1977).

15. Vegreville *Observer*, December 21, 1932.

16. Woywitka, p. 18.

17. Potrebenko, *No Streets of Gold*.

18. Woywitka, p. 19.

19. Vegreville *Observer*, March 7, 1934.

20. Ibid., November 7, 1934.

21. Ibid., November 14, 1934.

22. Ibid., November 21, 1934.

23. Ibid.

24. Ibid., April 29, 1931.

25. Ibid., April 22, 1931.

26. Howard Palmer, ed., *Immigration and the Rise of Multiculturalism* (Toronto: Copp Clark, 1975), p. 106.

27. Vegreville *Observer*, December 12, 1934.

28. Ibid.

29. Ibid.

30. Ibid.

31. Ibid., June 12, 1935.

MOTHERS AND DAUGHTERS

MARY MEIGS

From *Lily Briscoe: A Self-Portrait* (1981)

In Lily Briscoe, *the painter and writer Mary Meigs describes her dual struggle to become an artist and to accept her sexuality. It is not a conventional memoir, like, for example,* That Summer in Paris *or* My Life With the Eskimo. *It is a book about emotions and character and relationships. Events are described only incidently; no coherent life chronology emerges. As Meigs writes: "It is not a book about my life's events, of which I hardly speak." Rather, it is a memoir of an internal life.* Lily Briscoe *reveals all of its author's insecurities, faults, and second thoughts. As a result, it is at times painful to read. Meigs sees herself as an outsider: in her family, as an artist, and as a lesbian.* Lily Briscoe *is about how she comes to terms with this situation. The following selection from the book examines Meigs's relationship with her mother. Miss Balfour was the family's governess.*

Mary Meigs was born in 1917 and grew up in Washington, D.C. Following the Second World War she determined to become a painter and lived for many years in Wellfleet, Massachusetts as part of an artistic community which included Mary McCarthy, Edmund Wilson, and Marie-Claire Blais. She did not begin publishing books until she was in her sixties, by which time she was living in Quebec, where she now resides. Her latest book, In the Company of Strangers *(1991), describes her experience of being in the highly-acclaimed 1990 National Film Board production,* The Company of Strangers.

Our poor mother spent the years after Miss Balfour's departure yearning for her lost children and not knowing how to go about getting them back. By then, we were miles away from her, keeping our lives secret from her, punishing her, it would seem, for having given us away. After my father's death, she lived alone in the big house, trying to carry on her old life, as brave as a soldier, and I can't think of it now without pain. How little we knew of each other; how incapable we were of talking! I remember again the bitter accusation that shot out of her, when, questioning the imminent marriage of a friend and her doubts, I said, "Does she really love him?" "Cold heart," she said, "what do you know about love?" I hated her at this moment—and yet, what evidence did my unloved mother have that I knew anything about love? And if she had any evidence, wouldn't her bitterness have been even greater, as it was on another occasion (I was going to visit a friend I loved, but of love I could say nothing) when she said, "Another woman?"

Even my sister was unapproachable, embarrassed, and cool when our mother suddenly said to her (they were sitting on a park bench and it was after our father's death), "Can't you love me a little?" We all felt—and I knew—that she couldn't possibly understand our lives, that there was no use in trying to talk to her, for hadn't she always been shocked by even the tiniest infraction of her rules? It was much easier to stay on safe ground, to talk about my teaching, about my painting, to go to concerts with her—yes, like schoolgirls—and stay away from dangerous subjects. But why did even these safe subjects create conflicts? Why did it seem to me that there was nothing in the world about which my mother and I agreed when, now, I have the impression that I never bothered really to draw her out? Hadn't she read all the French classics, seen innumerable operas and plays (my mother liked naughty drawing-room comedies and laughed at behaviour that shocked her in real life. "But it's a play," she said when I pointed this out to her); couldn't she recite the names of the kings of England and France? Didn't she love chamber music, and go, year after year, to the concert series at Coolidge Auditorium? But something prevented me from believing that this cultivation of hers was real, for she was unable to discuss why or how she loved books and music. A few years before her death, when she was paralyzed and talked with difficulty, I arranged with a violinist friend to come and play for her in her house and warned him that she might be impatient, or even rude, as she was at times with visitors. He played the Bach partita in B minor, perhaps the most exacting of all Bach to listen to, and my mother, far from being impatient, sat enthralled and afterwards thanked him with all the words she could muster. Once again, I felt horribly ashamed of my arrogance, of the false idea I had had of my mother's feeling about music. And I realized that even if she found the Bach partita hard to listen to, there was something graciously receptive at the very core of her being, stronger than her sickness, that recognized great music played by a master.

My mother had always been humble—much too humble, I thought. She was impressed by any kind of accomplishment, as long as it was accomplished by an outwardly virtuous person, and this humility appeared in her either as a strength or a weakness. In its strong aspect, it made her capable of listening to the Bach partita, of a silent worship of great art. But her character was fatally shaped by the humility that made her deny her own value and accept the impersonal judgements of society. When she married, because my father was a Democrat, she switched her political allegiance from Republican to Democrat, and from then on, she accepted everything the Democrats did without question. Humility was her primal matter and out of it was fashioned her self-denial, her ferocious loyalties, and her snobbishness. She had been humiliated by Mater because she came from a small town and her life in Washington was one long effort to keep a high place on the social ladder. But her friends were often not the great ladies of Washington, but rather relatively simple people of sterling character, who gave me the impression of having stepped from the pages of Dickens, and whom she never called by their first names.

Those friends whom she did call by their first names were all summer friends; with them she laughed and was happy. But even here, there was one whose name brought forth my mother's humility. This was Helen L., who knew Thornton Wilder and other giants, and who founded the Reading Club, of which my mother was a member. As I chase after wisps of memory, think of the high seriousness my mother put into doing homework for the meetings of the club, think of her real awe of Helen L., a genuine intellectual, and think of her awe of another friend, whose mother had been the first editor of Emily Dickinson, I see her in all her touching innocence and see how offensive I was with my mocking sarcasm. Sometimes I would overhear conversations between the friends which touched, not on literature, but on the "servant problem" (a problem which in those days could hardly be said to have existed) or about their husbands' little foibles. I remember noticing uneasily that their indulgent remarks about their husbands always implied their own sense of themselves as *wives*. One and all (including Helen, whose husband was a distinguished scientist, who believed in the superiority of their husbands to themselves), I saw with disgust, and within this rigid framework, like Japanese or Spanish wives, they were quite happy to live and turn any spark of rebellion into a tender joke. These were the terms then of happy marriages—and they were all happily married, for my mother's moral canon excluded unhappily married people. It was the wife's fault, she firmly believed, if a marriage failed.

In the warm summer sunshine, in the gaiety of picnics and parties, in the joy of her garden full of heliotrope and lavender, lemon verbena, rose geranium, all my mother's sweetness seemed to flourish. True, her loyalty to the Episcopal Church provoked a certain grimness, and I see her now of a Sunday morning, wearing her hand-knitted white wool suit, her hat adorned with plastic cherries, and her narrow, pointed shoes, rounding up a cranky flock of children and grandchildren (the latter in starched seersucker and kneesocks, with doleful expressions on their faces) for the eleven o'clock service. That was the trouble: the superego was always at hand telling her how to behave, telling her that she had to go to church every Sunday until she could no longer walk, telling her to badger her children and grandchildren and to be gravely offended if one of them refused her. It was I who refused, and that created another rift between my mother and me, for I refused first to take communion, and then, to go to church at all. There was always in my mother a threshold where laughter stopped, where the rules were invoked and where discussion became impossible. Her summer gaiety was illusory. (Hadn't it been in summer that she scolded me for saying I had seen my sister in her pyjamas?) Alas, none of us ever succeeded in turning this intractable morality of hers into a joke, and the sins we committed remained fresh in her mind, like prehistoric animals preserved in a glacier.

The summer mother and the winter mother were the same person, but in winter there was a concentration of loyalties that preoccupied her. In society, she became a redoubtable hostess; in politics, she became president of the Women's National Democratic Club. As a mother, she worked to see that her daughters could ride horseback, dance, speak French and go to the best boarding schools. Our brothers were not polished in the same way and continued to go to our first Quaker school; to be ignorant of the arts of riding and dancing. It was obvious that she was grooming us to be wives, for she drew the line at a college education (we rebelled, however) and put her ambitions and energies into our "coming out," which failed signally to get us husbands. I am grateful to her now for her zeal, and thankful that, among her failures, was the failure to make us carbon copies of herself. None of us believe in the things she believed in with the same fierceness. And how surprising it is that a person so modest could be so fierce! "Your mother is the sweetest, loveliest person!" her friends would say. At her grand dinner parties, she always prevented conversations from becoming heated ("I never talk about politics at the dinner table," she would say), and I can see her beaming face at the end of the long table, her head graciously turning from left to right, or, spotting a guest who hadn't spoken, launching a question that would draw him out. She was much loved for these qualities by the courtly gentlemen of Washington.

It amazes me that she could put so much moral energy into the most insubstantial beliefs. I remember the summer mother, the light-haired one, and her fury, when, one Sunday, the curly-haired, black-eyed minister of our church began intoning the Creed. She and her friends assembled and inveighed against the dangers of becoming "high church," seeing the minister, with his love for music, for sculpture and flowers, as an emissary of the Pope himself. To him, it was natural to inject a little art into the Episcopal service; to my mother, it was a crime. She won, of course, and eventually the minister, the only one of his kind I ever felt close to, changed to a church that was "higher," where he could let himself go, and an uninteresting and non-artistic man took his place.

Just as there was a right and wrong about the smallest details of the church service, just as these details engaged my mother's full moral attention, so too there was a rigid sticking to society's rules, as exigent as the laws of the land. I have said that my mother played the social game, but it seems to me that her psyche was geared to success or failure, that she was vindicated in a deep personal sense if she was invited to the White House and humiliated if she was *not* invited to something she considered a test of her social standing. During the war, a garden party was held at the British Embassy to honour the King and Queen and it became the kind of event that provokes intrigues, family quarrels, the kindling of furious social ambitions. Despite her efforts, my mother had not been invited, but worse still, her niece, who was married to the third son of a duke, had been, and the fortunate couple was staying in our house. The day of the garden party, it rained so persistently that the ladies' big hats collapsed and the collars of the gentlemen's morning coats turned green. Our bedraggled cousins appeared at the dinner table and as they told about the disaster of the party, we all began to laugh, helpless releasing laughter, and I remember my mother laughing until tears rolled from her eyes. It was over, this terrible test, and perhaps, at that moment of relief, she saw how little it mattered.

I have staked out in my mind an area where my mother felt unthreatened, for I see now that every day had its threats, that, if we seemed to be walking across a minefield, it was because our mother had this feeling herself. I see her now in the innocence and isolation of her safety spots, opening her tea basket in the compartment of a European train, heating water over a can of Sterno, handing us enamel cups of weak tea and Klim, the powdered milk of that time whose mirror name delighted me, and Petits Beurres. I see her outdistancing us all with her loping tourist gait, like a Tennessee walking horse, and, white-faced, sitting on a broken column at Hadrian's Villa, overcome by the Italian sun. I can feel her confiding arm in mine on the last trip we took together, during which I puzzled her by behaving like a sulky child; and the softness of her hand which so irritated me by gently stroking mine. In her mind, it seems to me, I had been changed into my father, with his depressions and his endless arguments, but with his power to protect her. In *my* mind, I was the unmarried daughter whose duty it was to take care of her mother, and the fact that I was compelled to fill this unwelcome role infuriated me. But by then, when she was in her seventies, my mother was an angel of patience and whatever differences we had were invariably my fault. These came from my feeling that we belonged to different species and that I was yoked to my so-different mother by an obligation which I could not accept.

Could we, I wonder, by some kind of consciousness-raising, have reduced all those threats that my mother felt? I am still convinced that I could not have told her any of my secrets (my sister, to whom I have told them, disagrees. "Mother knew more about you than you think," she says, but has no evidence to prove it), that she could never have understood my love for women, that, just as she had refused to speak to her oldest sister for twenty years because her sense of justice was outraged in a quarrel over their mother's will, so she would have refused to speak to me, and would have read me out of the family circle as well. Hadn't she had her first stroke at her club, watching McCarthy on television, the man who was abominable to her not only because he was a demagogue, but also because it was rumoured that there was a homosexual relation between him and Roy Cohn? To me, the convulsions that my mother had then were the outward sign of her loathing; and I was glad I'd kept my secret tightly locked away. And yet, there are Miss Walker's words, "Your mother was clairvoyant," and my sister's insistence that I could have talked to our mother, that she would have understood. Even now, my heart begins to thump with the old fear and sickness that came over me at the very thought of talking, that made it impossible to talk to my twin sister until recently—the old fear provoked by my mother's grimness, by an alarming sideways twitch of her set mouth that made us all tremble. I think of Lesbian friends with mothers who are still alive, who live near their mothers at their own risk, who spend themselves in a futile effort to placate them, consenting to hypocritical silence and coming to believe in the necessity, imposed by their mothers, of lying low and pretending to be invisible. I know mothers who have sent their daughters to psychiatrists, mothers who denounce their daughters behind their backs, mothers who take the fact of having a Lesbian daughter as an excuse to feel martyred. Which one of these stereotypes would my mother have chosen, she who cared with her whole soul about society's rules?

Too often, it is the mother who makes the rules and the daughter who cares about her who compromises and in so doing, permits her mother to become a tyrant. A veritable snakepit of taboos prevents the mother of a Lesbian daughter from loving her with any constancy. One might expect the fact that mothers naturally love their daughters the way women love each other (*i.e.,* with passionate tenderness) would help them to understand love between women. On the contrary, every woman is seen as a threat to this love, which, since it is "virtuous," is prevented by a taboo from ever becoming incestuous. The mother of a Lesbian stands between her daughter and her daughter's lovers like a dragon; it is as though she were snarling, "Keep away from my property!"—for she, the mother, is the only woman a daughter may legitimately love. Unfortunately, Freud was too busy with the Oedipus complex and too baffled by the psychology of women, who, for some strange reason, kept rebelling against their conventional role, to go into this other complex, to which no one has yet given a name. No doubt, Sappho had a mother who was anxious about Sappho's women lovers, and if her name had survived, the complex could have been named for her. No doubt, this anonymous mother was glad that Sappho had men lovers, too, just as a contemporary mother of a married Lesbian daughter swallows her aversion to the idea of women lovers as long as her daughter is "faithful" to her husband. Since she has been fashioned by the patriarchal society we live in, her first reaction to her daughter's marriage is delight (she need no longer be ashamed of her); if her daughter continues to have Lesbian attachments which aren't too visible, the mother prefers to think of them as adventures in which love plays no part. How strange it is that the purest element of a relationship between women is seen as the most threatening, the love that binds them together; and yet, it isn't strange, for it is this love which excludes the mother. The nameless complex which makes mothers love and hate their Lesbian daughters simultaneously, can never, like the Oedipus and Jocasta complexes, be said to be resolved, for society never sanctions Lesbian love as it does heterosexual love. When a son or daughter marries, the mother's bond with her son or daughter is dissolved in the ceremony of marriage and this official sanction helps her to bear the pain. Since she had been taught to accept the idea that a husband or wife takes priority over a mother, she must at least make an effort to play second fiddle. But a daughter's love for another woman is condemned by society, and a mother simply cannot believe that her daughter loves another woman more than she loves her own mother. One sees the mothers of Lesbians making frantic efforts to win back their daughters: bribing them, making them feel guilty, placing themselves bodily between the lovers in an act of non-violent resistance by living in the same house with them, this last, the worst punishment that a Lesbian couple has to endure. I have observed this and have seen the hate it spawned between the mother and the daughter's friend; I have seen the daughter wrap herself in a protective silence that made communication and honesty impossible. I've suffered from the mealy-mouthed atmosphere of respectability in which it is not permitted to show any signs of affection, to hold hands, to touch the person one loves in front of the dragon-mother, who pretends that she is fond of the daughter's friend, the mother always there as a super-spy, who gives you the impression, even in the night, of keeping her ears cocked for telltale sounds. It is drama quietly playing itself out below the surface of politeness and compromise and it leads me to this uncompromising conclusion: that Lesbian daughters should keep a safe distance between themselves and their mothers and should not harbour the illusion that they can share their lives, even if they seem to love each other. And I will continue to doubt that I could have talked with my mother or that any good would have come of it. My sister, married, with four children, her life a reflection in some ways of our mother's, of course could talk to her, could feel that anything she said would be understood. But I am thankful that I lived those last years of her life in a dishonest shadowland and am convinced that its air was the only air she could breathe. It was not only to protect myself, but also to protect her from the killing force of the word or words: homosexuality, Lesbian, that could not be said or attached to a person without triggering a sort of moral madness.

There is a beautiful episode in *Through the Looking Glass*, a little parable about the power of words to change love into fear. Alice finds herself in the wood, "where things have no names," and meets a fawn, who shows no fright, for he cannot remember what he is. "So they walked together through the wood, Alice with her arms clasped lovingly round the soft neck of the Fawn, till they came out into another open field, and here the Fawn gave a sudden bound into the air, and shook itself free from Alice's arm. 'I'm a Fawn!' it cried out in a voice of delight. 'And, dear me! You're a human child!' A sudden look of alarm came into its beautiful brown eyes, and in another moment it had darted away at full speed." People of my mother's generation were armed in their minds at the sound of certain words, and the triggers cocked to go off. How could she possibly have endured the naming of her daughter with a word she could not say herself? Like Alice and the Fawn, we could only be friends in a wood "where things have no names."

MAPS OF DREAMS

HUGH BRODY

From *Maps and Dreams* (1981)

During 1978-79 Hugh Brody lived on a Beaver Indian reserve in northwestern British Columbia. A natural gas pipeline was planned to cut through the area and the federal government funded Brody as a consultant to discover what he could about the ways the people made their living from the land. His book, Maps and Dreams: Indians and the British Columbia Frontier, *is an account of his time with the Beaver. In alternating chapters it mixes first-person reportage with more "objective" information about the history, economy and social conditions of the Peace River Country. It represents a development of the personal style of non-fiction writing used by Heather Robertson, Farley Mowat, and Maria Campbell, to name just three. Not only is the author present in the work, he is openly struggling with the difficulty of capturing in words the essence of the subject he is trying to convey. Can we know another culture and how do we express that knowledge? The following extract describes a hunting trip on which Brody came to understand something about the close relationship between the natural world and Beaver spirituality.*

Hugh Brody was born in England in 1943 but for many years has lived at least part-time in Canada. In the early 1970s he worked as a federal government researcher in the North, and 1974-76 was a consultant to Tom Berger's Mackenzie Valley Pipeline Inquiry. He is the author of several books about the North, including The People's Land *and* Living Arctic, *as well as one collection of short fiction; he is also a filmmaker.*

The rivers of northeast British Columbia are at their most splendid in the early fall. The northern tributaries of the Peace achieve an extraordinary beauty; they, and their small feeder creeks and streams, are cold yet warm—perfect reflections of autumn. The banks are multi-coloured and finely textured; clear water runs in smooth, shallow channels. The low water of late summer reveals gravel and sand beaches, textures and colours that are at other times of the year concealed. Such low water levels mean that all these streams are easily crossed, and so become the throughways along the valleys that have always been at the heart of the Indians' use of the land. In October those who know these creeks can find corners, holes, back eddies where rainbow trout and Dolly Varden abound.

The hunter of moose, deer, caribou (and in historic times, buffalo) does not pursue these large animals without regard to more abundant and predictable, if less satisfying, sources of food. The man who tracks and snares game, and whose success depends on his constant movement, cannot afford to fail for much more than two days running. On the third day of hunger he will find it hard to walk far or fast enough: hunger reduces the efficiency of the hunt. Hunger is inimical to effective hunting on foot; yet continuance of the hunt was, not long ago, the only means to avoid hunger. This potential source of insecurity for a hunter is resolved by his ability to combine two kinds of hunting: he pursues large ungulates in areas and with movements that bring him close to locations where he knows rabbits, grouse, or fish are to be found. These are security, but not staples. Hunting for large animals is the most efficient, the most rational activity for anyone who lives in the boreal forest. But such a hunter would be foolhardy indeed to hunt for the larger animals without a careful and strategic eye on the availability of the smaller ones.

In October, only a month after Joseph Patsah and his family first spoke to us about their lives, they suggested that I go hunting with them—and, of course, fishing. By now the rainbow trout would surely be plentiful and fat. Joseph said that he also hoped we could go far enough to see the cross. One evening, then, he proposed that we should all set out the next day for Bluestone Creek.

Between a proposal to go hunting and actual departure there is a large and perplexing divide. In the white man's world, whether urban or rural, after such a proposal there would be plans and planning; conversation about timing and practical details would also help to build enthusiasm. In Joseph's household, in all the Indian households of northeast British Columbia, and perhaps among hunters generally, planning is so muted as to seem nonexistent. Maybe it is better understood by a very different name, which is still to suppose that planning of some kind does in fact take place.

Protests against the hunting way of life have often paid hostile attention to its seemingly haphazard, irrational, and improvident nature. Before the mind's eye of agricultural or industrial man loom the twin spectres of hunger and homelessness, whose fearsome imminence is escaped only in the bright sunlight of planning. Planners consider many possibilities, weigh methods, review timing, and at least seek to deduce what is best. To this end they advocate reason and temperance, and, most important, they are thrifty and save. These ideas and dispositions, elevated to an ideal in the economics of nineteenth-century and secular puritanism, live on in the reaction of industrial society to hunters—and in the average Canadian reaction to Indians. And a reaction of this kind means that a person, even if inclined to be sympathetic to hunters and hunting, has immense difficulty in understanding what planning means for hunters of the North.

Joseph and his family float possibilities. "Maybe we should go to Copper Creek. Bet you lots of moose up there." Or, "Could be caribou right now near Black Flats." Or, "I bet you no deer this time down on the Reserve . . ." Somehow a general area is selected from a gossamer of possibilities, and from an accumulation of remarks comes something rather like a consensus. No, that is not really it: rather, a sort of prediction, a combined sense of where we *might* go "tomorrow." Yet the hunt will not have been planned, nor any preparations started, and apparently no one is committed to going. Moreover, the floating conversation will have alighted on several irreconcilable possibilities, or have given rise to quasi-predictions. It is as if the predictions are all about other people—or are not quite serious. Although the mood is still one of wait and see, at the end of the day, at the close of much slow and gentle talk about this and that, a strong feeling has arisen about the morning: we shall go to Bluestone, maybe as far as the cross. We shall look for trout as well as moose. A number of individuals agree that they will go. But come morning, nothing is ready. No one has made any practical, formal plans. As often as not—indeed, more often than not—something quite new has drifted into conversations, other predictions have been tentatively reached, a new consensus appears to be forming. As it often seems, everyone has changed his mind.

The way to understand this kind of decision making, as also to live by and even share it, is to recognize that some of the most important variables are subtle, elusive, and extremely hard or impossible to assess with finality. The Athapaskan hunter will move in a direction and at a time that are determined by a sense of weather (to indicate a variable that is easily grasped if all too easily oversimplified by the one word) and by a sense of rightness. He will also have ideas about animal movement, his own and others' patterns of land use. . . . But already the nature of the hunter's decision making is being misrepresented by this kind of listing. To disconnect the variables, to compartmentalize the thinking, is to fail to acknowledge its sophistication and completeness. He considers variables as a composite, in parallel, and with the help of a blending of the metaphysical and the obviously pragmatic. To make a good, wise, sensible hunting choice is to accept the interconnection of all possible factors, and avoids the mistake of seeking rationally to focus on any one consideration that is held as primary. What is more, the decision is taken in the doing: there is no step or pause between theory and practice. As a consequence, the decision—like the action from which it is inseparable—is always alterable (and therefore may not properly even be termed a decision). The hunter moves in a chosen direction; but, highly sensitive to so many shifting considerations, he is always ready to change his directions.

Planning, as other cultures understand the notion, is at odds with this kind of sensitivity and would confound such flexibility. The hunter, alive to constant movements of nature, spirits, and human moods, maintains a way of doing things that repudiates a firm plan and any precise or specified understanding with others of what he is going to do. His course of action is not, must not be, a matter of predetermination. If a plan constitutes a decision about the right procedure or action, and the decision is congruent with the action, then there is no space left for a "plan," only for a bundle of open-ended and nonrational possibilities. Activity enters so far into this kind of planning as to undermine any so-called plans.

All this is by way of context or background for the seemingly straightforward proposal that we should set out the next morning to hunt moose and fish for trout at Bluestone Creek. Since there are many such apparent decisions in the following chapters, it is important that they be understood for what they are: convenient—but often misleading—reductions to a narrative convention of intimate and unfamiliar patterns of hunters' thought and behaviour.

"The next morning" came several times before we set out in the direction of Bluestone. Several individuals said they would come, but did not; others said they would not come, but did. Eventually, we drove in my rented pickup to a stretch of rolling forests, where hillsides and valley were covered by dense blankets of poplar, aspen, birch, and occasional stands of pine or spruce. After studied consideration of three places, Joseph and Atsin chose a campsite a short walk from a spring that created a narrow pool of good water in a setting of damp and frosted leaves.

There we camped, in a complex of shelters and one tent around a long central fire. It was a place the hunters had often used, and it had probably been an Indian campsite off and on for centuries. It was a clearing among thin-stemmed pine, a woodland tangled and in places made dense by a great number of deadfalls lying at all heights and angles to the ground. Night fell as we completed the camp. The fire was lit and was darkly reflected by these dead trees that crisscrossed against the forest.

Long before dawn (it cannot have been later than five o'clock), the men awoke. The fire rekindled, they sat around it and began the enormous and protracted breakfast that precedes every day's hunting: rabbit stew, boiled eggs, bannock, toasted sliced white bread, barbecued moose meat, whatever happens to be on hand, and cup after cup of strong, sweet tea. A little later, women and children joined the men at the fire and ate no less heartily.

As they ate, the light changed from a slight glimmer, the relief to predawn blackness to the first brightness that falters without strength at the top of the trees. As the light grew, the men speculated about where to go, sifting evidence they had accumulated from whatever nearby places they had visited since their arrival. Everyone had walked—to fetch water, cut wood, or simply to stretch the legs a little. Atsin, at the end of a short walk that morning, returned with a rabbit. He had taken it in a snare, evidently set as soon as we arrived the evening before. It was white already, its fur change a dangerously conspicuous anticipation of a winter yet to come. Conversation turned to rabbits. All the men had noticed a proliferation of runs and droppings. It was an excellent year for rabbit, the fifth or sixth in a cycle of seven improving years. It might be a good idea to hunt in some patches of young evergreens, along trails that led towards the river. There could be more rabbits there. Lots of rabbits. Always good to eat lots of rabbit stew. And there could be rainbow trout in that place, below the old cabin, and in other spots. Or maybe it would be good to go high up in the valley. . . . This exchange of details and ideas continued off and on throughout the meal. When it had finally ended and everyone had reflected a good deal on the day's possibilities, the men set off. Perhaps it was clear to them where and why, but which possibilities represented a starting point was not easily understood by an outsider.

Atsin's younger brother Sam set off alone, at right angles to a trail that led to the river by way of a place said to be particularly good for rabbits. Two others, Jimmy Wolf and Charlie Fellow—both relations of Joseph's wife Liza—also set off at an angle, but in the opposite direction. I followed Atsin along another, more winding trail: Liza and her oldest child, Tommy, together with two other women and their small children, made their way behind the men on the main trail; Atsin's son David attached himself to Brian Akattah and his ten-year-old nephew Peter. The choice of partner and trail was, if possible, less obviously planned than direction or hunting objective. Everyone was plainly free to go where and with whom he or she liked. As I became more familiar with this kind of hunt, though, I found that some individuals nearly always hunted alone, whereas others liked a companion, at least at the outset. A sense of great personal freedom was evident from the first. No one gives orders; everyone is, in some fundamental way, responsible to and for himself.

The distance between camp and the particular bend in the river that had been selected as the best possible fishing place was no more than a mile and a half. No time had been appointed for a rendezvous. Indeed clock time is of no significance here. (Only Joseph had a watch and it was never used for hunting purposes.) Everyone nonetheless appeared from the woods and converged on the fishing spot within minutes of one another. This co-ordination of activities is not easily understood, although it testified to the absence of big game, of moose, deer, or bear. If any of the hunters had located fresh tracks, he would have been long gone into the woods. Atsin, who seemed to be an expert at the job, appeared with two rabbits he had shot after glimpsing their helpless whiteness in the dun-coloured undergrowth. But fishing was going to supply the next meal.

The river at this place flows in a short curve around a wooded promontory that juts from the main forest. Both sides are deeply eroded banks, where sandy rubble is given some short-lived firmness by exposed tree roots. On the far side the landscape is barer, with meadowy, more open land for fifty yards before the forested slopes rise towards the mountains. Where the trail meets the creek (sometimes no wider than ten rushing yards), it deepens into a pool. There, the water is held back by a shallow rib of rock over which it quickens and races to the next pool.

The fishing spot itself turned out to be a platform of jumbled logs that must have been carried by the stream in flood, and then piled by currents until they reshaped the banks themselves. The sure-footed can find precarious walkways across this latticework platform. At their ends the logs offer a view down into the deepest part of the hole. Through the sharp clearness of this water rainbow trout could be seen, dark shadows, hovering or moving very slowly among long-sunken logs and roots.

Joseph studied the water and the fish, then produced a nylon line. It was wound tightly around a small piece of shaped wood, a spool that he carried in his pocket, wrapped in cloth. Along with the line were four or five hooks (size 6 or 8) and a chunk of old bacon. On his way along the trail he had broken off a long thin branch, and by the time we had arrived at the creek he had already stripped off its side twigs, peeled away the bark, and broken it to the right length. He tied some line to this homemade rod and handed other lengths to Brian and David. The three of them then clambered along the log platform, found more or less firm places at its edge, and began to fish.

The baited hooks were lowered straight down until they hung just above the stream bed. They did not hover there for long. Almost immediately the fish were being caught. The men could watch a trout swim towards a bait and, with one firm turn of its body, part suck and part grab the hook. The fisherman, with a single upward swing of the rod, would pull it straight out of the water and onto the logs. Then each fish was grabbed at, and missed, fell off the hook among the logs, was grabbed again. . . . The fish, and the fishermen, could easily slip between the gaps of the platform. As the trout thrashed and leaped about there were shouts of excitement, advice, and laughter.

The trout were plentiful, as Joseph had said they would be, and fat. One after the other they came flying through the air into someone's hands, then to shore, where Atsin and Liza gutted them. A dozen or more, fish of one or two pounds each, every one of them with a brilliant red patch on its gills and red stripes along its sides—rainbow trout at their most spectacular. Then the fishing slowed down. Enough had been caught. Joseph, Brian, and David climbed back to the bank. We sat around the fires to eat rabbit stew and cook some of the fish.

By this time it was early afternoon, but the meal was unhurried. Perhaps the success of the moose hunt was doubtful, while a good supply of rabbit and fish had already been secured. Conversation turned again to places where it might be worth hunting, directions in which we might go; many possibilities were suggested, and no apparent decision was made. But when the meal ended, the men began to prepare themselves for another hunt. Having eaten and apparently rested and stared into the fire, one by one the hunters, unhurried and apparently indecisive, got up, strolled a little way, and came back. Then each began to fix his clothes, check a gun—began to get ready. By the time the last of the hunters was thus occupied, some had begun to drift away in one direction or another. After a last conversation, the rest of them left, except for Joseph, Brian's wife Mary, Liza, and the children, who stayed by the fire. Perhaps the afternoon was going to be long and hard.

This time a group of men walked in single file, Atsin in front. After a short distance, one went his own way, then others did so, until each of them had taken a separate direction. I again stayed close to Atsin, who made his way, often pushing his way, through dense bushes and small willows, along the river bank. He said once, when we paused to rest and look around, and think, that it was disappointing to find so few signs of moose, but there might be more fishing.

It must have been an hour before the men regrouped, this time on a high and eroded sandbar. The beach here was strewn with well-dried driftwood. Atsin and Robert Fellows began to gather enough of this wood to make a large fire. Brian fetched water for tea. Atsin's brother Sam, together with Jimmy Wolf, cut fishing poles, fixed up lines, went a short way upstream to a spot where the water turned and deepened against the bank, and began to fish. Their lines hung in the water, baits out of sight and judged to be close to the bottom. From time to time they changed the angle of their rods to adjust the depth at which they fished; and by taking advantage of the pole's being longer than the line, they periodically pulled the bait clear of the water, checked that all was well in place, and then dropped it easily back to where the fish should be.

But the fish were not there, or not hungry, or not to be fooled. Sam and Jimmy waited. There was no sudden upward whips of the pole, no bites, no shouts, no laughter. The others sprawled around the fire, watching the two fishermen, drinking tea, limiting themselves to an occasional squinting look towards the river and remarks about the dearth of game. The afternoon was warm and still. There seemed to be no reason for any great activity. Soon Jimmy decided to abandon the river in favour of a rest beside the fire. Sam forded the stream, crossed the sandbar, and tried his luck on the other side. From where we sat and lay we could see his head and shoulders, and the lift and drop of his long rod. It was easy enough to tell whether or not he was catching anything; he was not.

Moments, minutes, even hours of complete stillness: this was not time that could be measured. Hunters at rest, at ease, in wait, are able to discover and enjoy a special form of relaxation. There is a minimum of movement—a hand reaches out for a mug, an adjustment is made to the fire—and whatever is said hardly interrupts the silence, as if words and thoughts can be harmonized without any of the tensions of dialogue. Yet the hunters are a long way from sleep; not even the atmosphere is soporific. They wait, watch, consider. Above all they are still and receptive, prepared for whatever insight or realization may come to them, and ready for whatever stimulus to action might arise. This state of attentive waiting is perhaps as close as people can come to the falcon's suspended flight, when the bird, seemingly motionless, is ready to plummet in decisive action. To the outsider, who has followed along and tried to join in, it looks for all the world as if the hunters have forgotten why they are there. In this restful way hunters can spend many hours, sometimes days, eating, waiting, thinking.

The quality of this resting by the fire can be seen and felt when it is very suddenly charged, just as the nature of the falcon's hover becomes clear when it dives. Among hunters the emergence from repose may be slow or abrupt. But in either case a particular state of mind, a special way of being, has come to an end. One or two individuals move faster and more purposively, someone begins to prepare meat to cook, someone fetches a gun to work on, and conversation resumes its ordinary mode. This transformation took place that afternoon around the fire on the pebbled beach at just the time Sam gave up his fishing and began to walk back towards us. Atsin, Jimmy, and Robert all moved to new positions. Robert stood with his back to us, watching Sam's approach, while Atsin and Jimmy squatted where they could look directly at me.

In retrospect it seems clear that they felt the right time had come for something. Everyone seemed to give the few moments it took for this change to occur some special importance. Plainly the men had something to say and, in their own time, in their own way, they were going to say it. Signs and movements suggested that the flow of events that had begun in Joseph's home and Atsin's cabin, and continued with the fishing at Bluestone Creek, was about to be augmented. Something of significance to the men here was going to happen. I suddenly realized that everyone was watching me. Sam joined the group, but said nothing. Perhaps he, as a younger man, was now leaving events to his elders, to Atsin, Jimmy, and Robert. There was a brief silence made awkward by expectancy, though an awkward pause is a very rare thing among people who accept that there is no need to escape from silence, no need to use words as a way to avoid one another, no need to obscure the real.

Atsin broke this silence. He spoke at first of the research: "I bet some guys make big maps. Lots of work, these maps. Nobody knows that. White men don't know that."

Silence again. Then Robert continued: "Yeah, lots of maps. All over this country we hunt. Fish too. Trapping places. Nobody knows that. White men don't know that."

Then Jimmy spoke: "Indian guys, old-timers, they make maps too."

With these words, the men introduced their theme. The tone was friendly, but the words were spoken with intensity and firmness. The men seemed apprehensive, as if anxious to be very clearly understood— though nothing said so far required such concern. Once again, it is impossible to render verbatim all that they eventually said. I had no tape recorder and memory is imperfect. But even a verbatim account would fail to do justice to their meaning. Here, then, in summaries and glimpses, is what the men had in mind to say.

Some old-timers, men who became famous for their powers and skills, had been great dreamers. Hunters and dreamers. They did not hunt as most people now do. They did not seek uncertainly for the trails of animals whose movements we can only guess at. No, they located their prey in dreams, found their trails, and made dream-kills. Then, the next day, or a few days later, whenever it seemed auspicious to do so, they could go out, find the trail, re-encounter the animal, and collect the kill.

Maybe, said Atsin, you think this is all nonsense, just so much bullshit. Maybe you don't think this power is possible. Few people understand. The old-timers who were strong dreamers knew many things that are not easy to understand. People—white people, young people—yes, they laugh at such skills. But they do not know. The Indians around this country know a lot about power. In fact, everyone has had some experience of it. The fact that dream-hunting works has been proved many times.

A few years ago a hunter dreamed a cow moose kill. A fine, fat cow. He was so pleased with the animal, so delighted to make this dream-kill, that he marked the animal's hooves. Now he would be sure to recognize it when he went on the coming hunt. The next day, when he went out into the bush, he quickly found the dream-trail. He followed it, and came to a large cow moose. Sure enough, the hooves bore his marks. Everyone saw them. All the men around the fire had been told about the marks, and everyone on the Reserve had come to look at those hooves when the animal was butchered and brought into the people's homes.

And not only that fat cow moose—many such instances are known to the people, whose marks on the animal or other indications show that there was no mistaking, no doubts about the efficacy of such dreams. Do you think this is all lies? No, this is power they had, something they knew how to use. This was their way of doing things, the right way. They understood, those old-timers, just where all the animals came from. The trails converge, and if you were a very strong dreamer you could discover this, and see the source of trails, the origin of game. Dreaming revealed them. Good hunting depended upon such knowledge.

Today it is hard to find men who can dream this way. There are too many problems. Too much drinking. Too little respect. People are not good enough now. Maybe there will again be strong dreamers when these problems are overcome. Then more maps will be made. New maps.

Oh yes, Indians made maps. You would not take any notice of them. You might say such maps are crazy. But maybe the Indians would say that is what your maps are: the same thing. Different maps from different people—different *ways*. Old-timers made maps of trails, ornamented them with lots of fancy. The good people.

None of this is easy to understand. But good men, the really good men, could dream of more than animals. Sometimes they saw heaven and its trails. Those trails are hard to see, and few men have had such dreams. Even if they could see dream-trails to heaven, it is hard to explain them. You draw maps of the land, show everyone where to go. You explain the hills, the rivers, the trails from here to Hudson Hope, the roads. Maybe you make maps of where the hunters go and where the fish can be caught. That is not easy. But easier, for sure, than drawing out the trails to heaven. You may laugh at these maps of the trails to heaven, but they were done by the good men who had the heaven dream, who wanted to tell the truth. They worked hard on their truth.

Atsin had done most of the talking thus far. The others interjected a few words and comments, agreeing or elaborating a little. Jimmy told about the cow moose with marked hooves. All of them offered some comparisons between their own and others' maps. And the men's eyes never ceased to remain fixed on me: were they being understood? Disregarded? Thought ridiculous? They had chosen this moment for these explanations, yet no one was entirely secure in it. Several times, Atsin paused and waited, perhaps to give himself a chance to sense or absorb the reaction to his words. These were intense but not tense hiatuses. Everyone was reassuring himself that his seriousness was being recognized. That was all they needed to continue.

The longest of these pauses might have lasted as much as five minutes. During it the fire was rebuilt. It seemed possible, for a few moments, that they had finished, and that their attention was now returning to trout, camp, and the hunt. But the atmosphere hardly altered, and Jimmy quite abruptly took over where Atsin had left off.

The few good men who had the heaven dream were like the Fathers, Catholic priests, men who devoted themselves to helping others with that essential knowledge to which ordinary men and women have limited access. (Roman Catholic priests have drifted in and out of the lives of all the region's Indians, leaving behind fragments of their knowledge and somewhat rarefied and idealized versions of what they had to preach.) Most important of all, a strong dreamer can tell others how to get to heaven. We all have need of the trail, or complex of trails, but, unlike other important trails, the way to heaven will have been seen in dreams that only a few, special individuals have had. Maps of heaven are thus important. And they must be good, complete maps. Heaven is reached only by careful avoidance of the wrong trails. These must also be shown so that the traveller can recognize and avoid them.

How can we know the general direction we should follow? How can anyone who has not dreamed the whole route began to locate himself on such a map? When Joseph, or any of the other men, begin to draw a hunting map, he had first to find his way. He did this by recognizing features, by fixing points of reference, and then, once he was oriented to the familiar and to the scale or manner in which the familiar was reproduced, he could begin to add his own layers of detailed information. But how can anyone begin to find a way on a map of trails to heaven, across a terrain that ordinary hunters do not experience in everyday activities or even in their dream-hunts?

The route to heaven is not wholly unfamiliar, however. As it happens, heaven is to one side of, and at the same level as, the point where the trails to animals all meet. Many men know where this point is, or at least some of its approach trails, from their own hunting dreams. Hunters can in this way find a basic reference, and once they realize that heaven is in a particular relation to this far more familiar centre, the map as a whole can be read. If this is not enough, a person can take a map with him; some old-timers who made or who were given maps of the trails to heaven choose to have a map buried with them. They can thus remind themselves which ways to travel if the actual experience of the trail proves to be too confusing. Others are given a corner of a map that will help reveal the trail to them. And even those who do not have any powerful dreams are shown the best maps of the route to heaven. The discoveries of the very few most powerful dreamers—and some of the dreamers have been women—are periodically made available to everyone.

The person who wishes to dream must take great care, even if he dreams only of the hunt. He must lie in the correct orientation, with his head towards the rising sun. There should be no ordinary trails, no human pathways, between his pillow and the bush. These would be confusing to the self that travels in dreams towards important and unfamiliar trails which can lead to a kill. Not much of this can be mapped—only the trail to heaven has been drawn up. There has been no equivalent need to make maps to share other important information.

Sometime, said Jimmy Wolf, you will see one of these maps. There are some of them around. Then the competence and strength of the old-timers who drew them will be unquestioned. Different trails can be explained, and heaven can be located on them. Yes, they were pretty smart, the men who drew them. Smarter than any white man in these parts and smarter than Indians of today. Perhaps, said Atsin, in the future there will be men good enough to make new maps of heaven—but not just now. There will be changes, he added, and the people will come once again to understand the things that Atsin's father had tried to teach him. In any case, he said, the older men are now trying to explain the powers and dreams of old-timers to the young, indeed to all those who have not been raised with these spiritual riches. For those who do not understand, hunting and life itself are restricted and difficult. So the people must be told everything, and taught all that they need, in order to withstand the incursions presently being made into their way of life, their land, and into their very dreams.

TROPICAL GOSSIP AND KEGALLE

MICHAEL ONDAATJE

From *Running in the Family* (1981)

Running in the Family *is poet and novelist Michael Ondaatje's history of his Ceylonese family: his father an utterly charming, completely undependable dipsomaniac; his flamboyant grandmother swept to her death on the back of a monsoon flood; the rest a wild collection of indiscreet lovers, heavy drinkers and carefree socialites. The book is structured loosely around two trips which Ondaatje made back to Ceylon, now Sri Lanka, at the end of the 1970s. The narrative is fragmented, a compilation of memories—his own and other peoples'—photographs and poems. Unlike earlier memoirs represented in this collection, which are meant to be reliable accounts of their subjects' lives,* Running in the Family *illustrates the illusiveness of memory, the uncertainty of knowing what actually happened in the past. The following selection describes the family home in the town of Kegalle.*

Michael Ondaatje was born in Ceylon in 1943. He moved to England as a youngster, then came to Canada when he was nineteen and has lived here ever since. His first book of poems was published in 1967 and since that time he has won several awards—Canadian and international—for both poetry and prose. In 1992 his most recent novel, The English Patient, *won a Governor-General's award and shared the prestigious Booker Prize in England.*

It seems that most of my relatives at some time were attracted to somebody they shouldn't have been. Love affairs rainbowed over marriages and lasted forever—so it often seemed that marriage was the greater infidelity. From the twenties until the war nobody really had to grow up. They remained wild and spoiled. It was only during the second half of my parents' generation that they suddenly turned to the real world. Years later, for instance, my uncle Noel would return to Ceylon as a Q.C. to argue for the lives of friends from his youth who had tried to overthrow the government.

But earlier, during their flaming youth, this energy formed complex relationships, though I still cannot break the code of how "interested in" or "attracted" they were to each other. Truth disappears with history and gossip tells us in the end nothing of personal relationships. There are stories of elopements, unrequited love, family feuds, and exhausting vendettas, which everyone was drawn into, had to be involved with. But nothing is said of the closeness between two people: how they grew in the shade of each other's presence. No one speaks of that exchange of gift and character—the way a person took on and recognized in himself the smile of a lover. Individuals are seen only in the context of these swirling social tides. It was almost impossible for a couple to do anything without rumour leaving their shoulders like a flock of messenger pigeons.

Where is the ultimate and truthful in all this? Teenager and Uncle. Husband and lover. A lost father in his solace. And why do I want to know of this privacy? After the cups of tea, coffee, public conversations . . . I want to sit down with someone and talk with utter directness, want to talk to all the lost history like that deserving lover.

✧

My paternal grandfather—Philip—was a strict, aloof man. Most people preferred his brother Aelian who was good-natured and helpful to everyone. Both were lawyers but my grandfather went on to make huge sums of money in land deals and retired as he said he would at the age of forty. He built the family home, 'Rock Hill,' on a prime spot of land right in the centre of the town of Kegalle.

"Your great uncle Aelian was a very generous man," says Stanley Suraweera. "I wanted to learn Latin and he offered to tutor me from four until five every morning. I'd go to his house by cart every day and he would be up, waiting for me." In later years Aelian was to have several heart attacks. In one hospital he was given so much morphine that he became addicted to it.

My grandfather lived at Rock Hill for most of his life and ignored everybody in Kegalle social circles. He was immensely wealthy. Most people considered him a snob, but with his family he was a very loving man. The whole family kissed each other goodnight and good morning, a constant tradition in the house—no matter what chaos my father was causing at the time. Family arguments were buried before bedtime and buried once more first thing in the morning.

So here was 'Bampa,' as we called him, determined to be a good father and patriarch, spreading a protective wing over his more popular brother Aelian, and living in his empire—acres of choice land in the heart of Kegalle. He was dark and his wife was very white, and a rival for my grandmother's hand remarked that he hoped the children would be striped. The whole family lived in terror of him. Even his strong-willed wife could not blossom till after his death. Like some other Ondaatjes, Bampa had a weakness for pretending to be 'English' and, in his starched collars and grey suits, was determined in his customs. My brother, who was only four years old then, still remembers painfully strict meals at Rock Hill with Bampa grinding his teeth at one end of the table—as if his carefully built ceremonies were being evaded by a weak-willed family. It was only in the afternoons when, dressed in sarong and vest, he went out for walks over his property (part of a mysterious treatment for diabetes), that he seemed to become a real part of the landscape around him.

Every two years he would visit England, buy crystal, and learn the latest dances. He was a perfect dancer. Numerous aunts remember him inviting them out in London and taking great pleasure in performing the most recent dance steps with a natural ease. Back home there was enough to worry about. There was Aelian, who was continually giving his money away to ecclesiastical causes, the cousin who was mauled to death by his underfed racehorse, and four star-crossed sisters who were secret drinkers. Most Ondaatjes liked liquor, sometimes to excess. Most of them were hot tempered—though they blamed diabetes for this whenever possible. And most were genetically attracted to a family called Prins and had to be talked out of marriage—for the Prins brought bad luck wherever they went.

My grandfather died before the war and his funeral was spoken about with outrage and envy for months afterwards. He thought he had organized it well. All the women wore long black dresses and imported champagne was drunk surreptitiously from teacups. But his hope of departing with decorum collapsed before he was put into the ground. His four sisters and my recently liberated grandmother got into a loud argument over whether to pay the men two or three rupees to carry the coffin up the steep slopes to the cemetery. Awkward mourners who had come from Colombo waited as silent as my supine grandfather while the argument blazed from room to room and down the halls of Rock Hill. My grandmother peeled off her long black gloves in fury and refused to proceed with the ceremony, then slid them on with the aid of a daughter when it seemed the body would never leave the house. My father, who was overseeing the cooling of the champagne, was nowhere in sight. My mother and Uncle Aelian retired in a fit of giggles to the garden under the mangosteen tree. All this occurred on the afternoon of September 12, 1938. Aelian died of his liver problems in April of 1942.

For the next decade Rock Hill was seldom used by my family and my father was not to return to it for some years. By that time my parents were divorced and my father had lost various jobs. Bampa had willed the land to his grandchildren but my father, whenever he needed to, would sell or give away sections of land so that houses were gradually built up along the perimeter of the estate. My father returned alone to Kegalle in the late forties and took up farming. He lived quite simply at that time, separate from the earlier circle of friends, and my sister Gillian and I spent most of our holidays with him. By 1950 he had married again and was living with his wife and two children from his second marriage, Jennifer and Susan.

He ended up, in those years, concentrating on chickens. His dipsomania would recur every two months or so. Between bouts he would not touch a drink. Then he would be offered one, take it, and would not or could not stop drinking for three or four days. During that time he could do *nothing* but drink. Humourous and gentle when sober, he changed utterly and would do anything to get alcohol. He couldn't eat, had to have a bottle on him at all times. If his new wife Maureen had hidden a bottle, he would bring out his rifle and threaten to kill her. He knew, even when sober, that he would need to drink again, and so buried bottles all around the estate. In the heart of his drunkenness he would remember where the bottles were. He would go into the fowl run, dig under chicken straw, and pull out a half bottle. The cement niches on the side of the house held so many bottles that from the side the building resembled a wine cellar.

He talked to no one on those days, although he recognized friends, was aware of everything that was going on. He had to be at the peak of his intelligence in order to remember exactly where the bottles were so he could outwit his wife and family. Nobody could stop him. If Maureen managed to destroy the bottles of gin he had hidden he would drink methylated spirits. He drank until he collapsed and passed out. Then he would waken and drink again. Still no food. Sleep. Get up and have one more shot and then he was finished. He would not drink again for about two months, not until the next bout.

The day my father died, Stanley Suraweera, now a Proctor at Kegalle, was in Court when a messenger brought him the note:

Mervyn has dropped dead. What shall I do? Maureen.

We had spent three days in Upcot in beautiful tea country with my half-sister Susan. On the way back to Colombo we drove through the Kadugannawa Pass and stopped at Kegalle. The old wooden bridge that my father drove over without fear ("God loves a drunk" he would say to anyone who sat by him white with terror) had been replaced with a concrete one.

What to us had been a lovely spacious house was now small and dark, fading into the landscape. A Sinhalese family occupied Rock Hill. Only the mangosteen tree, which I practically lived in as a child during its season of fruit, was full and strong. At the back, the kitul tree still leaned against the kitchen—tall, with tiny yellow berries which the polecat used to love. Once a week it would climb up and spend the morning eating the berries and come down drunk, would stagger over the lawn pulling up flowers or come into the house to up-end drawers of cutlery and serviettes. Me and my polecat, my father said after one occasion when their drunks coincided, my father lapsing into his songs—baila or heartbreaking Rodgers and Hart or his own version of "My Bonnie Lies over the Ocean"—

My whisky comes over the ocean
My brandy comes over the sea
But my beer comes from F.X. Pereira
So F.X. Pereira for me.
F.X. . . . F.X. . . .
F.X. Pereira for me, for me. . . .

He emerged out of his bedroom to damn whoever it was that was playing the piano—to find the house empty—Maureen and the kids having left, and the polecat walking up and down over the keys breaking the silence of the house, oblivious to his human audience; and my father wishing to celebrate this companionship, discovering all the bottles gone, unable to find anything, finally walking up to the kerosene lamp hanging in the centre of the room at head level, and draining *that* liquid into his mouth. He and his polecat.

Gillian remembered some of the places where he hid bottles. *Here*, she said, *and here*. Her family and my family walked around the house, through the depressed garden of guava trees, plantains, old forgotten flowerbeds. Whatever "empire" my grandfather had fought for had to all purposes disappeared.

The family home of Rock Hill was littered with snakes, especially cobras. The immediate garden was not so dangerous, but one step further and you would see several. The chickens that my father kept in later years were an even greater magnet. The snakes came for the eggs. The only deterrent my father discovered was ping-pong balls. He had crates of ping-pong balls shipped to Rock Hill and distributed them among the eggs. The snake would swallow the ball whole and be unable to digest it. There are several paragraphs on this method of snake control in a pamphlet he wrote on poultry farming.

The snakes also had the habit of coming into the house and at least once a month there would be shrieks, the family would run around, the shotgun would be pulled out, and the snake would be blasted to pieces. Certain sections of the walls and floors showed the scars of shot. My stepmother found one coiled asleep on her desk and was unable to approach the drawer to get the key to open the gun case. At another time one lay sleeping on the large radio to draw its warmth and, as nobody wanted to destroy the one source of music in the house, this one was watched carefully but left alone.

Most times though there would be running footsteps, yells of fear and excitement, everybody trying to quiet everybody else, and my father or stepmother would blast away not caring what was in the background, a wall, good ebony, a sofa, or a decanter. They killed at least thirty snakes between them.

After my father died, a grey cobra came into the house. My stepmother loaded the gun and fired at point blank range. The gun jammed. She stepped back and reloaded but by then the snake had slid out into the garden. For the next month this snake would often come into the house and each time the gun would misfire or jam, or my stepmother would miss at absurdly short range. The snake attacked no one and had a tendency to follow my younger sister around. Other snakes entering the house were killed by the shotgun, lifted with a long stick and flicked into the bushes, but the old grey cobra led a charmed life. Finally one of the old workers at Rock Hill told my stepmother what had become obvious, that it was my father who had come to protect his family. And in fact, whether it was because the chicken farm closed down or because of my father's presence in the form of a snake, very few other snakes came into the house again.

The last incident at Rock Hill took place in 1971, a year before the farm was sold. 1971 was the year of the Insurgence. The rebels against the government consisted of thousands from every walk of life—but essentially the young. The age of an insurgent ranged from fifteen to twenty. They were a strange mixture of innocence and determination and anarchy, making home-made bombs with nails and scraps of metal and at the same time delighted and proud of their uniforms of blue trousers with a stripe down the side, and tennis shoes. Some had never worn tennis shoes before. My cousin Rhunie was staying at the Ambepussa resthouse with the Chitrasena dance troupe when fifty insurgents marched up the road in formation chanting "we are hungry we are hungry," ransacked the place for food, but did not touch any one there because they were all fans of the dance company.

The insurgents were remarkably well organized and general belief is that they would have taken over the country if one group hadn't mixed up the dates and attacked the police station in Wellawaya a day too soon. The following day every police station and every army barrack and every radio station was to be hit simultaneously. Some gangs hid out in the jungle reserves at Wilpattu and Yala where they survived by shooting and eating the wildlife. A week before the uprising they had broken into local government offices, gone through the files and found the location of every registered weapon in the country. The day after the revolt broke out, a gang of twenty marched from house to house in Kegalle collecting weapons and finally came up the hill to Rock Hill.

They had ransacked several houses already, stripping them of every-thing—food, utensils, radios, and clothing, but this group of seventeen-year-olds was extremely courteous to my stepmother and her children. My father had apparently donated several acres of Rock Hill towards a playground several years earlier and many of these insurgents had known him well.

They asked for whatever weapons the house had and my stepmother handed over the notorious shotgun. They checked their files and saw a rifle was also listed. It turned out to be an air rifle, wrongly categorized. I had used it often as a ten-year-old, ankle deep in paddy fields, shooting at birds, and if there were no birds, at the fruit of trees. While all this official business was going on around the front porch, the rest of the insurgents had put down their huge collection of weapons, collected from all over Kegalle, and persuaded my younger sister Susan to provide a bat and a tennis ball. Asking her to join them, they proceeded to play a game of cricket on the front lawn. They played for most of the afternoon.

BACKYARD BALL HOCKEY

KEN DRYDEN

From *The Game* (1983)

Canadian hockey, Canadian sports generally, have failed to produce a substantial literature. There is no shortage of player biographies, picture books, and reminiscences about the "glory days" of this or that team, but there is almost no writing that repays attention as writing. An exception is Ken Dryden's memoir, The Game.

Dryden played in goal for the Montreal Canadiens from 1971 to 1979, excluding one season which he sat out in a contract dispute. The Game *is an account of his final season, and a summation of his life in hockey. It is not a conventional "season in the life of." It is about hockey, of course, but it is also about life after hockey, about the effect of celebrity, about coping with fear, about the chemistry of a team.*

Ken Dryden was born in Hamilton, Ontario in 1947, and grew up in suburban Toronto. He attended Cornell University and broke into the National Hockey League late in the 1970-71 season. During his career with Montreal the Canadiens won the Stanley Cup six times, and he won or shared the Vezina trophy for top goaltender five times. Dryden retired from hockey at the end of the 1978-79 season. A lawyer, he has written two other books.

In the following selection from The Game, *Dryden recalls winters in the backyard playing ball hockey with his brother Dave and every other kid in the neighbourhood.*

I get out of bed and pull back the curtains. It has snowed overnight and traces are still gently falling. For several minutes I stand there, my forehead pressed to the window, watching the snow, looking out at the backyards of the houses behind, where the Pritchards, the McLarens, and the Carpenters lived, and down below at the winter's depth of snow, and at the backyard where I spent my childhood.

"Dryden's Backyard." That's what it was called in our neighbourhood. It was more than 70 feet long, paved curiously in red asphalt, 45 feet wide at "the big end," gradually narrowing to 35 feet at the flower bed, to 25 feet at the porch—our centre line—to 15 feet at "the small end." While Steve Shutt and Guy Lafleur were in Willowdale and Thurso on backyard rinks their fathers built, while Larry Robinson was on a frozen stream in Marvelville and Réjean Houle on a road in Rouyn under the only street light that his street had, I was here.

It was an extraordinary place, like the first swimming pool on the block, except there were no others like it anywhere. Kids would come from many blocks away to play, mostly "the big guys," friends of my brother, a year or two older than him, seven or eight years older than me. But that was never a problem. It was the first rule of the backyard that they had to let me play. To a friend who complained one day, Dave said simply, "If Ken doesn't play, you don't play."

We played "ball hockey" mostly, with a tennis ball, its bounce deadened by the cold. A few times, we got out a garden hose and flooded the backyard to use skates and pucks, but the big end was slightly lower than the small end, and the water pooled and froze unevenly. More important, we found that the more literal we tried to make our games, the less lifelike they became. We could move across the asphalt quickly and with great agility in rubber "billy" boots; we could shoot a tennis ball high and hard. But with skates on, with a puck, we were just kids. So after the first few weeks of the first year, we played only ball hockey.

Depending on the day, the time, the weather, there might be any number of kids wanting to play, so we made up games any number could play. With four and less than nine, we played regular games, the first team scoring ten goals the winner. The two best players, who seemed always to know who they were, picked the teams and decided on ends. First choice of players got second choice of ends, and because the size of the big end made it more fun to play in, the small end was the choice to defend. Each team had a goalie—one with goalie pads, a catching glove, and a goalie stick; the other with only a baseball glove and a forward's stick. When we had more than eight players, we divided into three or more teams for a round-robin tournament, each game to five. With fewer than four, it was more difficult. Sometimes we attempted a regular game, often we just played "shots," each player being both shooter and goalie, standing in front of one net, shooting in turn at the other. Most often, however, we played "penalty shots."

In the late 1950s, the CBS network televised NHL games on Saturday afternoon. Before each game, there was a preview show in which a player from each of the teams involved that day would compete in two contests, one of which was a penalty-shot contest. The goalie they used each week was an assistant trainer for the Detroit Red Wings named Julian Klymquiw. Short and lefthanded, Klymquiw wore a clear plexiglass mask that arched in front of his face like a shield. None of us had ever heard of him, and his unlikely name made us a little doubtful at first. But it turned out that he was quite good, and most weeks he stopped the great majority of shots taken at him. So, during backyard games of "penalty shots," we pretended to be Julian Klymquiw, not Terry Sawchuck or Glenn Hall. And before each of our contests began, we would perform the ritual that Klymquiw and announcer Bud Palmer performed each week:

"Are you ready, Julian?"
"Yes, Bud."

But the backyard also meant time alone. It was usually after dinner when the "big guys" had homework to do and I would turn on the floodlights at either end of the house and on the porch, and play. It was a private game. I would stand alone in the middle of the yard, a stick in my hands, a tennis ball in front of me, silent, still, then suddenly dash ahead, stick handling furiously, dodging invisible obstacles for a shot on net. It was Maple Leaf Gardens filled to wildly cheering capacity, a tie game, seconds remaining. I was Frank Mahovlich, or Gordie Howe, I was anyone I wanted to be, and the voice in my head was that of Leafs broadcaster Foster Hewitt: " . . . there's ten seconds left, Mahovlich, winding up at his own line, at centre eight seconds, seven, over the blueline, six—he winds up, he shoots, he scores!" The mesh that had been tied to the bottoms of our red metal goal posts until frozen in the ice had been ripped away to hang loose from the crossbars, whipped back like a flag in a stiff breeze. My arms and stick flew into the air, I screamed a scream inside my head, and collected my ball to do it again—many times, for many minutes, the hero of all my own games.

It was a glorious fantasy, and I always heard that voice. It was what made my fantasy seem almost real. For to us, who attended hockey games mostly on TV or radio, an NHL game, a Leafs game, was played with a voice. If I wanted to be Mahovlich or Howe, if I moved by body the way I had seen them move theirs and did nothing else, it would never quite work. But if I heard the voice that said their names while I was playing out that fantasy, I could believe it. Foster Hewitt could make me them.

My friends and I played every day after school, sometimes during lunch and after dinner, but Saturday was always the big day. I would go to bed Friday night thinking of Saturday, waking up early, with none of the fuzziness I had other days. If it had snowed overnight, Dave and I with shovels and scrapers, and soon joined by others, would pile the snow into flower beds or high against the back of the garage. Then at 9 a.m. the games would begin.

There was one team in the big end, another in the small; third and fourth teams sat like birds on a telephone wire, waiting their turn on the wall that separated the big end from Carpenter's backyard. Each team wore uniforms identical to the other. It was the Canadian midwinter uniform of the time—long, heavy duffel coats in browns, greys, and blues; tuques in NHL team colours, pulled snug over ears under the watchful eye of mothers, here rolled up in some distinctive personal style; leather gloves, last year's church gloves, now curling at the wrist and separating between fingers; black rubber "billy" boots over layers of heavy woollen socks for fit, the tops rolled down like "low cuts" for speed and style.

Each game would begin with a faceoff, then wouldn't stop again. Action moved quickly end to end, the ball bouncing and rolling, chased by a hacking, slashing scrum of sticks. We had sticks without tops on their blades—"toothpicks"; sticks with no blades at all—"stubs." They broke piece by heart-wrenching piece, often quickly, but we still used them. Only at the start of a season, at Christmas (Dave and I routinely exchanged sticks until one year he gave me a stick and I gave him a pair of socks) and once or twice more, would we get new ones. All except John Stedelbauer. His father owned a car dealership and during hockey season gave away hockey sticks to his customers as a promotion. Stedelbauer got all the new sticks he needed, fortunately, as they weren't very good. One year he broke nineteen of them.

A goal would be scored, then another, and slowly the game would leapfrog to five. Bodies grew warm from the exertion, fingers and toes went numb; noses ran, wiped by unconscious sleeves; coats loosened; toques fell off; steam puffed from mouths and streamed from toqueless heads. Sticks hacked and slashed; tennis balls stung. But in the euphoria of the game, pain disappeared. Sitting on the wall that overlooked his backyard, Rick "Foster" Carpenter, younger and not very athletic, gave the play-by-play, but no one listened. Each of us had his own private game playing in his head. A fourth goal then a fifth, a cheer, and the first game was over. Quickly, four duffel coats, four toques, four pairs of weathered gloves and rubber "billy" boots would jump from the wall to replace the losers; and the second game would begin. We paused at noon while some went home and others ate the lunch that they had brought with them. At 6 p.m., the two or three who remained would leave. Eighteen hours later, after church, the next game would begin.

When I think of the backyard, I think of my childhood; and when I think of my childhood, I think of the backyard. It is the central image I have of that time, linking as it does all of its parts; father, mother, sister, friends, hockey, baseball, and Dave—big brother, idol, mentor, defender, and best friend. Yet it only lasted a few years. Dave was already twelve when the backyard was built; I was six. He and his friends played for three or four years, then stopped; I played longer but, without them, less often. Yet until moments ago, I had never remembered that.

The backyard was not a training ground. In all the time I spent there, I don't remember ever thinking I would be an NHL goalie, or even hoping I could be one. In backyard games, I dreamed I *was* Sawchuk or Hall, Mahovlich or Howe: I never dreamed I would be like them. There seemed no connection between the backyard and Maple Leaf Gardens; there seemed no way to get there from here. If we ever thought about that, it never concerned us; we just played. It was here in the backyard that we *learned* hockey. It was here we got close to it, we got *inside* it, and it got inside us. It was here that our inextricable bond with the game was made. Many years have now passed, the game has grown up and been complicated by things outside it, yet still the backyard remains— untouched, unchanged, my unseverable link to that time, and that game.

Seventeen years after we played in the backyard for the first time, my father took a train to Montreal, hoping that something special might happen. He went to see a game between the Canadiens and the Buffalo Sabres, and in the middle of the second period, Canadiens' goalie Rogie Vachon was injured and had to leave the ice. I had been called up from the Voyageurs less than two weeks before, and was sent in to replace him. As I skated to the net, Sabres coach Punch Imlach motioned the goalie, Joe Daly, to the bench, and Dave skated out in his place. It was like it had been all those times before.

I didn't enjoy that game very much. I had played only two previous NHL games, and seeing Dave in the other end was a distraction I didn't want or need. And while I became more comfortable and the game went on, I was surprised and disappointed that I didn't feel more. All those hours we had spent in the backyard, all our childhood fantasies, the different routes we had taken, the different careers we had seem destined for; then, years later, Montreal, the Forum, our father in the stands—the unexpected climax. Yet try as I did, I couldn't feel that way. I could sense the curious excitement of the crowd, I could feel its huge vicarious pleasure, but my own excitement was vague, it had no edge to it, as if somehow it wasn't new, as if in fact we *had* done it before.

When the game was over, proud and relieved we shook hands at centre ice. A few hours later, I began to feel differently. What had surprised and disappointed me earlier, I found exciting and reassuring. It *really* had been no different. Those backyard games, the times we stood at opposite ends of the yard, the times we dreamed we were Sawchuk and Hall, we *were* Sawchuk and Hall, there *had* been a connection, we just never knew it.

Now, when the snow melts in the spring, the backyard looks like an old abandoned runway. The red of the asphalt has been worn away to grey, roots from nearby poplar trees have heaved and cracked its surface and clusters of tall grass have pushed their way through. Along the base of the bank that rose to McLaren's backyard, the concrete block wall that was our "boards," the target of balls and pucks in the winter and baseballs in the summer, has slowly pitched forward from the pressure of the bank, and soon will fall. Over much of the big end, where games opened up and skills were freed and given their chance, a huge compost heap lies like an ancient earthwork under the snow, growing faster each year then my father can use it. And a few feet from it, up against the back of the garage and under its eaves where I can't quite see it, a net, red with rust, its mesh completely gone; the other one loaned away years ago and not yet returned. It was been twenty years since Dave played here for the last time; fifteen years since I did. With no children or grandchildren to use it, fixing it up, restoring it as a monument to ourselves, doesn't seem right. Still, it's the most vivid memory I have of my childhood, and now when I come home, when I stand at this window and look out at the backyard as I sometimes do, I don't like to see it without its snow.

LIFE IN A NEW LANGUAGE

EVA HOFFMAN

From *Lost in Translation* (1989)

Eva Hoffman grew up in Poland after the Second World War. In 1959, at the age of thirteen, she emigrated with her family to Canada and lived her teenage years in Vancouver. Following graduation from high school, she attended university in the United States and did not return to Canada. Lost in Translation *is a personal essay in three parts. The first section describes Hoffman's Polish childhood; the second part, a sometimes bitter meditation on the interplay of language and personality, covers the Vancouver years; and the third section of the book deals with her life in the U.S.*

Lost in Translation *does not follow the conventional pattern of an immigrant's "rags-to-riches" success story. In the end Hoffman does succeed: she goes on to Harvard University and a job at* The New York Times Book Review. *But her book is more concerned with the psychological trauma of emigration than the material rewards. Like Mary Meigs in* Lily Briscoe, *Hoffman is concerned with the personal landscape of ideas and emotions, not the outer world of public events.* Lost in Translation *is a much more self-conscious book of memoirs than, say,* That Summer in Paris. *At the same time, her tart reflections on Vancouver will amuse and/or irritate anyone familiar with the city.*

The selection below describes Hoffman's arrival on the West Coast.

B y the time we've reached Vancouver, there are very few people left on the train. My mother has dressed my sister and me in our best outfits—identical navy blue dresses with sailor collars and gray coats handmade of good gabardine. My parents' faces reflect anticipation and anxiety. "Get off the train on the right foot," my mother tells us. "For luck in the new life."

I look out of the train window with a heavy heart. Where have I been brought to? As the train approaches the station, I see what is indeed a bit of nowhere. It's a drizzly day, and the platform is nearly empty. Everything is the colour of slate. From this bleakness, two figures approach us—a nondescript middle-aged man and woman—and after making sure that we are the right people, the arrivals from the other side of the world, they hug us; but I don't feel much warmth in their half-embarrassed embrace. "You should kneel down and kiss the ground," the man tells my parents. "You're lucky to be here." My parents' faces fill with a kind of naïve hope. Perhaps everything will be well after all. They need signs, portents, at this hour.

Then we all get into an enormous car—yes, this is America—and drive into the city that is to be our home.

The Rosenbergs' house is a matter of utter bafflement to me. This one-storey structure surrounded by a large garden surely doesn't belong in a city—but neither can it be imagined in the country. The garden itself is of such pruned and trimmed neatness that I'm half afraid to walk in it. Its lawn is improbably smooth and velvety (Ah, the time and worry spent on the shaving of these lawns! But I will only learn of that later), and the rows of marigolds, the circles of geraniums seem almost artificial in their perfect symmetries, in their subordination to orderliness.

Still, I much prefer sitting out here in the sun to being inside. The house is larger than any apartment I have seen in Poland, with enormous "picture" windows, a separate room for every member of the family and soft pastel-coloured rugs covering all the floors. These are all features that, I know, are intended to signify good taste and wealth—but there's an incongruity between the message I'm supposed to get and my secret perceptions of these surroundings. To me, these interiors seem oddly flat, devoid of imagination, ingenuous. The spaces are so plain, low-ceilinged, obvious; there are no curves, niches, odd angles, nooks, or crannies—nothing that gathers a house into itself, giving it a sense of privacy, or of depth—of interiority. There's no solid wood here, no accretion either of age or dust. There is only the open sincerity of the simple spaces, open right on to the street. (No peering out the window here, to catch glimpses of exchanges on the street; the picture windows are designed to give everyone full view of everyone else, to declare there's no mystery, nothing to hide. Not true, of course, but that's the statement.) There is also the disingenuousness of the furniture, all of it whiteish with gold trimming. The whole thing is too revealing of an aspiration to good taste, but the unintended effect is thin and insubstantial—as if it was planned and put up just yesterday, and could just as well be dismantled tomorrow. The only rooms that really impress me are the bathroom and the kitchen—both of them so shiny, polished, and full of unfamiliar, fabulously functional appliances that they remind me of interiors which we occasionally glimpsed in French or American movies, and which, in our bedraggled Poland, we couldn't distinguish from fantasy. "Do you think people really live like this?" we would ask after one of these films, neglecting all the drama of the plot for the interest of these incidental features. Here is something worth describing to my friends in Cracow, down to such mind-boggling details as a shaggy rug in the bathroom and toilet paper that comes in different colours.

For the few days we stay at the Rosenbergs', we are relegated to the basement, where there's an extra apartment usually rented out to lodgers. My father looks up to Mr. Rosenberg with the respect, even a touch of awe due to someone who is a certified millionaire. Mr. Rosenberg is a big man in the small Duddy Kravitz community of Polish Jews, most of whom have made good in junk peddling and real estate—but none as good as he. Mr. Rosenberg, who is now almost seventy, had the combined chutzpah and good luck to ride on Vancouver's real-estate boom—and now he's the richest of them all. This hardly makes him the most popular, but it automatically makes him the wisest. People from the community come to him for business advice, which he dispenses, in Yiddish, as if it were precious currency given away for free only through his grandiose generosity.

In the uncompromising vehemence of adolescence and injured pride,

I begin to see Mr. Rosenberg not as our benefactor but as a Dickensian figure of personal tyranny, and my feeling toward him quickly rises to something that can only be called hate. He had made stinginess into principle; I feel it as a nonhuman hardness, a conversion of flesh and feeling into stone. His face never lights up with humour or affection or wit. But then, he takes himself very seriously; to him too his wealth is the proof of his righteousness. In accordance with his principles, he demands money for our train tickets from Montreal as soon as we arrive. I never forgive him. We've brought gifts we thought handsome, but in addition, my father gives him all the dollars he accumulated in Poland— something that would start us off in Canada, we thought, but is now all gone. We'll have to scratch out our living somehow, starting from zero: my father begins to pinch the flesh of his arms nervously.

Mrs. Rosenberg, a worn-faced nearly inarticulate, diffident woman, would probably show us more generosity were she not so intimidated by her husband. As it is, she and her daughter, Diane, feed us white bread with sliced cheese and bologna for lunch, and laugh at our incredulity at the mushy textures, the plastic wrapping, the presliced convenience of the various items. Privately, we comment that this is not real food: it has no taste, it smells of plastic. The two women also give us clothing they can no longer use. I can't imagine a state of affairs in which one would want to discard the delicate, transparent bathrobes and the Angora sweaters they pass on to us, but luscious though these items seem—beyond anything I ever hoped to own—the show of gratitude required from me on receiving them sours the pleasure of new ownership. "Say thank you," my mother prompts me in preparation for receiving a batch of clothing. "People like to be appreciated." I coo and murmur ingratiatingly; I'm beginning to master the trick of saying thank you with just the right turn of the head, just the right balance between modesty and obsequiousness. In the next few years, this is a skill I'll have to use often. But in my heart I feel no real gratitude at being the recipient of so much mercy.

On about the third night at the Rosenbergs' house, I have a nightmare in which I'm drowning in the ocean while my mother and father swim farther and farther away from me. I know, in this dream, what it is to be cast adrift in incomprehensible space; I know what it is to lose one's mooring. I wake up in the middle of a prolonged scream. The fear is stronger than anything I've ever known. My parents wake up and hush me up quickly; they don't want the Rosenbergs to hear this disturbing sound. I try to calm myself and go back to sleep, but I feel as though I've stepped through a door into a dark place. Psychoanalysts talk about "mutative insights," through which the patient gains an entirely new perspective and discards some part of a cherished neurosis. The primal scream of my birth into the New World is a mutative insight of a negative kind—and I know that I can never lose the knowledge it brings me. The black, bituminous terror of the dream solders itself to the chemical base of my being—and from then on, fragments of the fear lodge themselves in my consciousness, thorns and pinpricks of anxiety, loose electricity floating in a psyche that has been forcibly pried from its structures. Eventually, I become accustomed to it; I know that it comes, and that it also goes; but when it hits with full force, in its pure form, I call it the Big Fear.

After about a week of lodging us in his house, Mr. Rosenberg decides that he has done enough for us, and, using some acquired American wisdom, explains that it isn't good for us to be dependent on his charity; there is of course no question of kindness. There is no question, either, of Mrs. Rosenberg intervening on our behalf, as she might like to do. We have no place to go, no way to pay for a meal. And so we begin.

"Shut up, shuddup," the children around us are shouting, and it's the first word in English that I understand from its dramatic context. My sister and I stand in the schoolyard clutching each other, while kids all around us are running about, pummelling each other, and screaming like whirling dervishes. Both the boys and the girls look sharp and aggressive to me—the girls all have bright lipstick on, their hair sticks up and out like witches' fury, and their skirts are held up and out by stiff, wiry crinolines. I can't imagine wanting to talk their harsh-sounding language.

We've been brought to this school by Mr. Rosenberg, who, two days after our arrival, tells us he'll take us to classes that are provided by the government to teach English to newcomers. This morning, in the rinky-dink wooden barracks where the classes are held, we've acquired new names. All it takes is a brief conference between Mr. Rosenberg and the teacher, a kindly looking woman who tries to give us reassuring glances, but who has seen too many people come and go to get sentimental about a name. Mine—"Ewa"—is easy to change into its near equivalent in English, "Eva." My sister's name—"Alina"—poses more of a problem, but after a moment's thought, Mr. Rosenberg and the teacher decide that "Elaine" is close enough. My sister and I hang our heads wordlessly under this careless baptism. The teacher then introduces us to the class, mispronouncing our last name—"Wydra"—in a way we've never heard before. We make our way to a bench at the back of the room; nothing much has happened, except a small, seismic mental shift. The twist on our names takes them a tiny distance from us—but it's a gap into which the infinite hobgoblin of abstraction enters. Our Polish names didn't refer to us; they were as surely us as our eyes or hands. These new appellations, which we ourselves can't pronounce, are not us. They are identification tags, disembodied signs pointing to objects that happen to be my sister and myself. We walk to our seats into a roomful of unknown faces, with names that make us strangers to ourselves.

When the school day is over the teacher hands us a file card on which she has written, "I'm a newcomer. I'm lost. I live at 1785 Granville Street. Will you kindly show me how to get there? Thank you." We wander the streets for several hours, zigzagging back and forth through seemingly identical suburban avenues, showing this deaf-mute sign to the few people we see, until we eventually recognize the Rosenbergs' house. We're greeted by our quietly hysterical mother and Mrs. Rosenberg, who, in a ritual she has probably learned from television, puts out two glasses of milk on her red Formica counter. The milk, homogenized, and too cold from the fridge, bears little resemblance to the liquid we used to drink called by the same name.

Every day I learn new words, new expressions. I pick them up from school exercises, from conversations, from the books I take out of Vancouver's well-lit, cheerful public library. There are some turns of phrase to which I develop strange allergies. "You're welcome," for example, strikes me as a gaucherie, and I can hardly bring myself to say it—I suppose because it implies that there's something to be thanked for, which in Polish would be impolite. The very places where language is at its most conventional, where it should be most taken for granted, are the places where I feel the prick of artifice.

Then there are words to which I take an equally irrational liking, for their sound, or just because I'm pleased to have deduced their meaning.

Mainly they're words I learn from books, like "enigmatic" or "insolent"—words that have only a literary value, that exist only as signs on the page.

But mostly, the problem is that the signifier has become severed from the signified. The words I learn now don't stand for things in the same unquestioned way they did in my native tongue. "River" in Polish was a vital sound, energized with the essence of riverhood, of my rivers, of my being immersed in rivers. "River" in English is cold—a word without an aura. It has no accumulated associations for me, and it does not give off the radiating haze of connotation. It does not evoke.

The process, alas, works in reverse as well. When I see a river now, it is not shaped, assimilated by the word that accommodates it to the psyche—a word that makes a body of water a river rather than an uncontained element. The river before me remains a thing, absolutely other, absolutely unbending to the grasp of my mind.

When my friend Penny tells me that she's envious, or happy, or disappointed, I try laboriously to translate not from English to Polish but from the word back to its source, to the feeling from which it springs. Already, in that moment of strain, spontaneity of response is lost. And anyway, the translation doesn't work. I don't know how Penny feels when she talks about envy. The word hangs in a Platonic stratosphere, a vague prototype of all envy, so large, so all-encompassing that it might crush me—as might disappointment or happiness.

I am becoming a living avatar of structuralist wisdom; I cannot help knowing that words are just themselves. But it's a terrible knowledge, without any of the consolations that wisdom usually brings. It does not mean that I'm free to play with words at my wont; anyway, words in their naked state are surely among the least satisfactory play objects. No, this radical disjoining between word and thing is a desiccating alchemy, draining the world not only of significance but of its colours, striations, nuances—its very existence. It is the loss of a living connection.

The worst losses come at night. As I lie down in a strange bed in a strange house—my mother is a sort of housekeeper here, to the aging Jewish man who has taken us in in return for her services—I wait for that spontaneous flow of inner language which used to be my nighttime talk with myself, my way of informing the ego where the id had been. Nothing comes. Polish, in a short time, has atrophied, shrivelled from sheer uselessness. Its words don't apply to my new experiences; they're not coeval with any of the objects, or faces, or the very air I breathe in the daytime. In English, words have not penetrated to those layers of my psyche from which a private conversation could proceed. This interval before sleep used to be the time when my mind became both receptive and alert, when images and words rose up to consciousness, reiterating what had happened during the day, adding the day's experiences to those already stored there, spinning out the thread of my personal story.

Now, this picture-and-word show is gone; the thread has been snapped. I have no interior language, and without it, interior images—those images through which we assimilate the external world, through which we take it in, love it, make it our own—become blurred too. My mother and I met a Canadian family who live down the block today. They were working in their garden and engaged us in a conversation of the "Nice weather we're having, isn't it?" variety, which culminated in their inviting us into their house. They sat stiffly on their couch, smiled in the long pauses between the conversation, and seemed at a loss for what to ask. Now my mind gropes for some description of them, but nothing fits. They're a different species from anyone I've met in Poland, and Polish words slip off of them without sticking. English words don't hook on to anything. I try, deliberately, to come up with a few. Are these people pleasant or dull? Kindly or silly? The words float in an uncertain space. They come up from a part of my brain in which labels may be manufactured but which has no connection to my instincts, quick reactions, knowledge. Even the simplest adjectives sow confusion in my mind; English kindliness has a whole system of morality behind it, a system that makes "kindness" an entirely positive virtue. Polish kindness has the tiniest element of irony. Besides, I'm beginning to feel the tug of prohibition, in English, against uncharitable words. In Polish, you can call someone an idiot without particularly harsh feelings and with the zest of a strong judgment. Yes, in Polish these people might tend toward "silly" and "dull"—but I force myself toward "kindly" and "pleasant." The cultural unconscious is beginning to exercise its subliminal influence.

The verbal blur covers these people's faces, their gestures with a sort of fog. I can't translate them into my mind's eye. The small event, instead of being added to the mosaic of consciousness and memory, falls through some black hole, and I fall with it. What has happened to me in this new world? I don't know. I don't see what I've seen, don't comprehend what's in front of me. I'm not filled with language anymore, and I have only a memory of fullness to anguish me with the knowledge that, in this dark and empty state, I don't really exist.

For my birthday, Penny gives me a diary, complete with a little lock and key to keep what I write from the eyes of all intruders. It is that little lock—the visible symbol of the privacy in which the diary is meant to exist—that creates my dilemma. If I am indeed to write something entirely for myself, in what language do I write? Several times, I open the diary and close it again. I can't decide. Writing in Polish at this point would be a little like resorting to Latin or ancient Greek—an eccentric thing to do in a diary, in which you're supposed to set down your most immediate experiences and unpremeditated thoughts in the most unmediated language. Polish is becoming a dead language, the language of the untranslatable past. But writing for nobody's eyes in English? That's like doing a school exercise, or performing in front of yourself, a slightly perverse act of self-voyeurism.

Because I have to choose something, I finally choose English. If I'm to write about the present, I have to write in the language of the present, even if it's not the language of the self. As a result, the diary becomes surely one of the more impersonal exercises of that sort produced by an adolescent girl. These are no sentimental effusions of rejected love, eruptions of familial anger, or consoling broodings about death. English is not the language of such emotions. Instead, I set down my reflections on the ugliness of wrestling; on the elegance of Mozart, and how Dostoyevsky puts me in mind of El Greco. I write down Thoughts. I Write.

There is a certain pathos to this naïve snobbery, for the diary is an earnest attempt to create a part of my persona that I imagine I would have grown into in Polish. In the solitude of this most private act, I write, in my public language, in order to update what might have been my other self. The diary is about me and not about me at all. But on one level, it allows me to make the first jump. I learn English through writing and, in turn, writing gives me a written self. Refracted through the double distance of English and writing, this self—my English self—becomes oddly objective; more than anything, it perceives. It exists more easily in the abstract sphere of thoughts and observations than in the world. For a while, this impersonal self, this cultural negative capability, becomes the truest thing about me. When I write, I have a real existence that is proper to the activity of writing—an existence that takes place midway between me and the sphere of artifice, art, pure language. This language is beginning to invent another me. However, I discover something odd. It seems that when I write (or, for that matter, think) in English, I am unable to use the word "I." I do not go as far as the schizophrenic "she"—but I am driven, as by a compulsion, to the double, the Siamese-twin "you."

FIRE

DAVID MACFARLANE

From *The Danger Tree* (1991)

David Macfarlane was born in Hamilton ("an unexceptional place") in 1952. Growing up, he was fascinated by the garrulous Newfoundland relations on his mother's side. "Whenever my Newfoundland relatives got together there were stories," he writes. The Danger Tree *combines these stories with Macfarlane's own recollections and historical research in a discontinuous narrative which moves back and forth between Ontario and Newfoundland, the present and the past, memory and imagination. It is a subtle and moving family history, focussing on the author's great-uncles and their experiences in the First World War but rippling out to become a history of Newfoundland in the twentieth century. Just as Michael Ondaatje manages to conjure up a version of Ceylon, so Macfarlane succeeds with Newfoundland: in both examples, readers are invited to engage imaginatively with another place and another people. Like much recent non-fiction writing, the author is present in the book, trying to make sense of the material as he presents it to the reader.*

David Macfarlane lives in Toronto where he is a successful freelance writer, the winner of several National Magazine Awards. The Danger Tree *was his first book.*

A match is struck, then held out between cupped hands. Necks crane forward, heads slightly twisted. One face, then another, is illumined briefly. The heads draw back and the smoke is exhaled upward. Then the flame is whisked out, well before its slender shaft of fuel is spent. For a third cigarette, a second match is required.

Three on a match is thought to be bad luck. If the injunction is something of a rarity these days, that's only because three smokers are seldom in one place at one time any more. But on the occasions that they are, the old superstition is often observed.

Today, this is a kind of gallantry, like taking off a glove when shaking hands. In the First World War, when the custom began, it was a precaution against snipers. At night, in a front-line trench, the tiny flare of a match was enough to attract the enemy's attention—sometimes from as far away as a quarter of a mile. The German marksmen had a reputation for hawk-like concentration and stubborn, sleepless patience. They squatted at the lips of observation posts or hid in the crooks of trees, peering into the darkness for hours to catch sight of a glint of moonlight on a helmet, or a shadow passing in front of a careless lantern, or the bobbing, telltale pinpoint of light that meant a few sentries were having a smoke.

Their rifle was the Mauser 98. It was actually called "the Sniper," and is considered one of the most successful bolt-action designs ever produced. It weighed nine pounds and was just over four feet in length. The calibre of its ammunition was 7.92 mm and its standard clip held five cartridges. The jacketed bullets were just over three inches long.

"Here," said a tall, sandy-haired lieutenant. He was with two Australians, accompanying them through the network of old German trenches, from Rosières back toward the Somme. It was just before dawn, late in the summer of 1918. The Canadian 102nd Battalion was under orders to link more closely with the Australians on the left, and the thirty-one-year-old lieutenant had volunteered to meet a reconnoitering party. He stopped and took a crumpled pack of Woodbines from his breast pocket. Through some mysterious oversight of Canadian Transport, the 102nd had been suffering from what their commanding officer, Colonel Fred Lister, called "a match famine" since the fifth of August. Now, with the sky growing brighter beyond Lihons and Chaulnes, it couldn't be dangerous. The lieutenant held out his smokes. "Anyone have a light?"

The Mauser 98 was a reliable, accurate weapon, and when, across a black field of mud, a match flared into visibility and a soft, round glow marked the spot where it was held in front of a man's face, the grooved thirty-inch barrel was quickly shifted into position. Lighting the second cigarette took long enough for the sniper to swing the almost imperceptible dot of yellow light into his steadying aim. The Mauser's scope had a range of almost 2,000 metres, and its sights showed a circle divided in half by the horizontal line of a T. The shafts of the T did not quite intersect and the gap where the three slender lines would have met was the bull's-eye. This meant that the light of the match could be held precisely on target when it was still, and tracked within the broader periphery of the circle when it moved. The sniper curled his index finger around the trigger, touching the steel but impressing no force upon it. The extended crook of his elbow and the angle of his head ensured that the act of taking aim was always accompanied by the strong, sour odour of his armpit.

One eye was shut. His breathing was shallow and steady. As the match moved to the third smoker, he followed its passage—the end of his barrel may have shifted a quarter of an inch—and when the match stopped, he steadied the barrel and drew a breath. He knew that the vague interruption in the darkness was a soldier's face, craned forward to the light cupped in a hand. He centred his aim on the dull glow. He had only a second before the head drew back, the match was extinguished, and his target disappeared. He tightened his index finger around the trigger, squeezing it equally from its front and two bevelled sides.

The trigger of the standard-issue Mauser required some pressure. But most experienced snipers filed the two steel pimples that acted as levers on the rifle's sear in order to quicken its action and minimize the barrel's movement during firing. Once lowered by the trigger, the sear released the cocked spring inside the bolt, which, extended to its full length, released the firing-pin. The impact ignited the shell's primer charge. Then the cordite exploded. The blast, which kicked the rifle's butt back against the sniper's shoulder with the force of a sudden shove, shot the copper-jacketed bullet through the spirals of the rifle's barrel, spinning it clockwise as it passed through the .323-inch bore. The spin kept the bullet's trajectory flat and accurate, the slight arc and the natural drift to the right compensated for by the sights. The bullet had a velocity of just under 3,000 feet per second, which meant that, from the striking of the firing-pin to the point of impact 300 yards away, less than a third of a second had elapsed. The Mauser could kill at more than 1,000 yards. At

300 yards, a bullet's weight was travelling at almost full force. Upon impact—against the right side of the young lieutenant's head, just behind the curve at the top of his ear and just below the rim of his helmet—it dimpled the flesh and, as the dimple deepened to a hole, it tore the surrounding hair and skin toward its point of entry. Skin, then bone, then brain slowed the bullet's passage, but as the bullet's velocity was reduced, it transferred its kinetic energy to the cranium. This commotion radiated out from the bullet like a shock-wave, and blasted the brain to unconsciousness before the sensation of pain had reached it from the point of entry.

Behind the bullet's deepening path a cavity opened that was many times wider than the projectile. In the case of a smaller-calibre bullet, the cavity would have closed again after a millisecond. This bullet was too big and fast for that. The impact of the Mauser's ammunition was far greater than the capacity of its target to absorb it. The cavity, widening like billiard balls on a break, would prove to be larger than the soldier's skull.

At the same time, the compression of brain, bone, blood, and skin that preceded the bullet's path was swelling the left side of the soldier's head. This bulge appeared while the spinning point of copper and lead was cutting through the midline of the brain. This was death. Pulse and respiration ceased as abruptly as if a vital strand of wires had been cut. Then the exit wound erupted. The fragments of brain and skull were drawn through the red, stellated wound. The soldier's hazel eyes began to roll back in their sockets and his lanky body began its collapse, just as the widening cavity behind the bullet's path broke out of its confines and blew his skull to pieces.

The exclusive dangers of three on a match were largely mythical. Three smokers were not necessarily a more likely target than any other number. One on a match was dangerous enough: a skilled German marksman could get off twenty-five aimed rounds a minute with the Mauser, which meant that the time it took for a soldier to strike a Swan Vesta, raise it to the oval end of his Woody or Mayo, draw a first puff, and then wave the match out was more than enough for a good sniper to take aim and fire. In these circumstances, two on a match should have been enough to have qualified for superstition. In different circumstances—if a sniper, for instance, was looking the other way when the match was struck—

certainly four on a hastily shared light would have been very bad luck indeed. If the sniper was slow and the match was put out before his aim was locked on target, a huddle of four or five smokers would probably have meant that even a haphazard shot would do some damage.

But it was three on a match that was said to be bad luck, and this had as much to do with the significance of the number as with actual fact. Threes were everywhere. They still are: three meals; three wishes; three chances; three witches; three cheers; three reasons why. There's morning, noon, night; faith, hope, charity; lower class, middle class, upper class; blondes, brunettes, and redheads. Dante divided his universe into hell, purgatory, and paradise. We speak of time past, present, future. There are, according to the ancient riddle of the Sphinx, three ages of man. There are three Graces, three Furies, three bears, three rings in a circus, and three blind mice. Races begin with ready, set, go, and end with win, place, show. In folk stories, it is often the third brother who slays the dragon, wins the princess, finds the treasure. In Christian iconography, there are three crosses on Calvary, three Magi, three temptations, three denials. And there is, of course, the Trinity.

In battle, three was the natural choice for superstition. The army seemed to run—hup, two, three—on a constant and ubiquitous trichotomy. On land there was infantry, artillery, and cavalry, with separate but sequential tasks in battle. Frequently battalions were divided into three groups. For every man on sentry duty, two were allowed to rest. There were front trenches, support trenches, and rear trenches. Soldiers routinely numbered off in threes, and the number a soldier called out could mean the difference between playing cards in the reserve trench or being blown to bits in No Man's Land. Military threes were prophetic, and every soldier knew it. They packed up their troubles in their old kit bags and smiled, smiled, smiled.

The bad luck of three on a match was the perfect superstition of the First World War, for it alluded to the war's, and the number's, most potent characteristic: finality. Three is the perfect number for chances or wishes or strikes because the figure represents the beginning, the middle, and the end. Implicit in all the myths, rituals, and superstitions that surround it is the understanding that the third is always the last. After three there is nothing. But the very existence of one and two ensures that three will some day come.

In the trenches, extinguishing a match after the second cigarette was cheating the inevitable. By the last year of the war, this was all a soldier could hope to do. The count toward his death had begun the day he enlisted, and any ruse or charm that would extend the interval between beats was welcomed. And perhaps this explains why the superstition has persisted for as long as it has: our century has kept its own count and, for the lifetime of my generation, has been suspended somewhere between two and three. We keep shaking out our matches. Our grandparents were ready and our parents aimed. Now we're afraid of fire.

By the end of the war, the significance of the number three was obvious enough to the Goodyear family: after a relatively brief period of shock, what had once been unthinkable became something that had somehow always been inevitable. After the war, the number three became, for Josiah and Louisa Goodyear, as much a way of summing up who they were as seven—the number of their children—had been a way of describing themselves before it. The three dead sons paraded past their parents, and on through the century. Now, two generations later, it is difficult for me to imagine the family without them. Their deaths cast everything I would ever hear and learn about the Goodyears—their inconsequential business disputes, their uncelebrated political feuds, their adventures and tall tales, and their little-known passion for the isolated, distant island of New-foundland—into high relief. They made everything seem important. Not that their deaths bestowed any particular meaning on events—quite the opposite. They were pointless. It's just that I come from a safe place, in the middle of a country where everything is foreign news. I live in danger of being entertained by the headlines of distant tragedies. When the wars described in newspapers and broadcast on cable television start to become prime-time abstractions to me, I think of my three great-uncles. They were ordinary men from an old, lost world. I come to them from far away. But they remind me that, in a war, death always matters more than the glorious cause that inflicts it.

Uncle Hedley may have noticed an ominous numerology on the night of August 7, 1918, although, judging from his marks in Math, Physics, and Chemistry at Victoria College in Toronto, and from the disastrous results of a brief real estate partnership with Roland in the spring of 1914, he was no good at arithmetic. Still, the numbers were there in front of him. By a strange quirk of fate, they were stamped in three places on the

revolver he carried in his leather holster that night. It was a .455-calibre
Webley Mark VI, produced in 1918. Its serial number, 332137, was
stamped at the base of the six-inch barrel, in front of the steel
trigger-guard, and on the rim of the revolving six-chambered magazine.
Hedley couldn't have helped but notice the figures as he cleaned and
loaded and checked his gun that night, preparing for what would become
known as the battle of Amiens.

By August 1918, there were rumours among the troops that the end of
the war was not far off. That spring, German offensives between the
Marne and Amiens, and further to the north, near Ypres, had been eerily
reminiscent of previous Allied offensives at the Somme and Passchendaele.
After the collapse of the Russian army, the German command had been
able to concentrate on the Western Front, and, with the American forces
growing steadily stronger, Ludendorff and Hindenburg were convinced
that the time had come for their big push. If they were going to defeat
Britain and France, it was going to have to be done now. Apparently
they had learned nothing from Haig's blunders. In March of 1918, as part
of an extravagant southern feint, German forces had pushed through the
Allied lines at the Somme. Haig, and the bulk of the British forces, were
waiting uselessly further to the north.

In the confusion that followed, the French general, Foch, consolidated
his position as the commander-in-chief of the Allied armies in France.
Immediately he proved that he, at least, had been awake for the previous
four years. In the face of the German advance, he held back his reserves.
Contrary to every tenet of nineteenth-century warfare, Foch let the
Germans come through. The advance won territory but it strained supply
lines and consumed reinforcements. The Germans paid for every mile
with appalling casualties. Then, with the restraint of a good poker player,
Foch finally put down his cards. His counter-attack came on both sides
of the bulge the Germans had fought their way into. It stopped the advance
dead.

In the months that followed, the Germans launched offensives in
Flanders, at the river Aisne, and at Rheims. In each case, they eventually
choked on their own initial successes, just as they had in March at the
Somme. By the summer, the war had shifted. In Germany there was talk
of a compromise peace; in the German trenches there was despondency.

In England, Lord Northcliffe—combining his penchant for publishing sensational half-truths with his enthusiasm for airplanes—was put in charge of dropping leaflets of propaganda over enemy lines, encouraging surrender.

By August of 1918, in the Canadian lines near Amiens, there was certainly cause for optimism. There was also cause for anxiety. The rumours of peace were welcomed, but, for the troops, hope only made each day more fateful than the one that had come before. Survival now seemed a possibility, but as the odds got better, the bets got higher and more dangerous. The thought of dying close to the end of the war was too cruel to contemplate. Superstitions and prophetic signs were everywhere, and even the most level-headed soldier found himself waiting out the long night before an attack, searching for some indication—in the stars, in his birthdate, in the number of letters in his name, in the games he played spinning the magazine of his revolver—that his luck would hold. Luck was everything, and guessing whether it was there was a pastime that may have caused Hedley Goodyear to consider the portents of a serial number while cleaning his Webley on the night of August 7. And, if he did, he could only have come up with one interpretation. The meaning of 332137 was too obvious to miscalculate: if the two represented the two wounded brothers safe in Scotland, and the one, the eldest still at home, if the seven was the sister who interrupted a mother's wish for seven sons, then it was clear enough what the threes were. And there were three of them.

Hedley sat on a groundsheet in Boves Wood, a few kilometres to the southeast of Amiens. He was surrounded by men in bedrolls and on groundsheets, sleeping outdoors or under the cover of camouflaged tents. As much as possible, noises were muffled. Lights were shielded. Everything depended on concealment. The Allied commanders—Haig, Pétain, Pershing, and Foch—had decided to counter the German offensives while the enemy was still reeling. As part of this plan, Canadian forces had been moved secretly to join the Australians near Amiens; their objective was to gain control of the railways to the east and to push the Germans back, possibly as far as the town of Roye. Hedley's commanding officer, Colonel Lister, estimated that fifty thousand men and twenty-five thousand horses were hidden in the woods. "The Canadian Corps," Lister noted in his diary, "was on the verge of the biggest operation in which it had yet been engaged and which figured as part of the most spectacular counter offensive yet launched against the Hun."

That night, Hedley wrote his farewell letter. He worked by the soft, yellow light of a hooded lantern, looking up to the chill, black sky between each sentence. There was no time for revisions. "Dearest Mother," he wrote, "This is the evening before the attack and my thoughts are with you all at home. But my backward glance is wistful only because of memories, and because of the sorrow which would further darken your lives should anything befall me in tomorrow's fray."

In the years since, copies of the page-long letter have circulated in the Goodyear family. It has been published in Newfoundland newspapers— usually on Memorial Day or on the eve of the November armistice—and once, seventy-one years and thirteen weeks after Hedley put down his pen, it was read with great dignity by the member for Bonavista-Trin-ity-Conception Bay on Remembrance Day in the Canadian House of Commons. The original seems to have disappeared. But the typed copies that family members keep in drawers and file-folders and scrapbooks and that the honourable member held when he rose from the Liberal benches on November 11, 1989, have been given the heading "The Last Letter of a Hero." The letter is twenty-three sentences long and concludes with a postscript. "P.S.," it reads, and instead of the expected *Please send more socks* or *Always short of fags* someone has added, "Hedley Goodyear was killed the following day, August 8th, 1918."

The letter's frequent publication was started, it seems, by E.J. Pratt. Less than two months after it was written, Pratt printed it in the Overseas Page of Victoria College's literary review, *Acta Victoriana*. He gave it the title "The Last Home Letter of Hedley Goodyear," and in his introduction Pratt wrote, "Of the thousands of farewell letters written from the trenches, few have surpassed, in noble feeling, this final message of Hedley Goodyear to his mother." Then, in a flight of rhetoric that must have floored Aunt Kate, amused a few girls in Scotland, and astounded anyone who had ever trapped young foxes out of season with my grandfather or had a few drinks in the Newfoundland Hotel with my great-uncle Ken, Pratt went on to tell *Acta*'s readers that "the sons of Josiah Goodyear were cast in heroic mould, every one of them a physical and moral giant."

I'm not sure what it is about death that brings out such extravagance in writers. Faced with something difficult and profound, the composers of eulogies often seem to choose the most windy and meaningless way of dealing with it. Pratt, who hadn't laid eyes on any member of the Goodyear family other than Uncle Hedley for more than a decade, and who had spent all of one week in Newfoundland since 1907, went on to tell his readers that Lord Northcliffe knew the Goodyears "personally" and that he had given "public testimony to their courage and resourceful-ness." This was probably not absolutely untrue, but it was certainly a stretch. And it was an odd point to raise in a tribute to the one Goodyear who, educated at Ladle Cove, the Methodist College in St. John's, and Victoria College at the University of Toronto, had spent little time in Grand Falls, had no involvement in the family company, and had probably never exchanged a word with Northcliffe in his life. The "personally" has a hollow, obsequious ring to it, as if the inclusion of a celebrity's name in an otherwise ordinary obituary might make the loss seem more important. Pratt's claim that the Goodyear brothers' "devotion to their country was equalled by their love for one another" was also suspect. He couldn't have had any idea whether such a claim was true. It sounded the kind of sentimental chord that almost everyone who appeared in print felt obliged to sound in 1918. In later years, it would have surprised anyone within earshot of one of the J. Goodyear and Sons board meetings in downtown Grand Falls.

Pratt, writing from the distance of his Toronto study, seemed to be idealizing the Goodyears, if not inventing them, and this may have been why my great-aunt held Canada's great poet in such disregard. She didn't begrudge him his debt to the family or his sale of calabogus to the victims of tuberculosis on Newfoundland's coast. And it wasn't that she disagreed with him when, in describing Hedley to the readers of *Acta*, he wrote of "the high principle and absolute candour of soul that was his." She may have simply begrudged him his survival: he never enlisted, and for that reason his life was allowed to extend beyond 1918. She had little time for those who, with no experience of war, use it as an opportunity to make political hay, sell newspapers, compose moving memorials, trot out their own sensitivity—or, for that matter, write a book. I don't think she ever forgave E.J. Pratt for being indiscriminate and therefore untrustworthy in his praise of the Goodyears in general and Hedley in particular. She knew that sometimes—in the face of an untimely death, for instance—silence was best.

If not a moral giant, Hedley was certainly a moral being. He was an earnest young man, dedicated to his studies but by no means a bookworm. "His victories with Latin, the Lit., and the ladies are duly recorded," *Acta* quipped one year. "Prominent in the Literary Society," it reported upon his graduation in 1913. "An outstanding debater. During his College course he was one of the best-liked members of his class."

Hedley was also an idealist. "My eye is fixed on tomorrow," he wrote to his mother from Boves Wood on the night of August 7, 1918, "with hope for mankind and with visions of a new world."

The terrible years that passed between 1914 and 1918 are remembered today as a steady process of disillusionment. It is generally assumed that by the end of the war there wasn't a soldier in the field who believed that what he was witnessing was anything other than a tragic waste. There is truth in this—the legacy of the war's poets is that the battles of stupid old men were fought by their innocent sons, and that it was all for nothing. But there were also soldiers—Hedley Goodyear among them—who never admitted to so bankrupt a possibility. The more horrible the war and the longer it dragged on, the more necessary it was to hope that it all meant something. He couldn't bring himself to believe that the carnage was pointless, and so he invested the war with his own idealism. He paused in his writing, raised the end of the pen to his lips, thought for a moment, and then bent forward again to his paper. "A blow will be struck tomorrow," he continued, "which will definitely mark the turn of the tide. . . . I shall strike a blow for freedom, along with thousands of others who count personal safety as nothing when freedom is at stake."

It was Hedley's idealism that was responsible for his being with the Canadians in the first place. He signed up for duty with the 102nd in Toronto when it would have been perfectly natural for him to have returned to Grand Falls to enlist with the Newfoundland Regiment. After all, his nationality—as written in his own hand on the University of Toronto's registration form—was Newfoundlander.

Being from so distant a place provided him with a slight foreignness which, like the roll of his accent, distinguished him from his classmates at Victoria. It was an identity he wore easily and naturally. He spoke frequently of Newfoundland, making its innate superiority to any place else on the face of the earth a running joke with his classmates. When he closed his eyes in Toronto, in the narrow bed of his sparse little room in a boarding-house on the corner of Yorkville and Hazelton avenues, he rememberd an island that had bluffs and hills and crags of rock like nowhere he knew. It had its own colours. They were the rust of kelp, the grey of the sea, the green of forests, the black of rattling brooks. It had its own smells—salt, cut spruce, dried fish, a curl of smoke. And it had sounds which, clear as dawn, came ringing—a hammer, a shot, oars against the gunwales of a dory—across the calm blue water of a little harbour. It had its own stories and jokes and ways of doing things. And it had means of description that were as various as its weather. New-foundland had a distinctiveness that he felt deeply and that he would never have dreamed of giving up.

And yet it was Hedley Goodyear's conviction that his country's fate was bound up with Canada's. Apparently, from the day he arrived at university, he was an ardent confederate. In the dining-hall, in common rooms, in seminars, and in debates at Hart House, he frequently argued the case for Newfoundland's joining Canada. In fact, his view on the subject—not a subject anyone else at Victoria would ever have spent much time discussing had Hedley Goodyear not constantly been bringing it up—was so well known that *Acta* took the occasional good-natured poke at him. On one occasion, ribbing him about his obsession with linking Newfoundland's fortunes more closely to Canada's, the editors even managed to include a caustic reference to Hedley's disastrous entrepreneurial fling with his older brother, Roland: "H.J. Goodyear has at last been successful in damming the straits of Belle Isle. This project, requiring six and a half million dollars, has been floated entirely on bonds guaranteed by Toronto real estate."

Uncle Hedley was a tall, sandy-haired young man. His vast black shoes were always carefully shined. His round collars were immaculate. His grey suit hung on his frame with a kind of shapeless dignity. In his academic gown, hands clutched at his lapels like a statesman, he cut an impressive figure. He was a forceful speaker and a clear, straightforward thinker, and usually, in debate, he was better informed than and twice as passionate as anyone who opposed him. He had a broad, serious face, and looked older than he was—until he smiled. Then, as he skewered his opposition on the well-turned point of his rebuttal, his expression was transformed by a boyish and mischievous grin.

"The leader of the opposition refers to Newfoundland's *manageable* public debt," he told an audience gathered for a student debate at Hart House one evening in 1913. "I fear that management is not the honourable member's strong suit, otherwise he would have *managed* to mount a more convincing argument." He moved away from the podium and took two deliberately paced steps across the polished hardwood floor. "Mr. Speaker, the public debt of Newfoundland bears over $1 million of interest annually. This, my mis-managed friend might like to know, is more than the country's combined expenditures for education, public works, fisheries, and the administration of justice and civil government." He let this sink in, looking up majestically to the leaded panes of the chamber's high, arched windows. "With managers such as these"—and here Hedley Goodyear extended an accusing finger at the opposition— "who needs natural disasters?"

No one was suprised when Hedley Goodyear chose "Newfoundland and Its Political and Commercial Relation to Canada" as the subject for his M.A. thesis. He worked at it steadily, sitting up late into the night in his room, his shirtsleeves rolled back and his little rickety table piled with books and notes. He completed it in 1914.

It is an impassioned, well-argued paper that reads more like a speech than an academic treatise. It is polite but blunt in its assessment of England's total failure with the island. Hedley was less deferential on the subject of Newfoundland's self-inflicted catastrophes. "The backward condition of the Island," he wrote, "is not due to the inherent shiftlessness of its people, but to . . . the selfishness of business men whose best means of escaping taxation and whose surest hopes of gain lie in the submission of the people to the old order." He expressed optimism about Newfoundland's industrial potential and about the wealth of its natural resources—sounding the theme that Uncle Roland, in a somewhat less orchestrated manner, would continue to sound in railway cars and hotel rooms and in letters to the premier for the rest of his life. But Hedley knew that much was seriously wrong with Newfoundland. He dismissed the island's denominational education system as a "festering disease," raged at its poverty and low standards of health, decried the absence of local governments, and criticized the country's failure of political will. "The greatest heresy and the worst treason," he said, "is to wink at the facts." And the facts were that Newfoundland was a political, social, and fiscal disaster.

Confederation with Canada was the only option that made sense to Uncle Hedley because it had an obvious geographic, historic, and economic logic, because Canada held great promise, and because Newfoundland was in such dire straits. "The fisheries could hardly have been more neglected; fewer and less efficient transportation facilities are out of the question; a more deplorable lack of industrial development is inconceivable; and education could not have been a more sorry affair. . . . "

In his thesis, Hedley implicitly dismissed the trappings of nationalism and the pride of imagined independence. He was passionate in his pragmatism, and, never doubting his own identity as a Newfoundlander, he believed that Newfoundland had everything to gain and nothing to lose by the union. A state, he claimed, was a political arrangement; the firmer its foundations and the broader its economic base, the more likely it was to fulfill its only responsibility: securing the prosperity, health, and freedom of its citizens. Any other claim to sovereignty—however ancient the traditions, however rousing the anthem—was emptiness. "A patriot's first duty to his country," he concluded, "is to know the truth about it."

All this, apparently, was too much for Newfoundland. According to the notes of family history that Uncle Roland was constantly scribbling and that were left after his death in the trunk in Gander, Hedley's professors thought highly of the thesis. They encouraged him to publish it. They thought it would be of interest in Newfoundland. Hedley was pleased. He took up their suggestion. He hoped that he would sell enough to recover his costs.

He printed several hundred copies, bound them in handsome, soft grey covers, and shipped them to St. John's. There, no shopkeeper would carry them. Every store that Hedley approached was either owned or influenced by the merchant families of St. John's. They felt the thesis was too controversial. The little grey pamphlets remained in their cardboard boxes. Then, on the day that Hedley began his military training in Toronto— marching in Queen's Park, across the dusty road from Victoria College and from the site of what would eventually become the E.J. Pratt Memorial Library—the half-dozen boxes were shipped from St. John's to Grand Falls. Uncle Roland picked them up at Grand Falls Station. He stacked them in the loft of an old, weather-bleached shed, between the back of the Goodyears' house and the company stables. When Roland wrote Hedley to tell him this news, he addressed the letter to Private H.J. Goodyear.

The First World War presented itself to Hedley Goodyear as exactly the kind of co-operative effort and union of strengths that lay at the heart of his belief in confederation. He believed the struggle was important. The real reasons for the war were so vague and unsubstantial that it was possible for rulers, politicians, and newspapermen to lay claim to the loftiest purpose in the call to arms. And Hedley took them at their word. He was young, strong, slightly naïve, and full of a student's dreams of a better world. In fact, he was a precise reflection of the forty-seven-year-old Canada. He was ready to take his place in the world. He was eager to prove his conviction to the highest of ideals.

It was time to pull together. Never doubting that he would always be a Newfoundlander at heart, he joined up with the Canadians. He rose from private, to sergeant, to lieutenant. And on the night of August 7, 1918, just before he addressed his men, he finished the letter to his mother. He wrote quickly. "I do not think for a moment that I shall not return from the field of honour, but in case I should not, give my last blessing to father, and my latest thanks for all he did for me. . . . I have no regrets and fear of tomorrow. I should not choose to change places with anyone in the world just now, except perhaps General Foch."

Before midnight on August 7, the 102nd left their position at Boves Wood. Two hours later, they reached their assembly point north of the Amiens-Roye road, at Gentelles. They waited there until just before dawn. Then, at 4:20 a.m., the Allied barrage opened up. The ground shook with it. The sky was breaking to the east and a white mist hung in the fresh, cool air.

The tanks went first. Behind them, the men crossed the shallow pool of the Luce, then headed southeast, in the direction of Roye. They flanked the road, making their way through orchards and fields of ripened corn. Shells burst in the harrowed soil. The woods were full of machine guns.

Their objectives were the Sunken Road and, beyond it, the woods at Beaucourt. The opposing fire was heavy, but they proceeded steadily. Shells screeched overhead. Bullets ripped through the air. Men cried and fell. But the battalion's discipline held. Bayonets remained fixed. The troops closed ranks on the gaps left by their casualties. The sun burnt away the mist. They moved forward.

On August 8, 1918, 110 men of the 102nd would fall in battle. And, in the remembrance of that day, the young Lieutenant Hedley J. Goodyear was numbered among the gallant dead.

But it wasn't true. He didn't die. Apparently everybody was wrong— E.J. Pratt, my Newfoundland relatives, and the editors of half a dozen newspapers. There had been an error. The postscript on the letter was incorrect. Against all odds, despite all signs, and contrary to accepted fact, his luck held. He survived the battle of Amiens without injury. Having done so, he cheerfully expected to last out the war. The worst was over.

As he had predicted, the tide had turned. Rumours ran wild. There were celebrations. Among the stores of supplies and ammunition the Canadians had captured that day were a few kegs of German beer and, amazingly, several cases of champagne. Hedley toasted his men. They hip-hip-hoorayed themselves hoarse. It was as if a wall of fear had come down within them. The gloomy anxiety they had lived with for so long disappeared in the roar of their three cheers. Things were changing, and changing quickly. Peace now seemed a possibility. The world wasn't going to end.

I learned this in Gander, not long ago. I was spending a few days there with my aunt and uncle. It was a Saturday evening, and they had worked late at their hardware store—the last of the Goodyear stores in New-foundland. It had been a busy day for them. The store was a popular spot with Poles and Bulgarians and East Germans—Aeroflot passengers who, supposedly on their way to a winter holiday in Cuba, strolled through the security doors of the Gander airport in their sports shirts, sunglasses, and beach sandals, approached the lone, beleaguered-looking Mountie there, and, in the broken English they'd been rehearsing for hours, asked for political asylum. The coming-down of the Berlin Wall had done nothing to stem this flow; more than one thousand refugees a month arrived in Gander that winter. They were put up by authorities in the airport hotels and given meal vouchers, and they could be seen every day, walking in single file through the swirling snow along the side of the Trans-Canada Highway. They wore towels around their heads for warmth. Their arms were bare. They looked bewildered. Stunned by the cold, bleak place they'd ended up in, they were on their way into town to buy ski-jackets, hockey toques, and snowmobile boots.

That Saturday night in Gander, after my aunt and uncle returned from their store and after our dinner, my uncle produced a cardboard box that contained a jumble of his father's—my grandfather's—possessions. It was the sort of disorganized, uninstructive collection of stuff that most people probably fear they will leave behind—old letters, ticket stubs, unused daily planners, odd cufflinks. There was a hairbrush and a meerschaum pipe. Half watching the colour television, with our plates of fruitcake perched on the sofa and the arms of easy chairs, we sifted through the contents of my grandfather's box for an hour or so.

My aunt put on more coffee. A squall of snow rattled against the picture window. My uncle said, "Well, what do you know."

He pulled out a letter that had been lodged beneath a file at the bottom of the box. He looked at it closely for a few moments, and then held it out to my aunt and me. "Will you look at this."

It was a letter from Uncle Hedley to his mother. It was dated after the letter that E.J. Pratt had called his last. We couldn't believe our eyes.

It was as cheery and bright as the one that preceded it had been somber. "Dear Mother o'Mine," it began. "The last letter I wrote you was before the big show. . . . Well, the big show is over, at least as far as we know. You need have no further fear for my safety."

My aunt and I sat together on the sofa, bent over the brittle old piece of paper. "So he didn't die," my uncle said.

"It was a great day," the letter continued, "and the company to which I belonged distinguished itself. There seems to be a Providence disposed to order things with justice. Strangely enough, I found myself the only officer left in the company early in the fight. When we neared our final objective, which was a wood, we found it full of the enemy. I had eight machine guns and over a hundred of the best troops in the world at my command. I ordered every gun to open up. . . . It took us ten minutes to gain superiority of fire. . . . I thought the moment opportune to charge so I gave the word and the boys went in with the bayonets. . . . I had no mercy—until they quit fighting, then I did not have the heart to shoot them. . . . But it was a great day, and we were terrible in our charge."

Reading the letter, I imagined Uncle Hedley returning to Scotland after the war was over. He would have arrived at Betsy Turnball's door in Hawick, a bouquet of flowers in his hand and his Military Cross gleaming on the breast of his uniform. He would have taken his fiancée in his arms and, with both her feet off the ground, danced her round in circles of happiness. A month after that, back in Canada, he'd have stood in Aunt Kate's doorway, laughing at her tears and telling her that you'd think she'd never had a visit from a brother before. He'd take off his cap and undo his covercoat and tell us we'd all been mistaken. We'd got the story all wrong.

The letter was dated August 17, 1918. "Don't worry about me," it concluded, "I'm Hun-proof."

To the two Australians who were with him, it looked as if a bomb had exploded inside his head. His lanky body crumbled. Three hundred yards away, a German soldier peered over the sights of his Mauser into the darkness. He lifted the barrel from the slender crook of a dead tree. He couldn't tell if he'd hit anything. It was just before dawn. The sky was breaking over Lihons and Chaulnes. He yawned and wondered about breakfast.

It wasn't very long afterwards that the shed between the Goodyear stables and the house in Grand Falls caught fire. No one knew how it started. It may have been a wayward cinder from the blacksmith's forge, or just a carelessly tossed match. At first, smoke crept though the cracks in the boards like ivy. The smell could have been the woodstove in the house. No one heard the crackling. By the time somebody realized what was burning, it was too late. The fire was too hot to get near. The sway-backed old building was lost. Its wood was dry and the loft was stacked with cardboard boxes full of little grey pamphlets.

FURTHER READING

I recommend the following books to anyone wanting to extend their reading of Canadian non-fiction writing in English. The list is in no way exhaustive; I have attempted to include books which strike me as particularly innovative or interesting, but these are matters of opinion, not fact. I will have ignored some titles and forgotten others. This is only to get you started.

Mark Abley, *Beyond Forget* (Vancouver: Douglas & McIntyre, 1986). Travel writing from the Canadian Prairie.

Edward Ahenakew, *Voices of the Plains Cree* (Toronto: McClelland & Stewart, 1973). Our very own *Black Elk Speaks*.

Thomas Berger, *Northern Frontier, Northern Homeland*, 2 vols. (Ottawa: Supply & Services Canada, 1977). It is not often that a government report becomes a best seller.

Laura Berton, *I Married the Klondike* (Boston: Little, Brown, 1954). The memoirs of Pierre's mom.

Sharon Butala, *The Perfection of the Morning* (Toronto: HarperCollins, 1994) Portrait of the artist as a nature worshipper.

Susan Crean, *Who's Afraid of Canadian Culture* (Toronto: General, 1976). An analysis of the politics of Canadian cultural industries.

Eli Danica, *Don't: A Woman's Word* (Charlottetown: Gynergy Books, 1988). A horrifying personal account of sexual abuse.

Modris Eksteins, *Rites of Spring: The Great War and the Birth of the Modern Age* (Toronto: Lester & Orpen Dennys, 1989). A quirky cultural history by an academic writing for a general audience.

George Faludy, *My Happy Days in Hell* (London: William Collins, 1962). A memoir of Faludy's Second World War experiences and his internment in the post-war Hungarian gulag.

Brian Fawcett, *Cambodia: A Book for People Who Find Television Too Slow* (Vancouver: Talonbooks, 1986). A split-level book, part fiction and part something else.

Daniel Francis, *The Imaginary Indian* (Vancouver: Arsenal Pulp Press, 1992). A history of the image of the Indian in popular culture.

John Franklin, *Narrative of a Journey to the Shores of the Polar Sea, 1819-22* (London: John Murray, 1823. Reprinted Edmonton: Hurtig, 1969). An account of his early adventures along the Arctic coastline.

W. Kaye Lamb, ed. *The Letters and Journals of Simon Fraser, 1806-1808* (Toronto:

Macmillan, 1960). Contains the famous account of his descent of the Fraser River.

Northrop Frye, *The Bush Garden* (Toronto: House of Anansi, 1971). A collection of essays about Canadian literature.

Don Gayton, *The Wheatgrass Mechanism: Science and Imagination in the Western Canadian Landscape* (Saskatoon: Fifth House, 1990). Ecology for the lay person.

Terry Glavin, *A Death Feast at Dimlahamid* (Vancouver: New Star, 1990). A first-rate book about B.C. Aboriginal people, fusing legend and land-claims politics.

George Grant, *Ocean to Ocean* (Edmonton: M.G. Hurtig, 1967. Reprint of 1873 original). Cross-Canada junket with Sir Sandford Fleming, scouting out a route for the CPR.

James H. Gray, *The Boy From Winnipeg* (Toronto: Macmillan, 1970). A veteran journalist's account of growing up the son of an alcoholic in post-First World War Winnipeg.

Frederick Philip Grove, *In Search of Myself* (Toronto: Macmillan, 1947). The novelist's autobiography, which won a Governor-General's award for non-fiction, turned out to be largely made up.

Sandra Gwyn, *The Private Capital* (Toronto: McClelland & Stewart, 1984). She manages to make Ottawa interesting; what higher praise can one give?

Daniel Williams Harmon, *Sixteen Years in the Indian Country* (Toronto: Macmillan, 1957). One of the more interesting fur-trade journals.

Alexander Henry, *Travels and Adventures in Canada and the Indian Territories Between the Years 1760 and 1776* (Edmonton: M.G. Hurtig, 1969). Blood-curdling adventure on the fur-trade frontier.

Ernest Hillen, *The Way of a Boy* (Toronto: Viking, 1993). Memoir of his childhood years in a Japanese prisoner-of-war camp in Java.

Bruce Hutchison, *The Unknown Country* (New York: Coward-McCann, 1942). An essay on the Canadian identity by British Columbia's most famous journalist.

Michael Ignatieff, *The Russia Album* (Toronto: Penguin, 1987). The story of the Russian side of his family; it won a Governor-General's award.

Diamond Jenness, *People of the Twilight* (New York: Macmillan, 1928). It has been called the best single book on the Canadian Inuit.

Rolf Knight, *A Very Ordinary Life* (Vancouver: New Star, 1974). About the author's mother.

Evelyn Lau, *Runaway: Diary of a Street Kid* (Toronto: HarperCollins, 1989). Life as a teenage prostitute on the streets of Vancouver.

W. Kaye Lamb, ed., *The Journals and Letters of Sir Alexander Mackenzie* (Cambridge: Cambridge University Press, 1970). Includes his *Voyages from Montreal*, published in 1801.

Charles Mair, *Through the Mackenzie Basin* (Toronto: Wm. Briggs, 1908). A travel book about the North at the turn of the century.

Nellie McClung, *Clearing in the West* (Toronto: T. Allen, 1935). The first volume of the famous suffragist's autobiography.

Marshall McLuhan, *Understanding Media* (New York: McGraw-Hill, 1964). The book that made him an intellectual superstar.

Christopher Moore, *Louisbourg Portraits* (Toronto: Macmillan, 1982). An unjustly-neglected work of popular history about daily life in the 18th-century Cape Breton fortress.

Gustavus Myers, *A History of Canadian Wealth* (Toronto: Lewis and Samuel, 1972. Reprint of 1914 original). An American muckraker turns his jaundiced eye on Canada.

Elfreida Read, *A Time of Cicadas* (Ottawa: Oberon Press, 1989). The first volume of a series of memoirs about her childhood in Shanghai, her wartime internment and her subsequent life in Vancouver.

Robin Ridington, *Trail to Heaven* (Vancouver: Douglas & McIntyre, 1988). A work of academic anthropology which offers the general reader a stunning insight into the Aboriginal world view.

Laura Goodman Salverson, *Confessions of an Immigrant's Daughter* (Toronto: Ryerson Press, 1939). The autobiography of an award-winning novelist, it won a Governor-General's award.

Maggie Siggins, *Revenge of the Land* (Toronto: McClelland & Stewart, 1991). This history of a particular plot of prairie land, and its owners, also won a Governor-General's award.

Joan Skogan, *Voyages at Sea With Strangers* (Toronto: HarperCollins, 1992). The view from the deck of a foreign fish packer in the north Pacific; the subject sounds unpromising but the result is terrific.

Donna E. Smyth, *Subversive Elements* (Toronto: Women's Press, 1986). A book about uranium mining and raising goats in Nova Scotia.

Sam Steele, *Forty Years in Canada* (New York: Dodd, Mead & Co., 1915). A memoir by the ubiquitous North-West Mounted policeman.

Richard Glover, ed., *David Thompson's Narrative* (Toronto: The Champlain Society, 1962). Another classic explorer's narrative.

Bruce Trigger, *Natives and Newcomers* (Montreal: McGill-Queen's University Press, 1985). The finest book of Aboriginal history written by a Canadian.

Merrily Weisbord, *The Strangest Dream* (Toronto: Lester & Orpen Dennys, 1983). Oral history of the Cold War meets family memoir.

George Whalley, *The Legend of John Hornby* (Toronto: Macmillan, 1962). The life and gruesome death of an old "Arctic hand."

Rudy Wiebe, *Playing Dead: A Contemplation Concerning the Arctic* (Edmonton: NeWest Press, 1989). Some thoughts about the North.

George Woodcock, *Gabriel Dumont* (Edmonton: Hurtig, 1975). A biography of the Métis leader by Canada's pre-eminent man of letters.

Ronald Wright, *Stolen Continents* (Toronto: Viking Penguin, 1992). The invasion of America from the Aboriginal point of view.

CREDITS

"A Backwoods House-Raising" from *The Backwoods of Canada* by Catherine Parr Traill (Toronto: McClelland & Stewart, 1989 edition).

"Backyard Ball Hockey" from *The Game* by Ken Dryden (Toronto:HarperCollins, 1989 edition). Reprinted with the permission of Macmillan Canada.

"Bathed in Bliss" from *Cosmic Consciousness: A Study in the Evolution of the Human Mind* by Richard Maurice Bucke, M.D. (New York: E.P. Dutton and Company, Inc., 1969 edition).

"Before We Were Famous" from *Memoirs of Montparnasse* by John Glassco (Toronto: Oxford University Press Canada, 1970). Copyright © Oxford University Press Canada, 1970. Reprinted with the permission of Oxford University Press Canada.

"Bingo" from *Wild Animals I Have Known* by Ernest Thompson Seton (New York: Grosset and Dunlap, 1966).

"Breaking Prairie Sod" from *Homesteader: A Prairie Boyhood Recalled* by James Minnifie (Toronto: Macmillan of Canada, 1972).

"Canlit Crash Course" from *Survival: A Thematic Guide to Canadian Literature* by Margaret Atwood (Toronto: House of Anansi, 1972). Reprinted with the permission of Stoddart Publishing, Don Mills, Ontario, Canada.

"Captured by the Iroquois" from *The Explorations of Pierre Espirit Radisson* by Pierre Radisson (Minneapolis: Ross & Haines, 1961 edition). Reprinted with the permission of Ross & Haines Old Books.

"Craigellachie" from *The Last Spike* by Pierre Berton (Toronto: McClelland & Stewart, 1971). Reprinted with the permission of Pierre Berton.

"D'Sonoqua" from *Klee Wyck* by Emily Carr (Toronto: Irwin, 1941). Reprinted with the permission of Stoddart Publishing, Don Mills, Ontario, Canada.

"The Diefenbaker Philosophy" from *Renegade in Power: The Diefenbaker Years* by Peter C. Newman (Toronto: McClelland & Stewart, 1963). Reprinted with the permission of Peter C. Newman.

"An Evening with James Joyce" from *That Summer in Paris* by Morley Callaghan (Toronto: Macmillan of Canada, 1963). Copyright © 1963. Reprinted with the permission of Macmillan Canada.

"Fire" from *The Danger Tree* by David Macfarlane (Toronto: Macfarlane, Walter & Ross, 1991). Reprinted with the permission of Macfarlane, Walter & Ross.

"The First of July, 1867" from *John A. Macdonald: The Young Politician* by Donald Creighton (Toronto: Macmillan of Canada, 1968 edition). Reprinted with the permission of the Estate of Donald Creighton.

"Hunger March to Edmonton" from *All of Baba's Children* by Myrna Kostash (Edmonton: Hurtig, 1977). Reprinted with permission of NeWest Publishers Limited, Edmonton.

"The Impulse of Savagery" from *A Whale for the Killing* by Farley Mowat (Toronto: McClelland and Stewart, 1978 edition). Reprinted with the permission of Farley Mowat.

"In Search of Whitemud" from *Wolf Willow* by Wallace Stegner (New York: Penguin, 1990 edition). Copyright 1955, 1957, 1958, 1962 by Wallace Stegner. Reprinted by permission of Brandt & Brandt Literary Agents, Inc.

"Jelly Roll and Me" from *Pilgrims of the Wild* by Grey Owl (Toronto: Macmillan of Canada, 1990 edition).

"June" from *A River Never Sleeps* by Roderick Haig-Brown (Vancouver: Douglas and McIntyre, 1974 edition). Reprinted with the permission of Douglas and McIntyre, Vancouver.

"Life in a New Language" from *Lost in Translation* by Eva Hoffman (New York: E.P. Dutton, 1989). Copyright © 1989 by Eva Hoffman. Used with the permission of Dutton Signet, a division of Penguin Books USA Inc.

"Maps of Dreams" from *Maps and Dreams* by Hugh Brody (Vancouver: Douglas and McIntyre, 1988 edition). Reprinted with the permission of Douglas and McIntyre, Vancouver.

"Mothers and Daughters" from *Lily Briscoe: A Self-Portrait* by Mary Meigs (Vancouver: Talonbooks, 1981). Reprinted with the permission of Talonbooks, Vancouver.

"A Night Crawl in Winnipeg" from *Canada Made Me* by Norman Levine (London: Putnam, 1958). Reprinted with the permission of Norman Levine.

"Nootka Customs" from *Narrative of the Adventures and Sufferings of John R. Jewitt* by John R. Jewitt (Ithaca, N.Y.: Andrus, Gauntlett & Co., 1851).

"Norway House" from *Reservations Are for Indians* by Heather Robertson (Toronto: James Lorimer & Company, 1991 edition). Reprinted with the permission of James Lorimer & Company, Toronto.

"An Ocean of Grass" from *The Great Lone Land* by William Francis Butler (Rutland, Vermont & Tokyo, Japan: Charles E. Tuttle Co, 1968).

"Ossification of Native Society" from *Prison of Grass:Canada from a Native Point of View* by Howard Adams (Saskatoon: Fifth House Publishers, 1989 edition). Reprinted with the permission of Fifth House Publishers.

"Shelter from the Storm" from *Death on the Ice* by Cassie Brown (Toronto: Doubleday Canada, 1972). Copyright 1972 by Cassie Brown. Reprinted with the permission of Doubleday Canada Limited.

"Sword Swallowing on the Tundra" from *A Journey from Prince of Wales's Fort in Hudson's Bay to the Northern Ocean* by Samuel Hearne (Toronto: Macmillan of Canada, 1958 edition).

"Tropical Gossip and Kegalle" from *Running in the Family* by Michael Ondaatje

PHOTO SOURCES

p. 23: *A Northwest View of Prince Wales Fort, Hudson's Bay, ca. 1797,* by Samuel Hearne. National Archives of Canada (C-041292).

p. 31: Maquinna. British Columbia Archives and Records Service (7931 A-2678).

p. 38: Catharine Parr Traill. National Archives of Canada (PA-802715).

p. 44: Susanna Moodie. National Archives of Canada (C-007043).

p. 61: Red River Cart Train, by William George Richardson Hind (c. 1862). Metro Toronto Reference Library, J. Ross Robertson Collection (T 33371).

p. 87: Vilhjalmur Stefansson. National Archives of Canada (C-086406).

p. 98: Grey Owl. Ontario Archives (ACC9291, S14232).

p. 107: Emily Carr. British Columbia Archives and Records Service (51765 C-5235).

p. 115: Roderick Haig-Brown. Photo by John Ough. Canadian Museum of Contemporary Photography (National Film Board Collection).

p. 202: The Hon. D.A. Smith (Lord Strathcona) driving the last spike on November 7, 1885. National Archives of Canada (C-003693).

p. 211: Breaking up the soil and bushes with horse-drawn plough and axe, n.d. National Archives of Canada (PA-038567).

DANIEL FRANCIS is a historian and editor, and author of ten previous books, including *The Imaginary Indian: The Image of the Indian in Canadian Culture, New Beginnings: A Social History of Canada, Our Canada: A Social and Political History*, and *The Great Chase: A History of World Whaling*. He lives in North Vancouver, B.C.